Here One Moment

ALSO BY LIANE MORIARTY

Three Wishes

The Last Anniversary

What Alice Forgot

The Hypnotist's Love Story

The Husband's Secret

Big Little Lies

Truly Madly Guilty

Nine Perfect Strangers

Apples Never Fall

FOR CHILDREN

The Petrifying Problem with Princess Petronella

The Shocking Trouble on the Planet of Shobble

The Wicked War on the Planet of Whimsy

Here One Moment

A NOVEL

Liane Moriarty

CROWN
NEW YORK

Copyright © 2024 by Liane Moriarty

Published in the United States by Crown, an imprint of the Crown Publishing Group, a division of Penguin Random House LLC, New York.
crownpublishing.com

CROWN and the Crown colophon are registered trademarks of Penguin Random House LLC.

Originally published in Australia by Pan Macmillan Australia Pty Ltd, Sydney.

Library of Congress Cataloging-in-Publication Data

Names: Moriarty, Liane, author.
Title: Here one moment : a novel / Liane Moriarty.
Description: First edition. | New York : Crown, 2024.
Identifiers: LCCN 2024017449 | ISBN 9780593798607 (Hardcover) |
ISBN 9780593798621 (trade paperback) | ISBN 9780593798614 (Ebook) |
ISBN 9780593800102 (International edition)
Subjects: LCGFT: Thrillers (Fiction) | Novels.
Classification: LCC PR9619.4.M67 H47 2024 | DDC 823/.92—dc23/eng/20240422
LC record available at https://lccn.loc.gov/2024017449

Hardcover ISBN 978-0-593-79860-7
International edition ISBN 978-0-593-80010-2
Barnes & Noble edition ISBN 978-0-593-80061-4
Signed edition ISBN 978-0-593-80016-4
Ebook ISBN 978-0-593-79861-4

Printed in the United States of America on acid-free paper

Editor: Amy Einhorn
Editorial assistant: Lori Kusatzky
Production editor: Abby Oladipo
Text designer: Andrea Lau
Production manager: Philip Leung
Copy editor: Lorie Young
Proofreaders: Karen Ninnis, Robin Slutzky, and Katy Miller
Publicists: Dyana Messina and Mary Moates
Marketers: Julie Cepler and Kimberly Lew

987654321

First US Edition

Jacket design: Chris Brand
Jacket photograph: (*butterfly*) tovfla; (*ripples*) Corbis/VCG

For Marisa and Petronella

I have noticed that even people who claim everything is predestined and that we can do nothing to change it look before they cross the road.

—Stephen Hawking, *Black Holes and Baby Universes and Other Essays*

When a man knows he is to be hanged in a fortnight, it concentrates his mind wonderfully.

—Samuel Johnson

Here One Moment

Chapter 1

Later, not a single person will recall seeing the lady board the flight at Hobart Airport.

Nothing about her appearance or demeanor raises a red flag or even an eyebrow.

She is not drunk or belligerent or famous.

She is not injured, like the bespectacled hipster with his arm scaffolded in white gauze so that one hand is permanently pressed to his heart, as if he's professing his love or honesty.

She is not frazzled, like the sweaty young mother trying to keep her grip on a slippery baby, a furious toddler, and far too much carry-on.

She is not frail, like the stooped elderly couple wearing multiple heavy layers as if they're off to join Captain Scott's Antarctic expedition.

She is not grumpy, like the various middle-aged people with various middle-aged things on their minds, or the flight's only unaccompanied minor: a six-year-old forced to miss his friend's laser-tag party because his parents' shared custody agreement requires him to be on this flight to Sydney every Friday afternoon.

She is not chatty, like the couple so eager to share details of their holiday you can't help but wonder if they're working undercover for a Tasmanian state government tourism initiative.

She is not extremely pregnant like the extremely pregnant woman.

She is not extremely tall like the extremely tall guy.

She is not quivery from fear of flying or espresso or amphetamines (let's hope not) like the jittery teen wearing an oversized hoodie over very short shorts that makes it look like she's not wearing any pants, and someone says she's that singer dating that actor, but someone else says no, that's not her, I know who you mean, but that's not her.

She is not shiny-eyed like the shiny-eyed honeymooners flying to Sydney still in their lavish bridal clothes, those crazy kids, leaving ripples of goodwill in their wake, and even eliciting a reckless offer from a couple to give up their business-class seats, which the bride and groom politely but firmly refuse, much to the couple's relief.

The lady is not anything that anyone will later recall.

The flight is delayed. Only by half an hour. There are scowls and sighs, but for the most part passengers are willing to accept this inconvenience. That's flying these days.

At least it's not canceled. "Yet," say the pessimists.

The PA crackles an announcement: Passengers requiring special assistance are invited to board.

"Told you so!" The optimists jump to their feet and sling bags over their shoulders.

While boarding, the lady does not stop to tap the side of the plane once, twice, three times for luck, or to flirt with a flight attendant, or to swipe frantically at her phone screen because her boarding pass has mysteriously vanished, it was there just a minute ago, why does it always do that?

The lady is not useful, like the passengers who help parents and spouses find vanished boarding passes, or the square-shouldered, square-jawed man with a gray buzz cut who effortlessly helps hoist bags into overhead bins as he walks down the aisle of the plane without breaking his stride.

Once all passengers are boarded, seated, and buckled, the pilot introduces himself and explains there is a "minor mechanical issue we need to resolve" and "passengers will appreciate that safety is paramount." The cabin crew, he points out, with just the hint of a smile in his deep, trustworthy voice, is also only hearing about this now. (So leave them be.) He thanks "folks" for their patience and asks them to sit back and relax, they should be on their way in the next fifteen minutes.

They are not on their way in fifteen minutes.

The plane sits on the tarmac without moving for ninety-two horrendous minutes. This is just a little longer than the expected flight time.

Eventually the optimists stop saying, "I'm sure we'll still make it!"

Everyone is displeased: optimists and pessimists alike.

During this time, the lady does not press her call button to tell a flight attendant about her connection or dinner reservation or migraine or dislike of confined spaces or her very busy adult daughter with three children who is already on her way to the airport in Sydney to pick her up, and what is she meant to do now?

She does not throw back her head and howl for twenty excruciating minutes, like the baby, who is really just manifesting everyone's feelings.

She does not request the baby be made to stop crying, like the three passengers who all seem to have reached middle age with the belief that babies stop crying on request.

She does not politely ask if she may please get off the plane now, like the unaccompanied minor, who reaches his limit forty minutes into the delay and thinks that maybe the laser-tag party is a possibility after all.

She does not demand she be allowed to disembark, along with her checked baggage, like the woman in a leopard-print jumpsuit who has places she needs to *be*, who is never flying this airline *again*, but who finally allows herself to be placated and then self-medicates so effectively she falls deeply asleep.

She does not abruptly cry out in despair, "Oh, can't someone *do* something?" like the red-faced, frizzy-haired woman sitting two rows behind the crying baby. It isn't clear if she wants something done about the delay or the crying baby or the state of the planet, but it is at this point that the square-jawed man leaves his seat to present the baby with an enormous set of jangly keys. The man first demonstrates how pressing a particular button on one key will cause a red light to flash and the baby is stunned into delighted silence, to the teary-eyed relief of the mother and everyone else.

At no stage does the lady make a bitter-voiced performative phone call to tell someone that she is "stuck on a plane"... "still here"... "no way we'll make our connection"... "just go ahead without me"... "we'll need to reschedule"... "I'll have to cancel"... "nothing I can do"... "I *know*! It's unbelievable."

No one will remember hearing the lady speak a single word during the delay.

Not like the elegantly dressed man who says, "No, no, sweetheart, it will be tight, but I'm sure I'll still make it," but you can tell by the anguished way he taps his phone against his forehead that he's not going to make it, there's no way.

Not like the two twentysomething friends who had been drinking prosecco at the airport bar on empty stomachs, and as a result multiple passengers in their vicinity learn the intimate details of their complex feelings about "Poppy," a mutual friend who is not as nice as she would have everyone believe.

Not like the two thirtysomething men who are strangers to each other but strike up a remarkably audible and extraordinarily dull conversation about protein shakes.

The lady is traveling alone.

She has no family members to aggravate her with their very existence, like the family of four who sit in gendered pairs: mother and young daughter, father and young son, all smoldering with rage over a fraught issue involving a phone charger.

The lady has an aisle seat, 4D. She is lucky: it is a relatively full flight, but she has scored an empty middle seat between her and the man in the window seat. A number of passengers in economy will later recall noting that empty middle seat with envy, but they will not remember noting the lady. When they are finally cleared for takeoff, the lady does not need to be asked to please place her seat in the upright position or to please push her bag under the seat in front of her.

She does not applaud with slow sarcastic claps when the plane finally begins to taxi toward the runway.

During the flight, the lady does not cut her toenails or floss her teeth.

She does not slap a flight attendant.

She does not shout racist abuse.

She does not sing, babble, or slur her words.

She does not casually light up a cigarette as if it were 1974.

She does not perform a sex act on another passenger.

She does not strip.

She does not weep.

She does not vomit.

She does not attempt to open the emergency door midway through the flight.

She does not lose consciousness.

She does not die.

(The airline industry has discovered from painful experience that all these things are possible.)

One thing is clear: the lady is a lady. Not a single person will later describe her as a "woman" or a "female." Obviously no one will describe her as a "girl."

There is uncertainty about her age. Possibly early sixties? Maybe in her fifties. *Definitely* in her seventies. Early eighties? As old as your mother. As old as your daughter. As old as your auntie. Your boss.

Your university lecturer. The unaccompanied minor will describe her as a "very old lady." The elderly couple will describe her as a "middle-aged lady."

Maybe it's her gray hair that places her so squarely in the category of "lady." It is the soft silver of an expensive kitten. Shoulder length. Nicely styled. Good hair. "Good gray." The sort of gray that makes you consider going gray yourself! One day. Not yet.

The lady is small and petite but not so small and petite as to require solicitousness. She does not attract benevolent smiles or offers of assistance. Looking at her does not make you think of how much you miss your grandmother. Looking at her does not make you think anything at all. You could not guess her profession, personality, or star sign. You could not be bothered.

You wouldn't say she was *invisible,* as such.

Maybe semitransparent.

The lady is not strikingly beautiful or unfortunately ugly. She wears a pretty green-and-white-patterned collared blouse tucked in at the waistband of slim-fitting gray pants. Her shoes are flat and sensible. She is not unusually pierced or bejeweled or tattooed. She has small silver studs in her ears and a silver brooch pinned to the collar of her blouse, which she often touches, as if to check that it is still there.

Which is all to say, the lady who will later become known as "the Death Lady" on the delayed 3:20 p.m. flight from Hobart to Sydney is not worthy of a second glance, not by anyone, not a single crew member, not a single passenger, not until she does what she does.

Even then it takes longer than you might expect for the first person to shout, for someone to begin filming, for call buttons to start lighting up and dinging all over the cabin like a pinball machine.

Chapter 2

It's been forty-five minutes since takeoff and the atmosphere on board is quiet, stoic, only a touch aggrieved. The delay, when time slowed and stretched and thinned so that every minute lasted its full quota of sixty seconds, is in the past. Time is once again ticking by at its usual brisk invisible pace.

A "light snack" of almonds, pretzels, crackers, and salsa has been served in the main cabin. The five business-class passengers have enjoyed a "light meal" (they all chose the chicken) and quite a lot of wine (they all chose the pinot).

In the main cabin, most of the garbage has been cleared and most tray tables are back up. The baby and the toddler are asleep. So is the bride, while the groom taps at his phone. The unaccompanied minor energetically plays a game on his device. The frail elderly couple bend their heads over separate crosswords. The crew chats in low voices about weekend plans and next week's roster.

People make use of the lavatories. They put shoes back on. They eat breath mints. They apply lip balm. They see the next steps of their journeys rolling out ahead of them: collect bag from baggage claim, line up for a taxi, order an Uber, text the person picking them up. They see themselves walking in the front door of their homes or hotels or Airbnbs, dropping bags with weary thuds. "What a nightmare," they will say to their partners or pets or the walls, and then they will step right back into their lives.

The lady unbuckles her seat belt and stands.

She is a lady about to get something down from the overhead bin. Or a lady about to head to the toilet. She is of no consequence, no concern, no interest, no danger.

She bows her head and presses a fingertip to the tiny brooch pinned to her blouse.

She steps into the aisle and doesn't move.

One person notices.

That person is a forty-two-year-old civil engineer with heartburn and a headache.

Leopold Vodnik, just Leo, never Leopold, to everyone except his maternal grandmother who is dead and an old university friend long gone from his life, is seated in 4C, directly across the aisle from the lady.

Theirs is the first row in the main cabin. They face a wall with a sign that declares BUSINESS CLASS ONLY PAST THIS POINT. A curtain is discreetly drawn across the aisle to conceal the luxury lifestyle on offer just a short distance away.

Leo looks like he belongs in business class. He is an olive-skinned man of medium build, with a large, definite nose and a high forehead that ends abruptly in a shock of mad-professor gray-speckled dark curly hair. One of his sisters recently sent him an article about scientists discovering the gene for "uncombable hair syndrome."

He wears a blue linen shirt with the sleeves rolled up to the elbows, gray chinos, and suede boots. His wife says he dresses better than her. (Not hard. Neve mostly dresses in the heedless, mismatched manner of someone who recently survived a natural disaster.)

Leo has spent the entire flight chewing antacids, massaging his forehead with his fingertips, and checking and rechecking the time.

It's all over. He must face facts. His eleven-year-old daughter's school musical is due to begin in five minutes. He will not be there because he is here: thirty-five thousand feet in the sky.

"Obviously I'll be home in plenty of time for *The Lion King*," he'd told his wife when he'd first raised the possibility of flying down to Hobart to take his mother to a specialist's appointment.

"Unless your flight back is delayed," Neve had said.

"It won't be," said Leo.

"Knock on wood," said Neve, without knocking on wood.

It kind of feels like the delay is her fault. Why even mention the possibility? He is meant to be the pessimistic one in their relationship.

Who could have predicted a *two-hour* delay?

Neve, apparently.

Leo checks the time once more. Right now, he should be shivering in his daughter's school hall, hissing at his teenage son to put away his phone and support his sister, exchanging good-humored banter about the arctic air-conditioning with the other parents, whispering to his wife to please remind him of Samira's dad's name, telling Samira's dad they must have that beer soon, which they both know will never happen because . . . life.

His head pounds with remorse. The lights are going down *right now*. The curtains are opening *right now*. He leans so far forward in his seat he is virtually in the brace position.

There is no one to blame but himself. Nobody asked him to do this. His mother said, Please, Leo, don't waste good money on a flight for just one day. His three sisters had not been grateful to him for taking on this familial duty. The opposite. They'd accused him of martyrdom on the family WhatsApp group.

But he'd had a strange strong feeling that something was not right with his mother's health and that he should be there to hear what the specialist said.

When his dad first got sick two years ago, he'd been distracted. He'd just started at his current position and work had been all-consuming. It's still all-consuming. He doesn't know how to stop it from consuming him.

And then: the strident ring of his phone ripping him from sleep at five a.m. and his mother's voice, so loud, assured, and awake. "You and your sisters need to get on a flight right now." She the grown-up, he the mumbling, half-asleep kid. "What, Mum, what, why?" He hadn't even properly processed the fact that his dad was seriously ill, let alone the possibility he might die, which he did, that day, while Leo and his sisters waited at the carousel for his middle sister's bag: she'd *checked* a bag.

Ever since, he's felt as though if he'd just concentrated more, if he hadn't been so focused on his work, he might have saved his dad. He is the oldest child. The only son. He is determined to get everything right with his mother.

So much for strange strong feelings. The specialist took five minutes and charged three hundred dollars to announce that Leo's mother was in perfect health.

Leo isn't *disappointed* by his mother's good health.

Of course not.

Look, truthfully, he *is* kind of annoyed by his mother's good health. It would have been gratifying if she'd been diagnosed with something serious but curable.

Also, painless. He loves his mother very much.

"Oh, well," Neve said when he called about the delay. At that point he'd still thought he'd make it, just a little late. He'd seen himself sprinting from the gate, line-jumping at the taxi stand—he would have broken his own moral code for his daughter! But then the plane continued to sit sullenly on the tarmac while the pilot made his infuriating intermittent "apologies, folks" messages and Leo lost his damned mind.

"There's nothing you can do." Neve didn't say I told you so. She never did. That was her power move. "Bridie will understand." He could hear Bridie in the background: "That better *not* be Daddy saying he's running late."

He has been helping Bridie rehearse for weeks. "It's a small but significant role, Daddy," she'd told him solemnly when she first came home with the script, and Leo had avoided Neve's eyes because Bridie is sensitive to shared parental smiles. She is playing "Zazu" (now, right now). Zazu is "a prim, proper hornbill bird," and the way Bridie instantly embodied the role was miraculous. She has gestures! Prim, proper gestures! She is Meryl Freaking Streep. She is that objectively good. Forget Mufasa. Forget Simba. Zazu will be the shining star of tonight's performance. Leo fully expects Bridie to receive a standing ovation. And he is missing it.

This is the sort of mistake people regret on their deathbeds.

He exhales noisily, sits back in his seat, and clicks the buckle of his seat belt open and shut, open and shut. The woman next to him lifts her head from her magazine and Leo locks his hands together. He's being annoying. It's the kind of thing his fourteen-year-old son would do.

His heart jerks at the thought of his son. For months now, he's been promising Oli they will do that beautiful national park walk they love, next Sunday, but it's always "next Sunday" because Leo so often needs to work on weekends, and this Sunday he'll need to catch up on everything he missed doing today, which does not, by the way, make him a "workaholic," just a guy with a job.

His boss believes it's important to achieve a healthy work-life balance. "Family always comes first, Leo," she said, when Leo mentioned he'd be taking today off, but one of Leo's key performance indicators is his "utilization rate." This is a measure of how many billable hours he logs each week compared to how many hours he has worked. His utilization rate is always in his thoughts: it's a buzzing mosquito he's not allowed to kill. Sometimes he works a fourteen-hour day but only bills eight. It's tricky. Life is tricky. He just needs to get a handle on time management. His boss, who has an interest in the topic, gives him book and podcast recommendations as well as useful tips. He's been working for Lilith for three years now. She's an impressive, inspirational woman in a male-dominated profession and he's trying to learn from her the way he learned from his very first boss, who would return Leo's drawings covered in red ink, which drove Leo crazy but ultimately made him a better engineer. Lilith recently told him the first step to improving productivity is a "comprehensive time audit," but Leo hasn't had time to do one.

Oli doesn't even look disappointed anymore each time Leo says, "Maybe we'll do the walk next weekend." He just responds with a cynical thumbs-up like he's dealing with a retailer's recurring broken delivery promises.

The woman in the middle seat clears her throat delicately and he realizes his left leg is jiggling up and down as if he's been electrocuted. He puts his hand on his thigh to still it.

He hears his wife's voice: *Do not spiral, honey.*

He couldn't believe it the first time she called him honey. The sweet feeling of that moment.

He smiles tightly in the vague direction of his seatmate, which he hopes she will take as an unspoken apology but not an invitation to chat.

Her name is Sue and her husband, in the window seat, is Max.

Leo knows this, and a lot more about them, because during the delay on the tarmac he had no choice but to overhear as the pair made an astonishing number of phone calls: "Wait, Sue wants a word!" "Let me give you back to Max!"

Max and Sue are a jolly, exuberant middle-aged couple just back from a trip driving a camper van around Tasmania. It was a blast! Sue is tiny, rosy-cheeked, bright-eyed, and big-bosomed. A silver bracelet loaded with charms jingles as she gesticulates. Max is tanned and white-haired, with a big firm proud tummy. Like Santa Claus back from his summer break. He has the same confident masculinity as the foremen Leo works with: strong, loud men who know what they're doing and have no difficulty managing their time.

At first, Sue tried to chat with Leo but gave up when he answered in barely polite monosyllables. He knows he could have told her about missing Bridie's concert, and he knows she and Max are the type to have offered instant sympathy and interest (he gathers from all the calls that they have grandchildren—"Grandpa and I can't wait to see you!"), but he'd been too tightly wound up to chat.

He looks again at the time. Bridie is onstage right now.

Stop thinking about it.

His stomach growls. He is starving. He refused the "light snack," because—and this is so stupid—he didn't want to slow things down. He'd been irrationally annoyed by all those people happily snacking on their nuts and pretzels. He wanted everyone to *focus* on getting to Sydney.

The lady across the aisle from him unbuckles her seat belt.

She stands.

Until now, she has been a blurred figure in his peripheral vision. If asked, he could have described her as a small lady with silver hair, but there is no way he could have picked her out of a lineup of small silver-haired ladies.

She moves into the aisle, right next to him, facing the back of the plane.

She doesn't move.

What's she doing?

Leo keeps his eyes politely on the seat pocket on the wall in front of him. He reads the top line of an advertisement on the back cover of the in-flight magazine: *What are you waiting for? Book your Jewels of Europe River Cruise today!* "We'll know we're old when those river cruises start to look attractive," Neve always says. Leo has not confessed that the idea of a river cruise already seems attractive to him.

The silver-haired lady is still not moving. It's been too long. She's kind of crowding him. Kind of bugging him.

He glances down. Her shoes are small, brown, well-polished, and neatly laced.

She says in a quiet, clear voice, "On the count of three."

Chapter 3

Well, I once loved a very tall, skinny boy with the most vulnerable of necks who gave me the courage to go to parties and dances when I thought I might pass out from shyness.

"On the count of three," he'd say while my heart pounded and my vision blurred, and he'd take my hand in his. "One. Two. Three."

And in we'd go.

That could explain why I counted myself in: I was thinking of him.

Chapter 4

On the count of three, what?

Leo studies the lady. Her face is pale and blank. She seems bewildered. Possibly distressed. It is hard to be sure. He checks over his shoulder to see if people are blocking her way, but the aisle is clear.

He looks back up at her. She is the same age, height, and body type as Leo's mother except that Leo's mother would not be seen dead wearing sensible shoes. (Literally. Leo's mother wants to be buried in her Jimmy Choos. Leo's youngest sister said, "Sure, Mum, we'll do that," while mouthing *No way* at Leo and pointing at her own feet.)

Leo's mother doesn't like it when people "patronize" her. Would it be patronizing to ask this lady if she needs assistance?

He notices a silver brooch pinned to her shirt.

His parents ran a jewelry store in Hobart for forty years, and although neither Leo nor any of his sisters had any interest in carrying on the business, everyone in the family automatically clocks jewelry. The brooch is small, possibly antique? It's a symbol of some kind. An ancient, old-world-y symbol. He can't quite see it without leaning forward, which would be inappropriate, but something about the brooch is distractingly familiar. It is somehow strangely related to *him*. It gives him a sense of . . . ownership. Vague pleasure? It must be something to do with Vodnik Fine Jewels, but what?

Or is it the symbol itself that means something? Wait, something to do with school? No. University? Thoughts of university lead inevitably to one of his most painful memories, himself on a street, outside a pub, shouting like he'd never shouted before or since, nothing to do with this symbol, although, wait, he nearly has it—

"One," says the lady.

Will she burst into song on the count of three? Is she in pain, perhaps? Trying to psych herself up to take a step forward? Neve's grandmother suffers from terrible foot pain, poor thing, but this lady is much younger than her.

Leo's dad always said that after September 11 he was "ready for trouble" whenever he traveled. "I crash-tackle anyone who behave even a little suspicious," his dad would say in his Eastern European accent, so earnestly, even though he was a five foot four, benign, dapper-looking city jeweler, a sweet man who never did crash-tackle anyone in his life. "I not hesitate, Leo."

Would his dad have crash-tackled this woman by now?

I not hesitate, Leo.

Jesus, Dad. She's a harmless lady! You would so hesitate!

"Two."

She's harmless! Of course she's harmless.

You can't get weapons through security anymore.

And women don't hijack planes.

Is that sexist? He hears his youngest sister: *I could hijack a plane better than you, Leo.*

No doubt about that.

Leo clears his throat. He is going to ask the lady if she's okay. That is the correct, most appropriate action.

"Excuse me," he begins, "are you—"

"Three."

The lady turns, stretches out one arm, and points directly at the passenger seated in the window seat of her own row, a wiry fiftyish man hunched over a laptop, pounding the keyboard with two fingers.

"I expect," says the lady. She pauses, still pointing straight at the man. It's as though she is accusing him of something.

She expects what?

"I expect catastrophic stroke."

The man looks up with a distracted frown and cups a hand to his ear. "I'm sorry, I didn't catch that?"

"I expect catastrophic stroke," she says again, diffident but definite, still pointing. "Age seventy-two."

The man's eyes dart about. "I'm sorry, catastrophic . . . ? I don't . . . How can I help?"

The lady says nothing. She drops her arm, pivots, and turns to face Leo's row.

The man meets Leo's eyes across the aisle. His mouth turns downward in faux alarm to indicate *Bit weird!* Leo grimaces sympathetically. The man shrugs and returns to pummeling his laptop.

Leo is calm now. No need for crash-tackling. He understands dotty old ladies. She is a welcome distraction from his misery over missing the musical. He knows how to handle this.

Leo's grandmother suffered from vascular dementia in the last years of her life and the family was advised to play along with her alternate reality wherever possible and safe. For someone as "uptight" as Leo apparently is (that word gets thrown his way a lot, thrown quite hard), he was unexpectedly flexible when it came to going along with his grandmother's delusions.

He will play along with whatever role this lady requires. "Catastrophic stroke": Did that mean she'd once been a doctor or a nurse? He remembers hearing about a retired doctor with dementia who spent his days diagnosing his fellow nursing-home residents. He walked around with what he thought was a prescription pad, efficiently scribbling out the same prescription for antibiotics.

"I expect," says the lady. She points at Leo's seatmate, Max, who is busy taking a photo out the window of the airplane.

Max turns from the window, grins, ready for a chat. "Eh? What's that, love?"

"I expect heart disease," says the lady. "Age eighty-four."

Max frowns. "Heart . . . ? Didn't quite catch that, love. Hard to hear over the engine!" He nudges his wife for help.

Sue smiles brightly at the lady and raises her voice. "Sorry, we didn't quite catch that?"

"Heart disease," repeats the lady, louder this time. "Age eighty-four."

"You've got heart disease?"

"No! Not me! *You!*"

"No problems with my ticker." Max bangs a closed fist hard against his barrel chest.

"Age eighty-four," says the lady. "As previously stated."

Max gives his wife a baffled look and Sue steps in, as good wives do, to rescue husbands from confusing social situations.

"I'm so sorry," she says. "Did you recently lose someone?"

The lady appears exasperated, but her tone is tolerant. "Cause of death. Age of death."

That's when it clicks for Leo. *She's not diagnosing, she's predicting.*

"'Cause of death, age of death,'" repeats Sue carefully. She puts her hand on the buckle of her seat belt. "Okay then."

"Holy guacamole," says her husband.

The lady points at Sue. "I expect pancreatic cancer. Age sixty-six."

Sue laughs uneasily. "You expect pancreatic cancer? As my cause of death? Goodness. At *sixty-six*? You expect that for me? No, thank you very much!"

"Don't engage." Max lowers his voice and taps his forehead. "She's not quite . . . ?"

"Something's not right," agrees Sue beneath her breath.

She looks back up at the lady and speaks in that very specific, commanding tone Leo remembers so well from the nurses who took care of his grandmother. "We'll be *landing* soon, *sweetheart!*" It is a voice designed to cut through confusion and impaired hearing. Leo hates it. He could never bear hearing his formidable grandmother spoken to as though she were a not-very-bright preschooler. "So if you want to use the *bathroom*, you probably should go *now*."

The lady sighs. She turns to appraise Leo.

Leo says, "You're telling us how and when we're going to die?"

Later he will berate himself. He will think he should have followed Sue's lead and shut her down, but his feelings are mixed up with memories of his beloved grandmother's confused face and how he—Leo!—could make it smooth and peaceful when he went along with her delusions. He was better at it than his sisters. Those were the last gifts he gave her. He will do the same for this lady. It doesn't matter what nonsense she is talking.

"Cause of death. Age of death," says the lady. "It's really very simple."

"Sounds very simple," agrees Leo. "Give it to me straight."

The lady points her finger like a gun at the center of Leo's forehead. Her hand is steady. "I expect workplace accident." Her eyes are a pretty color: the soft blue of faded denim. They don't look like crazy eyes. They look like sad, sensible, resigned eyes. "Age forty-three."

Forty-three! Leo does not experience it as a shock—he is taking all this as seriously as he would a fortune cookie or a horoscope—but he does feel a jolt. Fortune cookies and horoscopes aren't usually so specific. He turns forty-three in November.

"I'm going to die in a workplace accident? Might have to give up work then."

Max chuckles appreciatively while Sue makes the kind of worried "tch" sound of a mother seeing her child doing something mildly risky.

"Fate won't be fought," says the lady. Her gaze glides past Leo as her forehead creases.

"Better get my affairs in order then!" Leo is playing for the crowd now. This particular jolly persona normally only kicks in after two drinks. *This* guy is not uptight! He never spirals! He doesn't lie awake at night fretting about his utilization rate. No one accuses *this* guy of being a workaholic.

The lady doesn't answer. Her face is a door slammed shut. She is done with him. She takes a deliberate step forward.

Leo twists in his seat to watch. She's stopped at the very next row. Still close enough for him to touch.

"I expect." She points at a young woman wearing giant headphones over a headscarf. "Disease of the urinary system. Age ninety-two."

The woman unpeels one headphone away from her ear with her thumb. "I'm sorry?"

"Oh my word," marvels Sue as she also cranes her neck to watch the lady, while Max shakes his head and Leo grins inanely like the relaxed, easygoing guy he is not and tries to ignore the sensation of someone gently but insistently pressing an ice cube to the base of his spine.

Chapter 5

I have been told I pointed at passengers while repeating these four words: "Fate won't be fought."

I was always taught that pointing is bad manners, so I was skeptical about this, until I saw the photo, the one that eventually appeared in the papers, where I was most definitely pointing, in a rather theatrical manner, as if I were playing King Lear.

Embarrassing.

I noticed my hair looked very nice in that photo.

Obviously that doesn't excuse anything.

Anyhow, the phrase "fate won't be fought" was my mother's phrase, not mine. She was always saying things like that: *You can't escape destiny. It wasn't meant to be. It was meant to be.*

Supposedly that means she was a "determinist."

Or so I was told by a bearded man at a dinner party in the summer of 1984. I do not remember his name, just his magnificent lush brown beard. He caressed it tenderly and often, as though it were a beloved pet curled up on his chest.

We were eating overcooked apricot chicken and undercooked brown rice in a blond-brick house in the northern Sydney suburb of

Terrey Hills. It was a hot evening and our hosts had set up a rotating fan in the corner of the room. Every few seconds a violent gust of air whooshed back our hair so we resembled dogs with their heads stuck out of car windows and the bearded man's beard flapped to the left like a patriotic flag.

It's amusing, in retrospect, although as I recall, nobody laughed. We were young, so we took ourselves seriously.

I had accidentally shared a deeply personal story about my mother. I sometimes share personal stories when I'm nervous and drink too much and obviously both things are likely at dinner parties.

The story I shared prompted the bearded man to remark that my mother was "obviously a determinist," as was he. Nobody knew what this meant, so he delivered a benevolent mini-lecture (he was a university lecturer, he enjoyed lecturing even more than the average man) while our hosts argued in bitter low voices over whether brown rice was *meant* to be that crunchy.

The idea of determinism, he said, is that everything that happens, and every decision or action you make, is "causally inevitable." Why? Because everything is caused by something else: a preceding action, event, or situation.

Well. None of us knew what the heck he was talking about. He was ready for this. He made it simpler.

He said people can only act as they actually *do*. A murderer, for example, will inevitably murder because his childhood, his genes, his brain chemistry, his socioeconomic situation, his fear of rejection, the convenient proximity of a defenseless woman on a dark street corner, will all lead him, inevitably, to murder.

Someone said, quite passionately as I recall, as if we were speaking of a specific murder and not a hypothetical one, "But he *chose* to murder! He had free will!"

The bearded man said he himself was a "hard determinist" and therefore did not believe in free will. He had a grain of brown rice stuck between his two front teeth and nobody, not even his wife, pointed it out. Perhaps she thought it was causally inevitable.

This is what I wonder; this is what I would like to now ask the bearded man: If free will doesn't exist, if all your decisions and actions are inevitable, are you still required to apologize for them?

Chapter 6

What the actual? The tendons in Sue O'Sullivan's neck scream as she twists her head too fast to see what the crazy lady is doing now.

"Ow." She faces the front again.

Sue is an emergency room nurse, a mother of five adult sons, and a grandmother of three beautiful little girls and four beautiful little boys. She is the sort of person who regularly says, "Heard it all, seen it all" because she has heard and seen it all, but this is the first time a stranger on a plane has calmly informed her she only has three years to live.

She wouldn't have lasted long in her line of work if she took words to heart. She deals with angry, violent, distressed, drunk, high, and psychotic people every day. They spit terrible insults at her, along with the occasional sexually charged death threat. Water off a duck's back. Sticks and stones.

She is, however, feeling the most foolish desire to run after this lady and demand another prediction, please. A nicer prediction.

Sue's plan is to retire at sixty-six, not to die at sixty-six.

She and Max have never left Australia before. Sue hasn't seen it all. She hasn't seen a damned thing! A whole planet of castles and cathedrals, paintings and sculptures, mountains and oceans waits to be seen and admired by Sue and Max O'Sullivan. They're feeling especially positive right now about their future travel prospects because if they can so successfully drive a camper van around Tasmania, why not drive one around France? Why not *Italy*? They can drive on the wrong side of the road! They're pretty sure they can!

And now she hears there will be no trip because she is very shortly going to get very sick with pancreatic cancer.

The bad one. They're all bad, but that one is really bad. Hard to catch early. Outcomes are not great.

It's not true, of course, but it's a chilling reminder that people with plans get sick. Specialists hand out cruel diagnoses every single day. Things that happen to other people can also happen to her.

"I think she's doing predictions for the whole plane," says the man in the aisle seat beside her. He turns to face Sue and she meets his eyes for the first time. It's as though she has suddenly become a real person to him. He's been an annoying seatmate up until now: wriggling and jiggling like a toddler, tapping his fingers on his thighs, avoiding all eye contact and making it very clear he is very important and very late (yes, Mr. Important Man, we're *all* late!) and therefore not up for a chat.

"Should we call a flight attendant?" Sue asks him, always best to keep Mr. Important Men feeling important by asking for their opinions.

"Maybe?" says the man, at the same time as Max says irritably, "Just *ignore* her."

Max is spinning his phone in rapid circles against his armrest. He'll crack the screen in a moment. All very well for him. He's been given decades to live. It's Sue and this twitchy guy who are apparently living on borrowed time.

Sue looks for her favorite flight attendant, a stunning glossy-haired young woman called Allegra (Sue always reads name tags) who had chatted charmingly with them during the delay. She'd prefer to catch Allegra's eye than push the call button like an entitled "Karen."

She hears, "I expect cardiac arrest. Age ninety-one."

Sue twists farther to look, but she's not tall enough to see properly.

"I expect Alzheimer's. Age eighty-nine."

The lady's tone is increasing in confidence and volume with each prediction.

Fragments of mildly bemused conversation become audible over the roar of the plane. Nobody sounds too worried.

"She's got Alzheimer's?"

"She was saying something about urine before."

"Maybe needs the bathroom?"

The lady's voice again, almost triumphant: "I expect drug-induced death. Age thirty-seven."

"I'm twenty-seven, not thirty-seven."

"Bro. She's not saying your age. She's saying that's when you'll die of a drug overdose."

Sue unbuckles her seat belt.

"Sit down." Max pulls her sleeve as she stands up and faces the back of the plane. She brushes him away and hops onto her seat on her knees. The advantages of being of small stature.

"The seat-belt light is on," says Max.

"It is not!" She looks down the length of the plane, noting those passengers with whom she and Max chatted in Hobart. There's the pregnant woman who had to take off her shoes going through security, poor thing. Sue helped her out. It's the woman's first, she's feeling great except for heartburn, doesn't know the gender. From the way she's carrying the baby, all out in front, Sue predicts a boy. (She has an unblemished record on gender predictions.)

Farther back in the exit row is the very tall, lanky young man who is not a basketballer. Sue's boys all got that same awkward, sheepish look when they suddenly shot up: *I don't know how I got all the way up here!* Sue chatted with him and the big, military-looking guy with the buzz cut in the news agency. She assumed at first they were father and son, but soon worked out that they were not. As Max pointed out, not all tall people are related.

She can't see the poor young mother with the baby and toddler, but wow, they sure did hear that baby! Oh, wait, there's the sweet young girl who shook so badly when she was checking her bag she dropped her phone twice. Max picked it up for her, both times, and it didn't take Sue long to learn the poor child was terrified of flying and this was her first solo trip. Her name is Kayla. Sue knows a middle-aged Kayla who runs a rescue shelter, and told Kayla all about her, which gave Kayla the opportunity to show Sue photos of the puppy she got for her eighteenth birthday, so hopefully that distracted her.

The person in the middle seat directly behind Sue, whose brutally hard kneecaps have been intermittently digging into her lower back, doesn't see Sue. His attention is on the lady as she says to him, "I expect unintentional injury. Age seventy-nine."

The man's eyebrows pop. "You're injured?"

"Cause of death, age of death, as I think I've said, multiple times now."

Sue can't help but smile at her restrained tone. It's the tone of a professional woman with a job to do, dealing with people who don't listen. Sue knows the feeling.

She had not noticed the lady at the airport, but now she observes her as if she were triaging a patient who presented in the ER. Eyes clear but sunken, lips dry and chapped. Dehydrated? Sue would guess she is in her early seventies. Young for dementia, but it's a possibility. Not agitated, violent, restless, or confused. Nothing to indicate substance abuse. She looks ordinary and familiar and nice, like someone Sue would know from aqua aerobics or the local shops. Her blouse is beautiful. White with small green feathers. It's the sort of blouse that would appeal to Sue if she saw it on a rack, although she probably couldn't afford it. If they'd been seated together Sue would have complimented her on it.

"I expect." The lady points at a frowny fortyish woman wearing one of those wildly colored sequined caftan-type tops. *She* looks more like a fortune teller than the lady. "Pneumonia. Age ninety-four."

Sue feels resentful. Why does caftan woman get ninety-four? She doesn't look especially healthy. Sue would put good money on hypertension.

The lady moves farther down the aisle and Sue can no longer hear her over the roar of the plane.

Caftan woman looks up at Sue. "Do we know what that was all about?"

"She's predicting deaths," explains Sue.

"Oh, good for me. What about you?"

Sue pretends not to hear. She sits back down and refastens her seat belt. The man behind her is digging his knees even harder into her lower back. She can hear him saying, "So, wait, she's saying I'm living until I'm seventy-five? Is that what she said? Or was it seventy-nine?" As if he doesn't want to miss any extra years he's owed.

"You know she's talking gibberish, right?" Max puts his hand on Sue's thigh. "Don't get your knickers in a knot." His hand feels too heavy. "She does not have access to our health records. Unless she's a cyber hacker, of course. Always a possibility these days." He laughs hollowly.

"Well, she might be a psychic," says Sue. "Or think she's one."

"You don't believe in psychics."

"How do you know?" says Sue, just to be difficult. Max often blissfully assumes their politics, memories, food and television preferences will align, and mostly they do, but not always! They're different people!

"Have you ever been to one? No. You have not."

"I have, actually," says Sue. "I had my cards read. We all did it for Jane's fiftieth."

"Well, did those cards say anything about you getting . . . whatever she said?" asks Max. He doesn't want to say the word "cancer." Whenever he hears of a serious diagnosis, the first involuntary expression to cross his face is pure revulsion. Fear disguised as disgust.

"No," says Sue. It was more than ten years ago. The tarot card reader sorrowfully predicted that Sue's husband would have an affair with a short Italian woman in the next year. Sue never told Max. She didn't want to put any ideas in his head. She just upped the sex, kept him busy. Just in case. He'd seemed pleased. She may well have changed their destinies.

"There you go then," says Max.

"Well, I'm sure there are good and bad psychics," says Sue. "It's not an exact science."

Max bangs his phone on his armrest. "It's not a science at all!"

"Okay, keep your hat on."

Suddenly she gets it: Max is trying to convince her not to be upset because *he's* upset. Her husband is a self-employed plumber, the most practical of men. He can fix and build anything, from a cubbyhouse to a cake to a grandchild's "working model of the digestive system" due the next day, but he cannot bear it when there is something to worry about but nothing to be done, no way to fix it.

He's secretly worried the lady actually does know something about their future. Max's feelings always manifest as something different, like the way pain in the neck, jaw, or shoulder can mean a heart attack. It's been this way from the moment they met forty years ago, when a fair-haired, big-shouldered boy marched up to her at a church youth group and brusquely asked if she'd like to see a movie with him, please. To this day, she doesn't know why she said yes, because it seemed like someone was holding a gun to his head, his expression was so unfriendly. It wasn't until she said yes that his whole face transformed. "Really?" He smiled like a loon, revealing the famous O'Sullivan dimples he would pass on to all five of their sons and two of their grandchildren. *"Really?* I thought for sure you'd say no." She was a goner from the moment she saw those dimples.

"No one can see the future," frets Max.

Oncologists can, thinks Sue. Oncologists, neurologists, cardiologists, hematologists. All those damned "ologists." They're the fortune tellers. They don't read your cards, they read your blood tests, your scans, your genetic tests, and see terrible things in your future.

"I'm not dying at sixty-six, darling." She pulls the in-flight magazine from the seat pocket in front of her and points at the advertisement on the back page. "We'll be swanning about Europe."

"Exactly." Max's shoulders drop. "Poor old girl is unhinged." He holds his phone over the magazine and snaps a photo of the river cruise ad. "One of those cruises might be fun. We could work that into the itinerary."

He leans forward to address the man sitting next to Sue. "Not worried about your 'workplace accident,' I hope, mate? Don't believe in psychics, do you?"

"Not really," says the man. "But I guess I might take extra care at work next year. I turn forty-three in November."

"Do you have a dangerous job?" asks Sue.

"Civil engineer."

"Better keep that hard hat on then," says Max.

"Oh, well, I'm mostly at my computer, but yeah, sure, might be a good idea to—" He cups his hands over his head and pretends to duck from a flying object.

"Sorry we haven't introduced ourselves," says Sue. "I'm Sue, and this is Max."

"Leo." The man leans across Sue to shake Max's hand.

There is silence for a moment. Leo plucks at the fabric of his pants. Max clasps his hands over his stomach. A bit too much good eating and good wine in Tasmania. Lots of salads on the menu this week. Sue traces the letters of the alphabet in the air with her right foot. She tore a ligament in her ankle many years ago and tries to keep up her strengthening exercises whenever she remembers.

Now Leo turns sideways to face Sue formally, as if they're at a fancy dinner party and he's now addressing the guest to his left. He has lovely green eyes. Sue stops her ankle exercises and smiles. She feels maternal toward him as well as a mild attraction. It's disconcerting how often that happens these days.

"I'm sorry I haven't been good company," he says. "I've missed my daughter's school musical because of the delay."

"Oh, *no*," says Sue. "That's bad luck." She pats his arm. Forgets the attraction and goes full-on grandma. She's had him all wrong. He's not Mr. Important Man, he's a stressed young dad. "How old is she?"

Before he can answer, a troubled youthful voice rises over the plane's hum. "Wait, you expect *what*?"

"Okay, so I think we definitely need to—" begins Sue, but Max and Leo are already reaching for their call bells.

Chapter 7

Look, I can answer my own question. I don't need to ask the bearded man.

You should always apologize for your actions. Whether you believe in free will or not.

Manners matter.

A sincere apology has the power to save a friendship, a marriage, even a life.

Just say sorry. That's all you need to do.

I am sorry. Profoundly sorry.

I could not, in fact, be sorrier.

Chapter 8

The cabin manager, Allegra Patel, is in the lavatory when the call buttons first commence their peevish melody. So that's Murphy's Law. Or Allegra's Law, more like it. Her period has turned up a week early, and she is rummaging through her bag for a tampon and each time she thinks she has found one it turns out to be the same tube of lip balm, which is making her laugh softly and kind of demonically.

Today is her twenty-eighth birthday and she hadn't been expecting champagne and rainbows, but she had assumed it would be a pleasantly neutral Friday, not one of those days where everything consistently goes just a tiny bit wrong, where that scratchy sandpapery feeling starts to build up behind your eyes.

"Give me a break," she mutters as she feels the first cruel clench of a cramp. Her cramps are always worse when she flies.

She digs farther into the corner crevices of her bag.

Euphoric relief: one solitary, beautiful tampon. Thank you, universe.

She'd been pleased when she got the roster for her birthday: Sydney-Hobart, Hobart-Sydney. Home in time for dinner with her parents and brother. She likes this leg. The flight length is not too long but also not so short that you're rushed off your feet trying to get everything done. It had been a bonus when her friend Anders, who she's known since they trained together, was rostered on the same crew. He arrived at the preflight briefing with doughnuts and a metallic heart-shaped helium balloon.

Sadly, it was all downhill from there.

"Not these two tossers *together*," moaned Anders, when their two pilots swaggered into the crew room like movie stars. "There won't be enough room for their inflated egos in the cockpit."

Captain Victor "Vic" Levine addressed them with his usual brusque brevity. Unremarkable weather. Full flights. He's not rude. He just doesn't fully register anyone's existence unless they're a fellow pilot. To him, all cabin crew members are interchangeable. They're not quite real to him. They're like holograms.

"Birthday, eh?" said First Officer Jonathan "Jonny" Summers, instead of saying, "Happy birthday, Allegra," like an actual human. He accepted a doughnut, took a minuscule bite, scrunched up his offensively handsome face as if he'd eaten a lemon, and then *dropped it in the garbage can* in full view of everyone.

"I'll never love anyone as much as I hate that guy," Anders had whispered in Allegra's ear. He was especially distressed by the disrespectful treatment of the doughnut because he's currently undergoing an aggressive intermittent fasting regimen. He has a wedding next weekend where he'll come face-to-face with an ex he hasn't seen in five years. Allegra will be glad when this wedding is finally done.

The other two members of Allegra's crew today are fine: just mildly exasperating.

Kim is a placid, padded woman who has been with the airline since the eighties and ambles about the cabin as if she's hosting a backyard barbecue, leaning one elbow on the back of seats for long chummy chats with passengers. A quick service is a good service, but it's never going to be a quick service if you've got Kim on the other side of your cart. Ellie is at the opposite end of the spectrum, young and fizzy. She's only just got her wings, so is brimming with new knowledge, eager to impress and do every PA announcement.

On the first leg Ellie informed Allegra that Anders had taken a bag

of pretzels from the food cart, which Ellie understood was "technically stealing." Why are new flight attendants always such snitches?

"I was feeling faint!" said Anders, who was more ashamed that
he'd broken his fast with half a pretzel than that he'd broken the rules.

"Eat the rest of them, you look like a corpse!" Allegra hissed, wondering if his stupid diet was turning into an actual safety issue she
needed to address.

And then: the delay.

It would have been polite for the flight deck to keep her in the
loop, seeing as she was the one responsible for keeping control of an
increasingly agitated cabin, but she heard nothing for ages, while the
baby screamed like a broken car alarm and tempers simmered, bub-
bled, and boiled over.

The reason was finally revealed to be a broken seat belt in the
cockpit. They had to wait for someone to fly in from Sydney because
Hobart has no engineer on-site. If the passengers had learned that,
they would have been offering to fix it themselves. No doubt the
square-jawed guy Anders dubbed "Superhero" could have fixed it
with his eyes closed.

"He'll trek through the mountains to save us before we turn to
cannibalism," he'd whispered as they both watched the guy march
down the aisle. Allegra elbowed Anders. He didn't actually use the
words "plane crash," but he sure did imply them.

Allegra could have fixed the belt. She's handy. Sadly, that's not the
way safety protocols work. She was once on a flight where they had
to wait an hour for an engineer to fix a broken overhead bin, which he
did with a strip of *masking tape*. Took him three seconds, tearing it off
with his teeth while asking her out for a drink.

She washes her hands and studies her face in the mirror, then gets
that disconcerting but not unpleasant out-of-body feeling she's been
experiencing since she was seven. She would look at herself in the
bathroom mirror and float free of her body for a few seconds. "I left
my body!" she told her mother. "Did you, beta?" said her mother.
"That's nice."

"Do you know how insanely beautiful you are?" said the most recent man with whom she'd had sex (two weeks ago now, and never again, absolutely not, done with that) as he ran a fingertip back and forth across her collarbone.

"You're done with him, Allegra," she whispers to her reflection. "*Done.*"

He's like a junk food addiction: delicious at first, then regrettable.

Insanely beautiful.

I mean, that's a nice compliment.

Nope. Stop it.

People comment on her beauty often enough that it would be disingenuous not to believe she's attractive, but high school burns forever. Only tall, skinny blond girls were considered beautiful back then, the girls who, ironically, came back from summer holidays with tans that were exclaimed over and complimented, tans that made their skin nearly as dark as Allegra's, but her brown was not the right brown. Even Allegra's own mother would say, "Don't go out in the sun, Allegra, you'll get too dark." Her mum wouldn't say that now. She's evolved, like everyone.

She thinks of Sara Perkins in Year 8, saying, "Imagine how beautiful Allegra would be if she wasn't, you know . . ." Meaningful jerk of her head. She said this in front of Allegra. She thought it was a compliment, or at least not an insult. Allegra wonders if Sara Perkins ever wakes up in a cold sweat thinking, "Oh, God, did I really say that?" *You really did, Sara Perkins, you really did.*

Allegra finds Panadol in her bag, palms two tablets into her mouth, swallows them without water (life skill), and reapplies her lipstick. She only wears makeup at work. She is "required" to wear a "minimum" of foundation, eye shadow, and lipstick. Male flight attendants like Anders must only be clean-shaven with their hair cut above the collar, which is ironic because Anders taught Allegra everything she knows about makeup. He gave tutorials when they trained together in Melbourne. Allegra laughs each time she remembers him, makeup brush poised, shaking his head sorrowfully and saying, "I can't *believe* you girls don't know how to contour."

She will never forget the pure exhilaration she felt the day she got her wings. Her dream job. Not her mother's dream job for her. She'd always wanted Allegra to be a dentist, a strangely specific career choice, seemingly based only on Allegra's excellent toothbrushing as a child. Allegra's dad is happy for her—he loves the perk of free standby flights for family members. Thankfully, her brother got the medical degree, so they can show off about Taj to the grandparents, while Allegra makes them seem "interesting." She was flying the day after she completed Ground School. Walking through the airport that first morning she'd felt glamorous and alive. All these years later she still feels lucky and secretly sorry for her friends in nine-to-five office jobs. No one expects *them* to have interesting anecdotes about their work (and they sure don't), but people love to hear about Allegra's work as a flight attendant.

People always want to know if she's had the oxygen masks drop, and Allegra enjoys telling them about the one time she was working when they lost cabin pressure and the masks dropped, and she saw the horrified realization hit her passengers that maybe they should have listened during all the safety demonstrations they'd been ignoring. She also once had a pregnant woman's water break. Who knew there was that *much* amniotic fluid sloshing around in every "baby bump"?! Allegra had carefully studied the obstetrician's letter that today's hugely pregnant passenger handed over as she boarded. "I'm only twenty-five weeks," the woman sighed, "I just look gigantic."

Kim once had two passengers get into a brawl over the reclining of a seat—fists flying, yelling, police, viral video—but Anders trumps them all because he had a passenger die last year. It might even have been on this same leg. The man's poor wife was sitting right next to him. Thought he was napping. Anders said the man was old, but not, you know, Dumbledore old. Allegra has been keeping a careful eye on the ancient couple on this flight. They're retired doctors, don't require wheelchairs, their only walking aids are walking sticks, and they're both wearing fancy Apple Watches, which is endearing. She wants them delivered to Sydney alive and well.

She straightens her back, smacks her lipsticked lips together, and watches her face in the mirror go into work mode: professional, polite, do not fuck with me.

Please, universe, don't let these pinging call buttons mean a death or a brawl or a baby. I'm too crampy. Also, it's fun telling horror work stories *after* the fact, not so much when they're actually happening.

As soon as she leaves the lavatory, she checks the Flight Attendant Panel: a computerized screen showing her the exact location of the active call buttons. Three in the first two rows of economy. Another one pings as she watches. Something is going on. She knows Anders is packing up the back galley, but why isn't eager-beaver Ellie dealing with these? As Ellie would well know, they're meant to monitor the cabin and answer call buttons as fast as possible.

Kim is busy cosseting the business-class passengers with salted caramel chocolate balls and extravagant compliments about someone's earrings.

"Anything I should know about?" Allegra asks her. The curtain is drawn, so they can't see what's going on in economy.

"What should I know about?" Kim is oblivious. Of course she is.

A passenger holds up a wineglass. "Kim, could I trouble you for a top-up?"

"No problem, Mrs. Lee!" Kim beams. "Back in a flash."

Allegra grits her teeth, leaves business class to Kim. She pulls back the curtain and surveys the main cabin. She can't immediately see anything untoward. People are up in the aisle as you would expect at this time: heading to the lavatory, opening overhead bins. There is, however, a subtle change in the atmosphere. Nothing dramatic, but *something*. A low hum of voices. Not agitated as such, but more conversation going on than you would normally expect.

Right. Start at the front with the chatty husband and wife who told Allegra all about their Tasmanian holiday in maybe a little more detail than she needed during the delay. She knows their names because they introduced themselves so enthusiastically, as if they expected they'd all be staying in touch after this day: Sue and Max O'Sullivan.

She smiles as she leans over to turn off Max's call light. "What can I do for you, Mr. O'Sullivan?"

"There's a lady we think might be upsetting people." Sue answers on her husband's behalf. She points backward over her shoulder, as though discreetly pointing out someone behind her at a party. "Not us! *We're* not upset. We're perfectly fine."

"She's predicting deaths," explains Max.

"Deaths? She's threatening people?" Allegra blanches.

"No, no, love, more like a clairvoyant, thinks she's a fortune teller or whatever." He twirls a finger next to his ear. "Harmless."

Allegra's view of the back of the plane is blocked by a passenger in a sequined caftan top who is attempting to push her bulging carry-on bag back into the overhead bin.

The well-dressed anxious man in the aisle seat next to Sue says, "She's sitting across from me." He indicates the empty seat across the aisle from him. Four-Delta.

"Okay." Allegra tries to visualize the passenger. She switches off his call light too. "Thanks so much for letting me know."

A man's voice rises up from about three rows back. "*What* did you just say to me?"

Allegra feels her heart rate pick up. *You've got this,* she tells herself. *Kim handled a brawl; you can handle one wacky fortune teller.*

"Excuse me," she says to the caftan woman. "Could I get by?"

"Oh, sure, but could you help me here?" The woman dumps the bag back on the floor. Flight attendants are not technically meant to help passengers lift bags. *You packed it, you stack it.* But in practice, Allegra is always helping people.

"Wheels first is best," says Allegra. She goes to lift the bag, assuming the woman will continue to bear some of the weight, but she releases her hands and stands back, watching with a frown, as though

Allegra is a bellboy charged with the welfare of her precious bag: apparently packed with bricks.

Allegra, who changed into flats once they were in the air, is right on the airline's minimum-height requirement. She feels like she might have shrunk since she first did that terrifying "reach test" at the Assessment Day. It was the very first hurdle two hundred hopeful applicants faced at the door of the auditorium. They had to take off their shoes and touch a strip of tape with their fingertips. "Reach for your dreams, honey!" Anders had said in Allegra's ear, before she knew his name. Later he said he was worried she'd dislocated her shoulder.

"Ooof." She feels a distinct twang in her lower back as she stretches on tippy-toes to wedge the bag into place.

"I think that might be over the weight limit for carry-on luggage, ma'am." She slams shut the bin.

"Shoes," replies the caftan lady. "Us girls need our shoes."

"Check it next time," says Allegra, with her most charming smile, while she imagines pushing her thumbs into the stupid entitled woman's eye sockets the way she was taught in school self-defense classes.

The woman sits down, huffy rather than grateful. Allegra now has a clear view of the aisle.

A small gray-haired lady is midway down the plane, pointing at passengers on both sides of the aisle one by one, as if she's assigning tasks. It's clear she is leaving ripples of mild consternation in her wake. Virtually every single head turns to watch her progress.

Allegra walks rapidly down the aisle. Two more call buttons light up, but she doesn't stop. The lady is maybe seven rows ahead, still pointing, still making pronouncements. Allegra is gaining ground. A man wearing a Hawaiian-style shirt shoots up his hand like a student with the right answer. "Miss?"

"I'll be with you in just a moment, sir." She keeps walking, but once again she's suddenly blocked. This time it's the astonishingly pregnant woman, feet sturdily planted apart like a cowboy walking into a bar, hands on holsters, except hers grip the seats on either side of her.

"Just discovered I won't make forty, which is bad luck for me," she tells Allegra without preamble, as if they're old friends. The giant firm balloon of her belly pushes into Allegra's hip. Allegra thinks queasily of the gallons of water sloshing around in there. "That lady seems to think she's some kind of oracle."

"Yes, I'm so sorry," says Allegra, trying to see past her. "I'm trying to stop her."

"It's okay. I just laughed. Prefer that to the horror birth stories people think I need to hear." The pregnant woman chuckles. "Or the ones who say, 'No getting off that roller coaster now! Sleep while you still can! You look like you're about to pop any minute!'"

"You're welcome to use the business-class toilet." Allegra steps sideways and indicates the front of the plane.

"Oh, that's okay, no special treatment required!" The woman taps her fingers against her belly like she's playing an accordion.

Farther down the plane a woman calls out, "Jesus is the only true prophet, my dear!"

"Please." Allegra wedges herself in front of someone's knees to let the pregnant woman pass to the front of the plane unimpeded.

The owner of the knees takes this as an opportunity. "There's a lady—"

"Yes." Allegra doesn't look at the passenger. "I know about the lady."

Two more call buttons chime. A voice rises in consternation. The baby begins to cry again. Ellie and Anders are both still missing in action.

"Gosh." The pregnant woman frowns. "I wonder if some people are taking her seriously."

"Yep, I'm actually *trying* to—"

"Ah! You should have said!"

The pregnant woman shifts herself and her enormous belly out of the way and Allegra is once more walking down the aisle as fast as she dares without giving the impression that this is an actual emergency, although she's starting to wonder if it might qualify.

Chapter 9

"If my time's up, so be it!"

This was the facile comment that led me to accidentally share a deeply personal story about my mother while we ate our terrible apricot chicken at that long-ago dinner party.

The man opposite me had been experiencing a health symptom of some sort but was refusing to get it checked out by a doctor. His wife was concerned.

I cannot now recall the symptom. Don't worry about it. It's not relevant.

I said I thought it was stupid not to go to the doctor.

I had not spoken much prior to that point and my remark caused a lull. I immediately realized the word "stupid" was too harsh for the lighthearted tone of the discourse.

"Silly" would have been a better choice. It sounded like I cared too much about this man's health. He wasn't *my* husband! I'd only just met him! I worried people might think I was attracted to this man.

I was attracted to him. He was very handsome.

I was embarrassed, so I attempted to explain my strong feelings. I told the truth.

I explained that my mother had always hated doctors. She was squeamish and superstitious, so she willfully ignored the symptoms of the illness that would eventually kill her.

"Fate won't be fought!" she said, again and again, until I wanted to scream.

In fact, I remember once I did scream, in the car, as I drove to the shops to buy her some ginger beer, which was the only thing her stomach could handle in the last weeks. I remember a child in the back seat of the car stopped next to me at a traffic light, staring in horrified fascination as he watched me silently howl.

She died a week before her sixtieth birthday. It was a preventable death and she chose not to prevent it.

"Well, see, your mother was a determinist," said the bearded man, and off he went on his lecture about determinism.

"My mother was a fool," I said after he finished. I was still very angry with my mother at that time of my life. I needed her and missed her very much.

The bearded man remarked that Albert Einstein refused life-saving surgery at the age of seventy-six, the implication being, I assume, that no one would consider *Einstein* to be a fool.

"I have done my share, it is time to go," said Einstein. (Apparently.) "I will do it elegantly."

Everyone was impressed by that anecdote. As I said, we were young. We therefore believed seventy-six was a perfectly acceptable and possibly elegant time to choose to die.

But I do remember wondering how Einstein's children felt about his decision not to have surgery, if they maybe felt like screaming in the car, if they begged him, "Dad. Please. Have the surgery."

I see from the internet that the attractive man who refused to see a doctor is still alive. His time still isn't up. His symptom, whatever it was, turned out to mean nothing.

Symptoms often mean nothing because they are not, in fact, symptoms, they are just the normal niggles and quibbles of being alive.

The attractive man still has all his hair and a second, much younger wife, which any woman could have predicted.

Chapter 10

Jesus is the only true prophet, my dear!

Paula Binici opens her eyes. What the . . . ? Did she dream those words or actually hear someone say them?

She's thirty-six years old, although she's told she looks much younger; possibly it's something to do with the shape of her face (heart-shaped) or maybe it's her damned hair, which is wispy, flyaway, flummoxes hairdressers, and makes her appear permanently windswept. There is always the fractional lift of an eyebrow when she mentions she's a lawyer. Now she looks like a hapless stay-at-home mother, which is what she is, rather than the competent, respected, well-paid contract lawyer she previously was, and will be again, very soon, once her children start school, which people assure her will happen in the "blink of an eye." *The days are long but the years are short,* her mother says. This will apparently make sense to her one day.

She must have dozed, but she's not sure for how long. There is something going on. She has missed some kind of important development. But what?

Her baby and toddler are both still asleep, both still breathing. The seat-belt sign has not come on. No turbulence. No oxygen masks have dropped. She shifts carefully, trying not to disturb her children, who are both using her as a pillow. Their small beautiful heads are as heavy and hard as bowling balls. *It goes so fast,* people tell her. Hilarious. She's been on this plane for a thousand years. Time has never gone slower.

Timmy's cheek is sticky with drool against her chest, one dimpled hand gripping the fabric of her shirt, pulling it to one side and exposing the graying lace of her oldest nursing bra. The cold buckle of the seat-belt extender rests against Timmy's bare skin just above his nappy, but Paula has given up fiddling with the two belts to make him more comfortable. The main thing is he's secure. Willow's cheek, also sticky, is pressed against Paula's arm, her mouth wide open in a perfect oval, a rim of chocolate around her rosebud lips. Paula has bribed her with so many forbidden treats she will probably have an upset stomach soon. It will be the obvious next development in this nightmarish flight.

When they'd been waiting on the tarmac, Willow and Timmy had initially been cheerful, unaware they weren't getting anywhere, and that time therefore didn't count. She knew they were using up their precious reserves of good behavior, and had distracted herself by pondering the legal implications of the delay. *When would a flight delay be considered a breach of contract? When time is of the essence. It is of the essence. I'm flying to Sydney for my sister's wedding next Saturday. My daughter is going to be a flower girl and they need time to make any necessary adjustments to her dress. What is the relevant contract anyway? A contract of carriage. Wait, the consumer guarantees would apply. Section 62: In the absence of agreement, the service will be provided within a reasonable time. But what does "reasonable time" mean? That's always up in the air. Ha ha. Nobody here is up in the air. Nobody ever knows what "reasonable" means or who the reasonable man is. Where is that elusive reasonable man? Am I married to him? Matt likes to think he's so reasonable.*

She'd been looking up a German case where passengers stuck on a plane sued for false imprisonment when Timmy began to scream. No warning. It probably terrified the hugely pregnant passenger seated close to the front of the plane who Paula had observed cradling her bump with the prideful exuberance of a first-time mother-to-be, although the woman probably thought she'd never let *her* child cry like that. In fact, Paula had never heard Timmy cry so hysterically. She began to worry that he was actually dying, in her arms, from a burst appendix or something. Then Willow began to weep, piteously, as if she were a child on a television commercial appealing for foster carers. Paula heard someone say, without even bothering to lower their voice, "If you can't control your kids, don't fly, simple as that."

She'd never been so stressed and sweaty in her life. A vision of herself screaming in full-throated harmony with the baby appeared in her head and then got stuck, in that familiar well-worn groove, sliding endlessly back and forth like a marble in one of those office novelty toys for executives. She imagined the horrified faces, the flight attendants running to restrain her, police called, a doctor called, a mental health assessment demanded.

She reasoned with herself, one of those exhausting back-and-forth arguments in which she specialized.

You're not going to do that, you would never do that.

But what if I do?

But you won't.

But what if I do.

But you won't.

And she didn't, because a nice man from a few rows back stood up and handed Timmy his car keys, then said in a deep Chris Hemsworth voice, "Great pair of lungs, little mate," like it was a compliment, not a complaint. The keys calmed Timmy instantly. Paula suspected it was because a big strong man had given him the keys. Timmy is a man's man. He never looks more comfortable or smug than when he's sitting on his daddy's lap.

Paula is in the middle seat, with Willow in the aisle. "Don't let her sit next to some predatory stranger," Matt had said, so she'd dutifully put Willow in the aisle seat, but the man next to Paula is surely too distinguished and well dressed to be a predator. She'd guess he's in his sixties, his Scottish accent so thick it's like it's been squeezed from a tube, and he's wearing a beautiful blue tie, which he hasn't loosened even a fraction. He didn't look judgmental during the Great Crying Debacle, just winced occasionally as he steadily turned the pages of some densely written book. Meanwhile Paula has had to continually drag Willow back into her seat so she's not swiped by someone's carelessly swinging bag or elbow or knocked out by the drinks cart. Thanks a lot, *Matt*.

She thinks of her former job in a Hobart law firm. Right now, the thought of being in her quiet-as-a-library, air-conditioned, plush-carpeted city office, with a takeout coffee on the desk next to her and a tricky clause to unravel, is like remembering a glorious tropical holiday. She sees now that she didn't just enjoy work, she *loved* it. She is a person whose brain requires certainty and control, rules and procedures, perhaps more than the average person, but motherhood has none of that and some days she is bored out of her freaking mind.

No, don't think that, Paula, that's awful.

(A thought is just a thought.)

Motherhood is fulfilling, important work, and every day she experiences a moment of pure, piercing bliss. That is true. At least most days, anyway. Yes, there's certainty and control at work, and satisfaction, but no moments of bliss.

Willow whimpers in her sleep, and Paula thinks: sick bag.

She stretches her hand around Timmy toward the seat pocket, but she can't reach it without waking him.

"This lady coming down the aisle appears to be causing some kind of . . . kerfuffle," says her Scottish companion. He has closed his book with one finger keeping his place.

"What lady?" asks Paula after a second, because there is a slight delay while she deciphers his words through the accent. If she doesn't panic, she can understand perfectly.

"Heading our way." He indicates with his chin. "She seems to be talking to every passenger, insulting them, perhaps? Oh, I think a flight attendant might be attempting to detain her—no, flight attendant has been waylaid!"

He raises himself in his seat to see, brightly curious.

A voice from in front of them says, "She's telling people when they're going to die."

Paula and the Scottish man exchange wide-eyed looks and raised eyebrows. Suddenly they are audience members enjoying an impromptu performance piece.

They both watch as a gray-haired lady addresses every passenger in the row ahead of them.

"I expect heart failure. Age eighty-two. I expect diabetes. Age seventy-nine. I expect snakebite. Age forty-eight."

"This is a bit confronting," says Paula. "Snakebite! How likely is that?"

"Perhaps a clairvoyant gone rogue, do you think?" says her seatmate. "I believe there was a new age festival in Hobart this weekend."

"Oh, yes, I saw that advertised," says Paula. "Are you a believer in all . . . that?" She's finding this adult conversation as stimulating as a double espresso.

"I confess I enjoy all things occult," says the Scottish man. "But I'm not a true believer."

"What is your profession?" asks Paula, because he seems too distinguished a man to ask "What do you do?"

"I'm a professor of psychiatry in the University of Tasmania Sleep and Chronobiology Department. I'm speaking at a conference in Sydney this week. What about yourself? When you're not busy looking after these two? I'm guessing you probably don't get much sleep right now."

He's so lovely! Why didn't they talk earlier? She's so interested in everything he has to say!

"Contract law," begins Paula, but now the lady is nearly upon them.

"Did you just tell me I have *diabetes*?" says the passenger sitting directly in front of Paula.

"Cause of death, age of death," says the lady tersely. "I couldn't be clearer."

"Great way to derail someone's weight-loss journey!"

An older woman's voice cuts in, "Danielle, she does not mean you have diabetes."

"Well, I think that's exactly what she means, Mum!"

The Scottish man snickers. "I shouldn't laugh."

The lady is now talking to the three broad-chested men crammed shoulder to shoulder in the row diagonally opposite. "I expect heart disease, age eighty-four. I expect dementia, age eighty-nine. I expect skiing accident, age fifty-five."

Three heads turn in startled unison.

"Lots of heart disease," comments the Scottish man. "Perhaps she's sponsored by the Heart Foundation?" He chuckles generously at his own joke and Paula laughs along.

The lady steps forward.

"Ooh! Our turn!" The Scottish man rubs his hands together.

Paula thinks, *Wait, I know her.* Something about her mouth? She can imagine her smiling. Laughing. She's not smiling now, that's for sure. She looks grim.

Paula has always been excellent with faces and sometimes suspects she might be a "super-recognizer," one of the two percent of the population with such superior facial recognition skills that they get employed by the military. However, it's also likely she overestimates her abilities simply because she's just so good in comparison to her sister, who is notoriously bad with faces and once stood behind Paula in a supermarket line looking blankly at her for a good few seconds before Paula said, "Lisa, you idiot, it's me."

Paula is clearly not a super-recognizer because if she really has seen this woman before, she can't remember where. There goes her career with the military.

"I expect pneumonia." The lady points at the Scottish man. "Age ninety-one."

"Ah. Pneumonia. The old man's friend." The Scottish man nods with satisfaction as if that's exactly what he'd anticipated. "Very likely. I'm sure you're right."

The lady points at Paula. "I expect—"

"I don't want my fortune told," interrupts Paula. "Thank you anyway." She shifts the baby in her arms.

"I expect chronic obstructive pulmonary disease. Age eighty-four."

"Really?" Paula's not sure what chronic obstructive pulmonary disease means, but eighty-four does not seem particularly old to her. Her grandmother just turned eighty-eight and is in excellent health, still playing golf twice a week. She has far more energy than Paula.

"We actually have excellent longevity in our family." She's not sure if she's trying to be witty for the benefit of the Scottish man or if she's truly hoping to convince the lady to give her a different prediction. "So I would have thought I'd make ninety."

It doesn't matter because the lady is not interested. She points at Willow. "I expect—"

"No," says Paula. "No, thank you. Definitely not. She's too little. Please don't."

"Pneumonia. One hundred and three."

"Oh, snap!" says the Scottish man. "Although you would have thought they'd have a cure for pneumonia by then, wouldn't you?"

"One hundred and three," repeats Paula. "Well, all right." She looks at her daughter's matted dark curls and imagines her as a wizened old lady. She'll be so grumpy! The afflictions of old age won't suit Willow. The kid becomes enraged when her nose is blocked.

The lady looks beyond them to the next row. She goes to step forward and then does a double take when she notices the baby in Paula's arms.

She stops in her tracks. She points at the back of Timmy's head and for a moment says nothing. Her breathing quickens.

"What?" asks Paula. Surely she is about to say that Timmy will also live until he's over one hundred like his sister, but the lady says nothing. Does she look sad? Is that *sadness*?

"*What?*"

"I expect," she says.

Paula feels a sharp spike of panic. "No, stop, I don't want—"

"Drowning," says the lady. "Age seven."

Paula feels it like a blow to the solar plexus. "Don't say that. That is absolutely not true."

"Oh, of *course* it's not true." The Scottish man holds a protective arm in front of Timmy.

He says to Paula, "These people are charlatans. I'm so sorry. I should not have encouraged her." He addresses the lady in a louder voice, his accent thicker than before. "That's enough now, madam, move along, please. We have no interest in your so-called expectations."

The lady does not move. She is staring at Timmy with the most dreadful look of naked pain.

Paula shifts the baby to her side in a futile move to hide him from that awful gaze. The sudden movement causes Willow's head to slide off her mother's arm. She is instantly awake and upright, rubbing her eyes with her knuckles. Timmy unpeels his cheek from Paula's chest and his whole body tenses.

"You should not say that sort of thing!" Tears spring up in Paula's eyes. She always cries when she's angry, which is infuriating. It sends the wrong message.

"But you see, fate won't be fought," whispers the lady.

"Mummy?" says Willow shakily as Timmy begins to whimper, but Paula is not done with this lady, although the lady is apparently done with her and is stepping forward to the next row.

Paula turns in her seat and calls out, "That is a *terrible* thing to say to a mother!"

Chapter 11

It *was* a terrible thing to say to a mother.

When I put my hands to my cheeks, I can still feel the heat of my shame.

I brought my profession, the profession I love, into serious disrepute that day, and we already had an image problem.

Chapter 12

"Excuse me! Madam!" Allegra is gaining ground. The thud, thud, thud of her footsteps reverberates through her body.

There is something very wrong with her lower back. Or perhaps it's the middle of her back. She is holding it stiffly because it feels like the slightest movement will result in pain.

She can see the mother rocking the screaming baby. Her toddler, in the aisle seat, a little girl with flushed pink cheeks, is writhing about, arching her back in that way kids do. The man next to the mother is scrabbling for something in the seat pocket.

Allegra knows exactly what's about to happen a microsecond before it happens, but she has too much momentum to stop.

Chapter 13

The Australian Psychics Association, of which I am not a member, released a statement condemning my actions. As they should.

My mother never told anyone who sat for her anything terrible or distressing that she saw in their future.

"What would be the point of that?" she said. "They come to me for hope."

"If fate won't be fought," I said, "what's the point of any of it?"

I knew the point. The point was that it paid the bills.

Chapter 14

Paula rocks Timmy. She uses the breathing techniques she learned for childbirth.

What a creepy, cruel thing for someone to say about her baby. She will not let it worry her. She is not "spiritual." She is an Anglican.

If Timmy never goes near water he won't drown. Simple as that. They will move to the desert. She will lock him up. For God's sake, she doesn't *believe* this kind of rubbish.

"*Mummy?*" says Willow. "*Mummy?*"

"I think the wee lass might—"

Paula stares for a dull stupefied moment at the document the Scottish man is trying to hand her. She squints to read it, as if it's a contract or a file she needs to act on, but she really doesn't have the bandwidth for this right now.

Then she gets it. Of course it's not a document, idiot, it's a sick bag. She takes the bag. A flight attendant hurries down the aisle.

Willow turns her head.

"No," says Paula.

Chapter 15

In fairness, I don't think I can be held responsible for the toddler. I saw what she was eating in the departure lounge. You didn't need any special abilities to predict that particular outcome.

Chapter 16

Allegra shrieks, "*No!*"

Not the appropriate service language.

Ground School never covered this and Ground School was intense.

She extinguished real fires. She shouted, "*Brace, Brace, Brace!*" over and over, while imagining her workplace plummeting to the earth. She set up a life raft in a swimming pool while sprinklers poured heavy rain and fake lightning flashed overhead. She swam the length of a pool fully dressed, dragging the dead weight of Anders, who went full Method playing the role of an injured passenger, groaning and crying, and didn't help her out by kicking even a little bit.

She can resuscitate, placate, and charm. She is word perfect on every drill, every procedure. She is ready and willing to save her passengers' lives: even the whiny, grabby ones. She is not, however, prepared for a small child to projectile-vomit on her like she's channeling the kid in *The Exorcist*. It's the volume. The *velocity*. The epic revoltingness. It's all over her skirt. It's in her shoes. It's seeping through her stockings. It's between her toes.

The distraught mother has an expression of such horror you would think Allegra had been knifed by her child and is bleeding out in front of her, and that is the appropriate expression.

Now the mother is pulling wet wipes from somewhere on her person, like a magician producing a stream of colored scarves, and she is shoving them at Allegra. "Sorry. Sorry. Oh my God, I'm so sorry."

"It's not a problem." Allegra tries not to retch as she dabs at her clothes, recalling that she did not bring a spare uniform today because she didn't want to be bothered carrying her bigger bag. "It's really not a problem."

The lady is talking now to the elderly retired doctors, both thankfully still alive. They are nodding and smiling respectfully, seemingly unbothered by whatever she is saying. Perhaps their former professions and their ages mean they are not afraid to face their own mortality, or perhaps they can't actually hear a word she's saying and they're just nodding along, pretending to hear.

She bends forward and tectonic plates shift in her back.

It's my birthday, she thinks pathetically as her eyes fill with tears of pain and she attempts to smile at the glassy-eyed little girl now slumped back in her seat, with a relieved, stunned expression on her face and her thumb in her mouth.

"You okay, sweetie?" She deserves an Oscar for her caring tender tone.

"I'm so sorry," says the kid's mother again. "I was distracted by that awful lady."

"Please don't worry," says Allegra. "It happens." Her decision to remain childless is now set in stone.

The lady progresses down the plane as steadily and efficiently as a conscientious crew member distributing snacks.

Chapter 17

It was a cool clear April morning in Hobart.

That day. The day of the flight. The day I did what I did.

I did not eat breakfast. The previous day had not been a good one. There had been a distressing incident at the Fast Fitness Gym, followed immediately by a mortifying incident at the Everyday Fresh Market grocery store, and subsequently there was no food in the house.

I had a flight to catch. There is something about a day when you have a flight to catch. Even a short domestic flight to Sydney. Even when you fly frequently. It's an obstacle in your day and it's hard to see around it.

I was to spend just two nights in Sydney. My overnight bag was already packed. Carry-on luggage only. I'm an organized person and an excellent packer.

I don't know if this is significant, but I remember I had a great deal of difficulty pinning my brooch to my blouse that morning. No matter how I tried, I couldn't seem to manage it. I have worn that brooch every single day of my life for thirty years. I've pinned and unpinned that brooch on thousands of occasions. I've pinned it to good silk and cheap cotton, to denim and linen and wool and a whole lot of polyester. Before that day, I had done it every morning when I got dressed, without thinking, like cleaning my teeth.

Imagine if you suddenly found you couldn't clean your teeth. It might upset you too.

I have just now recalled that my grandmother lost the dexterity in her hands and used an elastic band to keep her toothbrush attached to her hand when she cleaned her teeth.

I'm not keen on that happening to me.

"What the heck?" I said out loud, to try to make it seem as though I were lightly amused, not wildly infuriated, by my predicament, as if it were something inconsequential like a jar lid that won't be opened, although in truth that can be quite consequential depending on your dinner plans. My voice, in the empty house, sounded hoarse, like a smoker's voice. I thought, Who's *that*? She sounded like my auntie Pat, who was a lifelong smoker, although the "ciggies" didn't kill her. She died of kidney disease caused by the large doses of phenacetin in the Bex Powders she took every day for her headaches. She worked at a dressmaking factory in Redfern and said all the girls took Bex. You might recognize their iconic advertisement aimed at women: *Have a cup of tea, a Bex, and a good lie-down.* It's an amusing pop culture reference but it wasn't so amusing for all those women who died of kidney disease.

Anyhow.

That was the first time my own voice had surprised me, although my face surprises me every day. There is always that one startled millisecond before I adjust: Oh, yes, that's right, I forgot, this is you, this is how you look now. I don't expect to see my twenty-year-old face. I think I expect to see my forty-five- or even fifty-five-year-old face looking back at me. It feels like an error, but I'm not disappointed. I have never been vain.

Correction: I have felt vanity regarding my professional abilities.

Correction: There have been times in my life where I felt beautiful and enjoyed feeling beautiful. For example, I once owned a flattering, slim-fitting, emerald-green crocheted dress. I was always wolf-whistled when I wore that dress, and a man referred to me as a "bomb-shell." I liked that very much. It's possible I was, and remain, somewhat vain about how good I looked in that dress. Wolf-whistling is no longer acceptable, and I think it may also be unacceptable to admit you once liked it, presumably because it belongs to the same category of behavior as the common, cheerful exhortation from a building site, "Show us your tits!" which nobody likes. Or perhaps some people do, I don't know. Each to their own.

I am also a little vain about my hair.

Anyhow. I finally placed my brooch on my dressing table and walked out onto my back veranda to calm myself down.

I live in Battery Point in a one-bedroom "workers' cottage" that was built in 1895. I had only recently purchased the property at the time of the flight. It didn't yet feel like home. It felt like a grave error.

I can see Mount Wellington from my back veranda if I turn side-ways. If I look straight ahead I can see the foreshore and right across the River Derwent. I can see yacht clubs and the marina, and if I look directly below I can see slivers of the backyards and back decks of the homes on the street that runs parallel to mine but farther down the hill.

There was snow on the mountain that morning. Hobart had just had its coldest Easter in eighty years. The white of the snow against the blue of the sky made me think of the whitewashed houses with bright blue roofs on the Greek islands.

The air was as crisp as a crunchy apple.

I do not care for apples.

I opened and closed my stiff hands, trying to loosen them.

Something caught my eye as I looked at my hands and I saw a woman on her back deck waving enthusiastically up at me. She'd misinterpreted my hand movements. She thought I was waving at her. I would never have waved at her! I think the polite thing is to pre-tend you can't see anyone else in the privacy of their own homes.

I could not properly see the features of her face, but she had fashionable dark hair and she wore a white silk dressing gown.

Look, there was no way for me to know if the fabric was silk or her hair fashionable. It was just something to do with the way she moved; she moved like a fashionably haired woman wearing a silk dressing gown. I could see some kind of earth-moving equipment in her backyard. So in addition to waving, she was *renovating*. There would be noise and dust. Wonderful, I thought.

At that point a younger man came out onto the back deck and handed her a coffee cup. (Could have been tea, but it seemed more likely to be coffee.) He looked up and I think he may even have lifted a hand to wave, too, but I quickly stepped back inside. That was quite enough waving for one morning.

I tried once more to pin my brooch to my blouse, and by now I was feeling extremely tetchy, and once again I couldn't seem to get a grip on the tiny sharp pin. I felt so frustrated! What was I doing differently? I remember meeting my eyes in my dressing-table mirror and *snarling* at myself. I remember the strange duality of it: me being so aggressively angry with me.

My reaction was oversized and unexpected. I threw the brooch in a fit of anger, as if it were the brooch's fault. It's not behavior you would expect from my personality type. Supposedly, the late Queen Elizabeth and I share the same personality type although I'm sure she wasn't actually required to take the Myers-Briggs personality test for her position. I assume somebody decided her personality type based on observation.

You can probably guess what happened after I threw that brooch across the room.

Exactly.

I couldn't find it. It's a very small, delicate piece of jewelry. I knew logically that it had to be somewhere in the room, but it felt like it had vanished into thin air.

I got systematic. I knelt down on my hands and knees. I started from the far corner of the room and divided the bedroom into imaginary grids of approximately thirty by thirty centimeters, and then I went grid by grid across the room, running my hands across the floorboards and the gray wool blend of my non-slip rug.

It took fourteen grids before I found it.

It was near the bed. Nowhere near where I thought it would be. I stood back up and calmly pinned the brooch to my blouse, no problem at all, just the way I'd always done those eleven thousand times or so before.

I then sat in the armchair in my study, my packed bag at my feet, until it was time for my taxi.

That would have been at least four hours, which is a long time to sit without moving, without thinking a single thought. I didn't eat breakfast. Or morning tea. Or lunch. I did not have a glass of water or even a cup of tea. I did not eat a Monte Carlo biscuit.

There was something not right with me that day.

But I guess you already knew that.

Chapter 18

Ethan Chang already has death on his mind when the Death Lady approaches his row.

So that's ironic, or coincidental, or possibly it's evidence he's living in a simulation.

He isn't just casually thinking about death, either. He's *fixated* on the topic. He's been thinking about nothing else all day.

One of the flight attendants on this morning's flight out of Sydney had asked if he were "off to Hobart for work or pleasure?" with a big friendly smile.

"Funeral," Ethan had answered, and the poor woman didn't know where to put her smile.

It was his first-ever funeral. At the age of twenty-nine. His flatmate, Jasmine, talked him through funeral etiquette. She said he should dress like it's a job interview, don't be late, don't chew gum, turn your phone to silent, and open every conversation with "I'm so sorry for your loss." She said his broken wrist was not an excuse to get out of a funeral. She said funerals weren't like birthdays. He wouldn't get another chance next year.

Jasmine has been to extravagant funerals all over the world. She's been to a memorial service where guests sipped champagne while the deceased's ashes were scattered by means of a magnificent fireworks display. She said it was touching, but it would have been better if they'd synced the fireworks to the music.

She moves in very different circles to Ethan because she's an heiress. A frozen-fish heiress. He's seen her described that way in the social pages: *Frozen-fish heiress Jasmine Dumas, arrives in Rome for lavish celebrity wedding.*

Frozen fish made Jasmine's dad rich, "richer than God," but he's keen for his children to learn "how the real world works." He therefore bought Jasmine a Sydney apartment with only stingy ocean *glimpses* from the master bedroom and made her responsible for all the other expenses like electricity, water, and so on. Jasmine is philosophically opposed to working nine to five (she is an entrepreneur and needs creative space), so she advertised on Flatmate Finders for someone to take the second smaller bedroom, and that's how she found Ethan.

Jasmine has turned out to be both a good landlord and flatmate.

She even cut up his steak after his rock-climbing accident. She just did it without even asking. She said her brother (who lives full-time in Paris now, his apartment has only stingy glimpses of the Eiffel Tower, once again "keeping it real") was also into extreme sports and he'd broken seven bones. Ethan didn't tell Jasmine that he is definitely *not* into extreme sports. It had been his first time at the rock-climbing center and he didn't even make it as far as the supposedly easy "bouldering wall" before he tripped over his own backpack while attempting to put on his harness, fracturing his scaphoid bone.

"Mountain biking? Skateboarding? Snowboarding?" guessed the hot flight attendant when he handed over his boarding pass to return home, and for some reason he told her the truth. The surprised, pleased sound of her laugh that followed him down the aisle made him think that maybe he should do the same with Jasmine. He'd noticed that when it came to women you should often do the exact *opposite* of what you intuitively thought you should do.

"Why do guys like us always fall for girls who are out of our league?" his friend Harvey had said after he met Jasmine for the first time.

Ethan kind of felt like punching Harvey when he said that.

(He thought he was playing it cool.)

(Yes, *obviously* she's out of his league.)

Harvey often says things that make Ethan's head explode. Like, "Guys like us never make it past middle management." "Guys like us don't drive cars like that." "Guys like us are never good at sports."

Of course, Ethan didn't punch Harvey, he has never punched anyone in his life ("Guys like us don't get into fights") and he never will punch Harvey because Ethan has just attended Harvey's funeral and right now Harvey is lying in a big shiny black coffin beneath a whole lot of earth, and Ethan can't believe it, he just can't believe it.

Harvey is dead. Harvey doesn't "say" things. Harvey "said" things. Harvey is forevermore in the past tense. He's said everything he will ever get to say.

Harvey will never again text Ethan some random, weird-angled photo of a sign or a tree or a street corner that means something to Harvey but nothing to Ethan. Harvey will never again ring Ethan at an inconvenient time, for no reason, like he's his grandmother, just to "catch up" or, more accurately, to sigh about his life and his decision to move back to Hobart, which had maybe not been the right decision, and should he change his name because girls brought up Harvey Weinstein whenever they heard Harvey's name and that didn't get things off to the best start, like, girls got weirdly *combative*, as if Harvey was about to misuse his power, when obviously, guys like us have no power. Harvey will never get a new job or a new girlfriend, a better haircut or a new perspective.

That's it! He's done!

It's unbelievable.

No matter how many times Ethan lets himself think those three words, *Harvey is dead,* they don't seem to lose their profound shock-ingness.

Ethan feels queasy but also hungry. He shouldn't be hungry. He gorged himself at the wake, which was unexpected, although he'd noticed a lot of people were eating in the same frantic, mechanical way, shoving food into their mouths. Ethan and one of Harvey's cousins ate a whole platter of mini chicken-and-mushroom vol-au-vents between them. "I'm so sorry for your loss," Ethan said, and Harvey's cousin said no need to apologize, it wasn't Ethan's fault, and besides, he only saw Harvey once a year at Christmas and he was kind of a douchebag, and he grinned as he said it, but then the shape of his mouth went all wonky, and Ethan had to look away fast.

It was an aneurysm. Ethan had looked it up, and as far as he can understand, it's like malware had been installed in Harvey's brain years ago and it sat there, waiting, and finally caused him to crash when he was in the foyer of his local cinema. He'd bought a ticket to see the latest Marvel movie. He was on his own. He often went to movies on his own. He'd bought a jumbo box of popcorn and all the popcorn went flying when he fell. All that detail came from Harvey's cousin.

Ethan tries to imagine the scene. Harvey falling. Was he scared? What were his last thoughts? *What's happening to me?* Harvey liked popcorn. Preferred not to share. He always said, "Get your own." It's distressing to think of him dropping his popcorn like that.

So he never got to see the movie. It wasn't good. Harvey would have taken the time to write a long vicious review on Rotten Tomatoes.

Dying is by far the weirdest, most interesting, most glamorous, and way-out thing that Harvey has ever done. It's like he's moved to Siberia or joined the priesthood or got into NASA.

"You must allow yourself to grieve," Jasmine had said solemnly, while she was cutting Ethan's steak into very tiny pieces. "Take time off work. Just a month or two."

Just a month or two. She's so cute. As if he could say to his boss, "I'm taking a month or two off work to grieve."

Ethan is weirded out by Harvey's death, but he isn't *grieving.* That feels too serious and dramatic a description for what he's feeling. Isn't grief just for family members?

He's only known Harvey for, what, four years? No. Five. They both got hired on the same day as junior software engineers at the tech company where Ethan still works. Harvey grew up in Hobart, and he'd moved back about six months ago.

Did he even like the guy all that much? He could be kind of a downer. Someone got up at the funeral and said, "Harvey always lit up a room," and Ethan thought, What the hell? Harvey never lit up a room in his life. He was the one skulking in gloomy corners making disparaging comments about the music.

Ethan had been wondering if he would make an excuse not to go to Harvey's thirtieth birthday party, over which there had been a lot of doleful, depressing discussion. *I dunno if I should be celebrating. Didn't you think we would have achieved more by thirty, Ethan?*

Now Harvey won't ever achieve anything new.

No more achievements for you, Harvey.

There had been parts of the funeral that felt operatic. Like when Harvey's uncle played the bagpipes and when Harvey's dad collapsed in slow motion, like the way an avalanche starts out slow and gets faster, and Harvey's grandfather tried to catch Harvey's dad by his elbow but he was too frail and instead Harvey's sister had gone running to help.

Harvey had never mentioned he had a hot sister.

Ethan hopes the hot sister didn't hear him embarrass himself by saying "I'm so sorry for your loss," to one of the caterers. She wore a white shirt, black pants, and carried a tray of ham sandwiches. There were a lot of clues.

Harvey would have found that hilarious. He would have laughed his silent, wheezy laugh that made him look like he was choking on a grape. A guy at work once tried to give Harvey the Heimlich maneuver when he was laughing. It was the funniest thing Ethan ever saw. Harvey reckoned he broke a rib.

The woman next to him swears.

"The baby," she explains, gesturing to the front of the plane. "It's started up again."

"Oh, yeah, right," says Ethan. He can hear the baby screaming—and he knows it cried for a while when they were on the tarmac—but it's just background static, it doesn't really bother him. "Sounds upset."

"The CIA torture prisoners with that sound," says the woman.

"I would never take a baby on a plane," says her friend in the window seat. "It's child abuse. I think it hurts their ears."

"I'm more concerned about *my* ears." The one in the middle seat clasps her hands to the back of her neck, drops her chin to her chest, and squashes her ears with her arms. She's got heart-shaped sunglasses on the top of her head.

In normal circumstances Ethan would have been hyperaware of the two attractive women seated next to him. They were a bit tipsy when they first boarded and he was vaguely aware of a long emotional discussion regarding a mutual friend "Poppy." He probably would have struck up a conversation. He can do that. It's a skill of his. Women don't find him intimidating. He would have given them his opinion on the issues with Poppy. He has an older sister and he grew up talking to all her friends, so it's possible he gives off "little brother" vibes, which could be a problem. It's been over a year since his last serious relationship. He's on the apps. Ready to make a commitment. He's not bad looking, apparently; it's hard to rate himself objectively.

"Guys like us always get friend-zoned," Harvey once said. "It's because we're beta males. No one wants the betas. They SAY they want the betas, but they're lying, they want the alphas."

That "beta male" comment is probably why Ethan decided to try rock climbing.

Thanks a lot, Harvey.

"I feel like this old lady heading down the aisle is having some kind of *episode*," says the woman in the window seat. "Ooh! Here comes the flight attendant to sort her out. Oh. My. God. That kid just threw up all over the flight attendant!"

"Gross," says the woman in the middle seat without lifting her head.

Ethan leans into the aisle. A lady is walking down it pointing at people.

"She's predicting deaths," says a sharp voice. "I heard her say 'Cause of death, age of death,' so *that's* not weird at all."

The woman in the window seat nudges her friend. "You hear that? She must be a psychic from that festival!"

Both women simultaneously lift up their phones and press record.

"If I could afford it, I'd go to a psychic, like, once a week," says the window-seat woman.

"Me too," says her friend. "I find it really calming." She turns to Ethan. "You into psychics? Bet you're not. Men are so . . ." She puts on a deep manlike voice. "I need *evidence!* I need *facts!*"

Ethan doesn't say anything, as his opinion is clearly unnecessary. Also: she's right. He is not into psychics, and yes, he does need evidence, he does need facts.

The lady points at the elderly couple diagonally across from Ethan. He hears her say, "I expect old age, age one hundred. I expect old age, age one hundred and one."

The elderly couple nod politely, seemingly unperturbed. Why would they be? Those predictions seem fairly benign and obvious. Isn't that the dream? To make one hundred and die of old age?

Now the lady is in the aisle next to Ethan. She is small. She seems harmless. In a hurry. A little irritable. She reminds Ethan of his grandmother when she learns she is required to download an app.

She points first at the woman in the window seat. "I expect melanoma, age seventy-nine."

"Gotta give up those sunbeds, babe," chuckles her friend, still filming. "Ooh—my turn!"

The lady points at Ethan's seatmate. "I expect liver disease, age eighty-seven."

"Gotta give up the espresso martinis, babe," says her friend.

It's Ethan's turn. He smiles automatically up at her, as he would at any older woman stopping to talk to him.

She says, "I expect assault."

"Assault?!" His smile vanishes. "You mean I'm going to die in a fight?"

"Assault," repeats the woman. "As I said. Age thirty."

Thirty? Ethan feels it in his stomach. A shadowy version of the feeling he experienced when he first heard the news about Harvey. "I don't really get into—"

"Fate won't be fought!" She steps forward.

His seatmate elbows him. "So, how old are you?"

"Twenty-nine," answers Ethan vaguely without looking at her.

"Well, that sucks for you," she says with such nonchalant sympathy that Ethan grins, but that's when it happens, because he thinks, like an actual idiot, *Wait till I tell Harvey about this.* Harvey loves this kind of left-field stuff. Harvey will do his quite good Morgan Freeman impersonation: "Ethan Chang was twenty-nine years old when he learned the manner of his death."

But he can't tell Harvey. There is no telecommunications platform on which to reach Harvey. It's like Ethan has only now realized he's dead, even though he's just been to his funeral, even though he's been thinking about literally nothing else but Harvey's death the whole day.

He hears a strange sound like a panting dog. It's him.

Ethan hasn't cried like this—proper salty tears sliding off his jaw—since he was a child. He didn't know his body still possessed the ability to cry like this. It's like he's lost control of his bladder. He is mortified. His glasses are fogging up. His nose is running.

Guys like us don't die young, Harvey. Guys like us get old and bald and paunchy. Guys like us peak in our fifties, standing around the barbecue in short-sleeved plaid shirts talking about cholesterol and interest rates.

"Aww, sweetie," says the woman next to him. "You're not going to die in a fight. They just make stuff up! None of it is true!"

She unbuckles her seat belt, stands up so fast her heart-shaped sunglasses slip back from her hair and over her eyes, and shouts, "Hey, *lady*, you made this guy *cry!*"

Which is pretty funny, and very embarrassing.

Ethan can see Harvey laughing. Somewhere in the multiverse Harvey is laughing his head off, but in this universe Ethan will never witness Harvey's stupid silent wheezy Harvey laugh again.

And now he's thinking of Harvey's mum and dad, and Harvey's grandfather, and Harvey's hot sister, and Harvey's cousin, and all their sad-as-fuck caved-in faces, and these are the people he should have met at Harvey's thirtieth, not at his *funeral*, and if Ethan is feeling this sad, how sad must *they* be feeling, and it is not right, death is not right, it's not fair, it is unbelievably painful. *Harvey, mate, come back, of course I was coming to your thirtieth, I wouldn't have missed it.* It feels like he will never stop crying. He doesn't know how to make it stop.

Ethan Chang is so very, very sorry for his loss.

Chapter 19

I have learned that I made the injured young man cry, which distresses me.

I remember him. I stood behind him in the security line at Hobart Airport.

People often become flustered at security gates, patting pockets in a panicked way, but he managed to put his phone, wallet, and keys into a tray, all while being restricted to the use of one hand. I admired his dexterity, especially after my experience with my brooch that morning.

Then when he turned and I saw him in profile—the black-framed glasses, the strong handsome line of his jaw—I got such a surprise.

I thought: *Henry!*

It was not Henry, of course.

Henry worked at the Hornsby Picture Theatre in the sixties, selling tickets from inside a varnished wood booth. I only ever saw the top half of him behind a pane of glass with a cutout circle. My friend Ivy and I used to go to the Saturday matinee. Two movies, a cartoon, a serial, and a newsreel for sixpence. Very good value. "Oh, no, I only need *one* ticket," I said kindly, the last time I bought a movie ticket, assuming the bored young man had made a mistake. "You only got one ticket," he said. Not as polite as Henry.

Henry smiled warmly each time he saw Ivy and me and said, "Hello again, ladies!"

We weren't ladies. We were very little. Eleven or twelve.

Ivy would say, "Hello again, Henry!" Too loudly, in my opinion.

I would whisper, "Hello." I was too shy to say his name out loud. Every week I would think, *This time I will say Henry's name.* I never once did, and I was ashamed of that.

One of my earliest memories is my mother unpeeling my fingers from her skirt. "She's *shy.*"

I knew the injured boy could not logically be Henry and yet the resemblance startled me. I wondered, could it be Henry's son? Or grandson?

I considered saying, *Excuse me, this may sound silly, but was your father's name Henry and did he work at the Hornsby Picture Theatre in Sydney?*

But then as a uniformed man nodded and beckoned for me to take my turn stepping through the metal detector, I saw a couple in the departure lounge, lining up to buy coffee, and my heart leaped with joy because I thought, *There's Bert and Jill, I haven't seen them for so long!*

I wanted to run to them, to throw my arms around them both, but again, I knew it could not possibly be them, any more than that boy could have been Henry, and yet they looked so similar I froze and stared and stared.

The man had white hair and a blue polo shirt and he looked like a big polar bear next to his wife, who was small and dark-haired, and even from a distance I could see she had the same sparkly, always-moving energy as Jill. She was doing some kind of exercise as she waited in line, standing on one leg and bobbing up and down. An ankle- or knee-strengthening exercise, perhaps, and I thought, Didn't Jill do that *exact* same exercise? I watched as she wobbled and the man who looked like Bert steadied her with one tender hand, just the way Bert would have, and I knew it wasn't Bert, it wasn't Jill, but it was, it *was*, I felt that it was them.

I didn't move until a woman behind me said impatiently, "You can go!" at the same time as the uniformed man barked, "Come on *through*, madam!"

It kept happening when I went to my gate. Every single person felt in some way significant to *me*. It began to feel eerie, as if I were part of an elaborate prank or a reality show where I was the star but didn't know it.

It wasn't just resemblances. There were symbols and signs. Everything meant something.

The man at the table next to me wore a patterned shirt, and when I looked closer, I saw that they were kangaroos. *Gray* kangaroos. I heard a man with a strong Scottish accent say to him, "Is that seat taken?"

Gray kangaroos and a Scottish accent. Those two things in tandem were only of significance to *me*.

An elderly couple tottered by wearing silver Apple Watches, followed by a beautiful serious-faced woman who could have been Korean and could have been in her forties.

A woman in a leopard-print jumpsuit sat on a high stool at the bar and I wasn't close enough to see for sure but her drink could easily have been a Brandy Alexander.

An incredibly tall young man loped by on long legs, followed immediately by a little boy carrying a backpack in gray and green military camouflage.

Then everyone stopped to stare because a beautiful young bride and groom came through the security gates. Still in their wedding finery, they were pulling along small wheeled bags that looked brand new.

Some people applauded and whistled.

The bride and groom weren't familiar, but I recognized her dress.

Because it was mine.

It was my wedding dress.

I told myself, *It's just a similar style.* But then, as I kept looking, I thought, *No, it's identical.* High neck, empire waist, bishop sleeves. Chiffon and lace. Everything about it was the same.

They walked directly past my table and that's when I saw the hem of her dress. I know I did not imagine it, because I was hoping I would not see it, but I did.

Six pale yellow dots forming the shape of a circle.

They were yellow pollen stains. My yellow pollen stains. Put there by my bridesmaid, my childhood friend, Ivy, who felt terrible about it. She was shaking her bouquet over her head to be charming for the photographer.

My mother said, "Those stains will never come out." Then she said, in a lower voice, to Auntie Pat, "I tried to tell her that lilies are *funeral* flowers."

Ivy said, "It looks like a little sunshine. I think it's good luck."

The photographer said, "I'm sure you're right," and lifted his camera and took her photo.

(It was good luck for Ivy and the photographer. They got married two years later. A high percentage of my wedding photos featured close-ups of Ivy.)

The bride and groom headed off to the bar and I looked away, and saw Ivy herself!

She was emerging from the bookshop, a paperback in hand, talking animatedly on her mobile phone, forty years too young to be Ivy, it wasn't Ivy, Ivy moved to America and she never had a daughter or granddaughter, but here's the thing: the woman who looked like Ivy wore an artificial *lily* in her hair.

Lilies are funeral flowers, said my mother in my ear.

A man in a black puffer jacket walked by swinging a long tube on a strap. It was canvas with a leather cap. It was my father's fishing rod tube! How did that man get ahold of it? He had my dad's worried expression, and then he saw someone in the distance and the worried expression vanished and he smiled with his whole face, exactly the way my dad smiled whenever he was waiting for me or my mother to get off the train.

No more, I thought, please no more.

But there was my childhood piano teacher. She drummed her

fingers anxiously on the table as if she were practicing scales. Same sweet face, same long fair plait, except she was wearing a big hoodie and she wasn't crying like my piano teacher cried, not at first, but as I watched she turned fast and knocked a can of soft drink over with her elbow, and then, as she tried to dab up the spill with paper napkins, her other elbow knocked her phone to the floor, and her face crumpled, as if she were about to burst into tears.

A man with Elvis Presley sideburns wearing a moss-green Ralph Lauren polo shirt stood with narrowed eyes checking the departures board. Ralph Lauren cologne in a green bottle and Elvis Presley sideburns. Once again, those two things together added up to something of relevance only to me and *my* life, *my* past, *my* memories, and I thought to myself, nobody has long sideburns like that anymore, nobody!

Everything meant something.

I closed my eyes and tried not to see all the signs, but it didn't help because then my other senses took over. I could smell my mother's scent (Avon: To a Wild Rose) and my auntie Pat's cigarettes (Pall Mall slims). I could hear my father's laughter when he saw the expression on my face when I caught my first fish (a good-sized yellowfin bream) and I could taste my grandmother's scones (approved by the Country Women's Association!).

I opened my eyes and saw my veiny, age-spotted hands and I told myself, *Stop it. You are being so silly. You are embarrassing yourself. You're imagining all this. This is just an ordinary departure lounge. You are not the center of the world and this is not all about you.*

I felt confused and fearful and lonely. I felt filled with rage and resentment about the errand I had to undertake. I needed a cup of tea and a Monte Carlo biscuit.

A cup of tea might have solved everything.

Chapter 20

Eve is asleep in a sticky scratchy heap of chiffon and lace, her cheek squashed against the side of the plane, when she wakes with a dramatic audible gasp for air, as though she's been pulled unconscious from the ocean and brought back to life by chest compressions.

So that is seriously embarrassing.

"Whoa!" says her husband, Dom. Her literal husband. He looks briefly away from his phone. "You okay?" He's catching up on all his puzzles. He doesn't want to lose any of his streaks.

"I'm okay." She sits up, wipes the back of her hand across her mouth, and fishes another red rose petal out of her cleavage.

The rose petal cannon launchers had been a big hit. Maybe too big a hit. Some of their friends had looked like crazed soldiers spraying bullets. Dom's friend Zeb had literally shouted "Attaaaaack!" outside the church, which was not romantic.

She tugs at the neckline of her dress.

Her mother had said, "Eve, you can't get on a plane wearing that dress! You'll be so uncomfortable. Change into something comfy!"

Could there be a more depressing word than "comfy"? As if anyone needs to feel "comfy" heading off on their honeymoon.

Her wedding dress had cost fifty dollars. It's beautiful. Not like anyone else's wedding dress. She likes to be different, although under-the-radar different, not I'm-making-a-point different. She tried to make her voice not show-offy each time she described her dress as "vintage."

"As in secondhand," said her mother.

"As in not made in a sweatshop," said Eve. "As in eco-friendly."

She'd found it in the back of a Vinnies store in Hobart on a rack with a sign that said PRE-LOVED WEDDING DRESSES. The woman in the shop said she thought it was around forty years old. "It's got the seventies look to it," she said. "Bishop sleeves were big back then."

Annoyingly, her mother had pointed out the tiniest, smidgiest little stain on the hem.

"It looks like a little sun emoji," said Eve.

"It looks like a little drop of urine," said her mother, but then she must have felt bad because she said, "Princess Diana had a stain on her wedding dress, so you're in good company."

Which, ah, no, not good company, Mum, she got divorced and died.

Everyone said Eve looked amazing and nobody mentioned the stain and she felt beautiful all day, but honestly, right now, she kind of wishes she'd changed into track pants at the airport. It's annoying when her mother ends up being right. She will not tell her.

Or actually she will tell her, one day, as a little gift, when her mum is stressed and needs cheering up.

It would have been fine if not for the long delay on the tarmac. They would have been in their hotel room by now. Probably without any clothes on.

It's not so much the dress but her new lingerie that's driving her crazy. She never normally wears this sort of scratchy, lacy, sexy underwear, but her friends convinced her it was like a literal legal requirement for your wedding night.

Dom might think if she's changed her underwear he's got to change his moves. Do more porn-y type stuff. Like choking. Choking is so fashionable right now. No, thank you.

"I think I was dribbling," she whispers to him.

"That's so hot." Dom keeps tapping at his phone.

"I can't wait to rip off my bra," says Eve.

Dom looks up, grins. "Sounds good."

"Then I'm throwing it in the trash," says Eve.

"Okay then." Dom looks back at his phone and chews his lip.

Eve scratches her head. Her hair feels like straw because of all the hair spray and there are a million bobby pins sticking into her scalp as if she's a hedgehog.

Dom is perfectly comfortable in his tux. He's unclipped his pre-tied bow tie so it's hanging loose, not quite obscuring a cheerful chocolate splotch in the middle of his shirt. He probably hasn't noticed, or if he has, he doesn't care. Their wedding cake was chocolate, three-tiered, with seminaked vanilla frosting and edible flowers. It looked amazing, but Eve couldn't eat any of it! She basically ate nothing at the wedding, she was too overexcited. It felt like she couldn't take a full breath the whole day. Now she's starving. She could have eaten forty of those "light snacks."

Dom gave her the window seat and he took the middle one, because he was being all husbandly and gallant. He maybe regrets that decision now, like she regrets her underwear.

Wearing their wedding clothes had been so fun at the airport because they'd felt like celebrities. Eve could feel people's eyes on her wherever she went. She'd liked the smiles and the waves and the comments, "Aww, young love!" but now she's feeling the pressure of fame and wants her anonymity back. What if someone took a photo of her asleep just then with her mouth wide open and posted it online? With a nasty caption? *UglyAssBride.*

She sighs.

"You okay?" asks Dom again.

"Yup," says Eve.

Oh my God, she sounded snappy. Eve had assumed that they would only speak in loving tones on their honeymoon. She knew they wouldn't speak like that *forever,* but she thought they'd at least last the day.

"Sorry," she says.

Dom doesn't reply. He keeps tapping at his phone. "Hmm?"

"Don't worry." She pats his leg. His knees are just about touching the seat in front.

They should have maybe said yes to the people who offered them their business-class seats, but Eve wasn't sure they were even serious. Like, what if they'd said "Sure thing" when they were meant to laugh because it was one of those weird older-generation jokes? How embarrassing. She and Dom both get awkward about that kind of stuff. Thinking ahead, Eve had asked her mother what the right etiquette was when they got to the hotel tonight. She has never checked in to a fancy hotel before. She's only been to the mainland, like, twice in her life. She is not sophisticated. She doesn't care. Okay, so she does care if people are secretly laughing at her.

"You sashay straight up to the desk and say your name," said her mother. "I guess you'll say, 'I'm Mrs. Eve Archer-Fern, checking in to the honeymoon suite!' Unless you're going full-on retro and taking your husband's first name as well as his last name? So then you'll say, 'I'm Mrs. Dominic Archer-Fern.'"

Eve's mother can be bitchy. Supposedly it's due to perimenopause (too much information, no need to share everything, Mum), but Eve reckons her mother might have been a mean girl at school. She denies that *so* vehemently, probably because she feels guilty.

Eve's mother "doesn't understand why girls these days are taking their husbands' names like fifties housewives." Eve's mother is a single parent, an excited fan of the #MeToo movement, and a proud feminist. Eve isn't *not* a feminist, and obviously well done everyone on #MeToo, although why did it take so long? It's just that if she starts agreeing with her mother, where will it end? People already talk about how much they look alike. Will she start wearing quirky statement necklaces and complimenting strangers on their shoes? Will her hips become . . . you know, like her mum's hips? There isn't anything wrong with her mum's body, it's fine for *her*. Body positivity and all that. It's just that Eve would rather die.

Eve's mum looked appalled when she and Dom announced their

engagement, which is not normal. Normal mothers cry with delight, press their hands to their mouths, and then walk toward their laughing daughters with outstretched hands. There is endless evidence of this online. Not Eve's mum. She said, "But *why*? Just move in together! Getting married at your age is bizarre!"

Eve found the word "bizarre" to be hurtful.

She thought her mother liked Dom. How could she not like Dom? He's objectively perfect.

They have signed a rental lease on an apartment in Glenorchy and set it all up, but they have not yet spent a night there. Dom is going to carry her over the threshold, which is not bizarre, it's romantic.

Interestingly, once Eve's mum accepted that the wedding was happening, she sure did have a lot of opinions about how it should proceed.

The baby is crying again. The noise level in the plane seems to be increasing. It feels like a party where everyone is subdued at first and then their voices start to rise along with their blood alcohol levels. Someone is literally shouting.

An announcement crackles: "Cabin crew, please prepare the cabin for landing."

"Not long now." Dom puts down his phone and takes her hand, and Eve is relieved because she feels romantic and sexy and loving again.

Maybe she *should* try choking? According to her friend Liv it's a rush. Liv says it's like when they used to make themselves hyperventilate in Year 7. Eve should try not to be so vanilla. Get a bit freaky. She puts her hand to her neck and squeezes tentatively.

No! Oh my God, it's definitely not for her. She only ever pretended to hyperventilate in Year 7. She drops her hands. She does not consent.

An old lady is standing in the aisle looking at her. She points directly at Eve as if she's done something wrong.

"Um . . ." Eve looks nervously at Dom. What rule has she broken? She sits up straight.

"I expect intimate partner homicide. Age twenty-five."

Chapter 21

I hope I didn't spoil their honeymoon. Honeymoons are meant to be special.

Obviously there is no guarantee.

Mine, for example, was a disaster. I would never wish that on anyone.

Perhaps the bride wasn't a believer. Supposedly, only four out of ten people believe in psychics. I can't verify that statistic. It's one of those "facts" I found floating about in the polluted sea of the internet. (To be clear: I love the internet in spite of the pollution.)

I think the truth is that feelings about psychic predictions can be as layered as a German Black Forest cake. Your rational mind says, *Nonsense!* Your subconscious says, *What if it's true?*

Sometimes it depends on the time of day. A person who scoffs in the sunshine can wake with a pounding heart in the dark depths of the night.

I don't know how the bride reacted to my terrible prediction. I don't know if she was skeptical or angry or offended or frightened.

I don't know if she remembered a particular incident, an incident she had been trying to forget, downplay, or justify, and thought, *What if it's true?*

Chapter 22

Cabin crew, please prepare the cabin for landing.

Someone has to respond to the flight deck to acknowledge the PA. Normally it would be Allegra, but she's stuck in the middle of the airplane, stuck in the middle of what may be the worst flight of her career. If no one responds to the PA, they'll do it again or phone the cabin to check if they're okay, and are they okay? Because there is still no sign of Ellie and Anders, and meanwhile the injured guy sobs and the fortune teller trots merrily on. She is currently talking to the bride and groom.

Allegra turns stiffly to face the front of the plane, and thankfully there is Kim, drawing the business-class curtain back. Allegra signals "phone" with her hand. Kim gets it, nods. So that's under control, and once again Allegra is walking down the aisle, her skirt damp against her thighs, trying not to breathe in the toxic, gut-twisting smell of that seemingly sweet child's vomit. (Is there some in her *hair*?) "Could you put your tray table back up, please, sir? Could you open your window shade, please, madam?"

Cabin prep must still be done, even while a passenger distributes deathly predictions.

Allegra sees Ellie finally emerge from the galley. *About time! Thank you!*

She comes face-to-face with the lady. They exchange a few words. Ellie puts her hand on the lady's arm.

Well done, Ellie, turn her around, get her back to her seat.

But Ellie smiles and nods at the lady, then steps around her and walks briskly toward Allegra. The lady continues on her way.

Allegra can't believe it. "Why didn't you *stop* her?" she hisses when they reach each other.

"Stop who?" says Ellie. "I've been with Anders." She lowers her voice. "He fainted."

"What?" For goodness' sake. "Is he okay?" She's going to kill him. Intermittent bloody fasting.

"I gave him something to eat," says Ellie piously. "He's fine now."

"Good. Well done. So now please help me stop this lady." Allegra points.

Ellie turns to look. "That lady? Why? She's fine. She's just on her way to the toilet. She mentioned something about having bladder cancer? And being eighty-eight? I said I was sorry and to let us know if she needed anything."

"No, she doesn't mean—" Allegra catches herself. "She's upsetting people. We need to get her back to her seat."

"The seat-belt sign isn't on yet," says Ellie. Her nostrils twitch and she looks aghast at the state of Allegra's uniform. "What *happened* to you?"

A passenger says, "You two need to stop the chitchat and get that freaky fortune teller under control."

A wave of something halfway between laughter and tears builds in Allegra's chest. She ignores the passenger and keeps walking toward the lady.

Ellie follows. "Sorry, I didn't realize—wait, was she telling my fortune just now?"

Allegra reaches the lady as she is pointing at a passenger in the second-to-last row.

"I expect—" she says.

"Excuse me." Allegra's voice is firm and loud. Her hand hovers respectfully over the lady's shoulder without actually touching her. "Madam?"

"Please don't interrupt." The lady glances back at her. "I need to focus."

The passenger in the aisle seat is a woman with a crazy mop of curly gray hair and red-framed glasses. "Yes, let her focus!" she says cheerily. "It's my turn! I want to hear what she has to say."

"Madam," sighs Allegra.

"I expect heart failure, age ninety-five."

The curly-haired woman lifts up her palm. "High-five! I'll take that! Ninety-five, woo-hoo!"

People are peculiar.

The lady ignores the offer of a high five and turns to the window seat on the other side of the aisle, where a man sits, hunched, his back curved. He's wearing a black hoodie and AirPods.

The lady points at him. "I expect road injury, age sixty-four."

He's oblivious, doesn't hear, doesn't respond, will never know he should make a point of looking both ways when he's sixty-four.

"I really need you to return to your seat now," says Allegra. "We're going to be landing in Sydney soon."

"I expect smoke inhalation, house fire, age fifty-nine." The lady points at a woman steadily working her way through a bag of chips.

The woman stops, one chip midway to her mouth. "Fire? Where?"

"There is no fire," says Allegra. "Absolutely not."

Superhero emerges from the lavatory tugging at the waistband of his jeans.

The lady points up at his big barrel chest. "I expect kidney disease, age ninety-three."

"Please sit back down now, madam," says Allegra.

"Once I've completed my task," says the lady.

"I think we'd better do what the flight attendants say," says the superhero in his deep superhero voice. "They're in charge."

He's like a brick wall. There is no way anyone is getting around him.

"I don't think I'm done yet!" says the lady. She attempts to peer around the man.

Ellie speaks up. "No, madam, it's fine, you are done. You've, uh, completed your task."

"I've completed my task?" Those words seem to be the magic charm. Apparently even freaky fortune tellers can be task-focused. The lady looks back at Ellie hopefully. "Have I?"

"Absolutely," says Ellie. "Good job! You probably need a glass of water."

"Hydration is so important at my age," says the lady thoughtfully.

"Very important. You sit down and I'll bring you one straight-away," says Ellie. Allegra may have underestimated Ellie.

"Thank you," says the lady. "With ice, please."

"No problem," says Ellie.

"I'm exhausted," the lady confides to Allegra as she leads her back to her seat.

"Me too," says Allegra.

Allegra feels the curious sideways glances of passengers. The baby is quiet. No one speaks or calls out. The atmosphere is like a class-room after a teacher's lost their temper.

The lady sits, capably buckles her seat belt, sighs.

Ellie appears with a plastic cup of ice water, which she hands to Allegra.

Allegra can now see Anders at the rear of the plane, apparently fine again, smiling and charming, back doing his job, leaning over to help get someone's seat into the upright position.

"There you go," says Allegra. She hands the cup to the lady, who drinks thirstily.

There is an empty seat next to her, which is fortunate, and the man in the window seat is busy packing away his laptop.

"Are you feeling okay?" asks Allegra.

"I'm in excellent health," says the lady. "I take no medication what-soever."

Might want to reconsider that, thinks Allegra.

"We'll be in Sydney soon, so—"

The lady points at Allegra's forehead. Her voice has become mumbly, as if a drug is taking effect. "I expect self-harm, age . . . age . . . twenty . . ."

Her voice fades. She looks down at the cup.

"Twenty what?" says Allegra in spite of herself. She leans closer, glancing at the man in the window seat to make sure he's not witnessing her unprofessional interest in her own fortune, but he's still busy packing away his laptop.

The lady rests her head against her seat. Her hand still grips the plastic cup. Her eyes close.

Self-harm. The phrase slithers into Allegra's consciousness like a parasite. She sees the mustard-colored walls of a small room coming toward her from all sides. That childhood sensation of her nose pressed flat, bones crushed, the air squeezed from her body.

The lady opens her eyes very briefly.

She says, "Age twenty-eight."

The pilot says, "Cabin crew, please be seated for landing."

Chapter 23

I have learned it was the beautiful flight attendant's twenty-eighth birthday that day.

My gift to her was to predict she would take her own life before she turned twenty-nine. If only I'd predicted a long happy life and a natural death. That would have been kinder. More festive.

Honestly, sometimes I feel so ashamed I can hardly breathe.

Chapter 24

It has just occurred to me that I haven't yet introduced myself.

I apologize. One should always introduce oneself quickly!

I once met a woman at an industry function who said, "Hello, I'm Jan." Her name may or may not have been Jan, I can't recall. Don't concern yourself, it was an unexceptional name.

I said, "Hello, Jan." I said it nicely, although I admit I may not have smiled. I was in the process of pulling out my chair to sit down next to her while carrying a glass of white wine, a jacket, my handbag, and a tall metal table number for my dinner order. My number was seven, which is not my favorite number, but it's likely yours. Most people pick seven if asked their favorite number. My favorite number is zero.

I had ordered the pesto linguine. It was not good.

Anyhow, this woman chuckled crossly and snapped, "Are you going to tell me *your* name?"

I *was* going to tell her my name! I know how introductions work! I just needed a second to compose myself and sit down.

Well.

It was a long time ago. I really should have forgotten such a trivial incident by now. It's just that I'm overly sensitive about any perceived criticism of my social skills. They don't come easily to some of us, and hurtful jokes are often made about my profession, people like me, coming across as "strange," "weird," or even "scary."

I will certainly introduce myself. Quick smart!

My name is Cherry.

Not Cheryl, if that's what you think you heard. Cherry. The night before I was born, my mother had a vivid dream about a pale pink cherry blossom tree silhouetted against a bright blue sky. My mother took her dreams as seriously as her complexion. Hence, Cherry.

I'm aware Cherry and Cheryl are similar names. Both have six letters and the first four of those letters are identical. However, the name that appears on my birth certificate is Cherry. Not Cheryl. No matter how much you want it to be. No matter how much I want it to be.

I once worked with a man who continually called me Cheryl even after I politely corrected him on several occasions. (Twenty-seven occasions.)

One day we had a "team-building" lunch at a Chinese restaurant called Wok n' Roll. He said, with his mouth full, "Pass the spring rolls, will ya, Cheryl?"

It was the twenty-eighth occasion he'd called me Cheryl, in spite of repeated polite corrections, and it was at a difficult time in my life. I lost my mind and my temper and threw a spring roll at him.

It landed with a terrific splash in his glass of soft drink and he leaped back with the most appalled expression on his face. I apologized, but he did not forgive me or ever bother to get my name right.

My name is Cherry.

As previously stated. But it bears repeating. It sure does bear repeating.

The astoundingly popular British singer Ed Sheeran has a wife named Cherry. I wonder if her mother dreamed of a cherry blossom tree, or if perhaps her parents liked the Neil Diamond song "Cherry, Cherry." I love that song. It came out in 1966, the same year Australia switched to decimal currency. Mum didn't want to switch. There was a jingle to prepare us: *In come the dollars and in come the cents, to replace the pounds and the shillings and the pence!* I found the jingle catchy. My mother would press her hands over her ears. I'd sing louder.

She liked Neil Diamond, though. We danced to "Cherry, Cherry" in the kitchen while we peeled potatoes and shelled peas. I danced badly but enthusiastically. Mum danced beautifully. This didn't happen every night, of course. Some nights we didn't speak, let alone dance. We were philosophically opposed on multiple issues. We also could not have had potatoes and peas every night for our tea. Although it feels like we did.

I expect my mother's fear of decimal currency was related to her dislike of math, which is a common fear often dating back to a cruel teacher. In fact, my mother was more mathematically inclined than she realized. She used probability every day of her life and called it intuition.

I was pleased to learn Ed Sheeran's wife and I share a name because I'm an Ed Sheeran fan. To be clear, I don't buy his CDs or go to his concerts. I just turn up the volume when his songs come on the radio, which I presume doesn't produce any income for him. Sorry, Ed Sheeran.

Well.

Sometimes, when I'm nervous, I become overly, even inappropriately, chatty. I veer off topic. I say whatever comes to my mind, I become too literal, I try too hard to be accurate when no one cares as much as me about accuracy, and I can see by people's faces that I am being "odd," and I am forced to pinch the skin on my wrist to make myself stop talking.

My name is Cherry.

That's all I needed to say.

Chapter 25

Leo waits at the Sydney domestic terminal taxi stand. He's in a long line snaking back and forth as if for a Disneyland ride. *The Lion King* is over. His son just texted from the car on the way home to say the show was boring and Bridie forgot one of her lines. Brotherly loyalty.

His boss has texted twice and sent three emails. In one of them she said she hoped Leo's mother had "recovered"; in another she said she hoped he was enjoying "his long weekend." She also informed him that an already tight deadline had become even tighter: *I know you'll manage it, superstar!* He feels the tightness of the deadline like a noose around his neck.

His seatmates, Max and Sue, had walked with Leo through the terminal and separated at the bottom of the escalators, as they had to go to the carousel to collect their bags.

"Memorable flight, eh? Don't forget that hard hat, will you, mate?" Max had shaken Leo's hand while Sue patted his arm and said, "Plenty more school concerts ahead of you, darling, you did the right thing taking your mum to the specialist. Don't regret your life away."

"Thanks, Sue." He'd almost hugged her. She is more motherly than his mother. "Good luck with the cake!"

Max and Sue have to make a "Bluey" birthday cake for their grandson. Apparently Sue bakes, Max does "construction," and they both decorate. They'd showed Leo some of their elaborate creations. The party kicks off at ten a.m. tomorrow! Leo is now fretting about their tight deadline in addition to his own.

He shuffles forward, wondering how much baking time the average cake requires. A guy in a high-vis vest with a whistle around his neck is wrangling the line. He says, "How many?" while holding up his fingers in a preemptive guess. "Two of you? Three?" He orders people to stand at different numbered sections. People stand at the wrong numbers and occasionally a driver leaps from his cab, yelling and gesticulating. The guy with the whistle yells back. High pressure. Leo would lose his mind.

"Excuse me?" Leo turns. It's the young man with the sling. Also a day-tripper. They were on the same flight out of Sydney this morning. He's memorable because of the injury.

"I think we were on the same flight." He's behind Leo in the line, but the line snakes back and forth so right now they're next to each other, separated by the chain-link dividers. He's in his twenties. Very cool-looking. Probably in web design or television production. Stylish glasses. They suit him. (Leo has 20/20 vision but sometimes wishes he needed glasses.) All his hair, of course, no doubt he takes it for granted. He looks tired. Dark shadows under bloodshot eyes. Probably out clubbing last night.

Leo knows what he wants to talk about.

"Delayed flight from Hobart," agrees Leo.

"That lady say anything to you?" He lowers his voice on the word "lady."

"Don't take her seriously, dude," says Leo, and is instantly appalled by his use of the word "dude." Is he pretending he's Keanu Reeves? He does, in fact, aspire to be more like Keanu Reeves. He seems very relaxed and possibly enlightened. Neve loves Keanu.

"No, I'm not," says Cool Guy. "Just . . . you know, weird." He gestures with his chin. "She's back there."

Leo turns. There she is at the back of the line, wheeling a small suitcase: innocuous, self-contained, sane. A grandmother who travels regularly. Not a fortune teller. Now that Leo is out of the claustro-phobic airplane and back in the familiar bland world the sinisterness of her words has almost dissipated, like the way huge emotions produced by a movie or a concert fade.

He had discreetly observed her across the aisle after the flight attendant brought her back to her seat. She'd shut her eyes and had apparently fallen into a deep sleep because the landing wasn't enough to wake her. Her closest seatmate, the man in the window seat, didn't try to wake her either. As soon as the seat-belt sign went off he nimbly slid in front of her knees and out into the aisle. Just before Leo left the plane he glanced back to see if she'd woken yet, but her eyes were still shut as the passengers filed past, many of them giving her curious looks, but no one attempting to speak to her.

"Yeah, so she told me I was going to die in a fight when I'm thirty."

"Don't worry about it," says Leo. "She told me I'm dying young too."

The line is moving again so they are no longer parallel.

"Put it out of your mind!" says Leo over his shoulder as everyone steps forward. He's nearly at the front of the line.

Cool Guy gives him a cool thumbs-up with his free hand. Leo wonders if it was his injury that caused the lady to choose that particular prediction for him. Did she honestly believe what she was saying? She *seemed* to believe it. He recalls the symbol on the lady's brooch and how it had seemed weirdly relevant to *him* in some specific way: How could that be? Now he can't even visualize it. Was it an infinity symbol?

She's obviously too far away for him to see the tiny brooch from here. Theoretically, he could have leaned over, put on his reading glasses, and studied it when she was asleep on the plane, but he didn't want to risk having an elderly lady open her eyes to the sight of a male passenger looming over her, staring at her chest.

The man in the high-vis vest holds up one finger.

"Just me," agrees Leo, but then on impulse he looks back for Cool Guy. "Where you headed?"

Chapter 26

I have described the phenomenon I experienced at Hobart Airport where I kept recognizing people or thinking I did, and how everything and everyone seemed to symbolize something of personal significance. I was relieved when it was time to board. Once I was on the plane the foolishness of my thoughts would surely end. I planned to do sudoku. I had an advanced "ultimate challenge" puzzle book in my bag.

I boarded behind a very tall young man wearing blue tracksuit pants and a white T-shirt. He reminded me of the very tall young boy I once loved. I told myself that many young men have vulnerable necks. It is the juxtaposition of their broad shoulders and boyish hairlines that breaks your heart.

Someone asked if he was a basketball player and he said that he was not. He answered patiently although something about his tone made me think he was asked that question a lot.

A woman said, "Hope you're in the exit row," and he said yes, he always booked the exit row, and the woman said that was sensible.

I thought about the first time my tall young man boarded a plane and how he would not have known anything about exit rows.

I felt in danger of being swept out to sea by a giant river of memory.

I showed my boarding pass to the flight attendant, who was so stunningly beautiful I wanted to stop and take her in like a water view.

"Welcome aboard," she said with a smile. "Four D. On your left."

I was relieved because she reminded me of no one from my past or my present, she symbolized or signified nothing except youth and beauty, and I thought all the foolishness was over and done, but then I saw the other flight attendant: a young man. Also attractive. Fair hair swooped artfully back from his forehead and green eyes. I felt the most awful plummeting sensation in my stomach, like when you step out onto nothing in a dream. He did not seem to recognize me, and I thought, But how could that be? How could he just . . . forget? There was no doubt at all in my mind. It was definitely him.

I didn't stop. When you're boarding a plane you are a can of soup on a perpetually moving factory production line. I found my seat.

A man with the demeanor of an army general helped put my bag in the overhead bin. I did not require his assistance, but I appreciated it. I think I may not have thanked him. Manners matter. I feel bad about that.

I sat. I buckled my seat belt.

A woman wearing a bejeweled caftan banged my temple with her elbow as she looked for her seat number. She did not apologize.

A well-dressed, distinguished, and worried-looking man with no luggage took the aisle seat to my left. He had a copy of a magazine called *Construction Engineering Australia,* which he did not open. His hair was curly and too gray for the youth of his face. I looked down and saw he was tapping one foot, the incessant shoe tap of an impatient man, a man who would rather die than wait. He wore beautiful oatmeal-colored suede boots. *Armani,* I thought, or perhaps I even whispered it.

The impatient man was seated next to the couple who were not my friends Jill and Bert but who radiated their same friendliness and good humor, their delightful joie de vivre.

I looked at the seat pocket in front of me and read the words: *What are you waiting for? Book your Jewels of Europe River Cruise today!*

Chapter 27

Eve and Dom stand at the baggage carousel at Sydney Airport surrounded by people staring grimly at their phones and occasionally looking up to scowl when there are still no bags. Nobody smiles or congratulates them like they did in Hobart. Now their wedding clothes feel like Halloween costumes and it's not Halloween. Nobody is thinking, *Aww, young love;* they're probably thinking, *Euuww, stupid losers.*

Eve fiddles with her new wedding ring, yawns hugely, and only remembers to cover her mouth at the last second. She is so tired she could lie down on this grimy airport floor right now and fall asleep.

Dom is quiet, staring off into the distance with blank eyes. What is he thinking about? The thing about her boyfriend, not her boyfriend, her *husband*, is that he can seem perfectly fine, laughing and carefree, and then, *snap!* He reveals something that has been on his mind for days, even weeks. It's always a shock. Eve is never sure if he's acting happy, or if he forgets about whatever issue is worrying him and then remembers it. Eve can't hide her feelings. If there's something on her mind Dom says, "Okay, what is it?" within about five minutes.

"Excuse me?" A girl in short shorts, with a long blond fishtail ponytail and thick black eyelash extensions, sidles up close to Eve. She tips her head toward Eve and talks in a low voice without moving her lips, like they're trying to have a secret conversation in a school as-sembly without the teachers noticing. "Did that psychic talk to you too?"

"The lady? I don't think she's a psychic," says Eve. She speaks nor-mally, because she is older than this girl, and married, and she is not in a school assembly.

"Shhh," says Dom, as if she is speaking too loudly or saying some-thing offensive.

Eve lowers her voice. "I think that lady was just—"

"You look so beautiful, by the way," the girl interrupts, and gently puts a fingertip to the lace on Eve's sleeve. It's an almost childlike move, as if she can't help herself. "That lace! I love it so much!"

"Thank you." Eve looks down at her dress. "It's vintage." Oops, she sounded too show-offy. "Secondhand."

"I *love* vintage wedding dresses," sighs the girl. "That's the kind of dress I'd choose, when I get married, but I don't even have a boyfriend right now, so I don't know why I'm even telling you that! Anyway, you don't think she was a psychic?"

"Definitely not," says Eve. "Just a little . . . you know." She looks about her, just in case the lady is actually here somewhere, waiting for her bag. She whispers, "Nutty."

Eve puts the lady into the same category of person as Junie.

Most days Junie can be found drinking a lurid green slushie while sitting on the edge of the fountain outside the medical center where Eve works as a receptionist. She addresses everyone who walks by, as if they're old friends in the middle of a conversation. Often in her lunch break Eve sits on the edge of the fountain and chats with Junie. You never know what Junie is going to come up with next: the moon landing was fake but aliens are real; some members of the Royal Fam-ily are definitely reptiles; Junie is under CIA surveillance, so she has to be really careful what she says; it's hard to find comfortable shoes be-cause she has very wide feet.

"Hey, so you remind me so much of this singer, that one dating—" begins Eve.

The girl's face lights up. "I know who you mean, everyone keeps saying I look like her! It's flattering. But I'm just boring old Kayla Halfpenny from Hobart."

"Kayla Halfpenny actually sounds like the name of a famous person," says Eve. It's kind of true. Sometimes you say things that are kind of true to be nice.

"Oh, I don't want to be famous!" Kayla shudders. "Anyway, I'm glad you don't think she's a real psychic, because that lady freaked me out so much. She told me I was going to die in a car accident. I got my license on the first go! I'm a good driver! I already have a super-bad fear of flying, I don't want to get a driving phobia now!"

"Don't worry," Eve reassures her. "She told me I was going to die of intimate partner homicide."

It takes a second for Kayla to decipher the phrase, and as soon as she does, her eyes fly to Dom. Her giraffe eyelashes flutter rapidly, like she's maybe even scared, and poor Dom goes red and takes a step backward, nearly knocking into someone. Eve feels absolutely terrible. She needs to explain that Dom is not like one of *those* men, he's into word games, he sings lullabies to his dog, he plays mixed netball, he absolutely respects women!

Eve tries to fix it. "Which is *impossible,* so that's how I know she's not—"

"Are you talking about that lady?" A woman in a leopard-print jumpsuit looks up from her phone. "She woke me up to tell me I was dying of alcoholism. I said, Excuse me! *Rude!*"

Their conversation is a flame that catches alight and races through the crowd. Suddenly everyone around the carousel is chatting, sharing stories of their predicted lifespans, talking about "her creepy eyes," and the "terrifying matter-of-fact way" she predicted deaths. Some people admit to being "kind of freaked out." Others claim to not even remember what she predicted. (Like, seriously?)

Eve notices that Kayla is now talking to the super-tall skinny guy in the blue tracksuit pants and white T-shirt, and she's touching her hair a lot, so that's nice, like watching a romantic movie, but Kayla is kind of short, so Eve's not sure how sex will work, and that is a really inappropriate thing to think, Eve, stop it.

"Psychics *never* tell people how they're going to die," says a woman, maybe in her thirties, with heart-shaped sunglasses on top of her head.

Her friend, who has a ridiculous large fake flower pinned in her hair, agrees. "Exactly. They consider that totally unethical. There's no way she's qualified. We tried to tell that to the guy with the broken arm sitting next to us. She made him cry. He couldn't stop, the poor thing!"

Are there qualifications for psychics?

"Where is she anyway?" says someone. "Is she here?"

"She was the last one on the plane," says a deep voice. It's the big strong muscly guy with the army buzz cut, who looks like he could save the world all on his own. "She was sound asleep. Probably mental health issues. We should forget what she said. It means nothing. Nothing at all."

There is a pause, as if everybody is thinking they have to do what this man says, because he's in charge, but then they remember he's actually not the boss of them, and they keep talking.

"I mean, it puts things in perspective, doesn't it? I've only got nine years," says a frizzy-haired lady, fiddling with her wedding ring.

"We are definitely checking our smoke alarms when we get home," says someone else.

"Well, the first thing I'm doing is putting a call through to my accountant," chuckles a man who looks like an accountant himself. "I wasn't budgeting on living until ninety-eight!"

Dom doesn't join in the conversation, just looks agitated, even as Eve tries to send him looks to tell him it's okay, there is nothing to worry about.

Finally the carousel begins to move and the first bag makes its proud, disheveled appearance and someone swoops in for it. The excited flurry of conversation abruptly ends. Being reunited with their luggage seems to click people back into their lives, and they leave quickly, without saying goodbye to the people with whom they'd just been conversing so animatedly.

At last there is only Eve, Dom, and the elderly couple who look way older than Eve's grandparents. The carousel is empty. Eve begins to feel panicky. Did they do something wrong when they put on their luggage tags?

They chat, although not about the psychic, thank goodness, because Eve feels embarrassed at the thought of talking to these people about dying when surely it's on the cards for them, like, sooner rather than later.

They want to know all about the honeymoon plans and they tell Eve and Dom they got married young too. It turns out they are both retired doctors and Eve went to their medical practice when she was a little girl and lived in that area for a few years!

"Did it have a red roof?" she checks, and the doctors say it did, and everyone is amazed. She can *sort* of see their relatively younger, slightly less wrinkly selves in their wrinkly old faces, although she would never have recognized them if they hadn't told her they were the Dr. Baileys. Doctors Brian and Barbara Bailey. Eve has a memory of her mother on the phone saying in a lowered voice, "I need Dr. *Barbara* this time."

"Did we cure you?" asks the lady doctor.

Eve tells them there was never anything wrong with her, she regularly faked stomachaches. As she speaks, she remembers they were both super nice, with twinkly eyes, gentle hands, and gigantic jars of jelly beans on their desks.

"You were so generous with your jelly beans!" says Eve.

Dr. Brian Bailey holds up a finger: *Wait.* He begins rustling around in his pocket, and she thinks, Goodness, what is he doing? And she's about to repeat what she'd said about the jelly beans in a louder, slower voice, in case he thought she'd asked for change or a tissue or something, and next thing he holds out a bag of jelly beans! "Take two! Take three!"

Eve is starving, so she takes three.

Dr. Barbara Bailey tells Eve to make sure she drinks lots of water on her honeymoon, and to go to the toilet straight after sex, because all her patients used to come back from their honeymoons with honeymoon cystitis, so that's embarrassing.

Finally their bags appear, all at once, and Dom quickly grabs the elderly couple's bag from the carousel before the man can protest. Eve is wondering if they should offer to take them somewhere because surely they are too frail to be out in the world on their own—someone might knock them over—but then a gray-haired woman in skinny jeans rushes toward them, calling out, "Mum! Dad! I'm such an idiot! I was at the other terminal!"

"It's all right, darling," says the old lady, and the old man says, "No, no, it's got wheels, sweetheart, I can manage," when she tries to take the bag from her father.

The daughter is still a daughter and the mum and dad are still a mum and dad! Even though they are all three ancient! Eve finds that quite profound.

Eve and Dom head out to the back of the taxi line, and Eve is pretty sure she sees "the lady" getting into a taxi, but she doesn't tell Dom because he's starting to look more cheerful, more like a guy on his honeymoon.

She is not going to say or even *think* another thing about those three awful, inaccurate, inconceivable words. She is locking them up in three separate boxes:

Intimate.

Partner.

Homicide.

Chapter 28

I have no memory of what happened in the time between seeing the Jewels of Europe river cruise advertisement in the seat pocket and then opening my eyes, my head pounding, my mouth dry.

The beautiful flight attendant was leaning toward me, her eyes now narrowed and worried, her face drawn, everything about her somehow disordered and different.

"Is anyone meeting you?" she was asking me.

I was confused. Why was that any of her business?

This is interesting: I had no sense of time passing. The only thing I can compare it to is the experience of a general anesthetic, when you're asked to count down from ten and you never get to zero, you get to eight, or seven if you count fast, and the next instant you're in the recovery ward and everything feels different. It's disconcerting. Like being teleported.

(My most recent experience of a general anesthetic was a colonoscopy. My doctor found no polyps or abnormal tissue. I am vigilant with health checks. You should be too.)

I had no memory of the long delay on the tarmac. I had no memory of the plane finally taking off. I normally enjoy the sensation of a plane taking off. I think many people do unless they have a fear of flying, which I do not.

I had no memory of being offered food and drink and apparently refusing both.

I had no memory of making a decision to stand up or of doing what I did.

I had no memory of the plane landing.

I had a very bad headache, my mouth was dry, and I felt extremely hungry. It felt as though something disastrous had happened. My first thought was that the plane must have crashed, although I soon realized that this was not the case, because the plane was intact and there was no smell of smoke, no wailing sirens.

And then I looked around and I was shocked to see that the plane was almost empty. I could see the last few passengers disembarking. Some of them were looking back at me. I thought they were probably confused as to why I was still sitting there, and I felt embarrassed.

The last person to leave the plane was a little boy wearing a backpack. I remembered him—and specifically his army camouflage backpack—from the departure gate. He was being led off the plane by another flight attendant and he was twisting around to stare back at me. His eyes met mine. I thought he was worried that I had forgotten to get off the plane, so I tried to give him a comforting smile and a wave, but he spun away, grabbed for the hand of the flight attendant. Then he was gone.

I've never been good with children.

"I'm sorry," I said to the beautiful, now unkempt flight attendant. "I must have fallen asleep."

I looked down and saw that I was holding a plastic cup, empty except for an ice cube. I felt so thirsty, I tipped the ice into my mouth and crunched it between my teeth. The sound was embarrassingly loud, but I kept crunching so as not to choke. It's possible to choke on an ice cube and stop breathing before the ice cube melts.

"Do you need more water?" The flight attendant held out her hand for the cup. She spoke as though I'd suffered a medical episode, not fallen asleep. I am in excellent health. I take no medication. I write NONE in proud capital letters on forms that require me to list my medication and then I draw a diagonal line across the space, just to make myself clear.

"No, no," I said, although I was still very thirsty, but I was not in a café. "No, thank you."

I unbuckled my seat belt. I stood and did not understand why my legs trembled.

"Do you need . . ." She studied my face as her voice trailed off. She had the fearful, flinching smile of someone in the front row of a performance by a cruel comedian. It was as though she believed I could do or say anything at any moment.

"Do you need medical assistance?" she asked.

"Absolutely not." I couldn't understand why she would ask this, but once you reach a certain age you come to accept strange behavior from young people. They either look straight through you as if you're a houseplant, or they treat you like you're made of glass, hands hovering in case you tumble.

I handed her the plastic cup and stepped out into the aisle. The overhead bin above my seat was open and only my bag remained. Before I could reach for it, she took it down for me. I saw a spasm of pain cross her face although I knew my bag was well under the weight limit for carry-on luggage.

I released the handle so I could wheel it behind me.

"Thank you," I said, and I sniffed, because there was a smell of vomit and it seemed to be emanating from her. "Thank you very much. I'm so sorry to have kept you waiting."

"It's no problem," she said faintly.

"Are *you* all right?" I said. "Allegra?"

Because that was the name on her badge and the poor thing looked unwell and unhappy, and obviously I am no longer that shy little girl at the Hornsby Picture Theatre and can say people's names, no problem at all.

She seemed to make a decision of some sort.

"I'm fine. Perfectly fine." She smiled. Her smile was stunning. "Thank you. You have a good evening."

I exited the plane. I walked straight to the taxi stand. I could see the injured boy ahead of me in the line. I noted he did not resemble Henry from the Hornsby Picture Theatre, or if he did, it was only in the most superficial way. I wondered if I was developing face blindness, which I understand to be an affliction suffered by the exceedingly handsome movie star Brad Pitt.

As I got into the cab I saw the young woman wearing my wedding dress and instantly solved the puzzle. There was no frightening mystery or conspiracy. How embarrassing. I had donated the dress to a charity shop in Hobart. She had bought it. Simple as that.

I did not have a good evening.

Chapter 29

"I went to my first funeral today," Ethan explains to the older man who has introduced himself as Leo. "So I was already feeling kind of . . . strange."

They're in the back seat of a cab, which will take Ethan first to his apartment in Waverley and then on to Coogee, where Leo lives. Ethan wouldn't have picked him as living at Coogee. He looks more inner-city, like a guy who doesn't appreciate sand in his shoes.

"I'm sorry. Was it a family member?" asks Leo solemnly.

"No. It was a friend." Ethan looks out the window and focuses on the giant billboards advertising luxury watches, hotels, and cars.

"A friend? A friend your own age died?" Ethan turns from the window to see Leo turning his whole body to face him so that his seat belt pulls uncomfortably across his neck. He looks horrified. Genuinely horrified. It's gratifying.

"Yeah," says Ethan. "Exactly the same age. He's turning thirty in August. I mean, he would have been turning thirty."

"Oh, mate, I'm so sorry, I thought you were going to say it was your grandfather or something—not that it's not sad to lose a grandparent, it's very sad, but to lose a friend at your age!" He pulls agitatedly at the seat belt. "That's something you'll never forget, you'll never get over it!" He grimaces. "I mean, of course you *will* get over it, what a stupid thing to say, I'm so sorry."

The taxi driver makes a sound that could possibly be a snort.

"It's okay," says Ethan. "Thank you." The streetlights reveal Leo's face. He's wincing as if he just stubbed his toe. He actually reminds Ethan of Harvey: they both belong to the same subspecies of slightly odd, deeply intense people. Ethan has always been drawn to people like this. He likes bouncing off the surfaces of their oddness, in the same way he prefers to play tennis against a hard-hitting player. It's more difficult to cope with the soft lobs of normal, well-adjusted people.

"I once had a friend," says Leo. He stops and wipes vigorously around his mouth as if he's worried he's got tomato sauce all over it.

The pause goes on too long.

"Did he . . . die?" guesses Ethan.

"Oh, no," says Leo. "He didn't die." He looks out the window wistfully. "We just lost touch."

Okay, so that was a weird thing to say.

"Sorry," says Leo. "You losing your friend, for some reason it just made me think of him. It's hardly the same."

No, mate, it's not.

Ethan changes the subject. "So, what about you? How long did the lady give you?"

"Oh!" Leo laughs. "Ha ha. Not long at all. Forty-three, which is this November. A workplace accident. You?"

"I don't have long either," says Ethan. "I turn thirty in October."

"And she said you're dying in a fight?" Leo does a dorky little boxing move: jab, jab, uppercut. "You get in many fights?" He nods at Ethan's sling. "What did you do to yourself?"

"She said assault. So I guess that's not necessarily a fight. I'm pretty conflict avoidant. I broke my wrist in a rock-climbing . . . mishap," says Ethan.

"My father always said if those psychics knew what they were doing they'd win the lottery," says Leo.

"Maybe some of them *have* won," says Ethan. "They just don't advertise it. But yeah, I'm definitely not a believer."

There is silence for a moment. A car changes lanes directly in front of the taxi. The driver slams on his brakes and simultaneously slams his fist against his car horn. Leo and Ethan are jerked forward. The driver opens his window and yells insults.

"Sorry about that, boys!" says the driver, who has the same cockney accent and thick wrinkled neck as a terrifying gangster in a movie Ethan saw with Harvey.

Two weeks ago.

When Harvey was just Harvey. Like, not that important. He had come up to Sydney for the weekend. Reviews were bad, but Ethan and Harvey thought the movie was pretty good.

"Not your fault, mate!" says Leo. "Idiots on the roads these days!"

They drive in silence for a moment before the taxi driver clears his throat.

"Hope you don't mind me eavesdropping. Was there a psychic on your flight?"

"Just a poor soul with dementia, we think," says Leo. "She was telling everyone how and when they're going to die."

"Is that right?" The taxi driver looks over his shoulder and deftly changes lanes. "A clairvoyant told an aunt of mine she'd die on her sixtieth birthday."

There is a pause, and finally Leo says, "And—ah—did she?"

"She did, mate!" says the driver happily. "Choked to death a minute before midnight on her sixtieth birthday. Eating a leftover party pie from her birthday party. Always a bit greedy, Auntie Carol, may the poor old chook rest in peace."

"Oh, dear," says Leo. "Very important to chew your food."

"Fortunately, the same clairvoyant told me mum she'd live a long, happy life."

"And she's still alive?" confirms Ethan.

"Alive and kicking!" says the driver. "Loves her lawn bowls."

"Well, you know, we're kind of hoping this clairvoyant does *not* have special powers," says Leo. "Because a few of us got earlier deaths than we would have liked."

"Got it, mate. So if her predictions begin to come true?" A passing streetlight illuminates the car so that Ethan can see his eyes, bright and interested, looking back at them in the rearview mirror. "*Then you'll know.*"

Chapter 30

I've checked my diary and the first death took place on the same day as my Introduction to Line Dancing class.

I was not aware of it at the time, or for several months after.

I don't mean to sound flippant.

I'm not flippant about death. You could argue that death has defined my life, both personally and professionally.

The line dancing was not a success. I don't know why I thought it would be.

Chapter 31

It is the morning after Leo's pointless day trip to Hobart and the tragedy of the missed *Lion King* concert.

A thunderstorm has caused flash flooding, power lines to come down, and, to the joy of parents throughout the suburbs, the cancellation of all Saturday morning outdoor sports.

Oli is at a friend's place down the road.

Bridie lies under a blanket on the couch in the living room, white-faced with purple smudges under her eyes, her earbuds in, the television on. The leftover makeup under her eyes gives the impression that she's a teenager who has been out clubbing rather than an eleven-year-old hungover from all the adrenaline and excitement of playing Zazu.

Leo used the unexpected gift of time to catch up on work and now he's having coffee and croissants with Neve, while the rain falls steadily and the wind howls.

He watches Neve putting jam on her croissant. His wife wears pajama pants—she says they are not pajama pants, but they sure look like pajama pants, and she wears them to bed, so it seems conclusive—and an old blue school hoodie that once belonged to Oli but is too small for him, and, of course, her Cartier watch.

He met Neve at a party and it was her watch that first caught his

eye. Rectangular face, eighteen-carat white gold, covered in white diamonds.

"That is a really beautiful watch," he'd said without thinking. Normally he agonized over the appropriate opening line for so long the
moment passed.

"Thank you," said Neve, before she was Neve and when instead
she was a moderately drunk pretty girl sitting precariously on a stool
at a high table. She wore crooked glasses with smudged lenses, a red
slip dress with a fraying neckline, and Birkenstocks. (Leo's mother
loves Neve, but she does *not* love her shoes.)

She held up her wrist so that Leo could look more closely at the
watch and said, "It was a twenty-first birthday present from my mum."

One strap of her dress had fallen off her shoulder, which was mesmerizing. Now it drives him mad when a bra strap slithers to her
elbow. He keeps adjusting her bras. She seems to have no understanding of how the tightening mechanisms work.

After they introduced themselves and determined how they knew
the party host, she put her hand on his arm and said, "What's worrying you?"

He tried to tell her that he wasn't worried about anything, it
was just something about his face—he suffers from "resting worried
face"—but she insisted, so he admitted he was worried he might have
accidentally parked illegally and he couldn't afford a parking ticket
right now; he was worried he couldn't remember the host's mother's
name and he'd been introduced to her many times before; he was
worried Neve was about to fall off her stool, could she please stop
rocking back and forth like that? And finally he was worried that she
might not be able to see properly through those glasses and could he
please fix them for her?

He cleaned her glasses with his handkerchief and straightened the
frame and when she put them back on she said it was a beautiful miracle. She discreetly determined the host's mother's name for him, en-
abling him to smoothly say, "Hello, Irene!" just in the nick of time,
and they went for a walk to double-check the parking sign. Basically

they laid down a template for the entirety of their future relationship. His role is to straighten and adjust, mitigate risk and worry, hers is to mollify and soothe, to unwind his wound-up self.

Their first kiss was under the parking sign, which he had, as he suspected, misread. The ticket was already there, under his windshield wiper, so he didn't move it and he didn't care.

As they walked back to the party through the narrow inner-city streets in the moonlight, she mentioned that it was the anniversary of her mother's death. She'd died when Neve was six. That was very sad, but also confusing, because wasn't the watch a twenty-first birthday present from her mother? But then Neve explained that on her twenty-first birthday, she had opened her car door when she had arrived home after a family birthday dinner, and there, right on the asphalt, was this pretty gold watch, as if it had been placed neatly there for her to find.

Neve picked it up, tilted her face to the stars, and said, "Thanks, Mum."

Leo was already half in love with her by then, so he didn't say, *Are you crazy? Do you know how much that watch is worth? You should have handed it in to the police!*

He's not sure if she knows how much it's worth now. She has zero interest in brand names. She's a staunch atheist, has no superstitions, no patience for activities like meditation or yoga, but she truly believed, and still believes, that her watch was not someone's valuable lost property but a gift from her dead mother. She wears it every day, an incongruous gleam of designer luxury for someone who dresses purely for comfort and economy, who avoids wearing shoes wherever possible.

Sometimes he looks up at the stars himself and thanks Neve's mother for the Cartier watch that brought them together.

Also, now he has had children and lost a parent, he kind of gets it. He and his sisters are always asking their deceased father to help them find parking spots. They send photos of amazing car spots on the family WhatsApp captioned: *Thanks, Dad!* Just the other day a miraculous spot appeared directly outside the building Leo needed to be in, as wondrous and valuable as a Cartier watch. A parent's love is surely strong enough to occasionally crash through the barrier dividing heaven and earth.

"So this strange thing happened on yesterday's flight," says Leo.

"What's that?" Neve looks at him. There is a smudge of butter on the lens of her glasses.

He tells her the story while he cleans her glasses, and she is into it—not frightened, she does not really believe in psychics, she thinks most of them are probably scammers—but she's fascinated to hear what the lady said and how the passengers reacted, and she's so focused on Leo that unfortunately, without her glasses, she's unable to see the child standing in the doorway, listening to every word, which is why they both jump out of their skins when Bridie says, in a heartbreaking, terror-trembled tiny voice: "Is Daddy going to die?"

Chapter 32

Some people lead charmed lives and think it is all due to them.

They stand, like ship captains, proud and tall, feet apart, one hand loosely on the helm of their destinies. They are often charming, charismatic people because why wouldn't they be? They have no need of fortune tellers. They have only ever faced clear seas and easy choices.

When the iceberg looms, when something finally happens that is outside of their control, they are outraged. They whip their eyes to the left, to the right, looking for someone to blame.

Try not to marry that sort of person.

Chapter 33

It's the fifth day of their seven-day honeymoon and Eve and Dom lie on top of the bedclothes, naked, spread-eagled, holding hands, watching the rotating ceiling fan as its cool breeze wafts across their sticky bodies. If they lift their chins a fraction they can see out through the half-open slatted-timber doors to an ocean view, framed by a splash of frothy purple bougainvillea and the elegantly drooping frond of a palm tree.

Right now they are honeymooners in an Instagram post. They are tanned, they have just had sex, Eve's hair looks great, the sky is pink and the setting sun has turned the water rose gold. Eve loves rose gold. Her phone case is rose gold! She didn't know it was an option for the sea.

Sadly, this view is also only temporary. It comes and goes with the tide. It's a life lesson about their wedding vows: good times and bad, good times and bad, over and over.

In the next hour, a giant parking lot of slimy black rocks and clumps of brown seaweed like piles of rubbish will slowly be revealed. Eventually, their view will resemble a nuclear waste site. Eve has never seen a nuclear waste site, but it seems an apt description.

This was the distressing sight that greeted them when they first arrived on the island: tired, cranky, grumpy, and married.

The night they'd arrived in Sydney, when they'd finally gone to bed in the "deluxe room" at their fancy hotel, all they had done was sleep. The uncomfortable lingerie was a total waste of money. They had *zero* physical contact. They slept like literal corpses. When they woke up all the sheets were still tucked in! They had to be up unbelievably early for their next flight, which had not seemed a big deal when Eve planned their itinerary but turned out to be a very big deal when their phone alarms went off. They didn't even have time for the free hotel breakfast.

It's okay about the sex. Eve looked it up. Loads of people are too tired for sex on their wedding night. It's practically a trend.

They are staying on Emerald Island, a newly renovated "affordable luxury" island resort in the Whitsundays. The previous resort was top end but went bankrupt and then got decimated in a cyclone. It's funny to think that rich celebrities who were once guests wouldn't be seen dead here now. But Eve and Dom get to walk on the very same sand for a fraction of the price—suckers.

Eve found it on a list of "great value packages for budget-conscious honeymooners." She booked a "standard view beach cabin."

After they checked in, a resort worker with a freaky resemblance to their friend Riley drove them in a buggy to their cabin and carried in their bags. Panicked, Eve whispered to Dom, "Do we tip him?" Dom shrugged, aghast. Dom's dad always insists you never tip *anyone* for anything in Australia because "we pay our workers a proper wage," but Dom's dad is not always a reliable source. (He sends texts like: *Hope you feel better soon, LOL, Dad.*)

After the Riley look-alike brought in their bags, he opened the wooden doors with a flourish and said, "Beautiful view, eh?"

Eve and Dom were stunned. Eve actually gasped in horror. Was he gaslighting them? Eve assumed it was climate change. Therefore, her mother's fault. Her mother's generation had done nothing about climate change. Or was it Eve's fault because she'd chosen the cheapest room? This was a "standard view." Get what you pay for.

She was the first to speak.

She said, "Thank you." She doesn't know why she said that: like, thank you for this terrible view. Then she gave him a ten-dollar note, which was the only cash she had in her wallet, and he looked amazed, which seemed to indicate that Dom's dad was correct, and she kind of felt like asking if she could have it back, please, she made a mistake.

Brownish rose petals were laid out in the shape of a wobbly heart on the bed and a small round table in the corner of the room contained a dusty bottle of room-temperature sparkling wine with a red $4.99 price tag on the back and a fruit platter, over which hovered a happy cloud of fruit flies.

"Think someone forgot the plastic wrap." The guy flapped at the fruit flies with Eve's ten-dollar note.

Eve took off her shoes and said, "Oh!" because the carpet oozed between her toes like damp cold forest moss, which was icky. It's only nice when forest moss feels like forest moss.

"That'd be the steam cleaning," Riley look-alike explained. "Last guests must have made a mess. Enjoy!"

Once they knew he was definitely out of earshot they couldn't stop laughing. The terrible view, the buzzing fruit flies, the icky carpet. "We could be on a reality show," said Dom. "*Honeymoons from Hell.*"

They had to flatten themselves against the walls to walk around the sides of the gigantic bed, but once they got in, the bed was actually amazing with crunchy-crisp but satin-smooth sheets. Who knew sheets could feel that good? They writhed about like dogs on carpets. They lay on opposite sides and called out "*Helloooo*" to each other over the mountain ranges of fluffy snow-white pillows, followed by fake fading echoes: "Hello, hello, hello."

Then they rolled into the middle of the bed and had sex, and because it was the first time since their wedding it felt laden with significance and they even stared romantically into each other's eyes like they were in a movie, proving the intensity of their love to their audience. Eve got the giggles first. Afterward they slept for hours.

Eve woke to the sound of Dom saying, "Babe. Wake up. Look what happened."

And there, like a miracle, was the stunning ocean view exactly as the pictures had promised. It didn't even need a filter, it was that beautiful, and the fact that the beauty came and went with the tide made it even more special.

Also, the carpet dried and no longer felt like forest moss.

They chucked the fruit in the bin.

Since then their honeymoon has been magnificent. Exactly like a real honeymoon. Eve knows it technically *is* a real honeymoon but it's weird to think she and Dom are the literal honeymooners. They've had sex seven and a half times, they've been snorkeling (they saw a turtle), they've been paddleboarding (they were both really good at it, they're so compatible!), they've had happy hour cocktails with all the other cheapskate honeymooners—some of whom are fun and will maybe be their friends forever—they've hiked the trails around the island and this morning they had the "signature couples massage," which was included as part of their package. They both found it painful but didn't like to complain, and now they know they don't like massages and will never do that again, so that's good.

Dom has also given Eve a few personal training sessions because he qualified as a personal trainer six months ago and he's building up his business and has awesome ideas for a fitness app. He already has lots of regular clients. He's popular with middle-aged mums because if they say, "It hurts, Dom!" he says, "Oh, well, have a rest, catch your breath," and they sit on the grass and tell him about their children and how they hurt their feelings and never stop looking at their phones, and Dom says, "Don't worry, they'll grow out of it."

Eve is worried the ladies are not going to see results if they just sit on the grass. She thinks he needs to be more boot-camp-ish and she's been trying to get him to practice yelling at her, but he can't do it, he's too nice. She tests him by moaning, "I can't do any more push-ups, Dom!" and every single time he lets her stop no matter how many times she explains he's meant to shout, "YES YOU CAN! WE NEVER SAY THE WORD 'CAN'T' AT DOM'S BOOT CAMP!"

"You know what I think we should do now?" says Dom. He looks at her with a mischievous, almost guilty expression.

Eve rolls onto her side to face him. "What?"

"Something really bad," he says. His eyes shine. "Something wild."

Eve feels sick. She knows exactly what he's going to say. He wants to try the choking thing. She knew it was coming. He's already bored. This beautiful honeymoon is an illusion, just like that rose-gold sea.

"I think," he says, "we should eat that Twirl from the minibar."

He leaps from the bed, his penis bouncing joyfully. "We're doing it, Eve, nobody can stop us."

Yesterday they'd talked about how, on the few occasions they'd stayed at hotels as children, their parents had made such a HUGE deal about never *ever* touching the minibar, like it might self-combust if they did.

"I mean, it's expensive, but it's not *that* expensive!" Dom studies the minibar price list.

He comes back to the bed with a chocolate bar and a bag of chips.

"I'm going to tell your dad," says Eve.

"I'd never hear the end of it," says Dom.

The chocolate tastes wildly good, probably because it's *forbidden fruit,* although it's not fruit. This is apparently why affairs are so good because the sex is forbidden, but Eve can't imagine ever wanting to sleep with anyone else, except a celebrity, of course.

Dom licks melted chocolate from his fingers and says, "What did you *think* I was going to suggest? You looked scared."

"Oh," says Eve. "No. It's stupid. It's just that I started thinking, on the plane, about choking. Or whatever the technical term is—"

"Autoasphyxiation. You want that?" Dom straightens up. Alert. Does he look alarmed or excited?

"No," says Eve. "I'm sorry. Liv and Riley are into it. I just don't think it would be . . . fun."

"Oh, thank fuck." Dom flops backward on the bed. "I don't get it."

"I don't get it either!" says Eve.

"I'm into breathing," they both say at the same time, and they spin their heads to look at each other with wide eyes and then they laugh and laugh, until Eve snorts, which always makes them both laugh even more.

They are such nerds. They are totally compatible nerds.

Eve starts to shiver, so they get back under the duvet and sit upright with their backs against the wall.

After a moment Dom says, "Were you thinking about choking before or after the psychic lady?"

"Before," says Eve. "Definitely before. It was nothing to do with her."

She opens the bag of chips and offers it to him.

"You're not worried about what she said?" Dom takes a chip.

"*Worried?* Of course I'm not," says Eve. "I do not think you're going to murder me, Dom."

She puts a potato chip on her tongue and lets the flavors seep into her taste buds. "Although I hope she's right about you and you live until you're ninety-three and die of respiratory whatever."

"Respiratory tract infection," says Dom. "But I'll be in jail, right, for killing you? So I'd rather die young."

"All psychics are fake," says Eve. "Remember what happened with my parents?"

"Your dad paid off someone?" Dom frowns, trying to remember the story. They know all of each other's stories. Or she thinks they do, anyway.

"Yes, he bribed a tarot card reader to tell my mum he was the man of her dreams on their second date!"

Her dad always told it as a funny story, which it is not, because he was definitely not the man of Eve's mother's dreams, and when he told her the truth after they got married, Eve's mum felt "deceived," and they had a big fight, and then he kept right on deceiving her with not one but *two* other women, and now Eve's mum has "trust issues" as well as perimenopause.

"Still, that's just one corrupt psychic," points out Dom.

"They're all scammers," Eve says with absolute confidence. "Anyway, remember a lot of those passengers thought she was just a bit loony tunes, not a psychic at all."

Remembering the conversations around the baggage carousel makes her think of Dr. Barbara Bailey telling her to drink lots of water. Eve finds the liter bottle she's kept on the floor next to the bed, due to the lack of a bedside table, and uses both hands to glug back as much water as she can manage.

As she drinks she glances at Dom. He is looking ahead with a vacant expression, munching on chips. She thinks, *Uh-oh.*

She drops the water bottle on the bed between her legs and swallows a burp. "Are *you* worried about what the lady said?"

Dom doesn't look at her. "I *wasn't* worried, but last night, in the middle of the night, I woke up and remembered something—and now I can't stop thinking about it."

Eve wipes the back of her hand across her mouth. "You remembered you want to kill me?"

"No." He's not laughing at her joke. Not even a little bit. He still doesn't look at her. "I don't want to freak you out."

"Tell me."

"Well, you remember what happened when we stayed at that Huon Valley caravan park with Liv and Riley, and we were drinking all that red wine and then—do you remember? What I did?"

"What?" Eve can't think. The caravan was musty. Liv couldn't stop sneezing. The red wine was disgusting. She and Dom aren't big drinkers. There was an argument of some sort. Over something stupid. It might have been the moon landing. Had Eve maybe been telling them about Junie's conspiracy theories? They all had headaches the next day.

Dom looks at her intently. He has the most beautiful brown eyes. She wants a baby boy with that exact color and style of eyes. She might actually have a baby soon. Why not? Babies are so cute, although she'll train hers not to cry like that one on the plane. Her mother will lose her mind if Eve gets pregnant before she has a "career," which adds to the appeal.

Dom says, "Remember?"

Suddenly she gets it. "Oh, Dom, no, *no,* wait, babe, that was *funny!* That doesn't mean anything! You don't need to worry about that!"

Dom folds the top of the chip bag into a firm straight line.

He says, "I am kind of worried about it."

"*Dom.*"

He says, "I don't think it's funny. It's not funny at all."

Chapter 34

My mother once had a customer who was engaged to be married.

She was a sweet, beautifully dressed young woman who was always angling her left hand so her sparkling diamond engagement ring caught the light. She had her cards read every few months and was always early, and she spoke to me like I was a grown-up, not an awkward child, and didn't require me to say much as she chatted, an endless stream of bubbly detail about her forthcoming wedding, the dress, the bouquets, you know the sort of thing. She glowed with anticipation.

She said it was a shame she would have to give up work with the public service but "the marriage bar" was still in place at the time, which meant she was required to relinquish her job straight after the wedding. (I know. I can't believe it either.)

I got so caught up in the excitement over this wedding that Mum ended up taking me to the church to watch. It was my first wedding. When the bride and groom kissed I felt faint with the romance of it.

The woman stopped coming for regular readings after that, and I must admit I forgot about her existence, until one day, maybe a year later, I saw her at the shops. I nearly didn't recognize her. She looked completely different: drab, slumped shoulders, a cardigan that didn't fit or flatter her. She smiled and waved but didn't want to talk. I thought, Is that what happens when you can't work? Is that what happens when you get married?

She died three years after her wedding. There was a house fire. Her husband made it out. He was never charged with her murder, but I heard a lot of talk I wasn't meant to hear.

Once, I asked my mother, "Did you *tell* her not to marry him? Did you see this happening?"

I probably sounded accusing.

She said, "I can't make anyone do anything, Cherry, and I don't always get it right."

I don't think she saw it.

I don't think anyone at that beautiful wedding could have seen it.

Chapter 35

The first liquid notes of a soulful cover of "Can't Help Falling in Love" trickle through the church, and all the wedding guests turn to see the tiny flower girl standing in the vestibule, illuminated by the molten light of a perfect April afternoon.

You would not believe this was the same sticky whiny child who threw up over a flight attendant eight days ago. Willow's face is creamy with self-satisfaction because she knows she looks like a princess. She wears a crown of white flowers in her hair, a royal-blue sash, and a full tulle skirt. She holds a basket of rose petals over one arm.

She walks slowly and deliberately down the aisle. She has been told not to rush and she has taken this instruction to heart. Every few steps she stops, pauses, smiles demurely, before taking a handful of petals and letting them fall one by one to the ground in front of her like she's trickling sand through her fingers.

"We're going to be here all day," says Matt in Paula's ear, glowing with pride, handsome in his best suit, with a blue tie to complement the wedding "color palette." He holds Timmy, who is dressed in a miniature little white dress shirt and blue bow tie and has one arm curled possessively around his dad's neck.

Willow is followed by three bridesmaids in slinky royal-blue dresses, with spaghetti straps, updos, spray tans, but who cares about them, Paula will only drag her eyes away from the flower girl for the bride. And here she comes, her little sister, luminous, radiant, perfect in every way, even though she didn't choose the dress Paula preferred, which would have looked even more perfect. Paula's face is already aching from smiling so hard. She watches their dad pat Lisa's hand in the crook of his arm and remembers her own wedding five years ago (no color palette, Paula has never been as fashionable as her sister), and she thinks about Willow walking down the aisle one day in twenty years or so, on Matt's similarly crooked arm, and in scuttles the thought, before she can stomp on it: *Will there be a toast at Willow's wedding for the bride's little brother who so sadly, tragically drowned when he was just seven years old?*

She sees the sorrow dragged like claw-marks down the lady's face.

As if in anticipation of Paula's future pain.

Where does Paula know her from? *Where, where, where?* And will it help if she works it out? It feels like it should come to her at any moment, the way a missing word or name appears like magic when you give up and stop thinking about it, but she is Paula, so she never stops thinking about it.

She has told no one about what happened. Not even Matt when he arrived last night. "Put it right out of your mind," said her Scottish seatmate, and she knew she wouldn't be able to do that, but she was determined to keep the awful prediction a secret so as not to cast any shadow over her sister's wedding. She knows the worried glances that would be shared, not because her family would be worried about the prediction itself, but because they'd be worried about Paula's reaction to it. She is meant to monitor her stress levels the way a fair-skinned person should monitor the UV index.

Willow, nearly at the front of the church, catches sight of her parents, and her face lights up with delight and surprise, as if she'd forgotten they'd also be in attendance.

Matt turns to say something to Paula's mum and Timmy chooses that moment to leap without warning from Matt's arms into hers, with absolute confidence his mother will catch him, which she does.

Later, at the wedding reception, speeches and toasts done, Matt on the dance floor with Willow, Timmy asleep in his stroller, Paula chats to a random cousin of the groom who is starting her own personally customized jewelry business.

"My clairvoyant says it's a good idea," she says as she shows Paula photos of her (dreadful) creations on her phone. "I never make a significant life decision without first consulting her."

Well, Paula is on her second glass of champagne and she doesn't drink much these days. She's out of practice. Her head is happily swimming and it is physically impossible not to share the story of what happened on the plane.

The random cousin listens. She purses her lips.

"You think I should be worried?" asks Paula.

"Well, sometimes they mean things metaphorically."

"How do you metaphorically drown?"

The cousin doesn't know.

And then it turns out that the person on the other side of Paula has been eavesdropping the whole time and next thing everyone at the table is weighing in on the story, and regrettably, Matt first learns of the prediction when a drunken bridesmaid throws her arms around him (hussy) and tells him she is so, so sorry about Timmy.

He is justifiably annoyed that Paula hasn't told him this story earlier and that so many other people know before him. She doesn't have a good answer.

Matt wants to know why Paula was talking to this lady in the first place.

"I wasn't talking to her!" says Paula. "I told her I didn't want my fortune told."

"So you were talking to her." He is a lawyer too. When they argue they look for holes.

Paula tries to explain that it happened so fast, she was trapped in her seat, what was she meant to do?

"Where were the flight attendants?" asks Matt.

"Well, where were *you*?" says Paula, which doesn't even make sense because it had always been agreed that she would go ahead to Sydney a week before the wedding so there would be time if Willow's dress needed alterations.

"Anyway, it's nothing to worry about," says Matt, already snapping out of his bad mood. He is good at that. "We shouldn't . . . make a thing of it."

"I'm not." Irritation swells. He means "you" shouldn't make a thing of it.

"What's this nonsense I hear about Timmy?" It's her dad. Bushy gray eyebrows forming a V shape.

Paula sees herself, at seventeen, holding the sharpest kitchen knife to his neck in a sweat-slicked hand, while the spaghetti sauce simmered on the stove.

"Bit closer," said her dad.

"Trust the science," said her mum.

"My turn next," said her sister.

Just another wholesome family memory.

Chapter 36

The consequences of my predictions were not necessarily negative.

After my identity became known, I received both "hate mail" and heartfelt thank-you cards.

I honestly don't know how to feel about the thank-you cards.

Chapter 37

Ethan Chang and a gorgeous frozen-fish heiress sit silently in the back of an Uber, driving through the Rocks under a canopy of red-gold trees, past historic sandstone buildings, cobbled laneways, and sapphire flashes of Sydney Harbour. The streets are blanketed with fallen brown leaves dancing in the chilly breeze and their car cuts through them like the bow of a slow-moving boat.

Ethan feels the kind of euphoria he's only ever experienced listening to certain music while high. It's a revelation that it can happen when you're stone-cold sober on a Saturday morning.

Oh, mate, don't pretend this is a religious experience. You've just got the hots for your unattainable flatmate.

Will Harvey always pop into his head with derisive comments like this or will he eventually drift away and Ethan will no longer think of him at all?

There it is again: the very bad feeling. He keeps thinking he's done with it.

"Grief comes in waves," his mother told him. Yes, but Harvey should only get ripples. Ethan never devoted this much thought to the guy when he was alive.

Ethan sneaks another look at Jasmine. She is writing on a Post-it note. Entrepreneurial ideas for new products and businesses strike her all the time. Ethan finds scribbled notes all around the apartment. Some make sense: *SOLO SUNSCREEN you can apply to your own back?* Some sound illegal: *Instant Fake Identity?* Others make no sense: *Yogurt Lip Balm Gin.* He guesses that last one might have been a shopping list.

She looks up, catches his eye, and grins, taps her pen against her teeth. He smiles back and looks away fast, as if something outside the car has caught his interest.

This is not a date. Do not give the impression you believe this to be a date.

The driver takes a tight roundabout too fast and the sudden swerve of the car gives him the chance to look at her again.

Her long brown hair is crazy-wild when she first wakes up (he sees her each morning in the kitchen, making green tea, a beautiful sleepy-eyed cavewoman in a T-shirt), but it's now smooth and glossy in a falling-down bun, as though she's on her way home from a drunken black-tie event. She wears three necklaces of different lengths, an oversized jacket over a knit sweater over a white silk shirt, and is it possible she's wearing *two* skirts? She feels the cold and keeps the heating in their apartment up very high. He sometimes feels like he lives in a sauna. Her shoes are military-looking black lace-up boots. Ethan's Nikes look pathetically ineffectual next to them.

They are on their way to see a psychic. It's the first time Ethan has ever been to one, if he doesn't count the lady on the plane, which he doesn't because he didn't sign up for that prediction. This time he has an actual appointment. He has basically agreed to be scammed for seventy-five bucks.

A few days after the funeral Ethan had offhandedly told Jasmine about what happened on the flight. He wasn't faking offhandedness— the more time that passed, the less significant it seemed—but Jasmine was instantly intrigued.

"So when do you turn thirty?" she asked, looking at him with such gravity and intensity he had to look away in case his body responded inappropriately. (The possibility of an involuntary inappropriate response while living with a girl like Jasmine is a cause of stress, especially when she walks around in a towel. He has to think of his grandmother a *lot*.)

"October," he said, and she caught her breath.

"*First* of October," he emphasized, in the hope she'd do it again, but she was already frowning and tapping at her phone like a NASA scientist accessing top-secret data. She told him a Mystics, Witches, and Oracles festival in Hobart ended the day of the flight. All kinds of psychics took part.

"That's why your lady was in Hobart," she'd said, and then she'd showed him photo after photo of mediums, clairvoyants, palm readers, and crystal-ball readers, none of whom remotely resembled the lady, but Ethan took his time considering each one, because it was very nice to have Jasmine sit that close to him on the couch.

"You know I don't actually believe in this stuff. I think the probability of me dying in a fight is zero," Ethan finally admitted. "I don't get in fights."

"I mean, sure, but you could be randomly attacked." Jasmine chewed the side of her thumb. "On the street?"

"I suppose I could," said Ethan, to be nice.

"You know what you need to do?" she said.

"Take up martial arts?"

"No, you need to get a *second opinion*. Dad says, 'Always get a second opinion.'"

It turned out that Jasmine sees "an excellent medium, aura and tarot card reader" at least twice a year, or more if she's going through a bad breakup or considering a new start-up. His name is Luca, he's *amazing*, so gifted and accurate, and he "only" charges seventy-five dollars for a half-hour reading. "Cheap as chips!"

Ethan wonders if Jasmine knows how much chips actually cost.

"It's hard to get in, but I'll explain it's an emergency," she'd said. "I'll make appointments for both of us—I was due to see him soon anyway. We can go together."

Of course he said yes. He's grateful to the old lady on the plane. You got me a date, lady. Although it's not a date. He knows it's not a date. But it's something.

Ethan told Jasmine to book him under a fake name because he's been reading up on how these scammers get away with it. They do "hot and cold readings." A hot reading is where they research you beforehand. A cold reading is where they ask open-ended questions and monitor your reactions. Ethan plans to sit there with a poker face.

"Yeah, good idea to go undercover," Jasmine had said, straight-faced. "Who knows what Luca could find out from your LinkedIn profile."

Did that mean *she's* looked at his LinkedIn profile? She's not on LinkedIn, of course, so he can't tell. They follow each other on Instagram. Ethan assumes she doesn't spend as much time examining his posts as he does hers.

"So . . . when you see this 'Luca,' is it what? Kind of like therapy?" he asks.

"I mean, no, because I see my therapist for therapy," says Jasmine. "She's amazing. Do you want me to get you an appointment?" She is already scrolling through her phone, ready to make the call. "You should probably get grief counseling. For Harry."

"Harvey," says Ethan. "I'm okay for now. I'll, uh, let you know."

The Uber drops them off in front of an arched doorway and Ethan follows Jasmine into what appears to be a dimly lit gift shop. It's fragrant with incense and adorned with mystical symbols and celestial images. The shelves shimmer with crystals, occult jewelry, candles, skulls, silver bowls, gold bells, and figurines of cats, wolves, angels, dragons, and demons. Mirrored walls behind the shelves refract prisms of red and purple light. It's like being inside a pirate's treasure chest.

"Jasmine!" A woman in a gray hoodie sits behind a desk eating a banana and working on an Apple Mac. Her vibe is all wrong.

"Althea! How are you? This is my friend Ethan. Sorry, I mean,

Jason. My friend Jason." Jasmine gestures back and forth so her brace-lets slide back and forth. "Jason Bourne."

Ethan splutter-coughs, meets Jasmine's dancing eyes, and for a moment they are schoolkids trying not to laugh in class.

"Been in the wars, Jason?" Althea nods at Ethan's wrist, and sticks her leg, which is strapped into a formidable-looking hinged and buckled brace, out from behind the desk. "Me too! Did my meniscus in the Coles car park!"

While Jasmine and Althea discuss her meniscus, Ethan wanders through the shop studying the titles of hardback books: *Beginner's Guide to Pendulum Magic, A Practical Guide to Psychic Self-Defense: The Classic Instruction Manual for Protecting Yourself Against Paranormal Attack.*

Ethan finds himself unexpectedly enthralled. He's remembering the magic kit he got for his ninth birthday. He picks up a miniature box of crystals, sees the price, reels, and quickly sets it back down, a little less enthralled.

"Luca is ready for you," says Althea. "Who wants to go first?"

"You go first," Jasmine says to him. "I want to make a quick call to a surgeon I know."

"Down the stairs, open the oak door on the *right,* through the purple curtains on your *left,*" says Althea, fastidiously peeling the last of her banana.

As he leaves, Jasmine has her phone to her ear. "You can't risk it with a cowboy, Althea, you need—" She holds up one finger. "*Dr. Geoffrey!* Yep, I've got another meniscus for you!"

Ethan goes down the stairs, ducks under a WATCH YOUR HEAD sign, opens the oak door, and draws back the purple curtains to see a clean-shaven, bald man about his dad's age wearing a black U2 *Achtung Baby* concert tour T-shirt and ripped jeans. He's sitting in a small white-walled room that could be for recruitment interviews, except for the fact that the table is covered with a purple cloth embroidered with gold stars and moons.

"Luca?" says Ethan.

"That's me! Have a seat. Jason, is it? How are you?"

"Not bad." Ethan is not giving anything away, not even his state of mind.

There is a framed typed sign sitting so that it faces the customer. It says: READINGS ARE FOR ENTERTAINMENT PURPOSES ONLY, AND NO GUARANTEE CAN BE GIVEN AS TO THEIR ACCURACY. I DO NOT GIVE MEDICAL, LEGAL, OR FINANCIAL ADVICE.

So they're not even *pretending* it's real?

"Broken arm?" asks Luca.

"Wrist," says Ethan. "Rock-climbing accident." Dammit! All he needed to say was "wrist." He's already given away information without even being asked!

"That's bad luck. Althea did her meniscus in the Coles car park," remarks Luca.

"Yes," says Ethan. "I, uh, heard."

"So just a general reading today?" Luca presses a button on a cheap plastic kitchen timer and picks up the deck of tarot cards. "Can you shuffle?"

Ethan waggles his fingers. "I think so."

"Left hand," says Luca. "Three piles."

Ethan puts the cards into three piles.

"Which one?" asks Luca.

"Ah. Middle one, please."

Luca bangs the pile of cards against the side of the table.

"You single? In a relationship?" he asks as he lays out the cards in overlapping rows as if he's playing an unusual version of solitaire, stopping every now and then to consider what he sees.

"Single," says Ethan.

"Star sign?" asks Luca.

"Libra," says Ethan.

"Ah, *Libra*." Luca shakes his head and chuckles.

What's so funny about Libra?

Luca has his hand across his mouth. He rubs his nose with his thumb, removes another card from the deck, places it down, and says, as if that's just what he expected, "Yup."

Without looking up, he says, "There's someone. Someone you see often. A work colleague? A friend in your circle? There is someone you would like to be more than a friend."

"Yes," says Ethan, and he finds he has to force himself to stop talking. This guy relies on people's natural desire to converse.

"Yes, yes. That's right. Someone physically close. But it's complicated. If you tell her how you feel it could jeopardize the friendship."

"Yes," says Ethan. "I don't know if she even . . . thinks of me that way."

He hears himself speaking humbly and respectfully, as if he's at the doctor. He's fascinated by his own collusion with the process.

"Exactly. You can't tell. Does she like you only as a friend or is there a possibility for something more? But listen—" Luca taps a card. "Good news: Knight of Cups. Love is coming into your life in the future. By September, October at the latest."

"With her?"

"It could be with her, it could be with someone else, it could be a friend of hers."

Ethan inwardly rolls his eyes. He's out. It's the sort of thing Ethan's grandmother says for free: *Be patient, the right girl is out there somewhere, Ethan, I just know it!*

"It's going to happen soon. Very soon. Make sure you open your heart."

"Right," says Ethan, as Luca pulls out another card with a macabrely cheerful image of a skeleton riding a white horse. It says baldly: *DEATH.*

Ethan remembers why he's here: for a second opinion. "What about that one? Does that mean I'm going to die?"

Luca looks up. "The death card is more likely to mean a period of transition. It could mean an ending. Or a beginning."

Ethan sighs. The guy is covering all bases. He may as well just tell him straight. "It's just that a psychic on a plane told me I was going to die soon."

Luca raises an eyebrow. "Psychic on a plane! Makes me think of that movie. What is it?" He snaps his fingers. *"Snakes on a Plane."* He chuckles again. "Hilarious."

"Ha ha."

"Do you have any health challenges?" asks Luca.

"No," says Ethan. "She said I would die in a fight."

Luca scrutinizes Ethan. Is he checking out his physique? Ethan subtly flexes his muscles the way he did in school photos.

Luca says, "You don't have the aura of someone who gets in fights very often."

It never worked in the school photos either. "So you think she's wrong?"

"I don't believe *anything* is preordained," says Luca.

"You don't?" *What is the actual point of you, then?* "You don't believe in fate?"

"To a degree, but I can't say: 'This is definitely your future.' Why? Because the moment I do, you change your behavior. You're no longer the same person you were a moment before. See the logic? So— all I can do is interpret the cards to help you see possible paths."

"Right," says Ethan.

Luca says, "Tell me: has a loved one recently passed?"

"Not so much a *loved* one," says Ethan. "A friend. I mean, I guess . . . yes, a loved one."

"I'm very sorry." There is genuine sympathy in Luca's bright blue eyes. It feels like a human moment, as if he's letting Ethan see the real person behind this charade.

Ethan follows his gaze to a ceiling so badly cracked it looks like the aftermath of an earthquake.

"Your friend had a special laugh. Unusual. A laugh that made other people laugh."

"He did," breathes Ethan. His voice breaks as he thinks of that absurd silent wheezy laugh he'll never witness again. "He really did."

(But maybe everyone thinks their friends have special laughs?)

Luca says, "Your friend is here. He's with you."

"Is he?" Ethan looks over his shoulder. Shouldn't Harvey be with his mum and dad and hot sister?

"Of course he is, and he says, *Have faith*. He keeps talking about *faith*."

"Really?" Ethan doesn't bother to hide his skepticism. There's a lot he could do with seventy-five dollars. Have faith? That doesn't sound like Harvey. Harvey had faith in nothing.

Luca puts his head on one side like he has a crick in his neck. He closes his eyes. Ethan shifts in his seat.

Finally Luca speaks. "Harvey says, 'Guys like us always wait too long to make the first move.'"

Ethan startles. The blood rushes from his face. *Guys like us*. Does Harvey mean he should make the first move with *Jasmine*? He always said, "In your dreams, mate," whenever Ethan mentioned her name. Was Harvey nicer now he was dead? Could he see from his other-worldly vantage point that Ethan and Jasmine actually had a future?

"He says, he'll enjoy watching you crash and burn, mate, but . . ."

"But what?"

Luca opens his eyes and grins wickedly. "But maybe you won't, Jason Bourne, maybe you won't."

Chapter 38

People are always intrigued when they learn my mother was a fortune teller.

Like Clark Kent racing into a phone booth and emerging as Superman, she closed her bedroom door and emerged as "Madame Mae."

Sometimes, in a social situation, a friend will suggest I tell other guests about Madame Mae and I will think, Wait. Is this why I was invited? Am I the entertainment? Is my mother the most interesting thing about me?

Possibly.

That's how it happened at that dinner party in 1984.

We broke into spontaneous applause when our hostess placed an extravagant multilayered lopsided concoction of chocolate flakes, cream, and sour cherries on the table. "It's a German Black Forest cake," she said tremulously. I seem to recall someone, I hope it wasn't me, attempting to amuse by responding in a poor German accent.

Look, it may well have been me.

We all make comments we regret at dinner parties.

The dessert was a triumph. I would go so far as to say it was a defining moment in our hostess's life. It became her signature dish. I have eaten it many times since then. Her eulogy will undoubtedly reference it.

Her name, by the way, was Hazel.

It still is Hazel!

She needs to watch her cholesterol but is otherwise in good health.

We developed a kind of friendship after I became a client at her hairdressing salon, which was called, unimaginatively, Hazel's Hair. She grew up in the same area as me and went to the same high school, although she was three years younger. We are not "kindred spirits" but that is okay. She is retired now, but still cuts and colors my hair whenever I am in Sydney.

People compliment my hair all the time and I accept those compliments as if they are for me, not for Hazel's skills. They assume it's my natural hair color. My natural hair color *is* gray, but Hazel "tweaks" it ever so slightly. She has a knack for color.

I realized very recently that I have often taken Hazel's friendship for granted, accepted it like a queen, as if it were my due, just like the compliments on my hair. You may have done the same with a friend. Give that friend of yours a call. If you find their conversation dull, you could always quietly unload the dishwasher at the same time.

Anyhow, Hazel's dinner party.

It feels like yesterday!

Not really.

I know it wasn't yesterday. It was a long time ago.

Our moods had improved. The wonderful cake helped, and also a late southerly buster had caused a dramatic drop in temperature, which meant the fan could be turned off and we could all fix our hair. Furthermore, the grain of rice in the bearded man's teeth had been dislodged, so that was a tremendous relief for all.

The southerly buster led to a discussion about the unreliability of weather forecasters.

"You'd have better luck with a *clairvoyant!*" Hazel gave me a flamboyant wink, which I pretended not to see.

The bearded man asked if we'd heard of "chaos theory." I had, but said nothing as I had contributed more than my fair allocation of conversation.

Chaos theory is the idea that a tiny change now can result in a large change later.

It was first observed by a meteorologist modeling a weather sequence. He mistakenly rounded his variables to three decimal places instead of six, and was shocked to discover this tiny change transformed his entire pattern of simulated weather over a two-month period, thereby proving even the most insignificant change in the atmosphere may have a dramatic effect on the weather.

"Could the flap of a butterfly's wings in Brazil set off a tornado in Texas?" asked the bearded man with a beatific smile, as if he'd just thought of this question himself when in fact he was quoting the alliterative title of the meteorologist's academic paper.

I happened to know the analogy originally invoked the flap of a *seagull's* wing. I'm proud to say I did not mention this.

"Well, could it?" asked someone finally, and the bearded man explained that theoretically it could, or it could *prevent* a tornado.

None of us had any experience with tornadoes, so there was a lull in the conversation.

"Shall we *lounge* about in the *lounge* room?" Hazel gave a sloppy wave of her arm. She had crossed that invisible line from charmingly tipsy to embarrassingly drunk.

Her husband said he would take care of the coffee, which was sensible, as we didn't want Hazel in charge of hot water.

There was not enough seating for everyone, so I sat on the floor next to the coffee table. As a young woman I enjoyed sitting on the floor and often did. I no longer do, although, ironically, it is now recommended that I should. A Brazilian doctor has developed something called a "sit-to-standing longevity test" where you are meant to rise from the floor to your feet without using your hands or knees. I tried it last year with my friend Jill and do not recommend it. We both failed. Although it made us laugh.

"Cherry!" ordered Hazel. "Tell everyone what your mother did for a living!"

"Everyone has heard quite enough about my mother tonight," I said firmly.

"Cherry's mum was a famous fortune teller. *Madame Mae!* Ooooh!"

"Did you inherit her skills?" The attractive man offered me his up-turned hand. "Can you read my palm?"

"No," I said. I resisted the temptation to take his proffered hand. "I didn't inherit her skills. My mother always said I had the intuition of a potato."

"A potato!" said the attractive man. "Well, you certainly don't *look* like a potato."

His eyes did that quick flick—down, up—that men did. I'm not sure it's allowed anymore.

I did look pretty that night and it was difficult to look pretty in the eighties. I wore a black pinstriped high-waisted skirt, a hot-pink shirt, and glittery triangle-shaped earrings. My hair was short at the sides and long and jagged on top. Hazel and I thought it looked marvelous. It's not our fault. It was the fashion.

His wife tucked a long annoying curl behind her ear and said, "Is fortune-telling even *legal*? Isn't it, no offense to your mother . . . fraudulent?"

I understood and fully accepted that this was her way of getting back at me for the way her husband had just looked at me.

"Of course it's legal," said Hazel. "Cherry's mum had a sign out the front of their house."

She was correct. The small handpainted wooden sign that hung on two chains beneath our letterbox read: MADAME MAE—PALMS, TEA-LEAF, AND TAROT. NO APPOINTMENT NECESSARY.

In fact, appointments were necessary, but my mother never liked to turn away a customer. During the years in which she became wildly popular, in fact briefly "notorious," there were sometimes as many as four people milling about our tiny sitting room. I had to offer refreshments, which was stressful.

"I believe fortune-telling *is* technically illegal," said the bearded man apologetically, but unable to resist sharing his knowledge.

Before Google you could toss about all kinds of unverifiable statements at dinner parties, but in this case he was correct. Fortune-telling was technically illegal but rarely if ever prosecuted. My mother certainly never encountered any problems with the police, although she knew stories from her childhood of police going undercover to try to catch fortune tellers. You could only be prosecuted if police witnessed money exchanging hands. Before women joined the police force some fortune tellers refused to see male clients to avoid this possibility. There are still some parts of Australia, and many places around the world, where fortune-telling is illegal. I recently read about convicted psychics in America sitting for interviews before parole boards. "It's all baloney, isn't it?" jeered the "commissioners" (who seemed to be all men), forcing the psychics (who seemed to be all women) to admit that, yes, it was "all baloney."

There has always been a special kind of fury and contempt reserved for women perceived to have supernatural powers. The last woman executed for witchcraft in the British Isles was stripped, smeared with tar, paraded through the town on a barrel, and burned alive.

To be clear: this was a legal execution.

The attractive man asked if I was descended from "a long line of fortune tellers"?

I said I was not, although in truth my grandmother also read palms. No sign on her letterbox, just whispered referrals, and my grandfather never knew about it. He wouldn't have burned her alive, but he would have put a stop to it. Grandma kept the money she made in a biscuit tin. Every Saturday afternoon, she'd go to the bookie in

Jersey Street, a few minutes' walk away from her house in Hornsby, invest two shillings each way, and listen to the horse races on the wireless back at home while she grilled chops for tea.

"Always find a way to make your own money, Cherry," she would say to me, shaking her biscuit tin.

I hear the faint jingle of my grandma's coins whenever I do my online banking: the sound of precious independence.

I did not argue the legality or otherwise of fortune-telling with the woman with the annoying curl. Instead, I shifted the spotlight of attention away from myself by asking the bearded man if he had any thoughts on how new technology might change our lives in the future. He had multiple thoughts, as I'd known he would.

He was explaining why the "mobile phone" would obviously never enjoy widespread use when the doorbell rang.

I wish I could say I felt a shiver of premonition at that moment, but I did not.

Chapter 39

It's mid-May, nearly a month since their glorious trip around Tasmania, and Sue O'Sullivan is having a midweek dinner with her friend Caterina Bonetti at a dimly lit new "rustic Italian eatery" in Haberfield. They haven't caught up for six months, so they have a *lot* to discuss—they practically need an agenda there is so much to cover. Their words trip, their thoughts veer, their voices overlap: *Did I tell you, I've been dying to hear about, how was Tasmania, how was Cairns, your hair looks great, I love that necklace, how is your mum, how is your sister, how is your ankle, how is your knee?*

An LED candle in a glass jar shines a spotlight on the white tablecloth and they lean forward, into the light and each other, and stir their ice-crammed bright orange Aperol spritzes with their environmentally friendly red-and-white-striped paper straws, and each time the waitress appears to take their order they say, "Oh, sorry, we haven't even looked yet, too busy talking!" The first three times she said, "No rush," but now she's annoyed and is ghosting them.

They put on their glasses and swap phones to flick through each other's photos: Sue's highly successful Tasmanian camper van trip and Caterina's mother's highly stressful ninetieth birthday celebration. They move on to complaining about their daughters-in-law, which is always necessary for therapeutic purposes, as they would never criticize these delightful but maddening women to their lovely young faces.

Sue tells Caterina how she and Max are required by one daughter-in-law to ask their eighteen-month-old granddaughter for "consent" before picking her up and how another daughter-in-law has put her family on a sugar-free diet, so right now, not a word of a lie, the children are banned from eating, wait for it: *fruit*.

Caterina tells Sue her daughter-in-law keeps asking if Caterina might cut back her hours soon. Caterina is a GP, and the daughter-in-law, who is also a GP, is hoping to increase *her* working hours while Caterina enjoys the privilege of providing free childcare. The other grandmother is already doing two days a week.

"I *do* want to cut back on my hours," Caterina confesses to Sue. "But not so I can look after toddlers! She told me the other day I could take the children to their swimming lessons, as if that would be a special treat for me! Didn't you just *hate* taking your kids to swimming lessons?"

Sue actually quite enjoyed taking her boys to swimming lessons, chatting with the other parents, and she'd love the opportunity to take her grandchildren, but she pretends to shudder. "Oh, yes. So noisy. All that . . . chlorine."

"*Exactly.* I've done my tour of duty!"

Caterina is consequently still working full-time, a ridiculous state of affairs: working to avoid her adorable, wicked grandchildren.

Sue tells Caterina to cut back her hours right now and *who cares* what the daughter-in-law or the other grandmother thinks?! Nothing wrong with day care. Caterina tells Sue to secretly feed those kids all the fruit she likes. Both of them know they will ignore each other's advice.

They finally stop talking long enough to use their phone flashlights to read the menu. Caterina catches another waitress's attention and instructs Sue to not start a conversation with her, so Sue resists complimenting the waitress on her lovely hair while they order bruschetta, garlic bread, butternut squash ravioli, pear and arugula salad, and a bottle of Tasmanian pinot noir in honor of Sue's trip.

Caterina is cutting the bruschetta in half when Sue tells her about what happened on the plane. It's been on Sue's agenda the whole time, but she has held off. She doesn't want to make it seem like a big deal.

"That is extremely creepy," says Caterina. She leans low over her plate, carefully holding her piece of bruschetta aloft. It's laden with tomato and basil and the whole structure implodes as soon as she takes a bite. "Right. I'm using a knife and fork." She looks up at Sue. "I assume you're not actually worried?"

"Oh, no, of course not," says Sue. She attempts to bite into her bruschetta, with similar results to Caterina's. "This sourdough is far too crunchy!" She wipes her mouth with her napkin. "We exchanged details with the man sitting next to me and he promised to get in touch if he ends up dying in a workplace accident. Ha ha. He'll go first if she's right."

"So, what, are you saying she made these predictions for *everyone* on the plane?"

"I don't know if it was every single passenger, but there were a lot of people at the baggage carousel talking about it. There were some honeymooners. The bride was still in her dress. The lady told her she was going to die of 'intimate partner homicide.'" Sue shakes her cocktail and drains the last mouthful.

"That's horrendous," gasps Caterina. She leans forward. "Did the guy look—"

"Violent? No, not at all," says Sue. "But they never look violent in their wedding photos, do they?"

"Some surprisingly intelligent people believe in psychics, you know," comments Caterina as she pushes her plate of bruschetta away. "I know this very successful surgeon who—hey, wait, didn't *you* see a psychic who predicted Max would have an affair with an Italian? You kept me away from Max for years!"

"It was a *short* Italian woman—you're taller than Max!" For some reason the thought of Max and Caterina in bed gives Sue the giggles. They are so incompatible it feels metaphysically impossible. "I never kept you away from him."

Caterina gives her a look of mock suspicion, wipes her mouth with her napkin, and drops it back on her lap. "I'd love to hear any *actual* evidence of accurate psychic predictions."

"Nostradamus?"

"He said the world was going to end in the nineties," says Caterina. "I remember reading he predicted the day of his own death—"

"Seriously? But that's impressive."

"No, but guess *when* he made the prediction? *The day before he died.* When he was sick and bedridden."

"Maybe not quite as impressive," Sue concedes.

Their ravioli arrives in giant steaming bowls, along with the salad and the wine. Sue takes the opportunity to compliment the waitress on her hair, and Caterina rolls her eyes.

"You are such a *grandma*," she says once the waitress has left.

Sue pretends to scratch her nose while giving her the finger: a maneuver taught to her by her oldest grandson. She decides to say nothing more about the plane incident. Caterina has complained before about people who bore her with their medical woes.

Sue understands. She once had a friend call to ask if Sue could please come over to bandage up her son's leg. Sue lived *half an hour* away and had five children at home. (She put the boys in the car and drove over. They had pizza for dinner and it was a fun night. But still. Come on.)

Sue says, "So how did you go with that—"

Caterina interrupts, "You've got no family history of pancreatic cancer, right?"

"None."

"And you're not experiencing any symptoms? Anything you're worried about?"

"No."

"None of the risk markers," says Caterina. She checks them off on her fingers. "You're not obese, you don't smoke, you're not diabetic, no family history."

"No," says Sue. "I know it's silly. Don't worry. I'm not worried." She takes a piece of pear from the edge of the salad bowl with her fingers.

"Aren't you?" Caterina looks at her steadily. In the dim light she could be the same woman Sue met when they took their first babies to their local baby clinic forty years ago and bonded over their dislike of the bossy clinic nurse.

"Well," says Sue. "I know it's hard to catch early. I know outcomes are not great. It wouldn't be my . . . preferred choice."

Caterina smiles ruefully.

Sue continues, "And I guess it's our age, but don't you find you keep hearing of people getting terrible diagnoses? It feels like we're all just waiting to see where the axe falls next."

"I know," says Caterina. "It's brutal."

"It's annoying because I've been in a really good mood since I turned sixty."

Caterina says, "You've been in a good mood as long as I've known you, Sue."

"No I haven't. And we're so excited about this trip. Can you believe I've never left the country? Imagine if I die before I even get a passport."

"You've been kind of busy, Sue," says Caterina. "Raising a beautiful family, working your socks off, saving people's lives. Don't buy into this idea that you've only truly 'lived' if you've traveled. As if taking the same photos at the same tourist spots as everyone else is the only thing that counts as *living*."

"I know," says Sue. She pauses. "Although I really *do* want one of those photos of me pretending to hold up the Leaning Tower of Pisa. I want it on my fridge. That's my dream. I want to see myself holding up the Leaning Tower of Pisa every time I open my fridge." She demonstrates with the palm of her hand, beaming at an imaginary camera.

Caterina snorts. She lifts her glass, swirls it, and puts it back down. "Okay. So let's do some baseline tests. An abdominal ultrasound. A breath test to check your blood sugars. Make sure you're not pre-diabetic. Blood tests to check how your liver and kidneys are functioning."

Sue puts down her fork. "Is it self-indulgent? I don't want to be like those people who turn up at the ER because they've got a bad 'feeling.' I haven't even mentioned it to anyone at work. Too embarrassing."

"We'll just do an overall health check," says Caterina. "Nothing wrong with that. For peace of mind. Everything we can feasibly check, we'll check."

"You are a very good friend," says Sue emotionally.

"Nope." Caterina holds up a hand like a traffic cop. She can't stand sentimentality. Although Sue sees right through her brusque exterior to her sentimental heart.

Sue spears one giant-sized ravioli with her fork and watches the juices pour free. "I know it's stupid to say this at my age, but I feel like I'm only just getting started."

"My mother used to say 'La vita va veloce: this life goes fast, much faster than time.'"

"Sometimes I worry I've lived the last forty years on autopilot," says Sue, "like I'm always thinking, okay, I'll just get through this next thing, then I'll start living: once I'm married, once the baby is born, once this kid sleeps through the night, once this one is at school, once they've all finished school, once Christmas is done, once Easter is done, you know how it goes. The hamster wheel."

"I do," says Caterina. "But you've never struck me as someone on autopilot. You've always seemed like a present little hamster, Sue."

"I'm just not ready to die," says Sue dramatically at the exact moment the waitress with the lovely hair appears to offer Parmesan and black pepper.

The waitress looks stricken.

"I'm not actually dying," Sue reassures her. "Oh, yes, please to Parmesan! There was this psychic—well, to be honest, we don't even know if she truly was a psychic—"

"Sue," says Caterina.

"Oh my God, I *love* psychics," says the waitress.

"Give me strength." Caterina sighs.

Chapter 40

That day, on the flight from Hobart to Sydney, I was the butterfly.

Actually, I was the less poetic seagull.

That seems more apt. I walked through that plane squawking my predictions, flapping my wings, and my actions had consequences, which had consequences, which had consequences.

I was an agent of chaos.

Chapter 41

"Your baby spent the first nine months of their life in a warm, cozy, aquatic environment!"

Paula shivers in her too-tight old one-piece, waist-deep in chlorinated, supposedly heated water, in a circle of parents each holding a swimsuited baby. The parents tip back their heads to listen to the instructor standing above them on the side of the pool. Their babies kick and bounce, wriggle and gurgle, chortle and whimper.

"Your baby has a natural affinity for water." The instructor is a fit wiry woman with close-cropped white hair, wearing a red long-sleeved rash guard over her swimsuit. Paula can see her matching red-painted toenails hanging over the edge of the tiles. The instructor, like the parents, also holds a baby, a chipmunk-cheeked girl in pink, who seems to be a handy prop baby, as Paula can't see a parent nearby.

All the babies are cute but Timmy, obviously, is the cutest. He is making his favorite tuneless "ah *ah* ah" sound and patting his palms against the surface of the water, startling himself each time he splashes his face. Tiny droplets of water cling to his dark eyelashes and Paula feels a knifelike stab of love.

She has enrolled Timmy in Tiny Fish Swim School, which is an inconvenient forty-minute drive from home. It's the closest swim school she could find that takes babies under six months. Willow does swimming lessons five minutes down the road and loves it. "We'll put Timmy's name down and see him in four weeks!" the manager at Willow's swim school had said, tickling Timmy's feet. "Look at those gigantic feet! You've got a swimmer there!"

But Paula found she couldn't wait. Her desire for immediate action was too powerful. Timmy must learn to swim *right now*. It's irrational because if she believes the lady's prediction, then she also believes he's not drowning until he's seven, which is years away. But that brings no comfort.

Since returning to Hobart after the wedding, she and Matt have not spoken about the prediction. After all, what more is there to say? She knows he wants her to forget about it but she thinks of it constantly. Even while she is chatting quite coherently and cheerfully about something else, a ticker tape of thoughts scrolls through her head: *I don't believe it. But what if it's true? Where have I seen her before? I don't believe it. But what if it's true? Work out how you know her! But how will that help? I don't believe it. But what if it's true?*

It's exhausting.

"Well, that sounds exhausting, Paula," said Dr. Donnelly when she was seventeen and explained her hours-long thought process regarding some long-forgotten issue. Paula was taken aback. Didn't everyone think like that? Apparently not.

"Your baby already *has* a natural ability to swim! Up until six months, the mammalian dive reflex stops water from getting into a baby's lungs." The instructor flips her baby onto her tummy the way Matt does with Timmy when he's playing Superman. She waves her through the air and the baby chuckles. "The amphibian reflex means their legs will move when you place them on their tummies in water."

"Ah *ah* ah!" agrees Timmy. At least he's happy to be here.

His new bracelet jingles on his plump little wrist. Paula can't decide if she finds the bracelet sinister, comforting, or amusing.

The instructor turns serious. "By coming here today you are giving your children a head start on a natural skill that may one day *save their lives.*"

"Timmy is too little for swim lessons," Paula's mother-in-law said when Paula dropped Willow off at her place this morning. "This is because of the witch on the plane, yes?"

Matt must have told her. The prediction is obviously still on his mind too if he's telling his mum, which makes Paula feel tenderly toward him. Perhaps he's not as unconcerned as he made out.

"Oh, no, no, it's just a fun activity for Timmy," said Paula. "Anyway, thanks so much—"

"Wait." Zehra held up an imperious hand.

Matt's mother is Turkish, dark-haired, dark-eyed, fashionable, and alluring.

"I have something for Timmy," she said. "I should have given one to both children when they were born, but Matt always said, Mum, don't embarrass me in front of Paula with your village superstitions."

"Matt said that?" Paula was surprised. She thought he understood his family—wealthier, more stylish—was demonstrably superior to hers. She was ordinary Paula Jones when she met him. Of *course* she was happy to change her name to Paula Binici and automatically become more glamorous. (She's still waiting to become as glamourous and interesting as her new name. Those plain vanilla Jones genes won't go down without a fight.)

"An evil eye bracelet. To protect him," said Zehra. She'd attached a silver bracelet with a blue and white pendant around Timmy's wrist. "I have one for Willow too."

"Thank you," said Paula, and then she said curiously, "Do you truly believe this, Zehra?"

Zehra shrugged an elegant shoulder. "They are Swarovski."

Everyone has superstitions. That sensible-looking, glasses-wearing guest at Paula's sister's wedding, a tax auditor apparently, was ecstatic to catch the bouquet, as if she truly believed it would bring her a marriage proposal.

Now the instructor walks to the edge of the pool. "What we teach at Tiny Fish is a concept called self-rescue."

The baby in the instructor's arms beams. Paula knows what's about to happen before it happens.

"Meet my granddaughter, Olivia, who learned to swim before she could crawl!"

The instructor drops the baby. Everyone gasps. She descends for a few terrifying seconds but then rolls sideways, kicks her little arms and legs, and her grinning wet tiny face emerges from the water as she floats on her back.

"Yeah, this isn't for us," says the man next to Paula as his baby buries her face into his heavily tattooed chest. "I thought we were going to sing 'I'm a Little Teapot.'"

But Timmy is in a frenzy of delight. He's trying to leap free of Paula's arms into the water and she has to hold tight to keep his slippery body in her grip. She has never seen him so excited.

"Well, *your* little man is keen," says the instructor to Paula.

Paula laughs, as if with pride and pleasure, but she is remembering her mother-in-law's muttered words, spoken so low that Paula had to lean close to hear her as she clasped the evil eye bracelet around Timmy's wrist: "It may not have been a prediction, Paula, it may have been a curse."

Chapter 42

I think my mother was wrong. Fate can be fought.

You go to the doctor. You do your health checks. You don't ignore symptoms. You eat your vegetables. You exercise. You take your medication. You stay on the marked trails. You wear your seat belt. You wear your sunscreen. You check your blind spots. You look both ways. You check your brakes. You download a dating app. You go to that party. You apply for that job. You speak to that person. You study as hard as you are able. You invest sensibly.

You won't necessarily *win* against fate, but you should at least put up a fight.

Chapter 43

"How is your back, beta? Are you still taking the painkillers? Your father and I just watched an excellent documentary about the opioid crisis. It was interesting, but also terrifying."

Allegra's mother is softly spoken, but her authority is so unassailable, Allegra finds she has to actively keep a grip on the grown-up version of herself even just talking with her on the phone.

She looks around the bedroom of the North Sydney apartment in which she once again finds herself, the one that she had promised she would never return to again, and yet here she is, not yet at the self-loathing stage, still at the to-hell-with-it stage.

All it took was some concerted texting on his part. He appears at the bedroom door holding up a bottle of wine, pointing at the label, eyebrows raised. For a moment he is illuminated only by the city lights from his window: stubbled, sculpted, gorgeous. It's always a relief and a surprise to note he doesn't have the rock-hard abs you'd think would go with his personality. He says he likes his food too much to ever get a six-pack.

He promised on his life not to make a sound while she takes this call from her mother. These days, if Allegra ignores a call from her mother for too long the next thing she might hear is rescue helicopters. She nods yes to the wine and he disappears.

"Remind me of the name of your medication, Allegra, I thought

I'd written it down, but I can't find it. I want to ask your brother what he thinks."

"Who cares what Taj thinks?" says Allegra instinctively. There you go. Two minutes into the call and she's already behaving like she's twelve.

It's been over a month since Allegra's twenty-eighth birthday: a day forever marked by the worst flight of her career to date. She had to miss her birthday dinner at her parents' place and go straight home to her apartment and to bed, and then the next morning she woke up and couldn't move. Her back felt like it had calcified. She had to crawl on hands and knees to the bathroom, whimpering dramatically, all the while thinking vengeful thoughts about the caftan-wearing passenger with the carry-on bag filled with shoes.

Allegra rang her mother, who came and helped her back to bed, then called one of Allegra's cousins, an orthopedic surgeon, who probably had better things to do, possibly even surgery to perform, but came straight over and prescribed the painkillers. It was while Allegra floated on a sea of blissful pain relief that she told her mother and cousin all about how a passenger had predicted her death by "self-harm" in the next twelve months.

Her mother took a rational, sympathetic approach. Of course that would be an upsetting thing to hear! But Allegra should not dwell on the words of elderly ladies.

It seems, however, that her mother has been dwelling. She's always been interested in Allegra's diet, sleep patterns, and menstrual cycle, but now she has an aggravating new interest in Allegra's state of mind. *How do you feel in yourself? How are your stress levels? Are you calm today? Are you worried about anything?* All different ways to ask the same question: Is the family curse coming for you?

Because it was horribly apt that the lady had predicted the particular cause of death she did.

A coincidence, of course, although could the lady have guessed? Seen it? Felt it? Was it just that Allegra was having a terrible day at work so she looked kind of glum?

It's not a secret that there is a history of depression on both sides of Allegra's family. There is no shame. Absolutely not. Theirs is a progressive modern Indian family and her parents understand the importance of being open about mental health issues. Yes, of course they can answer any questions, although there's little to say and there are more interesting things to talk about.

Her mother suffered postnatal depression after both Taj and Allegra were born. It was a challenging time, she got help, she got better, what do you mean why won't I talk about it, Allegra? I just *did* talk about it.

Her father has been on antidepressants since he was thirty. His brain chemistry got "out of balance," that is all, it's under control now, nothing to worry about, is that all you need to know, because I am quite busy, yes, I *am* busy, I'm not just sitting here, I'm about to run on the treadmill, would you like to watch me? (Allegra's father recently acquired a treadmill and is eager for an audience every time he uses it.)

And then there is Allegra's grandmother, her father's mother, who "accidentally" took too many headache tablets when she was fifty-six and not herself.

It was an aunt who informed Allegra and Taj that their grandmother had not made a mistake. She chose to end her life and therefore she would not go to heaven or hell, her spirit was stuck in a kind of in-between place, waiting for the day she was *meant* to have died.

"But is the in-between place nice?" asked Allegra.

"No," said Allegra's aunt emphatically. "It is not."

For months, possibly years, Allegra had nightmares about her grandmother being in a claustrophobic waiting room the size of an old elevator, containing only one chair upon which her grandmother sat, her handbag on her lap, looking straight ahead, as the mustard-yellow walls drew closer and closer, and then it was no longer her grandmother, it was *Allegra* in the waiting room, and the mustard-yellow walls were coming at her from all sides, her nose pressed flat, her bones crushed to dust, and just before she died, she would wake, gasping for air.

Their parents never forgave that aunt for Allegra's nightmares. She had never had one before!

Taj took a logical approach. He asked the aunt if they could work out when their grandmother *should* have died, so they would know how long their grandmother would be stuck, because their grandmother hated waiting. The aunt scoffed that no respectable astrologer would reveal your expected span of life on earth. Taj pondered and then said, "Wait."

He said if their grandmother's birth chart predicted she would die at another time, it would be wrong, because *that's not what happened.* Therefore, logically, the chart meant nothing. "Don't be disrespectful, Taj," said the aunt.

Taj went further. He said he didn't believe in heaven or hell or an "in-between place." He slept peacefully and dreamlessly and became entirely secular from that moment on.

Allegra is not religious, but she is happy to go with the flow. She still goes to temple now and then. Why not? It does no harm and it makes her parents happy.

Her grandmother would only be in her seventies now if she were still alive. The ordained date of her death might still be years ahead. She might still be waiting for release from the mustard-colored walls.

Now Allegra says, "I already told you, Mum, my back is good now. I'm back at work. I've stopped taking the tablets. No need to discuss my health with Taj."

"He's a medical professional, and he's your brother, Allegra, it's not like I'm discussing it with a stranger on the street."

Rationally, Allegra knows her brother must have some expertise. He has a degree, an office, patients. But he's still just *Taj.* What would he know?

Her irritation makes her reckless. "I shouldn't have told you what that passenger said. I will *never* 'self-harm.' I do not have depression, Mum, and I'm not getting it."

Her mother's tone is frosty. "Depression is not actually something you *choose* to suffer, Allegra, any more than you *choose* to catch a cold."

Now Allegra feels bad. "Yes, I know, you're right, I'm just saying—"

"I'm not concerned about what the passenger said." Her mother's voice is louder. She probably regrets saying what she said too, because isn't she therefore implying that depression floats invisibly in the air like cold germs ready to infect Allegra with her genetic susceptibility? Allegra knows her poor mother is walking a delicate line: Don't worry about this, but don't be cavalier about this.

"I'm not even thinking about it. I called to make sure you knew when Diwali is this year, so you're not working, because your cousins—"

"I know, Mum, I've got it in my calendar. I promise I won't be working."

A glass of wine is handed to her by the man about whom Allegra's mother knows nothing. Her mother is not old-fashioned about pre-marital sex, but she would not like the idea of sex for the sake of sex. Sex is meant to be an expression of love. *If you know for sure you have no future with this man, Allegra, if you're not sure you even like him, why waste your time sleeping with him?*

He carefully positions himself next to her on the bed, his back up against the headboard. He has smooth tanned calves. He shaves his legs because it "improves his aerodynamics" when he cycles. A surf-board is propped up in the corner of his bedroom. A dumbbell sits on a pile of military-themed books on his bedside table, along with a nasal spray. They could not be less compatible.

"You sound distracted," says her mother. "Are you in the middle of watching something? Your brother hates it when I call when he's in the middle of watching something, which, apparently, I always do."

"I'm just tired," says Allegra.

"You work too hard. Have you—"

"Eaten? Yes, I have." She preempts the next question. "I had the brown chicken you gave me the other night." She'll have it tomorrow night. "It was good."

"I will make more for you, *meri jaan*, sleep well."

Meri jaan. Her mother reserves this term of endearment for times of genuine illness or heartbreak. The translation is "my life." The love in her mother's voice makes Allegra feel terrible for snapping. She will visit tomorrow.

"Bye, Mum," she says, in a tone of voice that means *I'm sorry*.

She puts the phone face down on the bed next to her.

"Thank you," she says to the man with whom she is not compatible.

He smiles. "You sound different when you're talking to your mother."

"You mean I sound more Indian."

It's something Allegra and her family notice about themselves: their accent subtly shifts depending on their audience. "Listen to Dad doing his Aussie voice," her brother will chuckle. It happens naturally. Allegra can't fake it.

"Do you speak . . . any other languages?"

"I understand Hindi pretty well," says Allegra brusquely. "But I'm not fluent."

She doesn't want to talk to him about her family, her background, her *culture*. It's too personal. She's happy to be called "insanely beautiful" but not if what he really means is "exotic."

She picks up her phone again, begins to scroll. "Shall I order us takeout?"

"Nope. I'm cooking," he says.

"You're *cooking*?" She puts down her phone. "You don't need to do that."

"For your birthday," he says. "I felt bad when I turned up to work and saw your friend with the balloon and realized it was your birthday, I didn't know—"

"Why should you have?" She wants to make it very clear she has no misapprehensions about what is going on here. She kicks his calf with her foot. "Speaking of which, what was that performance with the *doughnut*? My friend . . ."

She catches herself. Mockery is the basis of their relationship, but there are surely limits. She can't tell him Anders said he'd never love anyone as much as he hated that man, in the same way that she can't tell her friends that she occasionally hooks up with First Officer Jonathan Summers.

They would be appalled. More disapproving than her mother. Please not a pilot, Allegra, and okay, fine, if it has to be a pilot, why him? He's the *worst*.

"I don't know why I did that." He puts his hand over his face and looks at her between his fingers. "I was thinking, *Play it cool, play it cool, Jonny*, because I know you don't want anyone at work knowing about us, and then I . . . don't know, I behaved like a jackass. I love those doughnuts."

"You should be good in a crisis," says Allegra. "You're a pilot. Our lives are in your hands."

"I'm excellent in a crisis," he says. "I'm just a terrible actor."

"It's fine," she says. "But you really don't need to cook for me. That's not necessary. That's not . . . what we do."

What they usually do is have astonishingly good sex, followed by fairly nice Vietnamese or quite good pizza from local takeouts and an expensive bottle of wine at his place. Never at her place. They never go out to dinner. Then she leaves his apartment in an Uber, satiated and a little drunk, and she promises herself that it won't happen again.

It has the feeling of an affair, but he's not married or in a relationship with anyone else, as far as she knows. No woman makes an appearance on his Instagram account.

There is no ban on work relationships. This happens all the time. They could go public with it, but it seems unnecessary to risk the humiliation and the gossip when it's not going anywhere.

"I've made you a pie," he says.

There is a beat.

A long beat.

"You've made me a *pie*?" She doesn't know why the word "pie" is suddenly so funny.

"Yes," he says. He's laughing a bit too. "I've made you a pie, Allegra. It's my signature dish. I make good pies. I make the pastry from scratch. It's chicken and vegetables with a lattice top. It will be ready in twenty minutes. I've also made a green salad."

"Well, that's all very, gosh, domestic . . . a *lattice* top, I'm not even sure what that means."

"Like a basket weave." He demonstrates by crisscrossing his fingers.

"Oh, yes, of course, I know." She takes a big mouthful of wine and avoids his eyes. She feels embarrassed. His cooking for her feels more intimate than what they just did, the moment she walked in the door, which was very intimate.

Something is not right. He seems unsure, when Jonny's defining characteristic is arrogance.

They ran into each other outside of work six months ago, when Allegra and a group of schoolfriends went to see a band. She recognized him right away, standing at the bar next to her: that conceited, good-looking pilot. She looked away fast, but he caught her eye.

He said, "How do I know you?"

She looks different outside of work. No makeup, hair down, jeans, nose ring, tank top, tattoo on her shoulder. (A tiny abstract Ganesha. She and her cousin got them together when they turned eighteen. Her mother said, You will regret that. So far: no regret.)

He worked out who she was with a snap of his fingers: "Allegra!"

"First Officer Jonathan Summers." She tipped a finger to her forehead.

He flirted. She mocked. He took it with good grace. They danced. He could dance. Of course he could. She went back to his apartment because she was just the right level of drunk, because it felt wicked but technically was not wicked, because of the way she felt when he looked at her, because she'd been single for two years and her body said, That's enough celibacy, Allegra, thanks very much.

This is the fifth time it's happened since then. The sex, unfortunately, is only getting better.

He says, "When you were talking to your mother, I overheard—

sorry if you don't want to talk about it—but did that passenger give you a prediction that day?"

He knows about the lady because, as is normal practice, the flight crew all waited for one another on the aerobridge and left the airport together, so there was plenty of time to fill one another in on what had happened. Even the captain was intrigued and acted less like an aristocrat talking to his servants and more like a regular workmate.

"I wouldn't want to know," he said as the staff bus jolted its way toward the car park. "My wife found this website called the Death Clock, where you enter your date of birth, your BMI—that sort of thing—and it predicts the date of your death. I told her, do not enter my data!"

Bet she did, thought Allegra.

"Bet she did," said Kim out loud, as she has no filter.

"I bet she did too," said the captain gloomily, and they all laughed.

"I'd like to know when and how I'm going to die," said Anders. "I'm so bummed I missed a prediction from the lady."

"It's not real," Ellie said, with such conviction you would think it was a rule she'd learned in Ground School. "She was just making it all up as she went."

Allegra remembers that Jonathan didn't contribute much to the conversation on the bus, just looked at his phone and avoided all eye contact with Allegra, who also didn't speak much, as she sat stiffly in her damp clothes, her back so fragile it felt like it could explode into a million pieces at any moment.

"So she predicted I'd die by self-harm at the age of twenty-eight," says Allegra now.

Jonny flinches. "That's *horrible*. You're twenty-eight now! That was your twenty-eighth *birthday*!"

"I'm aware," says Allegra. "It's fine. I'm not worried. I'm not . . . you know, depressed or anything. I will not be self-harming."

He frowns. "Imagine if she'd said that to someone experiencing mental health issues."

"But I'm not," says Allegra. "So it's fine."

He looks intently at her. "My brother got bad depression in high school. It was a scary time for our family."

Goodness. What is going on? He's basket-weaving pastry, he's sharing personal stories about his family, he's being *vulnerable*.

"Anyway," she says. She's certainly not going to share stories with him about her family's history of depression. She sees those claustrophobic mustard-yellow walls again from her long-ago nightmare, thinks of her grandmother, waiting, waiting, possibly still waiting.

"Did you do an incident report?" asks Jonny. "For a passenger disturbance?"

Is this his pompous work persona emerging? Good. He's being too nice. It's weird.

"I thought about it, but nothing really happened; it was all over before it began," she says. "I did a safety report for my back injury, and the vomiting kid, but the psychic lady . . . no."

He nods. "Sure."

"Do you think I should have?" She is momentarily anxious. "Maybe I should have."

"No, I'm sure it's fine," he says, and he puts a comforting hand on her arm. "Sorry. I don't mean to worry you. It would only be if a passenger complained or a video went online. That would have happened by now if it was going to happen. How long has it been?"

"Six weeks," says Allegra. "Yes. I guess it would have."

He puts his glass down next to his dumbbell and nasal spray, rolls onto his side, rests his head on his hand, and looks up at her with a smile.

Oh, no. Please. Stop it. You can't actually like-like him, Allegra.

The fragrance of baking fills the apartment. She imagines him carefully cutting strips of pastry and feels a weightless sensation, a roller coaster tipping forward of her heart.

Her mother taught her that relationships begin with mutual respect and friendship that leads to love and then, only then: sex. But if you started with sex, could you loop your way back to friendship? Could you do things out of order and end up at the same place? In an actual relationship? With *First Officer Jonathan Summers?* Of all people?

He says, "Tell me your life story, Allegra Patel."

He says it like he really wants to know.

Chapter 44

Tell me your life story, Cherry.

Said a man with liquid black eyes on a summer night while he topped up my red wine and nudged a basket of garlic bread toward me across a red-and-white-checked tablecloth, and he said it like he really wanted to know.

You do not want to know my life story, at least not in the same way that he did, because you are not hopeful that I will take off my green crocheted dress later tonight and go to bed with you.

But you do want to understand how I came to be "the Death Lady." I want to understand it myself.

I will therefore attempt to tell as accurate and concise a version of my life story as possible, and I will not try to be charming or funny, like I did that night in the Italian restaurant in Glebe.

(*Don't try to be funny, Cherry,* the liquid-eyed man said, years later. That's the way it goes sometimes. You no longer beguile.)

I promise I will circle back to the dinner party and the ringing of the doorbell.

My good friend Jill hated that phrase: circle back. She worked for a man who said it all the time: "Let's circle back to that, Jill." It made her grind her teeth. Sorry, Jill.

But the older you get, the less linear your memories, and the more everything seems to circle back to something else.

Chapter 45

Budget your time like it's money!

Leo looks at the text from his boss and tries to remember if he ever actually *asked* Lilith for help with time management strategies over the last three years, or if she has noticed it's a weakness of his and she's trying to mentor him, and if that's the case, he is of course grateful and open to constructive criticism.

He feels a little ill each time her name appears on his phone or computer screen. Does this indicate internalized misogyny because she's his first female boss? But he is used to bossy females. He has three younger sisters. He was their *horse*! He had to crawl around the house on hands and knees while they shouted, "Giddy-up!"

Neve says you can't call women "bossy" anymore, even though she's met his sisters.

Right now it's seven on a Friday night and he's at his desk getting some hours in before the family goes out to see a movie.

Budget your time.

He should skip the movie. He could spend that time more wisely. He'll just be sitting in a theater staring at a big screen; it's not like he'll be interacting with his family during the movie.

"You ready to leave soon?" asks Neve, putting her head around their study door.

"Ah," begins Leo.

"Leo." She comes into the room. "Bridie is looking forward to this."

"Bridie is fine now," says Leo.

The consequence of Bridie overhearing Leo tell Neve about the prediction he would die in a workplace accident had been close to two weeks of incredibly stressful parenting: insomnia, stomachaches, tears. Bridie constantly came to them with new evidence she'd found online about psychics who had accurately predicted deaths as well as all the ways that civil engineers could and did die in workplace accidents. (Kind of sobering, to be frank.) She wanted to know if Leo wore nonslip shoes.

"Don't shut her down," Neve said, whenever Leo interrupted to tell Bridie there was nothing to worry about, he wouldn't slip, most days he's just working at his computer anyway! "Just let her work through it. By the way, *do* you wear nonslip shoes when you're on-site?"

Thankfully Oli was not in the least concerned, coolly proclaiming the lady to be "a scammer," the implication being that Oli wouldn't have fallen for it.

Just when Leo and Neve were thinking they might have to get professional help for Bridie, she snapped out of it, losing interest like it was a fashion fad. She seemed to forget all about it. Didn't care about her dad anymore? "Stop that," said Neve.

Bridie's new obsession became her forthcoming math exam, which she was convinced she would fail (she did fail) and they'd all been swept up once more in the rapid-moving current of family life: school, work, weekend sports, bills, housework and homework and finding Bridie a patient math tutor.

Since then, Leo has been too busy to give much thought to the prediction, although perhaps he thinks about safety more than he normally would when he visits the site of the city underground railway station and shopping complex that has filled his days and his dreams for the last two years. *One of the most significant civil engineering projects awarded in the state this year!* Exciting. Also, stressful. He needs to be on-site, and the crews complain if he isn't there often enough, but Lilith says he should aim to be at his desk at least six hours a day, so that's another time-management conundrum he hasn't quite solved and none of the apps she recommends have the answer.

Neve leans against the wall next to his desk, arms crossed. "Do you want to know the most common deathbed regret for men? According to this palliative-care nurse?"

"Not especially."

"*I wish I hadn't worked so hard.*" She says it triumphantly, as if she has just proved a point and he will now leap up from his desk and stop working so hard.

Leo says, "Those dying men forget they *needed* to work and that's the reason they now have the money to pay for a nurse to listen to them bang on about their regrets. They're also forgetting they *wanted* to work. They can't actually remember the person they used to be."

Neve considers this. One of the things he has always loved about her is that she will always stop and consider an opposing view.

She says, "Maybe you're right."

"Thank you," says Leo. His eyes return to his computer screen.

"But, Leo," she says, "you don't want to miss seeing your children grow up."

Well, of course he doesn't want to miss seeing his children grow up. He's not! He's taking Oli to soccer tomorrow. He helped Bridie with her math homework tonight, which was extremely painful. What the hell is she talking about?

Sometimes he feels like he's one of those stretchy rubber-man toys and his boss has one arm and his wife has the other arm and every day they pull in different directions, demanding *more time, more time, more time.*

"Okay, fine, I'll come to the movie," he says, but he doesn't stand up.

"It's fine." Neve sighs. "I don't want you sitting there fretting over work all through the movie."

He rolls his chair closer, puts his arm around her waist, and looks up at her. "I'll come next time."

"Do you want to know another top five deathbed regret?" asks Neve as he drops his arm and scoots back to his desk.

"What is it?" says Leo, although he doesn't care, his hands are back on his keyboard, ready to do more in less time, to prioritize, to group tasks based on importance, to focus on what's important, not just urgent, except everything is both important and urgent.

"I wish I'd stayed in touch with my friends."

He grunts. Another point made. Another point ignored.

Chapter 46

When you imagine the life story of a fortune teller's daughter, you probably imagine red satin drapes and flickering candles, colored smoke and crystal balls.

Think this instead: a white, weatherboard, two-bedroom house with red terra-cotta roof tiles on a quarter-acre block, a kitchen wallpapered with vertical rows of fat bunches of purple grapes, a tiny mint-green bathroom, a backyard with a mandarin tree and a mulberry tree, a vegetable garden, a shed for the chickens, and a shed for Dad.

Think freckled noses and screaming cicadas, fishing rods and bubbling creeks, the nose-tickling fragrance of eucalyptus and freshly mown grass, an endless expanse of hopeful blue sky.

Think suburban Sydney in the 1950s.

My parents met in 1946, right after the war, at a New Year's Eve dance hosted by the Air Force Association. My mother kept the ticket, which I still have, faded and precious. It says: *Dancing 8:30-1:30, Liquor permitted in hall, Novelties for all, Confetti battle. Admission 10/6 Single.*

The dance was held at The Cab, which was what everyone called the Pacific Cabaret in Hornsby: an elegant, white, art deco–style building, designed so that when you walked inside it felt like you were stepping on board a cruise ship. The light fittings resembled ships' bows. Cut-out palm trees decorated the walls. The dance floor, made of tallow-wood, was considered the best in Sydney.

The Cab became a roller skating rink in the 1970s.

The building was demolished in the eighties and replaced by an office block.

It's often best not to think too much about "progress" or you may find yourself depressed.

My parents' names were Arthur Hetherington and Mae Mills.

Arthur, my dad, was a shy, deep-voiced, tall country boy from Lismore, with a head for figures, good with his hands, a careful, meticulous, logical man. His favorite things were fishing, canoeing, and chess.

Dad served in the war as an aircraft mechanic. Most of his time was spent in hangars and workshops on the island of Morotai in Indonesia. "Oh, I think he had a grand old time," Mum would say, as if his wartime experience was just an overseas version of the time he spent tinkering in his shed after tea. If asked about the war, Dad talked about the pilots anxiously, his forehead creased, as if he still felt the weight of responsibility for their safety. He remembered "a funny Queenslander called Gus" and "a young bloke called Les who sang like an angel." All the pilots had superstitions. Gus always flew with his childhood teddy bear. Wasn't embarrassed about it. Les never flew without first kicking the front tire three times.

Dad reckoned he knew enough that he could take off and fly one of the planes, but he'd have trouble landing it. People always chuckled when he said this, but I found it troubling. Landing is pretty important, I thought.

(Almost half of all men who took part in a recent survey believed they could successfully land a commercial aircraft in an emergency. It's their hubris that makes men both so adorable and exasperating, don't you think?)

Mae, my mum, was eighteen when they met, three years younger than my dad, and bright, beautiful, and effervescent. Her favorite things were dances, parties, library books, and the pictures. She and Dad got talking at the refreshment bar. Mum ordered a Kir Royale. Dad said, "That sounds good, I'll have the same." He said it was so sweet he nearly spat it out. (It must have had too much crème de cassis. I have one every year to toast their anniversary. I highly recommend, but the ratios must be correct.)

Mum introduced him to her older sister, my auntie Pat, who I'm sure was smoking a cigarette when she said, "Read Arthur's palm, Mae. See what's in his future."

Mum read Dad's palm and told him a dance was in his future.

Her flirting skills were impeccable.

She then got the surprise of her life—this was always my favorite part of the story—because Dad could dance, and he didn't look like a man who could dance, but he could do it all: the rumba, foxtrot, swing, the Canadian Three-Step, the Gypsy Tap.

Auntie Pat said it sure was nice to watch Arthur and Mae dance together that first time, like seeing something that was always meant to be.

You would think with parents like that, I would have turned out to be a good dancer, but sadly not. "Anyone can line dance," the teacher assured me when I signed up for his class, and you should have seen the expression on his face as I proved him wrong.

I was born right at the start of the mid-twentieth-century baby boom. This was when childbirth rates soared after all the servicemen came home in optimistic moods, ready to start families. I am therefore a baby boomer. We're not popular. Younger generations believe we've had more than our fair allocation of luck. Perhaps they are right.

Correction: And service*women*. It wasn't just servicemen coming home after the war. Sorry, Auntie Pat. My auntie Pat served as a nurse with the Australian Army Nursing Service. I remember her bandaging my grazed knee once and my mother trying to correct her technique. "I treated gunshot wounds in the Middle East, Mae." Auntie Pat blew smoke out the side of her mouth. "I think I can manage this."

My mother said, "Sorry, Pat." It was rare to hear my mother apologize. She liked to be right. I do too.

Auntie Pat's fiancé was taken prisoner by the Japanese in Singapore. He starved to death working on the Burma Railway. Auntie Pat never married, although she was deeply in love with Paul McCartney, but he wasn't available. I've read that your first experience of love permanently changes your brain. It does feel like that.

Mr. Brown, who lived three doors down from us, had a son who was also a prisoner of war, but he came home. Sometimes, on moonlit summer nights, he took off all his clothes and ran through the neighborhood. Poor old Basil Brown, we children said, obliviously.

There were a lot of "old maids" in our neighborhood, who had maybe lost their first loves like Auntie Pat, or maybe there weren't enough men to go around after the war and they never even got first loves. Miss Heywood had a long blond plait and often cried silently for no reason as she taught us piano. Of course, I'm sure there *was* a reason for her tears, we just didn't know it. Perhaps it was the sound of our playing.

Miss Piper, an angry, beautiful lady, kept six milking cows on a vacant block of land next to her house. She used to take the cows for "walks" across the bush and up our road, like they were her pets. She'd named all her cows after flowers: Buttercup. Lily. I can't recall any more names. *Primrose!* Well, you get the picture.

I'm glad we no longer say "old maids," and for the widespread availability of antidepressants, dating apps, sperm banks, and vibrators. It's much easier for young women to be single. Progress isn't always bad.

I had no brothers or sisters and never had a lot of friends, due to my personality, but I had my friend Ivy who lived next door to us on Bridge Road. I don't remember meeting her. She just always existed. Like a sister, I guess. She did the talking for both of us.

Back then Hornsby was a bushland suburb with a country village feel to it. Ivy and I ran along bush tracks filling our billycans with wild blackberries. We splashed bare feet in the big clear rock pools at the bottom of our street. We caught tadpoles, frogs, and lizards. Ivy and I had our own little tomahawks, if you can believe it, which we used to cut down tree branches to build bonfires.

The colors of my childhood memories are so rich and vibrant, but then again, yours probably are too. My eye specialist told me the lenses of our eyes naturally become yellower as we age, so colors are never as bright as they once were.

On weekends my dad took me fishing in a tinny boat he kept at Apple Tree Bay. I always had multiple thoughts to share with my dad as we waited for the fish to bite, and questions to ask. It's possible I never paused for breath. Once, I overheard him say to my mother, "Gosh, she's the funniest little thing."

I still feel the warmth of his love in those words.

Although I didn't inherit his dancing abilities, I did inherit my dad's head for figures. He said I could count to one hundred by the time I was two. I'm not saying I was a genius. I was just mathematically inclined.

I read that the delightful award-winning actress Jennifer Lawrence pretended to walk with a limp as a child and was so "committed" to her performance her teacher believed her to be permanently injured. I found this anecdote charming. Jennifer was already the actress she would one day become.

My father could see the person I was destined to become.

He played mathematical games with me when I was very small. He would set up bowls of sliced banana on the table. He'd eat a piece and say, How many now, Cherry? That's how I learned addition and subtraction and multiplication.

Dad worked for the railways. He started out as a third class machinist, I believe, and moved up and up, all the while taking classes offered by the Railway Institute. He said to me, Cherry, if ever there is an opportunity to learn something new, you must take it.

Dad was ambitious. His dream was to work for the Department of Railways in York Street as a suit-and-tie-wearing "businessman" in the green-tiled art deco building called Transport House. He studied for an accounting qualification by correspondence. He and I did our homework together each night at the kitchen table.

I was in charge of balancing the family checkbook by the time I was nine. I would bend my head over my task at the kitchen table and sometimes I caught my parents exchanging smiles; maybe they were even trying not to laugh. I expect I looked self-important.

One night Dad told me I might one day study mathematics at Sydney University, and my mother made a sound: a little exhalation of disbelief.

"Cherry *could* study mathematics at university if she so chooses," said my father sternly.

My parents didn't often argue. Sometimes, if Mum was in a mood, she would snootily correct my dad's country boy speech. "It's fish*ing*, not fishin'," and sometimes my dad would inform my mother that money didn't grow on trees. Surely she knows that, I would think to myself bemusedly.

Their most sustained, most significant source of conflict involved the salesmen who knocked on our door, every day except Sunday. Mum was their favorite customer. She bought herbs, spices, "healing balms," makeup, face creams, encyclopedias, a sewing machine, and a vacuum cleaner. The vacuum cleaner salesman carried in his own bag of dirt, spread it out on the carpet, and vacuumed it up. My mother was enthralled. I said I could actually still see some dirt, but nobody took any notice of me.

My mother would have loved online shopping. Oh my goodness, she would have bought truckloads of skincare. She would have embraced retinol like a "Real Housewife."

There was only one door-to-door salesman Mum didn't like: Jiminy Cricket. This was my mother's nickname for the insurance man who knocked on our door every month to collect our insurance payment. We all called him that. Once Dad accidentally said, "Bye,

Jiminy," as he closed the door. I believe Jiminy's real name was Brian, so that would have been embarrassing for Dad and confusing for the insurance man.

If you're of a different generation, it's possible we don't share the same cultural references, so I should tell you that Jiminy Cricket is a character from the Disney movie *Pinocchio*. He's a wisecracking cricket, dressed in a top hat. He's annoying. Consciences often are annoying.

The insurance man had short, fast little legs and he was smiley and bald. He wore a trilby hat that he removed when we opened the door to him. He did resemble the Disney character, although he wasn't green.

My mother *hated* him. She said Jiminy made her skin crawl. She said he was "oily." I think he must have been one of those unctuous, obsequious, patronizing men. Perhaps you know the type. When I was organizing her funeral, I wondered why I felt such antipathy toward the funeral director. Was it simply because I was paying him to bury my mother? That's when the word "oily" arose from my memory.

Every month my mother complained about Jiminy. She said life insurance was a waste of money. Like throwing it into the ocean. She said there were so many better things she could do with that money. "I bet," said Dad dryly.

She said life insurance was bad luck.

My dad said, "Bad luck? I assume you're not serious."

She was serious. It's not uncommon. Superstition is one of the three main reasons why people choose not to buy life insurance. People think it will make them more likely to die.

Investing in life insurance does not increase your risk of dying.

Correction: Investing in life insurance may increase your risk of dying if you are married to a murderer. I'm not trying to be funny. Just accurate.

My dad said, "It's for your security, Mae, for you and Cherry. Life is unpredictable. It's a small amount of money to ensure you're protected if I get hit by a bus or struck by lightning or—"

"Don't say that! Never, *ever* say things like that!" My mother rushed about the house knocking on wood wherever she could find it.

Dad gave her a cuddle and they stopped talking about it. Dad said we could start saving for a holiday, not our normal camping holidays on the Central Coast, but a holiday at a proper roadside motel where you hung your breakfast order on the outside door handle before you went to sleep and in the morning you opened the door to find a tray on the footpath, with tiny jars of jam and honey and little gold-wrapped rectangles of butter along with your toast in a paper bag, and a hot pot of tea. Mum and Dad had experienced this kind of breakfast on their honeymoon, and it sounded like a dream to me.

Dad never did take us to a roadside motel.

Not all dreams come true, even for lucky baby boomers like me.

Of course, arguing over money is not unusual in a marriage. Conflict over financial matters is a leading cause of divorce. Ask most couples, wealthy or poor, what they argued about last and they are likely to say money.

Ask that young woman who wore my wedding dress on the plane.

Actually, please don't ask her. She might say their last argument was about me.

Chapter 47

Six weeks after their wedding, Eve opens their credit card bill, shrieks, and claps her hand over her mouth like a girl in a horror movie. She drops the bill on the table, takes a few steps back, leans against the ugly peach-colored kitchen countertop, and tries to calm her breathing.

She is alone in their apartment. It's a Saturday morning. Dom has back-to-back personal training sessions all day today until five. She doesn't want to look at it again. She feels literally sick.

No. Grow up, Eve. She picks up the bill with her fingertips. A thought occurs: It's not their bill! She's accidentally opened someone else's mail! But no, it's their bill. Their shiny new names are right there: *Eve and Dominic Archer-Fern.*

There will be a mistake. She will find the mistake. She sits at the kitchen table and uses the straight edge of the envelope like a ruler, to go through the bill, line by line. So many lines. So much money. The bridesmaids' gifts, the groomsmen's gifts, the hairdresser, the makeup artist, two bottles of prosecco for the girls while they were having their hair and makeup done, three meat lover's pizzas for the boys when they got hungry waiting for the wedding to start, the stupid uncomfortable wedding-night lingerie she will never wear again, her wedding shoes, Dom's wedding shoes, the tuxedo rental, the taxis in Sydney, the painful couples massage they thought was included in their accommodation package (the words "additional cost" in tiny letters), the half-price happy hour cocktails (why did they buy drinks for that couple from Adelaide? That girl worked in a literal bank and her husband was up himself), the minibar bill (once they started, they kept taking stuff from the minibar, and it started to feel like it was free), the Uber home from the airport (Dom's dad *offered* to pick them up! Why did they say no?), the insurance they had to pay on all their stuff in their new apartment because apparently that's what you have to do, their phone bills, their first electricity bill (oh my God, why did no one tell them electricity cost so much, isn't it like a basic human right?), Dom's daily midmorning smoothie, Eve's daily midmorning coffee, the grocery bills (why were they buying so many groceries? Who knew eating regular food was so expensive?).

There is a huge bowl of fruit in the middle of the table: mandarins, bananas, oranges, apples. Dom eats an extraordinary amount of fruit every single day. "Aren't raspberries kind of expensive?" Eve said when they did their last shop. "We can afford it, can't we?" Dom was confused.

The next day Eve discovered half the raspberries were covered in white fur! Disgusting! What a waste of money.

Neither of them has lived away from home before and Eve's mother keeps reminding them of this, and giving them helpful advice, as if they are actual idiots. They are twenty years old, they can drink and vote and drive.

"Don't forget you'll have to pay all your other expenses, like electricity, groceries, car insurance," she said when they'd put in an application for this rental. "Have you done a budget?"

Budget. Such a Mum-type word. It isn't like they'd applied for a place somewhere expensive like Battery Point. They are a twenty-minute drive out of Hobart, on the first floor of a red-brick building without balconies.

It's not exactly charming, but there is a beautiful big tree directly outside their kitchen window and the sunlight filters through its flickering leaves so on breezy days it creates a disco ball effect of bouncing light and shadow, and on clear days they can see right through the big tree to the mountains. "That's a lovely outlook," Eve's mother had said approvingly, but hadn't been so thrilled by the discarded vapes, cigarette butts, pizza boxes, and empty glass bottles that littered the front of the building, which turns out to be a popular local hangout for teenagers. This wasn't mentioned on the list of features in the real estate advertisement. Sometimes Eve and Dom are woken in the middle of the night by raucous laughter, sobbing, and yelling: all those big raw teenage emotions.

The point is they didn't lease a fancy apartment, which is why Eve assumed they could afford, like, normal stuff. Not diamonds and designer bags. Just raspberries and electricity.

She finds a pen and notepad, opens her laptop, and sits upright in her chair, like she is at work. She is an organized, intelligent person. She was pretty good at math at school. She will do a boring "budget." She will get on top of this.

When they put in their rental application for this apartment, they had to submit their most recent pay stubs. At that time Dom worked full-time at a warehouse and did personal training after hours. The warehouse laid him off after their application was approved, but they weren't worried. The opposite. They were pleased. The plan was that Dom would expand his personal training business, and work on his fitness app, and make a lot *more* money. People sold fitness apps for millions!

He is getting more clients, but the problem is last-minute cancellations. Children seem to get sick *a lot* and cars often won't start, which Eve finds suspicious, as Dom's clients all drive better cars than they do. She thinks Dom should charge a cancellation fee if they send a *So sorry, Dom!* text when he's literally on the oval setting up equipment, but Dom won't even consider that. Often his clients say they don't have any cash and ask if they can pay next time, and Dom, being

Dom, always says, "Sure thing," but he doesn't keep records and he never chases up money. "Oh, it all works out in the end," he says, but Eve knows that none of his clients pay twice. So it does not work out in the end.

Nothing has come of the fitness app.

Apparently you need a wealthy investor to get started. Dom isn't sure where to find one.

She checks the balance of their joint account and whimpers. Their next rental payment is due on the twenty-sixth of the month. Their car payment is due on the twenty-seventh. Eve's salary is deposited on the twenty-eighth of the month. Unless they deposit some cash into the account they will not have enough money for the direct debit.

She picks up her pen, draws a line down the middle of the page. and lists income on one side and expenses on the other.

Fifteen minutes later she pushes the notepad away and rests her forehead on her hands. She feels fearful, overwhelmed, but mostly she feels deeply embarrassed.

They literally cannot afford to live their lives.

They have miscalculated. Well, they never actually calculated in the first place. They just thought that if you worked hard most days then you could afford the kind of stuff that everyone else had. They have messed up big time.

How will she tell Dom?

She needs to handle this carefully. Dom is the sweetest, most loving, easygoing, and stable of boys, except for those times when he's weird and complicated and stubbornly fixates on a wrongheaded idea.

The first time this happened was when they were seventeen and had been together for two years after they fell in love during a French lesson (so romantic, it's like they met in Paris, ha ha, no it's not).

It was all Dom's dad's fault. One night, after too much red wine, he delivered one of his famous after-dinner monologues about "life." Eve wasn't there. It was just Dom listening respectfully, like his dad was a priest delivering a sermon. The topic was relationships. Dom's dad explained that most teenage relationships were destined to fail and it was "a tragedy" that Dom and Eve had met so young (he later denied using the word "tragedy") because they'd most likely break up in their twenties when they realized they hadn't experienced enough of the world or dated enough other people to know that they were right for each other.

Other boys would have said, "I'll prove you wrong, Dad," or just ignored it as the typical tipsy ravings of a clueless Gen X parent, but not Dom. He took it to heart and lay awake all night worrying about it, until he came up with a stupid solution.

Eve will never forget Dom's cold, determined face as he broke her heart on the balcony outside the senior science lab. It was like he'd been body-snatched by aliens. "We need to break up," he said. She kept sobbing, "Why? *Why?* What did I do?" He didn't explain his reasoning because he knew she'd try to change his mind. It was the same kind of crazy no-pain-no-gain conviction that allows him to do an insane number of push-ups and chin-ups.

He seriously believed that if they broke up then, they could "quickly" have relationships with other people, get them over and done with, and be back together in six months, a year, tops. He said the breakup was like a vaccination.

Luckily Dom went home and told his dad, who was horrified that Dom had taken his ramblings so literally. He grabbed Dom's arm and said, "But you might lose her, mate!" and then delivered another monologue, sober this time, about how you can't *trick* destiny, you can't strong-arm your life in a different direction, some things are meant to be and some things are not meant to be, and you don't always get to choose, all you can do is enjoy the ride, and so on and so forth. (Dom's dad talks a lot.)

In the end their breakup only lasted nine hours and twenty-three minutes. They were the worst nine hours and twenty-three minutes of Eve's life.

Of course they were meant to be, and here they are, all these years later, happily married.

Blissfully happy!

So, so happy.

She takes a mandarin from the bowl, peels it, and chews on a piece. It's kind of sour, but she pretends not to notice and doesn't spit it out, not even the seeds.

Chapter 48

One sticky gray February day, a week after my tenth birthday, my father balanced a penny on his thumb and sent it spinning high.

He was thirty-two, a young man, although of course to me he was as grown-up as it was possible to be. His fishing rod in its smart canvas tube (Mum gave it to him for Christmas), his tackle box and swag were in the hallway next to the front door. He and his friends Ralph and Angelo were catching the train up to Gosford and then the bus to Avoca Beach, to camp overnight. The wives and children often went with them, but not this time because there was a school fete we didn't want to miss. (Now that I think about it, the mothers probably would have been very happy to miss the fete.)

Dad caught the penny and placed it on top of his hand. "Heads or tails, Cherry?"

I said heads, and I said heads the next time too, and got it right.

The third time I said tails.

"Why do you say tails?" asked Dad.

I said, feeling kind of proud and knowing, "Because we just got two heads, Dad, so now it's more likely to be tails."

Dad said, "I know it *feels* that way. It feels that way to me too! But the coin has no memory. If it's a fair coin the chances of it being heads or tails are *always* one in two."

The outcomes of a coin toss are statistically independent. That's what he was trying to say. He didn't use those words. He wouldn't have known them and I wouldn't have understood them. But that was the principle. I don't know why he chose that moment to talk about it. Perhaps he'd just learned it himself.

I thought for a moment and then I said, "But what if you got *ten* heads in a row? Then it would *definitely* be more likely that the next one was tails."

That's when he told me about what had happened in Monte Carlo.

There was initial confusion, because I understood Monte Carlo to be the name of my favorite biscuit from the Arnott's Assortment tin, not a famous district in Monaco, on the French Riviera, but we sorted that out.

It happened in 1913 at the Monte Carlo casino. The roulette table. The ball kept landing on black, causing more and more people to crowd around the table, placing bigger and bigger bets on red because they were convinced the streak was surely about to end. There were *twenty-six* consecutive blacks before the ball landed on red. People lost millions of francs.

The belief that the probability of future events changes based on past events (assuming those events are independent) is known as the Monte Carlo fallacy, or the gambler's fallacy.

I didn't *fully* grasp what my dad was saying as I was only a child.

In fact, history shows that many "financial gurus" don't understand the basics of probability. These highly successful, charismatic men (they are nearly always men) ride high on a streak of good luck that they attribute to their own remarkable intelligence, right up until the day the streak ends, and their clients' losses are catastrophic. But it's never the guru's fault. Then it's just bad luck. Past performance is no guarantee of future results, folks!

Maybe you've already guessed that this was the last conversation I had with my dad, and that's why I remember it so clearly and why I've thought about it so often, and given it more significance than perhaps it deserves.

My dad was struck by lightning while he, Angelo, and Ralph were rock fishing. They'd had a marvelous afternoon. The fish were biting. They'd all agreed on just five minutes more.

Never turn your back on the ocean, Dad always told me, but lightning doesn't care which way you're facing, it strikes the tallest thing it can find, whether it's a tree, a church steeple, or a human, and my dad was the most cautious of those three fishermen, but he was also the tallest.

It's rare to be killed by lightning, but it happens. Around two thousand people die by lightning strikes every year. I would say none of them expected it.

Nine out of ten people survive a lightning strike.

A cloud-to-ground lightning strike can contain up to one billion bolts of electricity. Cardiac injury is the main cause of death. The lightning stopped my dad's heart. My dad's big beautiful anxious worried loving ambitious funny heart.

I often wonder about the last thought he didn't get to finish. Was it about bait or statistical independence or homework with me or dancing with Mum or Monte Carlo biscuits or Gus the pilot from Queensland and his teddy bear or the beer he was looking forward to enjoying back at the campsite or swimming in the ocean or an itch he needed to scratch on the back of his knee? It doesn't really matter. He had millions of thoughts during his thirty-two years. I just wonder about that last one.

I have no memory of hearing the news that my dad died. There is an empty space where that memory should be, as if the lightning cauterized it. I was told I behaved "oddly": I didn't cry or ask questions. Apparently I nodded, as though to say *Message received,* picked up my pencil, and returned to my homework.

For years I was ashamed of this, as if I'd failed one of the most significant moments of my life, as if it meant I didn't love my dad, but later, when I'd just turned forty, I got talking to a friend of a friend at a party. We sat on white plastic chairs that sank into the grass and drank West Coast Coolers, and got into one of those strangely intimate conversations that sometimes happen between strangers when there is too much alcohol and not enough food, and we discovered we'd both lost our fathers as children.

She said, "It was too big for you to comprehend, you were in shock."

It's interesting how a simple kind comment from a stranger can make you feel better.

I do remember my mother's reaction. She fell, almost to the floor, as if the lightning had struck her heart, too, but Auntie Pat caught her with a chair, just in the nick of time, and Mum put her head down on the kitchen table and said, over and over again, No, no, no, no.

I looked away from her. I found it undignified. I didn't think Dad would like it.

The day after my dad's funeral, Ivy and I were heading to the creek when I saw Jiminy Cricket trot down the pathway of someone's house. I was thrilled. What good timing. I ran up to him and I said, "My dad died, so now *you* have to pay *us* money!"

Ivy said I had a big creepy smile on my face, as if I'd won a bet, and it was no wonder that Jiminy looked so alarmed.

Insurance *is* like a bet. You're betting on your own bad luck. The insurance company mostly wins because mostly you don't crash your car and mostly your house doesn't burn down.

Life insurance is a bet on when you're going to die.

We won, because it was unlikely a big strong clever man like my dad would die at thirty-two.

But that's what he did.

Chapter 49

It's a Saturday morning streaming with early winter sunlight when Ethan wakes to the smell of butter, vanilla, and sugar. Jasmine doesn't cook often, but she makes great pancakes. He's hungry, and his mood, as he opens his bedroom blinds all the way, is as bright and sunshiny as the day. Ever since their visit to the psychic, he and Jasmine have been talking more, spending more time together. She calls him Jason Bourne now. He still calls her Jasmine. No nickname has come to mind.

They have talked a lot about Luca's readings that day. Ethan told her about how Luca had channeled Harvey's words, "guys like us." Jasmine said the first time she saw Luca he told her that he could see someone behind her plaiting her hair. "That's Nana!" Jasmine had cried. Ever since then she has felt a wonderful sense of peace knowing her grandmother is with her at all times.

Ethan isn't one hundred percent convinced. Luca could have hit on that "guys like us" phrase by pure luck. It's not *that* specific. "It's pretty specific," said Jasmine. Also, when Luca read Jasmine's cards that day he told her to be prepared for "financial difficulties" later this year, which seems as likely as Ethan dying in a fight. (Does the guy really not know who Jasmine *is*?)

Ethan is still fairly chill about the lady's prediction, but he has no-

ticed that when he's out, he is more aware of the possibility of violence. He scans the streets like he's actually Jason Bourne on a
mission. He keeps an eye out for drunken angry thugs. On more than
one occasion he's crossed the road so he hasn't had to walk past the
entrance of a noisy pub. He's not sure how he feels about that. More
sympathetic to how women live their lives?

He reminds himself to never accidentally mention this revelation
to an actual woman.

He pulls on a T-shirt and jeans and heads to the kitchen. He can
hear the sizzle of butter. There is a skip in his step, a "Zip-a-Dee-Doo-
Dah" tone in his voice. "Do I smell pancakes?"

"You sure do, mate," says a deep voice, and Ethan fails to catch his
face before it falls like a disappointed child's.

There's a guy in the kitchen, in fucking Calvin Klein boxer shorts,
tanned bare rugby-player chest, private-school floppy hair, strong
jawline no doubt inherited from his dad along with his trust fund,
drinking coffee from Ethan's favorite mug, leaning back against the
counter, watching Jasmine cook pancakes.

"Morning, Ethan," says Jasmine. She gestures with her spatula.
"This is Carter."

"So you're the flatmate." Unmistakable animosity in the word
"flatmate." Carter puts down Ethan's mug, holds out his hand, and
Ethan knows what's going to happen and it does: Carter crushes his
hand, holding eye contact, letting Ethan know he's the highest-
ranking chimpanzee in this kitchen.

"Nice to meet you," says Ethan. "Wow. Good grip there, mate."

Jasmine glances over. "Watch it. Ethan broke his wrist rock climbing. He only just got the cast off."

Fury flares in Carter's eyes, because Ethan called him out on his
alpha male behavior, in front of Jasmine, and everyone knows women
hate that, but the guy isn't stupid. He comes right back at him with a
right hook of good-humored good manners. "Sorry. My old-school
dad is obsessed with firm handshakes."

"You want a pancake, Ethan?" says Jasmine. She's wearing a tank top and pajama pants, and her hair isn't as wild as it normally is in the morning, she's swirled it into a kind of topknot.

"Does she cook breakfast like this for you every day? Lucky guy!" Carter puts a possessive hand on Jasmine's shoulder, rubs up and down, up and down. Ethan's skin crawls.

Oh, Jasmine, thinks Ethan. He's trouble. Can't you see he's trouble?

When he first moved in he was ready to run into hookups in the kitchen. They are two single people, it had to happen at some point, but Jasmine had only just come out of a long-term relationship at the time. He'd stopped expecting it. He got comfortable. He got delusional.

"I'm good," says Ethan. "I'm about to go out."

Everyone knows it's a lie. His trilling "Do I smell pancakes?" still echoes.

"Take ours back to bed?" says Carter to Jasmine, his hand now low on her back. He gives Ethan a shit-eating grin. It says: I know how much you bench-press, your bank balance, the crappy car you drive, how badly you want her. You lose, I win. On every count.

Ethan gets out of the apartment as fast as he can and walks toward Bronte Beach, as if he really is meeting someone for breakfast.

What a loser he is, thinking he had a chance with a girl like that when she gave him *no indication whatsoever* that she had any interest. Carter is probably "someone," or his dad is. People like that date each other. They speak the same language, holiday in the same ski resorts. Jasmine and Carter are probably in bed right now imitating his hopeful nerdy tone: *Do I smell pancakes?*

Sorrow and humiliation make his throat catch. He pulls his phone from his back pocket, dials. As the phone rings he sees a couple passionately making out. The guy is sitting on a low brick fence. The girl is standing between his legs. It's nine a.m. It's unnecessary.

"Hello?" A woman's voice.

His heart plummets. He takes the phone away from his ear to look at the name of the person he has just called and the realization of what he has done crashes through him.

He has called Harvey. Harvey is the friend he calls when he's miserable. You don't call Harvey when you get a promotion, you call Harvey when you crash your car. Harvey loves misery. He never tries to make you feel better or downplays your feelings. He wants every detail, the more humiliating the better.

Ethan can't speak. That axe-like sensation of grief again. He wants to speak to *Harvey.*

The woman says, "Ethan? It's Lila. Harvey's sister. We met at the funeral."

Pocket dial. Pretend it's a pocket dial.

"I'm so sorry," he says, and he hears tears in his voice. "I just . . . forgot. For a moment I forgot. I can't believe I did that. I felt like talking to him."

"Don't worry about it. It happens to me all the time."

"I remember meeting you," says Ethan. "Hi, Lila. I really can't believe I did that."

"I've got his phone," says Lila. "Some people text. I mean, not accidentally, they know he's dead, but they text him. One guy texted: *Sorry about the hundred bucks, miss you, mate.*"

"Deano," says Ethan. "Tosser. Harvey wasn't going to let that go."

"I should get him to pay it to Harvey's estate," says Lila.

"You should." Ethan wipes his sweaty forehead, looks up at a cloud-scudded blue sky. How is it he still gets to be here in this solar system, is still allowed to stand on this planet as it orbits around the sun, when Harvey is in some other dimension? Or simply no longer exists? "How are you . . . managing?"

"You know what, I just can't believe it," says Lila. "It's nearly two months since the funeral and I still . . . I still can't get my head around it."

"I know," says Ethan. "I *know.*"

"Harvey never seemed the type to die young," says Lila. "He's been middle-aged since he was ten. He should have got to *be* middle-aged."

Ethan laughs. "I know exactly what you mean."

A seagull squawks raucously and someone honks their horn.

Ethan presses the phone to his ear. Is she crying? Please don't let her be crying.

"I should let you go," says Ethan. "I'm sorry, again—"

"Call him—call me—any time you feel like it. It's nice for me to know people are out there thinking of Harvey. Missing him too. Bye, Ethan."

She hangs up and Ethan walks toward the beach, past the couple who don't stop their rabid kissing. He feels better. Surely Carter won't be around for long, and if Jasmine falls for a guy like that, then she's not the girl for Ethan.

He catches sight of a quietly perched kookaburra, sitting regally on the branch of a white gum, almost completely camouflaged against the trunk. The bird's coolly calculating eyes meet his, and a childhood memory comes to him. Their next-door neighbors invited Ethan and his sister over to admire their fancy new pond filled with shimmery goldfish. The very next afternoon, as Ethan got changed out of his uniform, he looked out his bedroom window to see a kookaburra with something large, shimmery-gold and helpless in its mouth, which it was hitting, over and over, against the trunk of a tree.

Death and brutality in his own front yard.

He's never forgotten it.

Chapter 50

The Monte Carlo remains my favorite biscuit. I always think of statistical independence when I eat one. I pull the two layers of biscuit apart, so as to enjoy the creamy jam filling. I thought everyone ate Monte Carlos that way, so I was shocked, last year, to see my good friend, Bert, bite heedlessly through both layers at once. Crumbs flying. He winked at me and said, "I like to live dangerously, Cherry."

Chapter 51

For the rest of her life my mother believed she'd foreseen Dad's death.

She said that day when she and Dad were arguing about the pointlessness of life insurance and Dad made his comment "if I'm struck by lightning," she had *felt* his death in her chest. She knew right at that moment that he was going to die, and if Dad had just listened to her, if she'd been more insistent, if he'd closed the door on Jiminy Cricket's oily face, it would never have happened.

She said, "I knew it, I knew it, I knew it."

"You're not making any sense, Mae," said Auntie Pat.

Dad had also said, "If I'm hit by a bus," and he was not hit by a bus. These are just common colloquial phrases to indicate unlikely but possible events.

When I was an angry teenager I once shouted at my mother, "It meant *nothing*, you knew *nothing*!"

"I know what I knew! I know what I felt!" My mother banged her chest with her fist. By then my mother had become Madame Mae and foreseeing my father's death had become her origin story.

I was sixteen at the time, so I thought she was an idiot.

Chapter 52

Eve folds the credit card bill up tight and puts it in the back pocket of her jeans, as if she's hiding it from her mum. She goes into their bedroom and hops into bed. She always puts herself to bed whenever she is upset. Apparently she did this when she was a toddler. Back then it was *Aww, Evie, so adorable.* Now it probably means she has an actual disorder.

She has to wrench on the top sheet with all her strength just to get in. Dom always makes their bed and he does a great job. He pulls the sheets super tight, as though he's a soldier, although he also carefully positions the throw cushions just so, which is very cute. It was his dad who taught him to make a bed like this.

Dom is an only child brought up by a single father, and Eve is an only child brought up by a single mother. They discovered this in that fateful French lesson back in Year 10. In pairs, they had to get up and describe the other person's living situation in French. "Dom lives with his dad. He has no sisters or brothers. He has a dog called Tilly." "Eve lives with her mum. She has no sisters or brothers. She has a cat called Tilly." Oh my God, they were so bad at French, their French teacher hated them, but it was obvious, to, like, everyone in that class, except the teacher, because she had no soul, that Eve and Dom were two halves of a whole, two matching jigsaw pieces, two people *whose* pets, *although different species, shared the SAME NAME*, who were clearly destined to be together forever.

And now, here they are, married, living happily ever after.

They're so, so happy!

And then, bizarrely, a cruel, malicious thought appears in her head without her permission: *But, Eve, there is nothing to look forward to in your life.*

For the last eighteen months it has been nothing but wedding, wedding, wedding. Lists and appointments, so much to do, and a constant feeling of momentum, as if she has been sliding toward something, faster and faster, the wedding is a month away, it's a week away, it's tomorrow! And then: it's happening! She's walking down the aisle, she's doing the wedding dance, toasts, speeches, photos, and her face is aching from smiling so hard. And then the flight from Hobart to Sydney. No, let's not think about the flight. Think about the honeymoon: sex and cocktails and swimming. Coming home to their new apartment! Opening all those beautifully wrapped gifts and finding places to put them and going to the shops to exchange gifts from guests with crappy taste. Writing the thank-you cards: not quite so fun, but still, another task that needed to be done. And then picking up the photos, staring at themselves, feeling kind of pleased at how good they looked, watching the video with their friends!

Now what?

Now, nothing.

Nothing as big and glamorous as her wedding will ever happen again in her whole life. She'll just go to *other* people's weddings and, yes, she will hopefully have babies, but how will they ever afford babies? And what if she can't train them not to cry like that awful baby on the plane? She'll have to work two jobs and make her kids dinner and do their laundry and get old and die and what is the actual point of her whole life?

Is this what people mean when they say "existential crisis"? She didn't think she was complicated or cool enough for one of those.

She will not panic. She will work this out.

She googles: *Why am I sad after my wedding?*

The internet offers an instant diagnosis: *Post-wedding blues.*

Very common. Like postnatal depression but without the hormones or sympathy. Nobody is going to bring her a lasagna. The solution, according to the internet, is to *make plans*. Date nights and whatever. They are too young for date nights. She shudders at the thought. *Budgets. Date nights.* What next? Orthotics?

Anyway they can't afford to go out. Their credit card will explode.

She puts her hands behind her head and wonders how Dom will react to their financial crisis.

She will have to make sure he doesn't come up with a secret stupid solution like getting divorced, or worries all through the night, like he'd done on their honeymoon, fretting over what the lady said on the plane.

He promised her that he would stop thinking about it, but she knows it's still on his mind because just last night he sat upright in bed and said, very clearly, "I would never hurt Eve. Never in a billion years."

She said, "I know, Dom. I know you wouldn't."

She knew he was sleep-talking and that he would have no memory of it in the morning. His sleep-talking voice is very fast and mumbled, kind of sedated.

Fortunately he fell straight back to sleep. Sometimes when he sleepwalks she has to follow him around, gently suggesting he come back to bed.

The sleep-talking and sleepwalking started when he was six, which was when his mother left Dom and his dad. (She lives in Bali now and teaches yoga. Dom has forgiven her for disappearing from his life for *ten years*, but Eve has not.) One night Dom's dad got a knock on the door at three a.m. It was a neighbor, who had realized he'd forgotten to take his garbage cans out and rushed out into the night in his pajamas, to find little Dom, also in pajamas and bare feet, walking down the dark footpath, insisting to the neighbor that he was late for school.

After that his dad had to find ways to make sure Dom couldn't get out of the house. It got harder as he got older and kept sleepwalking. They locked windows and put a bell on his bedroom door. Occasionally his dad would catch him having a shower, fully dressed. Sometimes he made himself toast in the middle of the night, ate it, went back to bed, and woke up with no memory of it: just the plate with the uneaten crusts on the kitchen table as evidence. Sometimes months would go by and Dom and his dad would think he'd grown out of it, but then it would happen again. He couldn't go to sleepovers or camps, he was too embarrassed about what might happen, and his dad was worried that he'd walk off a cliff or in front of a car.

Once, when he was a teenager and had gotten his driver's license, *Dom drove in his sleep.* He woke up after he turned off the ignition and got out of the car in the moonlit empty parking lot at the local shops. He'd parked perfectly, but he had no memory of getting there. It terrified him. At Dom's request, Eve hides the car keys before they go to bed. It was his dad's job when he lived at home and sometimes his dad would forget where he'd hidden them the next day, which drove Dom crazy.

Mostly, it's not a big deal. He sits up in bed, says something nonsensical, and then lies straight back down. Since he started personal training most of his sleep-talking is about correcting someone's form. "Don't lock your elbows," he'll say in his sleep-slurred voice. "Focus on your core."

Sometimes he becomes a little agitated, but mostly he's calm. There was only one time that he'd sounded angry, which was on that camping trip in the Huon Valley in the stuffy caravan. Eve has noticed that his sleep disturbances are always worse in an airless room, and if he's been drinking.

That night they were sleeping on two bunk beds side by side in the on-site caravan. Eve and Liv had the top bunks and the boys had the bottom bunks.

Eve doesn't know what time it was when she opened her eyes to find Dom on his feet, standing next to her bunk, looking directly into her eyes.

He said, "I *will* kill you."

"You will what?" said Eve.

She sat up, and she never told him this and never will, but it terrified her. His face was illuminated only by the spooky green light from Riley's phone charger. She couldn't quite make out his features. His eyes were like black holes.

"I *will* kill you," he said again, and she could hear pure fury and conviction in his voice, and she scrabbled back so that she was up against the caravan wall and held her pillow in front of her, like that was going to help.

"Dom," she said. "Babe. Wake up. You're asleep."

He got really close to her face. She could smell his red-winey breath.

He said, "I have a very particular set of skills. I will look for you. I will find you, and I will kill you."

At which point she'd laughed out loud with recognition and relief, because now she understood. They'd all been quoting lines from movies that night, and that one was Riley's favorite: Liam Neeson's famous phone conversation with the kidnappers in that old movie *Taken*.

"You haven't got *any* skills, mate." Riley spoke up from the bottom bunk. "And your Irish accent is shit." He knew all about the sleepwalking and -talking, so he understood right away what was going on.

Dom dropped the accent and began muttering, "Let's stop here and buy some water. Pull over here, babe, I need water, you thirsty, babe?"

Riley got up and gave Dom a bottle of water, which he drained in one long gulp, spilling some on himself, which obviously woke him up because he said, in his normal voice, "Sorry. Was I sleepwalking?"

They all laughed about it. It was funny. Just another crazy Dom sleepwalking story.

That was until the lady on the plane made her prediction, and then, on their honeymoon, Dom woke up in the night, remembered the incident in the caravan, started researching, and discovered something truly terrible: a phenomenon called "homicidal sleepwalking."

"What if I do that to you?" he said, and he'd showed her all the news stories he'd found. A man who claimed he was dreaming about "aggressive ostriches" when he killed someone while asleep. A husband who killed his beloved wife and was now in jail with no memory of what he'd done. "I will miss her until the day I die," he said, which was extremely tragic.

"You won't kill me," Eve had said. "Anyway, I don't believe in psychics."

"Forget the psychic. I just think we should be aware I might hurt you in my sleep."

"You've never touched me when you've been sleepwalking," Eve comforted him. It wasn't technically true. Sometimes he'd kind of pushed her hand roughly away when she was trying to convince him to come back to bed, but she'd never once felt in danger.

Oh, gosh, it was all so silly!

He's still *Dom* when he's asleep.

Things that happen on the internet never happen in real life.

She picks up the framed wedding photo from their bedside table. She chose a "vintage-style" effect for this photo—it's in moody black-and-white, with a yellowish tinge—and this, combined with the fact that she's wearing a vintage dress, and Dom is wearing classic suspenders and a bow tie, makes it seem like their wedding took place decades ago.

Eve thinks about the first bride who wore her dress. Did she get post-wedding blues? Did she know that multiple affordable expenses add up to one big unaffordable total? Probably. Probably everyone knows that. This photo print cost forty-five dollars and the frame cost sixty dollars. She's been throwing her money around like a Kardashian.

What's that phrase people keep using? "Cost of living crisis." She didn't think it applied to them. She thought it applied to people with mortgages and school fees.

She remembers overhearing her mother talking to Dom's dad at their engagement party. "They're like babes in the wood, those two."

"I know," said Dom's dad sadly. "They don't know what they don't know."

Well, why didn't they just tell them what they didn't know?

"You're so, so stupid," she says out loud to her own smiling stupid face in the photo.

"Who's stupid?" says Dom from the bedroom door.

She drops the photo. "What are you doing back so early?"

"Last two clients canceled."

"You're kidding me," says Eve. "That is unbelievable, those people are so—"

"Oh, well, I got Thai for lunch." Dom lifts up the plastic bag looped around his wrist. "But it's maybe got a bit cold, because, I need to tell you, I had—"

"Not from the expensive place?" Eve sits up so fast she bangs her head against the wall. "Ow."

Dom looks alarmed. "Which one is the expensive place? I went to the one with the fish cakes you like."

"That's the expensive place!" wails Eve.

Dom puts down the bag. "What's going on?"

She pulls the credit card bill from the back pocket of her jeans and hands it to him.

Dom looks at it. "This is *our* bill? We owe that much money?"

"Yes," says Eve. "I feel like we've maybe kind of fucked up, babe, I didn't—"

"I smashed the car on the way home," says Dom. He sits down heavily on the bed. There is no color in his face. "And I think I forgot to pay the car insurance."

Chapter 53

This is how I know that it took me a long time to truly comprehend my dad's death.

One afternoon, when I was thirteen, after my dad had been dead for three years, I came home from school and my mother rushed to meet me, shiny-eyed and flushed. She said, "I have *wonderful* news, Cherry."

The most extraordinary sensation of relief suffused my entire body. My legs became so weak with joy I had to sit down. An enormous weight I didn't know I was carrying lifted from my shoulders. I thought, *Dad's back.*

That's what I truly thought, just for a second, before I came to my senses.

I read an article once about the dazzling pop star "Pink." She had recently lost her father and she said (according to the article, which may or may not have been fact-checked) that her first thought was this: No one would ever love her like that again. When I read that I thought, Yes, "Pink," I understand. Everyone loves a particular version of you and when that person is gone that version goes with them. My dad was so *interested* in me. Mum was interested too, but Mum loved a different version of me.

No one ever saw me the way my dad saw me, "the funniest little thing," the way he maybe still sees me, although I don't know if I believe in life after death. There is not enough data. But if there is such a thing, and my goodness it would be nice if there is, I wonder if Dad has ever run into Pink's dad?

Perhaps at the breakfast buffet. A breakfast buffet would be my dad's idea of heaven.

If you're wondering, my mother's wonderful news was that she'd saved up enough to book us a holiday at the Coffs Harbour Pacific Palms Motel so we could see the Big Banana.

This lurid yellow tourist attraction was the idea of an American banana plantation owner (who was inspired by a big pineapple he'd seen on top of a cannery in Hawaii) and at the time was the biggest banana in the world. I believe it still is. It began Australia's obsession with "big things." We now boast a big beer can, a big ram, a big guitar, a big apple, a big avocado, and many more "big things." If you are Australian, you may feel proud or embarrassed about this.

Many people are convinced the Big Banana was secretly replaced by a smaller version, so much so that journalists have written articles about it, but it's not true.

It just looks smaller when we visit again as grown-ups.

Nothing dazzles like the first time.

Chapter 54

It's a peaceful sunny Saturday afternoon three months after the flight.
Early July. A mild winter so far, which is nice.

Leo chops onions, coriander, and carrots for a curry while contemplating whether he can get a couple of hours of work in tonight,
but that will mean he has technically worked seven days this week,
which is an accusation from his wife he prefers to deny.

Neve comes through the back door carrying a laundry basket
laden with dry clothes from the clothesline. Oli steps out of the
shower after a muddy soccer game where he scored the triumphant
winning goal.

The dog snores.

Bridie's bloodcurdling scream is heard in all corners of the house
and probably by the neighbors too.

It sounds like she has suffered a cataclysmic injury.

Leo is so badly startled that he narrowly misses chopping off the
top of his thumb. He drops the knife and runs. Neve dumps the laundry basket, leaps athletically over it, and also sprints in the same direction.

Meanwhile Oli leisurely wraps his towel around his waist, wipes a
circle in the steamed-up mirror with the palm of his hand, turns to

one side to admire his flexed biceps, and wonders what's up with his sister.

The scream has come from the living room, where Bridie is sitting in the middle of the couch cocooned in a king-sized yellow blanket so that only the top of her head is visible.

Leo yanks the blanket away to reveal Bridie sitting cross-legged, head dropped so low her forehead is practically touching her damned phone, which they unwillingly gave her when she started catching the bus to school but which has now become the bane of their existence. Leo has installed all the latest parental controls on both kids' devices, but he suspects Bridie and Oli can both hack them with their superior technological skills. He and Neve keep coming up with new agreements—no phones after dinner, no phones before breakfast, no phones in the car—but the kids also know how to hack the agreements.

"What is it? What's wrong?" Neve examines Bridie's hairline with her fingertips, lifts and turns her limbs back and forth.

"What happened?" says Leo. "Where does it hurt?"

Neve looks around suspiciously. "Did your brother do something? I thought he was in the shower."

Bridie looks both angry and vindicated. Her face is red, as if she's been slapped. "Daddy is going to die, just like that lady said."

"Oh, please, not this again." Neve plonks herself down next to Bridie. "You frightened the life out of me."

"I'm not going to die." Leo sits on the other side of Bridie. "I told you. Why are you still thinking about this?"

He rubs his face, smells onion on his fingertips.

Bridie holds up her phone.

"Nope! We don't need to see any more proof of psychic predictions coming true," says Neve at the same time as Leo says, "Maybe show us after dinner?"

"I think she was on the plane," says Bridie.

"On your dad's plane?" asks Neve sharply.

"Look." Bridie gives them her phone. Then she picks up a cushion and holds it in front of her face. "I'm not watching it again." Her voice wobbles. "It's very bad."

Leo and Neve look at each other.

"Press play," says Bridie, her voice muffled by the cushion pressed against her face.

Chapter 55

It's probably happened to you at least once. You've had a premonition. You knew exactly what was about to happen before it happened. You knew you were going to win the raffle just before your ticket was called. You were thinking about someone the moment before they phoned or emailed or texted. You had a feeling something dreadful or wonderful would happen on a particular day and it did.

If listening to your intuition results in something of monumental significance, it changes you. Of course it does. How could it not?

Once, my grandmother was pinning washing on the clothesline. She had her beautiful baby, my mother, in a basket at her feet. Everything was lovely. The baby cooed and blew bubbles. The magpies warbled. Then my grandmother sensed danger.

How could there be danger?

She looked down just as a red-bellied black snake slithered across her precious baby's stomach toward her tender neck. Grandma reacted instantly, instinctively. She grabbed the hem of her baby's smock. She hoisted her out of the basket in one swift movement. She spun her above her head like an Olympic discus thrower.

"I don't think you really spun me above your head," Mum would say.

"Excuse me, were you there, Mae?"

"Yes, I was there, Mum."

"Very funny."

"No wonder Mae's brain is scrambled," Auntie Pat would chortle.

"I just *knew*," Grandma would say. "I sensed it. I had this dreadful feeling of *doom*."

"No, you didn't," Grandpa would argue, "you *heard* something, like a rustle, or you caught a tiny movement out of the corner of your eye."

Grandma would cross her arms, stick out her bottom lip, and say nothing more until Grandpa said, "All right, Lizzie, you're right, you knew, you just somehow knew."

He wasn't silly.

Then he'd get his cup of tea.

Before my father was struck by lightning, my mother was ordinary.

Well, not to me. She was charismatic and clever, clearly the prettiest of all the mothers I knew, with the most beautiful complexion, and she was the first mother on our street to learn to drive, which made me very proud, but what I'm trying to say is she wasn't "unusual." She spent her days on domestic tasks: sewing, cooking, laundry, and gardening. She swore when the magpies dropped mulberries from our tree over her clean washing on the line. She cried over the brick-sized romance novels she borrowed from the library.

Yes, she read palms, but it wasn't serious. She was mimicking Grandma. She never charged a fee and if she did a reading for her girlfriends they normally ended up in fits of giggles. I think Mum predicted wicked things about tall, dark, handsome men. She read my tea leaves, because I begged her to, but it was like asking her to tell me a story. I don't think either of us truly believed it.

We had the same superstitions as most people we knew. We knocked on wood. If we spilled salt we threw some over our left shoulder. If we cracked a double-yolk egg we said, "Someone is having twins!" and we never checked if anyone actually did have twins. We crossed our fingers for luck. It was all in good fun.

But after Dad died, everything changed. All our superstitions got serious.

I don't know. Maybe Mum really did foresee his death.

But you'd think if she *truly* believed Dad would be struck by lightning she might have suggested he avoid rock fishing on a day with the possibility of a summer storm heavy in the air.

A heads-up might have been helpful, Mum.

Chapter 56

"Have you done those tests yet?"

Sue has dumped her shopping basket on the floor and taken the call in the middle of the fruit and veg section of the supermarket, where she is squeezing rock-hard green avocadoes in the hope of finding one likely to ripen this century. It's Caterina, sounding unusually tense.

"Not yet," says Sue.

After their dinner, she'd felt a weight lift. Knowing she had the forms to do the tests somehow meant she didn't need to actually *do* them. Her concerns about the lady had come to seem absurd.

Is Caterina annoyed with her for wasting her time writing out the referrals? Or, and this seems more likely, is she concerned she recommended unnecessary tests?

"I don't need to do the tests if you're worried—"

Caterina interrupts. "You haven't seen this video that's going around today?"

"What video?" Sue's phone is beeping. She replaces the avocado and glances at her phone. Her youngest son is trying to call her.

She puts the phone back to her ear.

"It's a girl. Seems like she was on your flight," says Caterina. "It's . . . distressing. I'm surprised it hasn't been taken down yet."

Now Sue's phone is buzzing and vibrating like a child's toy.

"It's probably just a coincidence," says Caterina. "Like Nostradamus getting lucky."

Someone approaches the avocados with a determined expression, and Sue steps aside, kicking her plastic shopping basket across the floor.

"Sue?" says Caterina.

"Has someone died?" says Sue. "From the flight? Is that what you're saying?"

A pause.

Sue hears someone in the background say, "Excuse me, Dr. Bonetti?"

"Just one moment," says Caterina, her voice muffled.

"Look. It's silly. It's probably fake." Her voice is loud and clear again. "But do the tests, Sue, you should do the tests."

Chapter 57

This is the thing with a heads-up.

The person has to believe. The person has to change their actions.

What if my mother had actually said, with certainty, *You will get hit by lightning, Arthur.*

Would he still have gone rock fishing?

He might have looked up at that cloud-heavy sky and said to his friends: *Let's call it a day.*

Mum might have saved Dad the way Grandma saved her from the red-bellied black snake.

Dad might have lived until he was one hundred.

Chapter 58

Paula's sister texts: *Passing this on from that weirdo cousin, haven't watched, something you talked about at wedding? Feel free to ignore! x*

The only potentially "weirdo" cousin that Paula spoke to at Lisa's wedding was her new brother-in-law's cousin, the one who never made a significant life decision without checking in with her clairvoyant.

Paula feels a sense of foreboding. Should she ignore it? It will be something about psychic predictions and she doesn't want to tumble back down that anxiety rabbit hole.

She's just about over it, or she hopes she is.

Both Timmy and Willow wear their evil eye bracelets every day. Willow *loves* hers and holds out her wrist for people to admire it. Matt looked quizzical when he saw the bracelets but didn't object. Perhaps he even likes them. It turns out he and his brother both wore them when they were kids.

Paula can now make the same boast as that swim instructor did about her granddaughter: Timmy swam before he walked. He's still not shown any interest in walking, crawling suits him fine, but he can float, seemingly forever, and dog-paddle the width of the pool, grinning and gurgling.

The power of the lady's prediction, or curse, is steadily fading, the way the pain of a hurtful remark becomes muted, although never for-gotten, the more time passes. She no longer thinks about it every day. It's all a little embarrassing.

The children are asleep.

Paula and Matt are watching a brooding Scandi series. It feels like they'll never finish because each night they have to rewind it after one of them falls asleep and wakes to confusing plot developments the other one can't satisfactorily explain.

Paula looks over at Matt stretched out on the opposite couch. Sure enough, he's sound asleep, his forearm across his forehead, his chest rising and falling.

She pauses the show, presses the link on her phone.

It's a video of the side profile of a very upright fair-haired young woman behind the wheel of a car. The person filming is next to her in the passenger seat. It seems to be a small car. There isn't much space between them.

The person filming says, "Why are you driving so slowly today, Kayla?"

The girl doesn't glance sideways. Her focus is all on the road ahead.

Her hair is in a sleek low ponytail with a ruler-straight center part. Her eyelashes are long and Bambi-fake, her skin young and dewy, and she grips the steering wheel so hard her knuckles are white.

"Because yesterday I turned nineteen," she says without turning her head.

"And why does that mean you have to drive so slowly people keep honking their horns at us?"

"Nobody is honking at us," says the driver.

The girl filming whips the phone in front of her own face. She's a dark-haired, dark-skinned version of the driver: exact same hairstyle and curly long eyelashes.

"They totally are," she whispers, and returns to filming the driver. "Why are you driving like a senior citizen, Kayla? What is your totally rational explanation for this?"

The driver still doesn't look at the camera. She checks over her shoulder to change lanes. "Three months ago, I flew to Sydney—"

You were on the flight, thinks Paula.

"Which you were really chill about."

"I was not chill, I have a super-bad fear of flying, it's a phobia, and this was my first time flying on my own—it was only my second time on a *plane*—and there was this psychic on board and she said—"

"Wait, do they offer psychics on *all* flights these days?"

"Shut up." Kayla grins. "Anyway. She told me I was going to die in a car accident when I was nineteen, so I'm driving extra-extra cautious until I turn twenty. Just, like, as a precaution."

She bites her lip, stops at a traffic light, waits a moment, and then turns to face the camera. She is very pretty. Big guileless cornflower-blue eyes.

Paula doesn't recognize her. There are only three faces she can remember from the flight: her Scottish seatmate, the beautiful Indian flight attendant who suffered the consequences of Paula's bad parenting, and the lady herself.

"Because I don't want to die." Kayla pulls a mock "dead" face: eyes crossed, tongue out, head on one side. She is adorable.

Paula has been so obsessively worried about Timmy that she has not given a thought to anyone else on the same flight who also received a scary prediction. It's easy to be cool and rational when scary things happen to other people. She should get in touch with Kayla, tell her, sure, it's a good idea to drive carefully, but don't worry, there is no evidence anyone has the power to see the future.

"Why don't you just stop driving?" asks the girl filming.

"That's what Mum said, she's like, Kayla, just stay off the roads altogether until you're twenty, and I'm, like, Yeah, thanks, Mum, I'd rather be dead."

Paula feels a throb of sympathy for the mother.

"I mean, what am I going to do? Stay home for a year? I've got to live my actual life, and we live in the sticks."

"Totally. Oh, and what *else* happened on that flight, Kayla?"

Kayla giggles. "I don't know what you're talking about."

Once again the friend speaks into the camera. She whispers, "She got a boyfriend. Six foot six! Like a giant. A skinny giant. But a hot skinny giant. I'm jealous! Looks like a basketball player but he's not."

The traffic light turns green. Kayla looks straight ahead. She drives forward.

The other car appears like the sudden leaping, snarling attack of an animal.

It collides without mercy into the driver's side of the car.

Kayla's careful hands fly from the steering wheel.

Crash of metal against metal.

Kayla's shoulder slams sideways toward the camera and the vision becomes choppy and blurred, as if the phone has been knocked out of its owner's hands.

There are quick flashes: Strands of Kayla's blond hair. The side of her face? The stitching of a seat. Someone's flesh. Then fuzzy gray material, as if the phone has landed face down in the passenger footwell. The sound of someone's ragged breathing.

The video stops abruptly. The screen goes black.

Matt sits up, rubbing his eyes. "What is it? What happened? What are you looking at?"

Paula can't speak. There is no air in her lungs.

She reads, in jarringly inappropriate cheerful pink curly cursive:

RIP KAYLA HALFPENNY
TAKEN TOO SOON.
FOREVER MISSED.
FOREVER NINETEEN.

Chapter 59

The flap of a seagull's wing and everything changes.

Chapter 60

"No, no, please, no," says Sue under her breath.

She watches the video on her phone in the grocery store, surrounded by the bright colors of fresh fruit and vegetables. Ladyfinger bananas on special, death on her phone.

She remembers Kayla dropping her phone in the check-in line, her polite gratitude when Max picked it up for her; telling Sue about her flying phobia.

You're more likely to die in a car crash, darling.

Sue is pretty sure she didn't actually say that to her, she probably just thought it, although what does it matter if she did. Sue wasn't the one making awful predictions that day.

She thinks about Max teaching the boys to drive: "You still look, mate, even if you get a green light. You can't trust other drivers to do the right thing."

She and Max tossed out last-minute warnings like hopeful lifebuoys every time their sons left the house, from when they were bike-riding kids to newly licensed young drivers to young dads with new babies. "Wear your helmet!" "Don't drink too much!" "Drive slowly in the rain!"

But you could never say it all and you could never say it enough.

Check, double-check, triple-check, please protect your vulnerable beautiful heads that we once cupped so tenderly in our hands.

Sue knows her children often ignored their boring parental advice, yeah, yeah, sure thing, Mum, got it, Dad, she knows they took risks Max and Sue never knew about, and it's only pure luck they got away with it.

She thinks of Kayla's parents but only momentarily because she could never have worked in the ER for all these years if she took on everyone's pain. It won't help them. Nothing will help them. There is no pain relief she can offer.

Instead, she returns to grocery shopping while scenes from the video continue to flicker behind her eyes.

This doesn't mean her own prediction will also come true, of course it doesn't, but as soon as she gets home she will make the appointments. She will do the tests.

Chapter 61

It feels wrong to be sharing my life story, without acknowledging the life story of Kayla Halfpenny.

I saw Kayla in the departure lounge in Hobart. She was the one who reminded me of my tearful piano teacher. The one who knocked over her drink and then her phone.

I have learned a lot about her. It's all still there, online, if anyone cares to look.

Kayla Halfpenny lived in Lauderdale, a town on the outskirts of Hobart, with her parents and her two younger sisters. She was studying for a Diploma of Beauty Therapy. She was a "Swiftie" (a passionate fan of the extraordinary performer Taylor Swift, whose music I also find extremely catchy). Kayla was terrified of flying, but that weekend she was bravely flying alone to Sydney for a friend's party. She had a good time at the party. She told everyone about the very tall boy she'd met at the baggage carousel.

Her younger sisters worshipped her. Her parents adored her. They had surprised her with a puppy for her eighteenth birthday. Kayla was so pleased and surprised she cried hysterically. I have seen the footage of this. It's touching. She called the puppy "Ruby Tuesday." I don't know why. "Ruby Tuesday" is a Rolling Stones song that came out in 1967. I don't know if Kayla loved the song, but I love that song.

Ruby Tuesday grieved so badly for Kayla the vet put her on antide-pressants. Kayla's sister posted this online. She's doing better now. Ruby Tuesday, that is. Not the sister. I know I'm rambling. I'm upset.

Kayla died in a car accident on a Thursday afternoon at an inter-section in Primrose Sands, Hobart. It was not rush hour. It was a clear, cold July day. Visibility was good. She was not speeding. We know exactly what happened because her friend, who survived, al-though she was seriously injured, livestreamed the accident on social media. If, like me, you are over the age of fifty—or even if you're over the age of thirty?—you will not understand why she would be "livestreaming" a conversation in a car, its only significance to share with "friends" that Kayla was driving slowly because of a psychic pre-diction.

The accident was not Kayla's fault. She obeyed every road rule. She should have been able to trust the green light.

It was not technically my fault, either, although it has occurred to me that if Kayla had been driving faster that day, not so cautiously, she might have been at a different intersection at the moment a forty-year-old man, more than three times over the legal alcohol limit at ten in the morning, with two previous drunk-driving convictions, drove straight through a red light at over one hundred kilometers an hour.

I wish this thought had not occurred to me and I hope it has not occurred to her parents.

Chapter 62

"It's only money, babe," says Dom when he finds Eve crying, her phone pressed to her collarbone. "We'll work it out. What is it? Another bill?"

She has played the video at least five times, as if hoping something different will happen. It feels like her heart is breaking and she doesn't know this girl, so her heart has no right to break!

"No, it's nothing to do with money." Eve wipes her disgusting snotty nose with the back of her hand. Her teeth are chattering. It's a cold day and they're trying to save money by not turning on the heating because every volt of electricity, or whatever you call it, costs so much. "It's that girl from the plane. She . . . she . . ."

She can't speak. She is remembering Kayla at the baggage carousel, touching the lace on Eve's wedding dress with that delicate fingertip and then how she touched her hair when she talked to the tall boy.

"I don't want to be famous," she'd said, when Eve told her Kayla Halfpenny sounded like it could be the name of a famous person, and now she's gone viral.

Dom takes the phone.

He watches the video and she watches his face, and then she thinks to herself, Oh, Eve, you stupid, *stupid* girl.

Chapter 63

A "hard determinist," like the bearded man, would say the driver responsible for Kayla Halfpenny's death could only have behaved as he actually did. His actions were the inevitable result of a genetic tendency toward alcoholism, perhaps, along with a childhood that gave him little or no moral code, an argument with a girlfriend that brought up infantile memories of abandonment, leading him to drink all through the night and then get behind the wheel the following morning.

A series of inevitably falling dominoes.

However, I was taught God gave us free will, and although I have complicated feelings about the existence of God, I believe in free will.

That man chose to drink and drive.

He could have stopped that last domino.

I hate him for making my dreadful prediction come true.

I hate him for making me accurate.

Chapter 64

Ethan is in his bedroom with the door shut, avoiding Jasmine's buffoon of a new boyfriend, when the text comes from Leo.

He has him saved as *Leo Anxious Flight Guy*.

He texts old-person style. Fully punctuated sentences.

Hi Ethan, it's Leo here, from the Hobart flight. We shared a taxi home. I just wondered if you had seen the distressing video doing the rounds on the internet? Wondering if it's fake?

Ethan has seen it. He nearly scrolled past it, but something made him stop. Maybe he subconsciously recognized the girl from the plane. It seems genuine. He checked and found a Tasmanian news site reporting the accident. *Woman killed, another in critical condition after two-vehicle crash.* He suspects Leo knows perfectly well it's not fake.

He answers: *Yes. Very bad. Reckon pure chance lady got one right?*

Leo answers: *Yes. Not worried yet! Remind me when you turn thirty?*

Ethan answers: *Oct 1. Not long! Will be watching my back! When u 43?*

Leo answers: *Nov12. Keep in touch, mate.*

Ethan can't seem to make himself feel properly frightened. He's still skeptical, or at least relatively skeptical. It just feels so unlikely he and Harvey would *both* die young. Wouldn't that be too much of a coincidence? Statistically unlikely?

He thinks about a long-ago statistics class where the lecturer asked students to estimate how many people in the packed hall shared the same birthday. Nobody was even close. The lecturer said everyone always gets it wrong. They wildly underestimate the likelihood because people have a tendency to put themselves at the center of the universe.

It's called "the birthday paradox." You think, *What is the probability someone else in this room will have the same birthday as ME?* You don't think of all the possible permutations.

In fact, there is close to a one hundred percent chance that at least two people will share a birthday when there are just seventy-five people in a room.

Ethan is *not* the center of the universe.

Harvey's death does not make Ethan any less or more likely to die. Ethan's chances of dying are just the same as they always were.

So that's maybe sobering. But still, he's not worried.

He hears Carter's booming voice from somewhere in the apartment and shudders.

He picks up the grip-strengthening tool his surgeon recommended he use three times a day after his cast came off, and squeezes. Five seconds on. Five seconds off.

His wrist aches.

He hasn't been diligent enough with his exercises.

Chapter 65

Accuracy has always mattered to me. As a child I often corrected teachers when they made mistakes. I thought I was being helpful, but my teachers were rarely grateful. The opposite.

"Did I ask your opinion, Cheryl?"

I'd say, "It's Cherry, and no you didn't ask my opinion, but you switched the nine and the six, sir."

It perplexed me. Didn't they want to get it right?

Accuracy is what made me, "the Death Lady," go "viral."

The same thing happened on a slower, more local scale to my mother when she transformed herself from ordinary Mae Hetherington to Madame Mae, the fortune teller.

Mum refused to touch a single penny of the life insurance money. She wanted nothing to do with it. She behaved as though it was somehow ill-gotten, as if Dad had robbed a bank, not insured his life.

People behave oddly when they are grieving.

Auntie Pat arranged for the money to be deposited in a bank account for "my future." It wasn't a life-changing amount. Even if Mum had used the money she still would have needed to find a way to support us. I guess she made a decision at some point, but she never actually said out loud: *I'm going to become a fortune teller.* It just happened.

She stopped borrowing romance novels from the library. Instead she came home with piles of books about "connecting with spirits," "accessing your occult gifts," and "interpreting tarot." She studied them, as though for an important exam, taking copious notes.

She transformed the closed-off back veranda of our house into her "office." She pinned cloth over the windows and set up three soft-lit lamps.

Mum knew the power of appearances. She created a "look": shiny scarves, jangling bracelets, and dangling earrings along with bright red lipstick and plenty of black eyeliner.

Then she did what would now be called a "soft launch."

She offered "half-price" readings to a select group of chatty, not too churchy but very influential women in our neighborhood. "Influencers," they would be called now.

The most successful of these turned out to be Mrs. Shaw, who worked at Shaw's Cake Shop on George Street. Mrs. Shaw was a widow, with seven children and three grandchildren. Her vanilla slices were to die for.

Mum told Mrs. Shaw that she saw these things in her future: an odd illness from which she would quickly recover as long as she rested, a small financial windfall, and an extraordinarily beautiful new baby.

In quick succession: Mrs. Shaw was struck by an odd illness from which she quickly recovered; she found twenty quid hidden in an old pair of her husband's socks at the back of a drawer; and her second daughter announced her first pregnancy.

Mrs. Shaw was *amazed*. She told the story to every single person who walked through the door of her cake shop. She was the sixties' version of a viral meme.

I couldn't believe people were so easily fooled. It was simple probability! Mrs. Shaw was a hypochondriac who was always suffering odd illnesses, *everyone* knew that! We also knew that ever since her husband died she'd been finding his hidden cash, and finally, three out of the six Shaw daughters had recently married so there was every reason to expect a new baby in the family soon, and of course all first grandchildren are "extraordinarily beautiful."

Word spread. (Word always spreads, it just happens faster these days.)

People began to travel long distances for a reading with Madame Mae.

Mum sat on the imposing high-backed leather winged armchair that had once belonged to my dad's dad. Her customers sat on a soft floral armchair, so that they were both comfortable and forced to look up at my mother as she spoke in her Madame Mae voice: deeper and slower than normal, and oooh, so spooky. I couldn't stand it. I found it ridiculous.

Some customers caught the train to Hornsby and walked from the station up the steep hill to our house, arriving nervous and breathless and in need of a glass of water. Others came by bicycle, car, and taxi. People began to waylay me at the shops to tell me my mother was remarkable, gifted, her readings were so accurate, she had changed their lives, even saved their lives!

My grandfather was horrified. Grandma wasn't pleased either. This was a big leap forward from Grandma's secret palm-reading. This was her daughter openly establishing an actual business.

Grandma and Grandpa believed Mum had lost her mind because of her grief, which I guess in a way she had. They asked the new parish priest to call on Mum to set her straight.

Over tea and a Shaw's Cake Shop vanilla slice (Mrs. Shaw brought along freshly baked vanilla slices whenever she came for a reading), Father O'Malley gently suggested that Mum lean on our Lord in her hour of need.

Mum said, "Father, I see a forbidden love in your future."

Father O'Malley got out of there fast.

He left the priesthood three years later, after he scandalously fell in love with a married red-haired woman, a respected member of the Parish Liturgy Committee. They went on to have six redheaded children, one of whom is now an MP I occasionally see on the news, nodding along in the background of more important politicians' press conferences.

You may be impressed by the accuracy of Mum's prediction, but I put it to you that perhaps my mother sensed Father O'Malley's eyes on her legs and intuited that celibacy was going to be tricky for him.

(My mother had beautiful legs.)

I was always looking for a more logical explanation. I believed logic was the answer to every question, the solution to every argument. Mum would say, "Sometimes there is no logical explanation, Cherry."

I still love logic, but I understand its limitations. I was nineteen when I first learned about Gödel's "incompleteness theorem," which states that in any reasonable mathematical system there will always be true statements that *cannot be proved.*

I was so disappointed!

I thought: Dammit, Mum.

Chapter 66

"Do psychics ever change their mind?" asks Paula.

She is on the phone to the random cousin of the groom from her sister's wedding, the one who forwarded the car accident video and whose name she hasn't bothered to remember, which is rude of her.

Paula just wants information, and this cousin, who spoke so gravely about checking in with her clairvoyant before she made a decision, not a hint of cynicism or this-is-all-just-a-bit-of-fun in her voice, is the only one she could think to ask.

"Sometimes," says the cousin. "Like if your circumstances change. Or if you make a different choice. My clairvoyant shows me different scenarios and it's up to me to manifest the outcome I want."

"Right," says Paula. "It's just that my baby boy can swim now. So I guess I just wondered if that would change her prediction? Like when you change your diet and get your cholesterol down, your doctor predicts you'll live longer."

"My doctor says diet only contributes like around twenty percent of the cholesterol in your blood," comments the cousin.

"Yes, well, that was just an example, but do you think this psychic would give me a different prediction now that Timmy can swim?"

"Sure," says the cousin. "It's possible. Also, my clairvoyant says that sometimes you might just have a different energy on the day. So that changes the prediction."

Different energy. All this woo-woo language. It's ridiculous.

But Paula needs to hear it from the lady.

She just has to find her.

Chapter 67

These were my grandmother's last words: "I have wasted my life."

"Thanks a lot," said my mother, who tended to make everything about her.

I said, "What do you mean, Grandma?"

I was interested, as I hoped to learn from her mistakes. I may even have gotten pen and paper ready.

(Perhaps my mother and I were more alike than we realized.)

"Of course you haven't, Mum," said Auntie Pat.

But my grandmother just sighed and fiddled irritably with the button on the blue brunch coat I'd bought her for her last birthday. She would really have preferred a paler blue but she supposed it would do.

Grandma never said another word. She died ten days later.

You never know what your last words are going to be, so try to choose them all wisely.

Chapter 68

Dom has bought handcuffs.

Naturally Eve thinks the handcuffs are for sex even though the tie from her dressing gown works perfectly well, and she's not unhappy about the purchase, although they are on a super-strict budget right now, but Dom says they're not for sex, as if sex is the last thing on his mind. The handcuffs are to protect Eve from the possibility of "sleep-related violence."

Dom's ludicrous plan is to handcuff himself to the headboard each night so he can't hurt her in his sleep.

"That's stupid," says Eve. "You won't sleep, you'll get stressed and then—oh, forget it."

She was an idiot to have shown him the video of Kayla Halfpenny's car accident.

That was enough for him.

One correct prediction and he's converted. He denies it but she knows.

Even if he isn't one hundred percent convinced the stupid lady has stupid magic powers, the thought of him hurting Eve in his sleep is now lodged in his stupid head.

In fact, everything he is doing is going to make sleep-related violence *more* likely. She's done the research too! He's meant to avoid alcohol and stress. He's meant to have a good sleep routine. He's drinking more than usual, working his way through a bottle of whiskey some stupid client gave him, and he is so, so stressed: mostly about money but maybe about everything. His eyelids look heavy and his skin has turned a strange kind of mushroom color, as if he is sick beneath his sunburn. He doesn't have a sleep routine because she thinks he might be trying to *stay awake.*

She hasn't told him this but when he does fall asleep, late, he is sleepwalking more than ever. Mostly he walks around the apartment, looking for an important unnamed object. "Where is it?" he mumbles as he opens cupboard doors and looks behind the curtains. "Got to find it, babe, it's really important." Eventually she gets him back to bed by telling him not to worry, she will find the really important thing. He tells her he loves her and gets back into bed. He is never violent, just agitated.

She knows what he's trying so hopelessly to find: a solution.

This is not how she imagined their first year of marriage. They have both taken on extra work and now they hardly see each other. Eve works at the medical center during the day and waitresses three nights a week. Dom still does his personal training wherever possible—it's hard without a car—but he's also picked up some laboring work as well as a part-time job as a night road worker.

They can't afford to make the car roadworthy. If they'd paid the car insurance they would have only had the excess to pay, but they did not pay it, and it's not clear who is to blame for this, because they never actually specified who was in charge of paying bills. Now it's Eve's job and she has a good system. She is an idiot for not having set one up in the first place. She would never have made this sort of mistake at work.

They still owe Dom's dad money for the car they can no longer drive until they can afford to fix it and they are chipping away at the astonishing credit card bill. They managed to pay last month's rent, but you have to keep paying rent, over and over, every single month.

Maybe Eve subconsciously believed landlords were like parents and would let you off now and then.

She has taken to yelling at herself: THIS IS NOT HOW THE REAL WORLD WORKS, EVE.

Just in her head. But it's still giving her a headache.

They don't go out for drinks or dinner or anything. They make excuses when friends suggest any activity that costs money. All activities cost money.

When Eve was doing grocery shopping last week and saw the total, the dismay she felt must have shown on her face because the girl at the checkout said, "I'm sorry." Not sarcastically, sympathetically!

The supermarket had a special on two-minute noodles so that's what they've been eating for dinner. They say yes whenever their parents ask them over for dinner and eat all the vegetables so their teeth don't fall out from scurvy. Who knew healthy food was so expensive? They have canceled all their streaming services. Supposedly one day they will look back on this time and say, "Oh! Remember when we were so young and poor! But we had each other!"

It's not romantic being poor, it's dreadful.

They haven't told anyone because it's too embarrassing. Their parents would make such a big deal about them forgetting to pay their car insurance. It would be unbearable.

Now Dom is in the bedroom practicing handcuffing himself to the headboard, and Eve is in the kitchen boiling water for two-minute noodles.

She can see her reflection in the kitchen window. It looks as black as outer space out there. It gets dark so early this time of year. She hates winter. She remembers how her mother admired the disco ball effect of the sunlight coming through the tree outside the window and then she told Eve some bizarre story about an apartment she and Eve's dad had rented when they were first married, and how they were "so happy" at that time. What the . . . ! Eve has never heard any mention before of "happiness"! She prefers to think her parents were always doomed to fail. Otherwise it means any couple who love each other can turn into bitter exes who can't stand to say each other's names.

She thinks of her dad bribing the tarot card reader to say he was the man of her mother's dreams. Paying for a lie.

She should do the same. Follow that fine family tradition. Except it wouldn't be a lie, it would be the truth this time.

Yes. That's the answer. She will pay the lady to tell Dom she got it wrong, and now here is the *right* prediction, and of course you're not going to kill your wife, for fuck's sake (she probably won't say "for fuck's sake," Eve can't imagine her swearing), you're going to live happily ever after and you won't die until you're as wrinkly and ancient as the adorable Dr. Baileys.

She just has to find her.

Chapter 69

Ethan wakes abruptly at three a.m. When he sees the time, he closes his eyes and tries to fool himself into falling back to sleep, but it's no good, he's as wide awake and buzzing as if it were ten a.m. and he'd just had his second coffee.

He sits up and chucks his pillow on the floor like it's to blame. He listens to the sounds of the apartment—the whir of the refrigerator, the agonizing drip of a tap. He should get up and turn it off, but he doesn't want to risk running into a shirtless Carter. The guy never wears a fucking shirt. This will be his fifth night in a row staying over, which most people agree is excessive for a housemate's new boyfriend.

Carter doesn't behave like a guest or even a grown-up. He behaves like a giant, spoiled preschooler. A permanent trail of Carter-related detritus snakes throughout the apartment: his half-eaten protein bar on the dining room table, his sopping-wet towel on the bathroom floor, his uncapped deodorant in the bathroom cabinet, his T-shirts draped over the backs of chairs. His booming voice is the first thing Ethan hears when he comes home. If Jasmine's bedroom door is closed Ethan puts on headphones fast, but once he wasn't quick enough to miss overhearing Carter moan, "Oh baby!"

Ethan has been avoiding coming home so he won't have to interact with him. He's been working late, going to the gym, making dinner plans with whichever friends are available, turning up un-invited at his parents' place. They're always happy to see him, but one time they were rushing out the door to meet friends for dinner, which made him feel pathetic, especially when they invited him along and he said *Yes, please* and had a good time. If this continues he'll have to move out. It's affecting his mental health. Maybe his physical health. He feels mildly sick all the time because the whole place reeks of Carter's aftershave. It's getting into his clothes. His mother sniffed his shirt and said he was imagining it, but he's not. This morning he liter-ally retched when he caught sight of Carter's underarm hair on his deodorant stick while he cleaned his teeth.

Jasmine never stays at Carter's place and Ethan doesn't know why. Perhaps Carter is one of those man-children who still live at home. He probably has his own wing in his parents' cliff-side Eastern Sub-urbs mansion, where the housekeeping staff discreetly picks up his shit. It's not clear what, if anything, Carter does for a living. He tosses meaningless words about like "consulting" and "investment." Jas-mine's lack of a job is cute, but Carter's lack of a job is offensive.

Ethan is suddenly irritable. Angry. He needs to sleep. Unlike Jas-mine and Carter, Ethan is a regular person, with a regular job requir-ing him to be up early, and tomorrow he's doing a boring in-house training course that will require concentration.

He gets out of bed. He will turn off the dripping tap. He will make himself a cup of tea with one of the Sleepytime tea bags that Jasmine is always offering him. He will not put on a shirt. He pays rent. He too will walk shirtless around his apartment like Carter.

He is toggling the tea bag in his mug while scrolling on his phone when Jasmine appears in the kitchen. He's only switched on the range's hood light above the cooktop so she is a shadowy, bundled-up figure.

"Are you wearing a scarf?" asks Ethan.

She shivers. "Carter likes the bedroom freezing."

"I'm trying out one of your tea bags," says Ethan. "Do you want one?"

"Yes, please," says Jasmine. He gets a second cup and when he turns she's illuminated by the bright light of the open refrigerator, like a beautiful actress under a spotlight on a dark stage about to deliver a dramatic monologue.

She says, "English muffin?"

"Sure," says Ethan. He wonders if Carter is asleep, if they just had *oh baby* sex, then banishes the thought.

Jasmine toasts the muffins. Ethan puts out two plates. She finds honey in the pantry. It's her special honey, made by a family friend who has started up beekeeping at their "hobby farm." The hobby farm has its own homestead and another one for the live-in managers. Carter is the right man for her, not Ethan. Carter also has family friends like that. He is not amazed by her life. Why is Ethan pining for a princess when he is a peasant?

Women don't find self-pity an attractive trait, says Harvey. *They like confidence.*

Please, you were the self-pity king, Harvey!

He remembers he hasn't had a chance to show Jasmine the video of the car accident. Obviously he hasn't wanted to talk about it in front of Carter. It's officially gone from the internet but he's kept a recording.

"Remember the lady on the plane?" he says as he puts the tea bags in the sink.

"Of course," she says. She turns to look at him. "Has something happened?"

He finds the video, offers his phone. She licks honey from her fingers and takes it.

The volume is low but loud enough for him to hear the sounds of the deadly collision. Jasmine gasps on cue.

"Oh, *Ethan,*" she says. They are standing close to each other, her hand on his bare chest.

The kitchen floods with fierce, blinding light.

Carter blinks and frowns, his hand on the light switch, and says with ferocious sarcasm, "Ah, sorry, guys, am I interrupting?"

Chapter 70

The screen recording of the TikTok LIVE video of Kayla's accident was eventually removed after a request from the family, but not before it had gotten a million views and three thousand "likes." I am told that this does not mean people "liked" the fact that Kayla died.

There was a lot of online "chatter" and one small article in a tabloid newspaper, but that was all. Kayla's family never spoke publicly about the prediction.

Her friend, the passenger who filmed the accident, had to spend weeks in the hospital and she shut down her social media during that time.

People soon got interested in other things, as they tend to do.

To put it in perspective: a video of a dog barking at its own reflection in an oven door got two million views and ten thousand likes.

People forgot. Only those who knew and loved Kayla continued to talk about her.

At this point no one had yet referred to me as "the Death Lady."

That was all to come.

Chapter 71

The second and third deaths were a day apart, in August, a month after the first.

News of the first diagnosis broke shortly after.

It was just like the roulette table in Monte Carlo, when that tiny white ball kept landing on black, again and again and again, and everyone gathered around, so certain it had to mean something.

Chapter 72

Leo learns about the next two deaths when he's at work.

He has set up a Google alert for the words "psychic," "plane," and "death."

The headline, from a Tasmanian newspaper, reads: "Plane Psychic Correctly Predicts Deaths of Married Doctors."

The article is behind a paywall, but he doesn't hesitate to sign up for a subscription, and as soon as the full article appears on his screen, he recognizes the elderly couple from the departure lounge in Hobart. He stood in line behind them while they ordered coffees and he noted their frailty, but also the Apple Watches on their wrists and the bright intelligence in their eyes. They were both warmly dressed and he'd thought about his grandmother and how badly she felt the cold.

The article says that the couple were both retired doctors who had run a joint medical practice in Hobart for sixty years and were well known in the local community, beloved by their patients. Dr. Bailey and Dr. Bailey had one daughter, three grandchildren, and seven great-grandchildren.

Their daughter is interviewed. She says her parents flew from Hobart to Sydney to attend their youngest great-grandchild's christening, and while on that flight, a lady informed them they would die at the ages of one hundred and one hundred and one respectively, which is exactly what happened.

"They were scientific people, being doctors, so they didn't take it seriously, they found it entertaining," she said, "and they were very philosophical about death. They got a kick out of hearing their cause of death would be 'old age,' just like Queen Elizabeth. They were proud royalists."

Leo feels emotional as he looks at the photos chosen to sum up the couple's lives: young and beautiful on their wedding day; as new parents holding a saucer-eyed baby daughter; standing back to back in white coats outside their brand-new medical practice, arms folded and professional, stethoscopes around their necks; as middle-aged parents of the bride at their daughter's wedding; as retired travelers holding up wineglasses to the camera, probably on one of those European river cruises; as the elderly patriarch and matriarch at their great-grandchild's christening, surrounded by family, the saucer-eyed baby now a grandmother herself.

He feels envy on behalf of his own parents, who should have gotten a long happy shared life together like this. Instead his mother will have to spend her last years alone. Their retirement plans never came to be. The other day she told Leo she is sick of people assuming she is over her grief by now. There was real fury in her voice, which surprised Leo, because maybe he assumed that too. He misses his dad, all the time, but he feels like he has passed through the really intense, dreadful period of mourning—he no longer cries in the car, for example—and he kind of assumed his mother had too. He sees now that was foolish. She lost her lifelong partner whereas Leo's immediate family structure remains intact. His mother is particularly incensed by the phrase "merry widow," although as far as Leo knows, nobody has actually used that phrase, or told her she should be one, she is just incensed by its existence. She recently made a new friend at aqua aerobics, also a widow. They are starting a club called The Angry Widows.

He hasn't told his mother or his sisters anything about the psychic. He doesn't want to upset his mother or give his sisters a reason to make fun of him when he doesn't end up dying.

"Tomorrow's site walk has been rescheduled until Thursday."

"Hmmm, what?" Leo looks up vaguely to see his office manager poking her head around his office door.

"Tomorrow's site—"

The words infiltrate. "Oh, yep, fine, good, thanks." He raises his hand in acknowledgment and looks back at his computer. This is rare for him. He works at work. This is not billable time.

The elderly couple's daughter is quoted: "Mum died peacefully in the hospital after a brief illness and my father didn't make it one night without her. He died in his sleep the very next night."

Up until their deaths, her parents had still lived in the house they'd moved into after their marriage. Their joint funeral, which is expected to be standing room only considering their positions in the local community, will be held in the same church where they'd married.

The woman said her parents had been blessed with long happy lives but she was still "devastated" to lose them. "It's never long enough, is it?" she said. "You'd still do anything for one more day, one more chat, one more phone call."

The article finishes with a reference to growing interest in the "so-called plane psychic" after a young Tasmanian girl's tragic death in a car accident was livestreamed on social media. The young girl was "allegedly" told by the psychic she would die in a car accident when she was nineteen.

Leo's phone rings.

It says: *Sue O'Sullivan (Hobart flight).*

"How are you, Leo, can you talk?" She launches straight in, as if they are old friends, not strangers who met once on a plane, and Leo feels the strangest longing for her and Max to actually *be* his old friends. He's messed up badly on the issue of friends. He's left "friends" to Neve, in the same way Neve has left "tax" and "lightbulbs" to him.

"I can talk," says Leo. "I'm just reading about the Baileys. The doctors in Hobart."

"Me too," says Sue. "What a great innings! Sad, but not a tragedy, not like the poor beautiful young girl in the car accident, which I assume you saw. I talked to her at the airport, she was so sweet. It was terrible to see . . . to see that."

Leo hears the horror of the video in her words.

"I did," says Leo. "That video was awful. My daughter found it first."

"Oh, no, and did Bridie understand the . . . implications?"

She remembers Bridie's name. He pauses. He is so touched by that.

"Sorry—it is Bridie, isn't it, I thought—?"

"Yes," says Leo. "You have a great memory! Unfortunately Bridie does know—she overheard me talking to my wife about it and got very worked up for a while. We thought she'd gotten over it, but obviously that video of the poor young girl in the car accident was just . . ."

"Kids are resilient," says Sue. "Try not to worry." She sighs. "I don't really know why I'm calling you, Leo, I guess I just wanted to talk to someone in the same situation. I've had all these tests and there is no indication that I've got any kind of cancer. I guess I just wondered, are you feeling—"

"Spooked?" says Leo. He looks at the framed photo he keeps on his desk of Neve and the children. It's nowhere glamorous, just the three of them on the couch, Neve in the middle, a kid tucked under each arm. Oli and Bridie are so much bigger now.

"Yes," says Sue. "I mean, it could all just be—"

"A terrible coincidence," says Leo. He needs to stop finishing her sentences. People prefer to finish their own. He pulls the photo closer to him. He can't die. He's necessary. Neve leaves flammable items near the hotplates, she never closes cupboard doors, and she's so happy when he comes home. Sometimes it gives him a kind of teenage boy's feeling of surprise: *Wow, this girl still really likes me!*

"Do you really think it's just a coincidence?" says Sue. She sounds younger on the phone than he remembers from the plane, less grand-motherly, more like someone the same age as him. He imagines invit-ing Sue and Max over for dinner. Ethan could come too! It's healthy to have friends from different generations. They could be *his* friends. Would that be weird? Yes, it's weird, what's wrong with him?

"It has to be a coincidence," says Leo. "But, yes, I'm feeling a little rattled. I shared a taxi with that injured guy and she predicted that he'll die in a fight when he's thirty, which is in October, and I'm meant to go in a workplace accident any time after my birthday in Novem-ber. I feel like we might be next on the chopping block!" Is this dark humor appropriate?

"Well, hopefully you two will prove her wrong!" says Sue robustly.

"I did hear her tell that flight attendant she'd die of 'self-harm' when she was twenty-eight," muses Leo. "But I think she was younger than that."

"Oh, no, please tell me it wasn't Allegra," says Sue. "The beautiful one? It was her twenty-eighth birthday that very day!"

Leo's phone beeps and he takes it away from his ear and sees Neve's name. She rarely if ever calls when he's at work. Has she seen the article? "Sorry, Sue, my wife is just calling—"

"You go, Leo," says Sue immediately. "Keep in touch."

Leo accepts Neve's call. "Hi," he says to her, and her words are a tumble of panic. The only time he can remember her ever sounding like this was in the final stages of labor with both babies, when both times she begged him to please make it stop, and he felt so terrible that he couldn't.

"You need to resign, Leo. Type up your letter of resignation right now."

"You're not serious."

"I am serious."

He can't believe it. Some kind of switch has been flicked. She'd been calm after they watched that terrible car accident video together.

"More people have died," she says. "Just like she predicted."

"I know, sweetheart, I just read the article myself, but they were an elderly couple, it wasn't actually that hard a prediction to make. I can't possibly give up work based on a random—"

"Why can't you? Of course you can. It's easy. Just stop working for a year."

"I'm not going to die in a workplace accident, I promise you."

"You can't promise me that. There was a story about a multistory crane collapse on a site last week. A man in his forties died. It could have been you. It could easily have been you."

"That was not one of our sites, and you know, Neve, you could be hit by a bus yourself."

"Well, if a psychic told me I was going to be hit by a bus, I'd avoid catching the bus!"

"Not if catching the bus was the only way to pay the mortgage!"

They seem to be in the middle of an argument. He tries to keep any emotion out of his voice. "This is all so—"

"You know what?" Neve interrupts. "If working for that woman ends up killing you, I will kill that manipulative, micromanaging bitch myself."

Leo reels. *Manipulative, micromanaging bitch?* What the hell? He thought Neve and Lilith liked each other. All that admiring of each other's hair at the office Christmas parties. He actually assumed Neve, as a woman, found Lilith even more inspirational than he does.

"What are you *talking* about, Neve?"

"Leo? Am I interrupting?"

And there she is, standing right in front of him. Lilith in her cream pantsuit and pearl earrings, frowning at a message on her phone.

"Have you heard about this drainage issue?"

She smiles. There is a minuscule fleck of red lipstick on one of her incisors.

Chapter 73

I have never really had a nickname before.

So it's unfortunate that my first was "the Death Lady."

I'm not keen on it.

It first made its appearance after the deaths of the elderly doctors.

That's when *Deathlady* became a trending hashtag across multiple social media platforms.

Which leaves me lost for words.

Chapter 74

It's late September. Spring in Sydney. Ethan is on the bus heading to work.

"Would you *look* at the color of that cherry blossom tree!" says the woman sitting next to him. She points through the window at the abundant froth of pale pink flowers.

"Beautiful," says Ethan.

"But they never last long, do they?"

"No," agrees Ethan, who has no idea how long cherry blossoms last.

He puts his AirPods in before the woman has the chance to point out more local flora.

Eleven days until his thirtieth birthday. It falls on a Monday, which is a shit day for a significant birthday. *Especially if it's my last.*

These morbid thoughts are like pop-up ads and he can't seem to access the right security software for his brain to stop them from appearing, even though he truly believes himself to still be unconcerned and skeptical.

Sometimes he catches himself hoping his "assault" will be quick, or that he at least gets one good punch in, although he still can't imagine himself hitting someone.

Guys like us—

Yeah, shut up, Harvey.

What with the pop-up thoughts and Harvey's interjections, Ethan never gets a word in.

Lately he's been thinking about the time in Year 7 when he accidentally kicked a soccer ball into the back of a scary Year 11 kid's head. "*Run, Ethan!*" cried his friends, so he did. It might have been better to have just said sorry? He'll never know. The scary kid didn't chase him, but word got out that he was planning to "get him." It was a terrifying time. Like knowing the Mafia had a hit out on you. Kids kept telling Ethan he should "watch his back" and consider leaving the school, leaving the country. Fate intervened and the Year 11 boy broke his leg snowboarding and by the time he came back he seemed to have forgotten all about Ethan.

It had become a funny story, but in truth there had been nothing funny at the time about waking up each day in fear of imminent but unspecified danger. Is his thirtieth year going to be a grown-up version of those two weeks in Year 7?

He is not having a thirtieth birthday party. He always assumed he would have one, most of his social circle seems to be doing them, but it just hasn't felt right.

There is the absence of Harvey, although the truth is that if Harvey had been alive and said he couldn't make it to his thirtieth, Ethan would never have canceled. Your status really improves when you die. There is also the fact that all his friends know about the psychic prediction, and none of his family do, so he doesn't want to risk getting them together in the same room. (He never told his parents or sister about the scary older boy either.)

Various small celebrations are planned in lieu of a party: a work lunch on the day of his birthday, drinks with one group of friends at a bar on the Friday night, a family dinner on the Saturday night and a dinner with another group of friends, his old high school friends, the ones who will never forget the ball-to-the-back-of-the-head story, on the Sunday night.

When Jasmine found out he had no plans for the night of his actual birthday she said she would make her "famous nachos" (this is the first he's heard of her famous nachos, but okay) and they could watch the first episode of *The Sopranos* together. A while back they discovered that neither of them had seen the series and both are sick of people making them feel inadequate about it.

Harvey had been a *Sopranos* fan. He had lots of *Sopranos* quotes. For example, whenever he saw Ethan wearing shorts he'd say, in his best Italian-American accent, "A don doesn't wear shorts." Harvey never wore shorts, although that was because he was self-conscious about his chicken legs, not because he was a member of the Mafia.

Ethan is looking forward to nachos with Jasmine more than he knows is good for him.

Carter will not be in attendance. Hallelujah. He has a regular Monday poker night with friends, so Mondays are blessedly Carter-free in the apartment.

He's been trying his best to *like* Carter. Jasmine could have any guy on the entire planet so Carter can't be as bad as he comes across. Ironically, the night of the incident in the kitchen, when Carter turned on the light with that murderous expression, ended up being the night that it first seemed possible they could become friends. Or at least friendly acquaintances.

Carter had said, in a tone of voice that honestly made Ethan's blood run cold: "Is there something going on I should know about?"

If Jasmine's blood was also running cold, she sure didn't show it. She appeared unbothered. She didn't take a step away from Ethan, although Ethan moved a little away from her. She clearly felt no guilt about possibly harboring a secret crush on her flatmate, so that was depressing.

"A psychic predicted Ethan's death at thirty," Jasmine explained. "And some of her other predictions have been coming true."

This seemed to really cheer Carter up. "Seriously?"

When he learned Ethan's thirtieth was only a few weeks away he became positively chipper.

"Sorry, mate," he said. "About my reaction. It just looked . . . for a moment, like something was going on between the two of you."

"Don't be ridiculous," said Jasmine with mortifying speed and conviction. Ethan agreed it was ridiculous.

The three of them ended up having English muffins and Sleepytime tea together, and Carter watched the video of the car accident and said, "You must be scared out of your mind." Then he paused and said, "But has it made you kind of grateful to be alive?"

Ethan admitted it really had *not* made him grateful to be alive, just occasionally nervous that he might soon be dead.

Then Carter became unexpectedly animated and informed Jasmine and Ethan that he *regularly* contemplated his own mortality. One of his poker buddies has gotten Carter into "the ancient philosophy of Stoicism." There was something charming, well, almost charming, about the self-conscious way Carter used the words "ancient philosophy," like when the school jock suddenly pipes up with an earnest contribution in English to the discussion about *Romeo and Juliet*. Carter even went to Jasmine's room and came back with a prop to demonstrate his point. It was a gold coin he "carries everywhere" inscribed with the words *Memento Mori*, which mean "Remember Death." Carter told them about the Roman generals who, after winning a big battle, would ride triumphant in their chariots, with some poor sod in the back, whose only job requirement was to whisper in the general's ear, over and over, "Remember thou art mortal. Remember you must die!"

"So that the dude didn't get a big head," explained Carter. He slurped his Sleepytime tea and said he looked at the coin every day to remind himself not to waste time thinking about trivial shit. (Like hanging up your bath towel, thought Ethan.)

"I'll tell you what I think," said Carter, in the manner of someone about to pass on something incredibly profound. "You've got to treat every day like a gift because it might be your last."

It was like he honestly believed he was the first person in the world to say that.

Then Jasmine talked about how her life coach (different guy from her therapist) got her to write her own obituary, which really clarified what she wanted out of life (success, fame, adulation), and how she'd once done this really cool death meditation workshop in LA, where she learned all about a Buddhist tradition where you visualize your dead body, like *rotting* and *decaying,* with *maggots* (she creepy-crawled her fingers across her beautiful face to demonstrate). The idea, she went on, was to help you lose your attachment to the material world. Afterward she'd just felt so *alive,* and by the way, the pancake station at the breakfast buffet at the Beverly Wilshire was amazing and she's experienced some pretty amazing pancake stations in her time.

"But didn't your friend die recently?" Carter asked Ethan delicately. "Doesn't that make you . . . I don't know, grateful it wasn't you?"

"No," said Ethan. "It just makes me sad it was him."

The three of them talked until dawn, at which point Jasmine and Carter went back to bed, secure in the knowledge that all their days were gifts, and Ethan got ready for work.

Since then there have been the deaths of the two elderly doctors, which Jasmine believes is further proof of the lady's special powers, but which Ethan doesn't find especially impressive. Anyone could have predicted those deaths. *He* could have predicted them. They don't count. Sorry, old doctors.

Carter is still staying over just as much but seems convinced that Ethan is his friend now. Whenever they come across each other, Carter offers Ethan a solemn fist bump and says, "Bro."

Sometimes there is *more than one fist bump a day,* which is excruciating. He's like that work colleague who brightly greets you every time you pass in the corridor, when everyone knows you should avoid eye contact after the first time, or at best exchange pained smiles.

Carter has also asked Ethan, on more than one occasion, to remind him of the exact date of his thirtieth birthday. Is he planning to get him a gift? Yeah, good one. Bro is gleefully counting the days.

The woman next to him nudges him, tapping at the bus window to indicate another cherry blossom tree.

"Beautiful," says Ethan again.

It actually is quite beautiful.

Chapter 75

Something extraordinary happened to me on a cloudy, breezy Saturday morning three days after my eighteenth birthday.

At the time I was studying for a double degree at Sydney University: a Bachelor of Science in Pure and Applied Mathematics and a Bachelor of Arts in Statistics. I was fulfilling my father's dream for me.

I don't mean to imply I only studied math to honor Dad's memory, and I would have preferred, for example, to be a ballet dancer. Imagine me dancing *Swan Lake* with my two left feet! That would defy the laws of physics.

(It is obviously impossible to defy the laws of physics, I was using hyperbolic language.)

I loved university. Not for the social life, of course. I didn't make any friends. Most of the time I was the only woman among hundreds of men, but that didn't bother me, and it's not why I didn't make friends. I can't recall making eye contact with a single person. I wasn't there to socialize. I was there to learn. If someone asked to borrow a pen or pencil I would hand it over without even looking. It was like I lost my peripheral vision. All I could see was the board or the figures on the overhead projector.

Everyone I knew thought my studies were useless, like learning a language nobody spoke. Math, by the way, *is* a language, I would argue a beautiful one, and it's the only universal language there is, because it's the same all over the world.

People said I would be qualified for only one job, and it was one I didn't want: teaching math to children who didn't want to learn it. I wasn't known for my love of children.

I didn't care. I was in seventh heaven.

One day, I was at home in my bedroom absorbed in my work. Auntie Pat was over, she was over more often than not, but this time she was there for a particular purpose: floating shelves. Mum had seen a picture in a magazine she wanted to replicate and she'd found a carpenter in the Yellow Pages: *Jack Murphy, EXPERIENCED CARPENTER, prompt, reliable service, quality work. For all your carpentry needs!* Auntie Pat was there to make sure this experienced carpenter didn't charge Mum an inflated price for these fancy shelves.

Nineteen years old. Tall, lanky, but graceful in his lankiness. The most vulnerable of necks and the kindest of eyes. Jack was the tallest man who had ever entered our house, which meant that he was the first and only person to nearly bang his head on our mother-of-pearl hanging light fixture. He swerved his head in a nimble, sporty way as if he were changing direction in a rugby game.

I saw this, because I happened to walk into the room at that exact moment, on my way to the kitchen to make myself a cup of tea. I stopped dead and looked down at myself in a panic. I wore bell-bottomed blue jeans, a tight blue-and-yellow-striped T-shirt, and silver hoop earrings. I'd washed my hair that morning. It reached the middle of my back, long and straight. I was relieved to find that, by pure chance, my appearance was excellent.

Mum said perfunctorily, "My daughter, Cherry."

"Cherry is a pretty name," said Jack.

My mother and I said, "Thank you," at the same time.

Jack held out his hand for me to shake, which was a little odd. Carpenters wouldn't normally shake hands with the potential customer's daughter as she walked by, but that's what he did.

I said, "Hi, Jack."

He said, "Hi, Cherry."

The handshake lasted perhaps one or two seconds longer than socially acceptable. I can still feel that moment in the palm of my hand.

That's all we said. I made my tea and returned to my abstract algebra. Jack took out his tape measure.

After he left, Mum and Auntie Pat shrieked and jumped about like girls in a teen movie.

"Did you *see* that?"

"Of *course* I saw it! Blind Freddy could have seen it!"

They talked about that moment for years.

I note with interest that something similar happened to the world-famous "Crocodile Hunter" Steve Irwin and his wife, Terri, on the day they met. I have seen interviews where they discussed that moment, and my experience with Jack was very similar to theirs, although obviously there were no crocodiles at our house in Hornsby.

Perhaps you think this is a commonplace story where two young people catch each other's eye and "sparks fly."

Perhaps you think describing this incident as "extraordinary" is hyperbolic language.

But I know you will understand if it has ever happened to you.

Chapter 76

Allegra is running along a boardwalk in Portugal at sunset, a gentle breeze in her hair.

A handsome African American man runs in front of her, turning often to grin back at her and offer advice and encouragement. His name is Jay. He reminds her to keep her elbows at ninety-degree angles and to enjoy the incredible views.

"I feel like I'm dying, Jay," puffs Allegra.

"You're doing awesome," says Jay. "You're crushing it!"

She is not really in Portugal at sunset, she is on a treadmill in her parents' garage in North Ryde, Sydney, Australia, and Jay is her virtual trainer on the monitor, while a fan blows a fake sea breeze in her face. She's on week two of a Basics of Running series. Jay says they're going on a "fitness journey."

"You feel the endorphins yet?" Her dad pops his head around the door separating the garage from the house. This is his third time checking on her. "How is Jay today? I love Jay! Where are you?"

"Go away, Dad!"

"Sorry, sorry!" He lifts up his hands. "Keep it up! Your form is good!" He puts his own elbows at ninety-degree angles.

Her dad is thrilled someone else is using his precious treadmill. The first time she came over to try it out he stood next to her the whole time, watching her run, offering an endless stream of enthusiastic commentary: "Feel how the incline is going up! As if you are running up a hill! Now the speed is increasing, see, you have to run faster! Careful!"

He wants to tell her all about his favorite trainers and the spectacular places he has run around the world. Maybe they can train for a half-marathon together!

"Whoa back, Dad," said Allegra, while her mother laughed and said she had never seen a drop of sweat on her daughter's forehead before, which is not an exaggeration. Allegra has never been into fitness or sports. She doesn't enjoy getting out of breath, has never crossed the threshold of a gym, and has always believed working as a flight attendant gives her all the exercise she needs. She's on her feet for hours at a time.

She had told her parents a doctor had suggested running for her back. He said it was great for those with a "structurally normal spine," like Allegra, who need to "improve their core."

This is true but Allegra isn't really interested in improving her core; her back is fine now. The reason for her new interest in exercise is her new interest in her mental health, which up until now she always believed to also be "structurally normal" but which she now fears could at any moment catastrophically fail her, just like her back did on that flight.

Anders sent her the shocking video of the poor Tasmanian girl in the car accident and the link to the story about the elderly doctors. He's *obsessed* with the psychic and has been sending Allegra daily messages. *RUOK? SERIOUSLY, RU?? DO NOT SELF-HARM TODAY! YOU ARE LOVED, DEAR HEART.*

Her parents, who inhabit different algorithms, have not seen the car accident video or the article, and of course Allegra has not told them about the deaths. She deeply regrets revealing the prediction to her mother in the first place.

Surely, she keeps telling herself, her particular prediction is easy to avoid: she simply will *not* self-harm. Every day that goes by is another day where she has refused to allow the lady's prediction to come true, and it's not like it's difficult to resist the temptation to hurt herself. She has never felt a desire to self-harm. There were kids at school who cut themselves and it always baffled her. Why would anyone deliberately choose pain?

She does not have depression. She is fine with her life. It's a good life. She likes her job. Her apartment. Her friends. Her mood has always been steady. She is calm in a crisis, she handles conflict well. She's snippy before her period, grumpy if she's slept poorly, but she rarely, if ever, feels melancholy.

She has always felt herself to be an almost boringly well-balanced person, like a solid little tugboat, able to right itself no matter how choppy the waters.

The last time she can remember feeling properly sad was when her ex-boyfriend broke up with her three years ago. He did it in a restaurant. She had not seen it coming. It was bizarre because there was no winding down of the relationship. It was as though he thought you were legally required to continue behaving as a loving, committed boyfriend—holding her hand as they walked from the car to the restaurant, talking about their plans for the weekend—until the very last moment. Then: BANG. Did he think the element of surprise was crucial for the most effective outcome? They had just placed their orders. They had agreed to share the seafood special. Another woman might have walked out, but she, the boring tugboat, did not make a fuss. She did not cry at the table. She had too much pride. She even ate some of the seafood. She thinks she might have a permanent seafood allergy as a result.

She had been devastated, but she did not miss a day of work and she got over it. She did not suffer from depression. She is not susceptible.

Now it's possible, although certainly not confirmed, that she has a new boyfriend. First Officer Jonathan Summers seems intent on seducing her even though it's not necessary—the job's done, Jonny—but the excellent lattice-topped pie was just the beginning. He is asking her on walks, to the movies, to dinner, and it's charming, it's almost irresistible, but she is holding back, keeping a piece of herself in reserve, just like a *Bachelor* contestant who refuses to give her whole heart, and will therefore not receive a rose, because everyone knows you've got to lay it all on the line and humiliate yourself on prime-time television if you want to be the last woman standing on a reality-TV dating show.

Now that she thinks about it, Jonny Summers is *exactly* the sort of bachelor producers would love to cast. Allegra watches *The Bachelor* to feel superior. If she was watching herself she'd be yelling at the television: "Refuse that guy's damned rose! Reject him before he rejects you!"

One morning she woke with a clear thought: "the Death Lady" has foreseen that Jonny is going through all this nonsense as part of a strangely elaborate plan to break Allegra's heart, and this time she *will* spiral into a depression serious enough to lead her to self-harm.

The next day she woke with another thought: a far more significant tragedy lurks in her future than a breakup. For example, she will be in a car accident with her parents and brother and she will be the only survivor. The subsequent grief will be unbearable. She thinks she's a tugboat only because life has never tested her.

She looks over at her parents' car, parked alongside the treadmill, a silver Volvo, bought ten years ago when both Taj and Allegra still lived at home. Naturally her mother did a ceremony to bless and protect the precious new car but they were running late for a family event and Allegra's dad lost his mind as Taj took forever to smash the coconut on the garage floor (he had a new technique he wanted to try out) and they sprinkled coconut water on all four tires while reciting a special travel safety mantra, put lemons under each tire, and then Allegra's mother lit a diya and waved incense inside the car, while her dad sat at the steering wheel, nostrils twitching, waving his hands, spluttering, "Prisha, *enough*, it's getting in the *upholstery*!" Allegra or Taj only have to say to each other, "Prisha, enough!" to have them both rolling about laughing.

In addition to her mother's blessing, her dad, besides being a careful driver, is meticulous about having the car serviced every six months. So, all bases covered, spiritual and earthly.

There will be no car accident and there will be no depression.

A couple of weeks ago, Allegra typed into her search bar: *How to prevent depression* even as she guessed all the answers that would appear. Regular exercise. Spend time with family and friends. Get outside. Avoid alcohol and drugs. Gratitude.

There is no sure way to prevent depression, the website warned, but Allegra still went ahead and made her own personal *Stay Happy This Year* plan as per the suggestion of some online psychologist. Why not? She might as well take control of her future happiness. Keep her mood stable. She has never been a huge drinker, but she is drinking even less. She runs on her dad's treadmill twice a week and catches up with her parents at the same time. Occasionally she remembers to look at a tree and think, *Nice*.

"Next interval coming up, we're increasing our speed for just thirty seconds," warns Jay as the treadmill picks up the pace and Allegra's legs are forced to run faster. There is always a moment of panic as her brain catches up with the rest of her body: *Why are we running so fast? What's the emergency?* But then she settles into it.

Did her grandmother need a treadmill? It's impossible to imagine Allegra's dignified grandmother on a treadmill, but could that have saved her? She never seemed sad at all! Was she hiding her true feelings, or did the sadness creep up behind her one day like a monster and wrap her in its malevolent arms?

Allegra's phone, on the treadmill console, rings and flashes the name: *Trina Tanaka*.

Trina is her crew manager. Allegra doesn't know her well, but the little interaction they've had has been pleasant and professional. Trina is responsible for a team of more than fifty crew members and Allegra only occasionally sees her face-to-face. It's one of the things Allegra appreciates about not being in a corporate environment: there is no possibility of a terrible boss having a daily impact on her life.

Allegra tugs the safety key free to stop the treadmill and grabs the phone.

"How are you, Trina?" she gasps.

As soon as she speaks, she realizes she should have let the call go to voicemail. For one thing, she needs to catch her breath, and more important, she knows why Trina is calling. Allegra should have called Trina first, got ahead of this situation as soon as the stories began appearing on the internet.

"Hi, Allegra. Listen, you were cabin manager on a Hobart-Sydney flight back in April where a passenger supposedly made predictions . . . about deaths of passengers, correct?" says Trina. "I assume you know what I'm talking about. The media is picking up on it. We're getting calls."

"Yes." Allegra steadies her breathing. Come on, Miss Supposedly So Calm in a Crisis. "Sorry. I was on the treadmill."

"That's okay, take your time."

Something about the tone and the words "take your time" reminds Allegra of a detective interviewing a suspect.

"It really didn't seem that big a deal." Allegra hears herself sounding defensive.

"Please just take me through it, Allegra."

Allegra blinks away a droplet of sweat that has run into her eye as she reads the error message on the treadmill monitor: *Uh-oh, looks like your treadmill has stopped.*

Uh-oh indeed.

Chapter 77

Six months after we met, I found it necessary to inform my devout Catholic grandmother I loved Jack Murphy more than God.

Sometimes you can't believe the things you said or the feelings you felt.

"Oh, darling," winced Grandma, and she patted my shoulder consolingly.

Everything was better because of Jack. Food tasted better. The stars shone brighter, my studies were even more fascinating and they were already so fascinating!

I never thought, *This can't last.*

I thought, *This is just how my life is now. Perfect.*

It was a special time. Jack was a social boy. He took me to parties and dances I would otherwise have avoided like the plague. With him by my side I found I could walk through any door, always on the count of three, and even enjoy myself, especially if I could find myself a spot in the corner with my back against the wall and a view of the nearest exit.

I took him fishing and canoeing and camping. He was very cowardly about cold water and wasn't a strong swimmer. I'd count *him* in—one, two, *three*—when it came to the ocean.

I remember standing with him at the blowhole at Avoca Beach, watching the water being sucked in and out and then exploding volcanically, splashing our faces, while a group of local boys with shiny tanned shoulders, their hair slick against their heads like seals, timed their moment to jump.

I wore a purple "ring and string" bikini. The top was two triangles connected by a plastic ring. The bottom was another two triangles tied together in loose bows on my hips. I had not a care in the world about melanoma.

Poor Jack said gamely, "So . . . we're going in there?"

He was so relieved when I said we were certainly *not* swimming in the blowhole (for one thing my bikini would not have withstood it) and he kissed me right there on the rocks while the boys hollered and whistled.

Blowholes can be treacherous, and blowhole swimming can be deadly. Please don't do it. Even if you are a young boy with shiny tanned shoulders and think you are capable of anything, you are not.

When I was a child, I saw a boy I knew by sight from the campground dragged from the sea by his father. His head lolled at a ghastly angle in his father's arms, and his gang of friends, who had been swimming in the blowhole with him, watched on in silence, when normally they were so noisy. He could not be revived. My dad hurried me away, but the sound of his mother's wails followed us.

Sometimes I think those wails may have followed me forever.

Jack said if he'd jumped in that blowhole he probably would have vanished like the Australian prime minister Harold Holt, who a few years prior had gone for a swim on a Victorian beach and was never seen again. There were many conspiracy theories, one of which was that he'd been a Chinese spy and was picked up by a submarine. People didn't believe a prime minister could drown. Prime ministers can drown. Princesses can die in car crashes.

Sometimes we went out in a foursome with Ivy and her boyfriend at the time. Jack was undeniably superior in every way to Ivy's boyfriend, so I enjoyed that. I take after my dad, but I am also my mother's daughter. (You may have noticed.)

Jack's dad was a ruddy man with a dodgy knee. He liked me, but Jack's mother preferred his previous girlfriend, a trainee nurse, who was more her sort of person.

She found me odd. "So you're saying you really don't want to be a math teacher?"

"That's what she's saying, Mum," sighed Jack.

"But what else can you *do* with a math degree, Clever Clogs?" That's what she called me. I called her Mrs. Murphy. I said I'd find something to do with my math degree.

I don't know if Jack loved me more than God, but I know he loved me. I still have the cards and notes he wrote during that time, in which he told me I was "his girl" and he was "keeping me forever" and "his heart belonged to me." His handwriting was beautiful. His spelling was not the best.

After my mother died I found a drawer full of notes my parents had exchanged from when they first met. I still have them too. There are notes about how excited they were about their upcoming wedding and then the arrival of the new baby (me). There are apologies for unspecified misdemeanors: *I'm sorry. I didn't mean it.* Some are suggestive. Even raunchy. I will protect their privacy by not repeating them here.

Some are sad, because they had both wanted more children but never got them. Dad wrote, *It doesn't matter, we already hit the jackpot first time round.*

To be clear: He meant me. I was their jackpot.

Jack wanted four children: two girls and two boys.

He said their names would be Harry, Henry, Helen, and Hope. I don't remember why all their initials had to be *H*. He just found that funny. I laughed along although I didn't really get it.

I will be honest: I think if I'd had the capacity to look deep into my heart back then, I would have found that I didn't actually want any children, let alone four of them, but I had no idea it was possible or permitted for a woman to feel that way. Everyone wanted children. I just assumed Jack would make children fun and bearable, in the same way he made parties fun and bearable.

My dad carefully dated each of his notes. My mother drew tiny love hearts all around the borders of hers. It seems like theirs was a happy marriage, perhaps the perfect marriage, but obviously I don't have all the data. There is a lot I never knew and can never know.

Marriage is a mysterious institution, even from the inside.

Sometimes it can feel like a softly furnished minimum-security prison.

That was my experience anyway.

Chapter 78

It's an icy gray Sunday in Hobart and Paula sits in the driver's seat of her car, parked a short walk from St. David's Cathedral, and considers going home and giving this spot to someone more deserving, like someone who actually knew Drs. Barbara and Brian Bailey, and is attending their joint funeral to mourn their deaths and celebrate their long lives, and not for her own strange, selfish reasons.

She is early. The funeral doesn't start for another twenty minutes, although she can already see people walking along the footpath with that somber well-dressed look that says *funeral*, not *celebration*. Paula is wearing an old work suit.

Matt has the kids. He thinks she's meeting a friend for coffee. Not worth explaining her rationale in being here. He refuses to talk about Timmy's prediction. He says there is nothing to talk about because he doesn't believe it. Her husband's dogged refusal to have even *one word* spoken about the psychic in his presence is, frankly, almost as strange as her own behavior. It's like he thinks talking about it will make it come true, which makes him just as superstitious and weird as her.

Of course, he didn't notice she was overdressed for coffee.

Paula had no interaction with the elderly doctors on the flight, although they boarded early together as they belonged to the special

category of "Passengers with small children or anyone requiring assistance." She thinks the old man may have smiled at her children.

She slides her stockinged feet back and forth in her sensible kitten
heels and yawns. She was up till four a.m. last night trawling through
psychic websites, looking for the lady, looking for that damned familiar yet strange face. No luck.

When she covers her mouth with her hand she smells chlorine.
Timmy is now enrolled at three different swim schools. He does six
lessons a week, all of which require her to get in the pool with him,
because he is a baby. Timmy is happy. He loves every opportunity to
get in the pool. Willow only does one swimming class a week and
she's happy to go to the pool center childcare, thank goodness. On
the two days Willow is at preschool, Paula takes Timmy for two lessons: one at ten a.m., one at two p.m. He sleeps so well.

Her thoughts spool endlessly: *Where will it happen? Pool? River?
Ocean? How will it happen? How can I stop it? How can I prepare?*

The only time her mind is truly at rest is when she's in the pool
with Timmy, watching him effortlessly "self-rescue," watching him
not drown, watching him float so peacefully, so confidently, his face
dreamy, as if he's back in the womb.

"Wow, he's a true water baby!" people say, and Paula says, "He
sure is!"

Paula picks up her phone and calls her sister.

"Just hold on a sec," says Lisa. Paula waits while she yells her order
at a McDonald's drive-thru, changing her mind, umming and ahhing.
She is surely driving the poor order-taker mad.

Paula rests her head against the window. She can just see the entrance to the cathedral from where she is parked. Strangely, this is the
second time she has been to a double funeral at this church. Last year
she went to support a friend, a work colleague who had lost both her
parents in a car accident. It was another driver's fault, just like in the
case of the young girl from the flight.

That was a desperately sad funeral and Paula nearly made herself
sick trying to hold it together, imagining the stares. *Why is she crying,*

she never even met them! Surely she won't feel like that today, when the two doctors are so much older and died of natural causes.

"How are you?" says her sister, with her mouth full, presumably of fries.

"How could you be eating fries at this time of the day?" asks Paula.

"Why not?" says her sister. "Life is short, and I don't need to fit into a wedding dress anymore. What are you doing?"

"Nothing," lies Paula.

"You never do nothing," says Lisa suspiciously.

"Are you driving?" asks Paula, imagining her sister distracted by her fries and Paula on the phone.

"It's fine, I've pulled over," says Lisa. "Everything okay?"

"I was just thinking," says Paula.

"Oh, dear," says her sister.

It bursts out of her. "I was just thinking that if Timmy drowns when he's seven I'll be too old to have another baby and Willow will be an only child."

"He won't, I promise you. This is really terrible, it's upsetting how this is affecting you, Paulie."

It's her childhood nickname and Paula suddenly wants to tell her little sister everything, that it's not just the endless swimming lessons; sometimes she feels like she might already be on that slippery slope to a strange, strange place. Her thoughts are getting darker and more twisty.

Her sister's voice is suddenly urgent. "Maybe you need to talk to someone about what you're going through at the moment. Like, a professional?"

"What? No. I'm not going through anything."

"You kind of are."

If anyone discovers the thoughts that flutter like bats across Paula's mind they will take her children away.

"I'm fine," she says.

"You could do a telehealth call with that doctor—what was his name? Dr. Donnelly."

It's humiliating how her sister remembers that name so easily.

A young woman crosses the road in front of Paula's car. She's wearing a black dress that is too big for her. Something is familiar about her.

It's the *bride*. From the plane.

"Actually, got to go, sorry, Lisa, I'll call you back later," says Paula, and opens her car door fast.

Chapter 79

I made Jack a pineapple upside-down cake for his twentieth birthday. It took me hours and it was a gluggy mess. I bake like I dance. You can imagine the expression on Mrs. Murphy's face when she saw it. She said Jack's last girlfriend had a "real knack" for baking.

Jack's twentieth birthday meant he was required by law to register with the Department of Labor and National Service. Registering didn't mean he would necessarily do national service. That was decided by a "birthday ballot." Numbered wooden marbles, each representing a day of the year, were placed in a barrel. It was the lottery you didn't want to win. The ballots happened twice a year and by this time were televised, so there could be no secrecy about the process, because people were beginning to say they were rigged. Conspiracy theories are not a new development.

Jack and I and his parents watched the ballot on their television in its wheeled wood-veneer cabinet.

"Don't worry, Mum, I've never won a raffle in my life," said Jack.

Jack's birthday was March 15. His number was 102.

Men in suits handled the ballot. Men in suits often handle your destiny.

The barrel was spun. Each marble was hand-picked, held up between fingertips. The second-last number called was 101.

Mrs. Murphy exhaled. She said, happily, "Well, the next one won't be 102, Jack, that's for sure!"

I said, almost to myself, "The coin has no memory."

"What's that, Clever Clogs?" said Mrs. Murphy sharply.

"Don't call her that, Mum," said Jack.

I said, "It makes no difference. Each time they spin it's the same probability—" I don't know what was wrong with me. *Shut up, Cherry,* I think now, when I remember my behavior. Mrs. Murphy did not want to hear about the gambler's fallacy. People can't grasp it. They look at me as if I'm crazy when I tell them my Lotto numbers are one, two, three, four, five, and six, because it is impossible for them to believe that this combination is as statistically possible as any other combination.

The next number was 102.

Mrs. Murphy burst into tears. She blamed me. I understood. I was to Mrs. Murphy as Jiminy Cricket was to my mother. I'd brought bad luck to her son and I couldn't even bake a simple pineapple upside-down cake.

Jack wasn't worried. Being balloted in meant you had to be in the Australian regular army for two years. It didn't necessarily mean he'd be sent to Vietnam.

Mr. Murphy said, "Like I've always said, national service will do the boy good, give him some discipline!" But his face was splotchy and his eyes were wild. He'd fought in France.

My only view on the ongoing war in Vietnam was that I did not want my boyfriend to have anything to do with it. I like solving problems. The war was a problem I had no way of solving. I have always felt like that about current events. I enjoy popular culture, you may have noticed. I like reading what a movie star eats for breakfast. It's soothing and silly and it doesn't really matter. However, I am distressed by the imprecise nature of current events because all relevant information is not available, and is possibly never available, and it *does* matter.

I didn't know what to think about the Vietnam War.

I can assure you the other women in my family knew exactly what to think.

Grandma said, "Let the Americans worry about it, nothing to do with us!"

Auntie Pat joined the protest marches along George and Macquarie streets, a neatly painted sign bobbing above her head: END THE WAR! ABOLISH CONSCRIPTION!

"Marching alongside those germy long-haired hippies," sniffed my mother, who approved of the war and thought it was a necessary evil "to keep the commies out." My mother was pretty conservative for someone who told fortunes for a living.

Jack did his training in Victoria and excelled, which Mrs. Murphy said was so stupid of him. He was subsequently selected for "special overseas service." Jack had never left the state before he went to Victoria, let alone Australia. He would not have been able to point out Vietnam on a map.

That's when my mother instantly changed her views, as though she were executing a graceful pivot on the dance floor. Conscription became an "abomination." She adored Jack.

Jack assumed the people in charge knew what they were doing. If they needed him, he'd help out. I remember him reading a NOT WITH MY SON, YOU DON'T sign in a shop window in Waitara and saying to me, "Well, whose son then?" He would have preferred not to put his carpentry business on hold just when it was taking off, but he was also excited to be leaving Australia for the first time. When he came back we'd get married, get on with our lives, and have those four children. It was all good with Jack.

We did not ask my mother to do a reading for Jack before he left with all the other "nashos" and she never offered. I never asked Mum if she saw or felt something, but when I said goodbye to Jack at the train station a thought came into my head:

You're never going to see him again, Cherry.

It was a cool, clear, cruelly definite voice.

I took no notice. I chose not to believe the voice. I went home and wrote him a letter. I told him all about an enthralling geometry lesson I'd done back in high school.

I know.

Not every boy would want to hear about a geometry lesson, but Jack was a carpenter. He had an innate understanding of geometry.

I told him about how our second form teacher, Miss Crane, drew the tiniest chalk mark on the blackboard and explained that a point is "zero-dimensional," meaning it doesn't actually exist. But once you have two points—two nonexistent points—you can fill in the space between with lots and lots of points, and you get a line, which has length, so it's now *one dimension,* which you could argue means it does now exist. Miss Crane dotted her chalk against the board, over and over, in a straight line, demonstrating how a series of nothings could become something. (Actually, you could also argue the line still doesn't exist, it's just a concept, but I'd learned by then not to add caveats to everything I said. This was, after all, a love letter.)

I told Jack how I leaned forward that day in class as if I stood with my toes hanging over the very precipice of enlightenment. In my naivete, I believed Miss Crane was about to explain something that explained everything. Something I felt I *almost* already knew, but could not articulate; it was related to infinity and God, the ocean and space, the universe and my dad.

Of course, I did not achieve enlightenment in my geometry lesson. Miss Crane put the chalk down and told us to take out our compasses and protractors.

I told Jack that when I was with him, I felt like I was close to understanding what I had nearly understood that day.

I told him I was a zero-dimensional, nonexistent point, floating in space, until I met him.

Yes, I know. What an embarrassing love letter! Attempting to be poetic about geometry! A modern woman would never write such a thing. You should most definitely exist before you meet a man! You should have your own career, your own hobbies, your own thoughts, and your own financial plan!

Never mind, no need to feel mortified on my behalf, because I don't believe Jack ever read or received my letter.

Jack had only been in Vietnam for twenty days when he and two other members of his platoon, both national service conscripts—"nashos" like him—were wounded in action by an enemy mine. Jack died in a field hospital early the next morning. The other two recovered.

Jack was born at a minute to midnight. Sixty seconds later and he would have had a different birthdate and the birthday ballot, the "death lottery," would have had no impact on his life. Jack Murphy would have been my husband and the father of my children. I wonder if I would have liked them.

Mrs. Murphy would have been my mother-in-law. I wonder if she would have ever learned to like me. I doubt it. I saw her just once, a decade later, when I got out of my car after parking on Albert Lane, Hornsby. She looked terribly old and drawn, but I recognized her straightaway. I know she saw me, I know she recognized me. We held eye contact for a good few seconds. Her lips moved. I assume she was muttering, *Clever Clogs.* I went to lift my hand, but she turned her head sharply and crossed the street to avoid me.

My mother never stopped marveling at the quality of her beautifully built, geometrically perfect floating shelves.

Chapter 80

"Excuse me! Hello?"

Eve is walking up the hill from the bus stop toward the cathedral when she turns to see a businesswoman jump out of her car, keys in hand, handbag looped over one arm. She looks like someone's capable but kind boss. She crosses the road toward Eve, all hopeful and urgent, as if Eve will be able to offer important assistance.

Eve straightens her mother's black dress, her go-to dress for funerals. Imagine having a go-to dress for funerals. That's what it's like to be old. As if wrinkles were not enough.

"Hi." The woman is now in front of Eve. She has wispy, fly-away hair escaping from a messy bun. Presumably she is in a state of terrible grief for the lovely doctors. Maybe she's their granddaughter? Oh my God, what is Eve going to say? But probably lots of former patients will be coming to the funeral. Eve will mention the jelly beans.

"I think we were on the same flight to Sydney," says the woman. "I'm Paula. I think . . . you were the bride?"

"Oh!" says Eve, relieved. "Yes, I was the bride. I'm Eve. Are you here for the funeral?"

"Yes, although I don't—well, I never met them, I just remember them from the flight. I was the one with the screaming baby." Paula tucks the wisps of hair behind her ears. "Did that lady—"

"Oh, yes," says Eve. "She sure did."

Paula breathes a little shakily and looks up at the spires of the cathedral tower. "Me too. I wondered if there was a chance she might turn up today. You know how murderers always lurk in the back of the funerals of their victims? Or they do on television, I don't know if they really do in real life."

"That was my exact thinking too," says Eve.

Paula says, "I'm desperate to find her."

"Me too," says Eve. "I'm going to pay her to give me a different prediction. I'm hoping she will do it for a hundred dollars, do you reckon that's enough?" It better be enough.

"But what if it's the same prediction?"

"No, no. I'm going to bribe her to say what I want her to say. I just need to find her."

"Oh," says Paula. "Right. But what if she won't?"

Doubt slithers. The story of Eve's dad bribing the tarot card reader has always been such an established fact in her family history, she has assumed *all* psychics are open to bribery, but what if that assumption is incorrect, like so many of her assumptions?

"So it sounds like you think she's definitely a fraud?" continues Paula. "Even though she's correctly predicted three deaths now?"

"I know she is," says Eve. "She said I was going to die of 'intimate partner homicide.'"

Paula shudders. "She told me my baby was going to drown when he's seven."

Eve is aghast. "That's way more horrible. He's not going to drown! Just make sure he knows how to swim, like, that's important . . . sorry, I'm sure you already knew that."

Paula smiles strangely. "It's okay, I'm definitely teaching him how to swim." She studies Eve. "So your husband, he's not . . ." She doesn't say the word "violent." She doesn't need to say it. "I assume he's never . . ." She doesn't need to say the words "hit you" either.

This is what keeps happening now. Eve sees awful questions in people's eyes. Questions convicting Dom without a trial. People who should know better, like her own mother, who said she was so sorry, but she just had to check, just in case there was something Eve wasn't telling her. The injustice of it makes Eve feel huge swells of rage on Dom's behalf. It is so wrong that her sweet Dom should be accused of something he would never do, and he can't even prove his innocence, because his guilt is supposedly in his future.

"I'm sorry." Paula looks at her keenly. "I shouldn't have asked that."

"I'm not even *one percent* worried," says Eve. "He would never, *ever,* hurt me, not in a million years."

"I get it," says Paula. She frowns. "So then, if you're so sure, why not just ignore it?"

"Oh, it's all so stupid. It's not me who's worried, it's him! Dom is a sleepwalker, and he's read these articles about 'sleepwalking murder.' It's, like, really rare, but it's real, it happens, and Dom is just . . . he's just . . ."

She stops because the cathedral bells have begun to toll. It's so somber and dramatic. Church bells always give her those feelings, like: Life! Big! Tragic! Mysterious!

"He wants to do all sorts of stupid things now, like sleeping in separate rooms, when we've only got one bedroom!" She hears the brittle, tense sound of her voice. It's familiar. She realizes she is sounding like her mother. "He suggested he lock himself up in the bathroom! Like he's a werewolf."

Paula nods. Something seems to be opening up in her face.

She says, "I get how Dom feels. It's because you can't control it. I've been a bit irrational too."

"How?" says Eve.

Paula says, "I've got Timmy enrolled at three different swim schools. It's the only time I feel calm, when he's swimming."

It's like she's admitting a huge secret.

"Does he not like the swimming lessons?" Eve tries to understand.

"Oh, no, he *loves* swimming, he's crazy about it," says Paula. "It's just . . . it's weird for me to do this many swimming lessons. I mean, if anyone knew, they'd think I'd lost the plot."

"But if he loves swimming, like, who cares what people say, whatever!"

Paula smiles as if Eve has said something amusing but also revelatory. For a minute they don't say anything. They listen to the bells and give each other kind of appraising looks, trying to work each other out.

"The lady is probably not coming to the funeral," says Eve.

"It's a long shot," agrees Paula. "She might not live in Hobart. She definitely doesn't advertise. I've looked at thousands of websites."

"She might not even live in Australia," says Eve. "Although I reckon she does. It felt like she did."

"Yes, you know, I actually thought I recognized her," says Paula. "But I can't remember from where." She scrunches her forehead so hard it looks painful. "I'm normally good with faces."

"Do you get a feeling when you think about her face?" asks Eve. "Once I saw a guy on TV who reminded me of someone and I got a sleepy bored feeling and I realized it was my history teacher."

"Oh," says Paula. She closes her eyes. "I think the feeling is a kind of sadness. But also, at the same time, maybe, joy? What could that possibly mean? I don't know. But, look, maybe we should join forces to try to track her down."

Eve is about to answer yes, she would like that very much, but her phone is vibrating with a message from Dom, and she glances down and reads the headline of an article he's sent her:

"*Woman Kills Beloved Parrot in Her Sleep.*"

His message says: *We need to talk.*

That's very upsetting, but she's not a parrot.

We need to talk. It's never good when your partner needs to talk.

She looks up at Paula. "We need to find her fast."

Chapter 81

I thought I couldn't live after I lost Jack, but I just kept right on living.

I had three women in my life—my auntie Pat, my mother, and my grandmother—who had all lost the men they loved, and they refused to let me sink too far into the dark muddy depths of grief and depression. There was always someone there to yank me back up by the elbow. It was a combined effort, involving endless cups of tea, long walks I didn't want to take, hot baths and hot water bottles, and sometimes just a hand on my back while I lay on my bed and cried a million tears for the future that was no longer mine.

And there was television.

Every weeknight at 8:30 p.m., the four of us watched *Number 96*, a racy, groundbreaking soap opera following the lives of the residents of an apartment block in Paddington, which caused us to gasp and laugh and my grandmother to make the sign of the cross, even as her eyes stayed glued to the screen. Its first episode was advertised with the tagline *Tonight Australian television loses its virginity,* and that was not an exaggeration. We were all four as deeply addicted as Auntie Pat was to her ciggies and Bex. I can still see the enthralled profiles of my mother, grandmother, and aunt illuminated in the flickering monochrome light from the television.

Of course, I kept up with my studies and my marks didn't drop, but I walked through the grounds of Sydney University in a daze. Nobody felt quite real to me. Bev, Don, and Aldo—characters from *Number 96*—felt more real to me than the people seated next to me in lectures.

It feels trite to admit a television series helped with my grief for Jack, but it's true. You can avoid grief but you can't do it for twenty-four hours a day. You need distraction, and as long as it's legal and doesn't hurt you or anyone else, I recommend you take that distraction where you can find it.

Ivy and I had a terrible falling out during this time. She wanted me to get on with things. One day she snapped, "You weren't even engaged to him, Cherry, stop *wallowing*! You will waste your life like your auntie Pat did for a man you hardly knew!"

I found that deeply offensive to both Auntie Pat and to me. Jack and I might not have announced an engagement but we planned to marry and have four children.

A year later Ivy sent me a letter of apology. It was a very nice letter and of course I forgave her.

It's never too late for an apology.

Correction:

Sometimes it is too late.

Never mind.

After I graduated, everybody smugly waited for me to accept the fact that the only job I was now qualified for was teaching math, but I was determined. I went through the White Pages and wrote down the names and addresses of any organization I thought might be able to find some use for someone with a math degree. I posted forty letters.

Two weeks later, the phone rang, and a man with a musical Scottish accent said, "Cherry Hetherington?"

That's how I got my first job. It was not teaching math.

It was counting gray kangaroos.

Chapter 82

Leo drives home at two p.m. on a Monday. It's a revelation. Traffic is great at this time of day! He glides through green light after green light like he's in a presidential motorcade. Sometimes rush hour feels like a personal attack, and he feels hatred toward every set of taillights blocking his way. He has to remind himself that every car represents another poor soul stuck in traffic, just like him.

"I won't be back in the office after the site meeting," he'd said, elaborately casual, to Kath, his office manager. "I'll work from home."

He is proving to himself and to Neve that he isn't micromanaged, but Kath seemed annoyingly taken aback when he mentioned his innocuous plan for the day, and then she said, even more annoyingly: "Does *Lilith* know this?"

He feels like he's losing his grip on what's appropriate workplace behavior. Surely at his level he doesn't need to ask Lilith's "permission" to work from home after a site meeting. Does he? No. She's interstate, speaking inspirationally at a Women in Engineering conference. It makes sense for Leo to plan his working day like this. But wait, is he being misogynistic? Would he ask permission if Lilith was a man? Surely not. He's not a junior employee. He doesn't need to clock in and clock out. Why is he even thinking about this?

Multiple safety issues had been on the agenda at this morning's meeting and Leo had mentioned—he's not sure if it was to entertain the team or genuinely to caution them—that it seemed he was destined to die in a workplace accident when he turned forty-three in a little over a month's time, so could everyone please bring their A game when it came to safety? (*Bring your A game.* What the hell? Every time he leaves a meeting there is always one particular phrase that comes out of his mouth that causes him anguish.)

"I hope it wasn't that plane psychic," said the project architect. "Did anyone see that terrible video of the kid in the car accident?"

"Well," said Leo, and he can't deny he enjoyed the moment. Mouths dropped. The meeting went nearly an hour over schedule. Turns out a lot of people had seen the video and read about the plane psychic.

"I'm not coming within ten feet of you, mate," said someone jocularly.

"If I were you, I'd give up work for a year," said someone else.

"That's what my wife wants," said Leo, and no one seemed surprised. He wanted to say, "But come on, would you *really* resign from a good job on the word of a psychic? You wouldn't, you couldn't."

He and Neve haven't talked about it since that strange argument on the phone last week. She was calm by the time he got home. Maybe even embarrassed. Or probably not. She rarely gets embarrassed, which makes him envious. He's been in a permanent state of embarrassment since he was five.

She's probably waiting him out. She does this sometimes to him and the children: waits patiently for them to come to the "right" decision. This is why she thinks Lilith is "micromanaging" him. Takes one to know one.

He stands in the driveway next to his car for a moment, keys in hand. Seagulls soar and dive; he smells the salty air. It's an easy walk to the beach. It's not an easy walk *back* from the beach, because it's all uphill—Coogee is so hilly—but still, it's amazing that he lives so close to an amazing beach with white sand and crystal-clear water.

When he and his sisters finished school and all of them left

Tasmania for the mainland, one by one, for study and work and op-portunities, they all fell in love with different cities. Leo remembers doing the Bondi to Coogee coastline walk on his first weekend in Sydney and thinking, Imagine if I could live *here*. It felt like it wouldn't be allowed.

But now he lives here. With his wife, his two children, and their cavoodle. Living the suburban dream. It's true he can't remember the last time he actually went to the beach, but it's there, right there, minutes away, and Neve and the kids are there all the time, so it's not like his family isn't enjoying it.

He looks at his front garden, described in the real estate advertisement as "coastal desert–inspired style." Palm trees and hardy native plants. Not much grass and little maintenance required, which is good, although sometimes looking at it does make him feel kind of hot and bothered. Sometimes he misses the misty skies and abundant green of his hometown. His mother is currently redesigning her backyard in Hobart "English cottage garden style." He's worried she's being scammed by a dodgy operator. He needs to get back down there again soon, but when? It doesn't seem possible. Lilith is always asking about his mother's "health," which feels like a subtle way to remind him of her benevolence when it came to that one day off, but she might have a problem with a future day off.

He pushes the edge of the key into the palm of his hand as if he can unlock the answer there, and studies his house, which certainly represents love and family, happy memories, home sweet home, yes indeed, but also represents a crushing debt.

They bought at the most recent peak, and probably overpaid, but everyone overpays for property in Sydney. The house is not huge, but it's modern, with three bedrooms and a "study nook" (a corner), sleek pleasing lines, and was designed by an architect Leo knows who is becoming very successful.

If he dies in a workplace accident there will be a worker's compensation claim. Neve will be able to use it to pay off the mortgage. That comforts him. He considers looking up what the payout would be.

He goes inside and finds Neve at her computer, headphones on, fingers racing across the keyboard, foot tapping in time to whatever music she is listening to. The dog is asleep at her feet, then lifts his head and lazily thumps his tail in acknowledgment of Leo's presence but then goes back to sleep. The days of toddlers and puppies running excitedly to the door to greet Leo are long gone. Did he appreciate those moments enough? He knows he loved it, anticipated it as he walked inside, felt like a king.

When he first met Neve she was a primary-school teacher, but after Bridie was born she reinvented herself as a designer of corporate training programs. She works from home and her current project is a training program for NSW Fisheries. He can see a half-complete PowerPoint slide on her computer screen.

He keeps standing there like a creepy stalker, watching the words *Illegal Use of Fish Traps in Inland Riv* appear on the screen, at which point Neve senses his presence, pulls off her headphones at the same time as she swings her chair around, screams, and falls off the chair onto the floor. The dog jumps up, excited.

It's generally accepted that Bridie's dramatic tendencies come from Leo, but sometimes he really does wonder.

"What are you doing here?!" In typical Neve style, she doesn't get up right away but instead continues to lie flat on the floor while the dog nuzzles her neck. "You scared the life out of me."

"Sorry," says Leo. "I was trying to work out how not to scare you."

"Wait, you're here." She sits up suddenly. "Did you get fired?"

"Don't look *hopeful*," says Leo. "It would be a disaster if I got fired."

"Mmm, not really," says Neve airily.

"Yes, really," says Leo. "We'd have to sell the house."

"Oh, well," says Neve. "We'd work it out."

He can feel his back teeth grinding. The mortgage is not a *concept*. It's a contract.

Neve shows no sign of getting up off the floor, so Leo takes her vacated chair, and as he cleans out crumbs and dust from her keyboard (unbelievable) he says, "Do you want me to leave work because you think the psychic's prediction is going to come true? Or because you hate Lilith? Or because I'm a 'workaholic'?"

"All of the above." She sighs. "I mean, I go back and forth on the psychic depending on where I am in my cycle. When I read about the elderly couple dying, I panicked."

His phone rings. He pulls it out of his pocket and confirms that it is, of course, Lilith. He looks at Neve. She opens her mouth and quickly shuts it again.

The phone stops.

Rings again.

"I guess it's urgent," says Neve dryly.

A text message appears: *CALL ME ASAP.*

"That woman," says Neve slowly, "is a bully."

Leo taps one knuckle against his lip. "There could be a crisis of some sort."

"You're in an abusive workplace relationship."

Leo feels his face heat up. It's as though she has pointed out something unmanly and unforgivably weak about him.

"That's not true," he says. Is it true?

"You work like a dog seven days a week."

"I work like a *dog*?"

He looks at the dog, who has never worked a day in his life.

The phone rings again. Leo can't stand it. He snatches it up. "Lilith?"

"Just checking in," says Lilith. "I hear you're working from home this afternoon? One of the children sick this time?"

"No." Leo clears his throat. "It just made more sense to come back here after—"

"What a relief! Have you seen that email about the cost overruns? *Little* bit of a concern."

"Ah, not yet." It must surely have been sent in the last five minutes. He can hear the clink of glassware. Is she out to lunch?

"How's the lovely Neve? She at home with you now?"

"She is," says Leo. "She works from—"

"That's so nice, spending time together in the middle of the day! Give her my love, won't you. Let's just make sure we stay on top of things, it's a crucial time, but I know I don't need to tell you that."

The phone goes dead. "Lilith sends her love," says Leo.

Neve sits cross-legged on the floor, looking up at him like a diligent student attempting to answer a tricky question.

"Do you really think I'm in an 'abusive' work relationship?" he asks.

Neve exhales. She pats the dog for a reflective few seconds and finally lifts her chin. "I remember how excited you were seeing your projects built. I remember when we drove past that overpass down south and you explained how you had to solve some issue with the piers. You were so happy about the piers!"

"The abutments," says Leo. "The height of the abutments, it was tricky because I had to—"

"That's okay, honey, I don't need to hear it all again, as fascinating as it was. My point is, I loved how you loved your work, I loved that about you."

"But now you don't love it anymore," guesses Leo. "Because I work too—"

"I don't think *you* love it anymore."

"What? I still enjoy my work," says Leo defensively.

"I don't think you do. Sometimes I think you don't enjoy your life that much. I think you're in a constant state of terror."

"*Terror?* Come on."

"She's got all of you. There's nothing left for us. Even when you're with us, you're not really with us. You're thinking about work."

"I'm not allowed to let a single thought about work cross my mind when I'm with my family?" He knows that's childish. He's also thinking about that cost overruns email right now.

Neve doesn't bother to answer. She gets to her feet and brushes dog hair off her pants. "Speaking of work, I should get back to my fishery trainees." She points at her computer.

Leo remains sitting in her chair. "So that's it, you're going to make all these allegations—"

"They're not allegations, they're just thoughts, and maybe I'm wrong about everything, maybe Lilith is a lovely, inspiring woman and I'm just . . . maybe I'm jealous? She looks so good in a pantsuit. Maybe I'm just tired? Maybe I'm scared to death about the fucking— excuse the language—psychic. I don't know. Give me my chair back, please."

He stands. He can't work out how to feel. He can't defend himself because Neve has effectively withdrawn all her comments. The woman is an evil genius.

She sits back at the desk, puts her hand on the mouse, then she swivels around.

"If you knew you really were going to die when you were forty-three, what would you do?"

He sighs. "I *promise* you there will be no workplace accident."

"But if you got a terminal diagnosis. If you were given, I don't know, six months to live—and money was no object and you still felt okay—how would you want to spend your time?"

He answers honestly.

"Nothing too crazy. I'd just want to hang out with you and the kids, with Mum and my sisters." He pauses as he really considers it. "So we really don't need to worry about money in this hypothetical scenario?"

"Leo. I just said. Forget about money."

"If only we could," says Leo. "But in that case, I would resign."

The thought of resigning makes his chest expand with air, as if he's just been released from a chokehold.

"I'd probably ask you if we could please move back to Tasmania," he says.

"Really?" says Neve. "Interesting. And what would we do there?"

"Well, the kids shouldn't miss school just because I'm hypothetically dying. We could just . . . relax. Maybe not so much rushing about, if that's possible. Maybe it's not possible. But Oli and I could do the

Bay of Fires walk. I'd like to take you for a weekend to that lodge in Coles Bay. And if I'm doing special trips with each of you then I would take Bridie to a musical in Melbourne, that would be so fun." He considers. "If money is no object, we could do one of those European river cruises!" He's getting into it now. "I'd call—" He catches himself, stops talking abruptly.

"Who would you call?"

"Doesn't matter."

She looks up at him. "Leo, I know who you would call."

He turns away. "I've got work to do and I don't have a terminal disease, which is *good* news."

"I've got his number. I can give you his number right now."

He feels sick. "I don't want his number. This was hypothetical."

"Let's do everything." Neve stands and puts her hands on his shoulders and gently shakes him. "Every single thing you just said, we can do. Except for the river cruise, you don't want to do a river cruise, you idiot, you'd go stir-crazy, you'd jump overboard."

"Neve, we can't do all those things."

"Yes we can." She pokes him in the middle of his chest with her index finger, a little harder than he expects. "Yes. We. Can."

Chapter 83

I like to tell people my first job was counting gray kangaroos because I think they imagine me in the outback, lying on my stomach, wearing an Akubra hat, peering through a pair of binoculars, and clicking a counter with my thumb each time a kangaroo bounded across the horizon.

The reality was far less glamorous. Reality tends to be far less glamorous.

I was employed by the National Parks and Wildlife Service as a junior biometrician.

A biometrician, if you don't know, applies statistical analysis to biological data. I was there to help my boss study Australia's population of western grey kangaroos.

The western grey kangaroo is one of the largest species of kangaroo. They are nicknamed "stinkers" because mature males have an unpleasant smell. During breeding season, the males compete for the females in a kind of boxing contest where they lock arms and try to push each other over, like sumo wrestlers.

Look, I'm not an expert on the western grey kangaroo, I just collected a few "fun facts" because people expect me to be one. The truth is, I could have been counting frogs or crocodiles or tubes of toothpaste. The math would have been the same.

Most of my time was spent at a desk, ecstatically analyzing data. When I first started I used a slide rule. I know this makes me sound ancient. But we all have to sound ancient at some point. Scientific calculators were about to make the slide rule obsolete, but I resisted for longer than most. By the time I left, every desk had a computer.

It was solitary work, but I was well suited to solitary work, and I couldn't believe I got paid to sit at a desk and do my favorite thing: problem-solving. To be paid to do what I once did so joyfully for free with Dad at the kitchen table! Nobody in my family could believe it either.

There was also occasional fieldwork required, which got me out of the office to see how my models were applied in the real world. I had to travel for my work! It felt very important, although I certainly wasn't staying in fancy hotels with breakfast buffets but in the corrugated-iron staff quarters of some of Australia's largest sheep and cattle stations.

Those big open landscapes gave me a not unpleasant sensation of vertigo. I enjoyed the feeling of being small and insignificant. It's healthy to be reminded of your insignificance.

I enjoyed talking to the farmers' wives. They were often "city girls," desperate for company, and once I had overcome my initial shyness, I was pretty chatty (as you would have noticed by now—although if you meet me at a noisy, crowded party, you may still find me odd).

(On that note, I recently watched a fascinating documentary about the making of the charity single "We Are the World," in 1985. There was the legendary Bob Dylan, surrounded by other "iconic pop stars," and he looked *exactly* like me at a party! Kind of hunted. Wanting the ground to swallow him up. Poor darling Bob Dylan! And then beautiful Stevie Wonder helped him overcome his nerves and sing his solo by impersonating Bob's unique style. He meant, *Just be you, Bob Dylan.*)

(It's the answer to many a question: Just be you. It sounds easy, but it seems even icons struggle to be their iconic true selves.)

There was one woman who invited me in for tea and scones. Very thin with wild curly red hair and watery green eyes. Her name was Suzanne. It was clear she was unhappy in her marriage. She reassured me, "He's not violent." She lowered her voice and said, "He just shouts, that's all. I'm not keen on the shouting."

She told me her mother had said to her, "You've made your bed, Suzanne, now you've got to lie in it."

She was older than me and clearly more sophisticated. I could see she was the sort of person who went to galleries and museums and stopped in front of paintings to make intelligent remarks. She didn't belong in the country. It seemed to me she'd accidentally fallen into the wrong life. In normal circumstances she probably would never have shared such personal information with someone like me, but she was lonely and bored and phone calls can't replace having another woman sit across the kitchen table from you, drinking your tea and eating scones. The scones, by the way, were rock-hard. The Country Women's Association and my grandma would not have approved.

I put down my teacup and did something that shocked me.

I asked her if she'd like me to read her palm. I told her my mother and grandmother were well-known palm readers and implied I had the same skills.

It's interesting when you suddenly behave out of character.

An example: I went tandem skydiving for my sixtieth birthday. It was exhilarating!

Obviously, I will never go skydiving again.

Not if you paid me. I still have nightmares about it.

Suzanne's was the first palm I ever read. As a child I never mimicked my mother or grandmother by pretending to read palms or see the future. I never read my friend Ivy's palm. I never read Jack's palm, not even when he left for Vietnam, which you'd think I would have done if I believed there was any chance it might have told me something.

Not believing had become an important part of my identity. After

Dad died, I never asked Mum to read my tea leaves. I swore allegiance to the sensible side of the family. The same side as Dad, Auntie Pat, and Grandpa.

And yet here I was, my hand out, waiting for her to give me hers, and Suzanne did, without hesitation, and I recognized the expression on her face because I had seen it on the faces of so many of my mother's customers: equal parts skeptical and hopeful, a nonbeliever desperate to believe.

It was strange how easily it came to me. It was strange, too, the sense of power I felt. My breathing slowed and my voice became deeper. Even as I had been scoffing, I had apparently been learning. There was no door to the back veranda where Mum saw her customers, just a purple curtain that she drew to give the illusion of privacy. I could hear every word, and in that first year after Dad died, I lay on the floor on my stomach and listened in, not because I was impressed by Mum's skills but because I was enthralled by the intimate, grown-up details her customers shared about their broken hearts, their disappointing sex lives, their pain, their dreams of something better, something more, something *different*.

I heard myself telling Suzanne, with absolute confidence, that her lifeline had nothing to do with the length of her life but with the richness of experiences that were in her future, and hers was deep, so there were many, many experiences ahead of her.

All of Mum's customers had rich experiences in their future.

I said her broken heart line suggested she would have multiple partners in her life.

Then I said those words I'd heard Mum say to some women, with more conviction than any of her other predictions.

I said, "I see you leaving."

I see you leaving. It's what my mother would say to women who cried into soggy, balled-up handkerchiefs while they asked, "Will I ever be happy, Madame Mae?"

She'd say it over and over, at every reading: *I see you leaving, I see you leaving, I see you leaving.* Until finally they saw themselves leaving too.

Some of her customers had violent husbands, and Mum's predictions for those women became very specific and instructive: "I see you packing a bag *without him knowing*. I see you catching the train to Gosford. I see you going to the first phone booth you find and dialing a number that I am writing down for you now. I see you never going back. I see you finding happiness and peace."

Well, those women weren't stupid. They knew Mum had slipped from fortune teller to counselor, but they nodded along respectfully and took the number for Mum's old schoolfriend Dulcie, who, with her mother, ran a kind of unofficial women's refuge on the Central Coast and helped many women and their children get back on their feet. Some of Mum's customers did exactly as she suggested and some of them only temporarily changed their destinies and returned to their unhappy marriages.

When I came back to the office after that field trip I was overcome with shame. I could not believe I'd taken that woman's hand in mine and behaved as I had. It was like I'd been drunk. Perhaps I got myself drunk on a shot of power. The power of Madame Mae. Seeing the truth *I* wanted to see and the future *I* thought was right for her. Perhaps she and her husband just needed better communication! Did she even ask him to please stop shouting? Perhaps he had hearing problems like my grandfather and didn't realize he shouted. What if she ruined her life because of my reckless meddling?

I never heard if she left, and I didn't read another palm for many years after that.

My boss with the musical Scottish accent was Scottish but of Pakistani descent. His name was Baashir and he was the first openly gay person I had ever met, if you don't count Don, the gorgeous gay character on *Number 96*. To be honest I *do* count Don. Gosh, I was fond of Don.

Baashir's passion was travel. He'd taken two years to reach Australia from Scotland. He'd hitchhiked all over Europe and North

Africa, via Greece, Turkey, the Middle East, India, Iran, Nepal, and Thailand. He planned to work in Australia for two years, and then take another two years to make his way back to Scotland.

Before I met Baashir, "travel" wasn't in my vocabulary except as a way to get places. The only people I knew who had left Australia did so to fight wars. Air travel at the time was impossibly expensive. Nobody took "gap years."

Baashir had no photos to show me. No slides, either. Thank goodness. If you think your friends post too many photos of their travels on social media, be grateful you won't ever have to sit in their living room watching those photos projected onto a wall while you eat hard cheese and cocktail onions. Those have been some of the longest nights of my life.

Anyhow, Baashir just told me stories, about visiting the Taj Mahal at sunrise, soaking in the steaming hot springs in Iceland, camping just outside of Cairo, eating crisp perfect Wiener schnitzel in the world's oldest restaurant in Salzburg. He was like a carpet salesman, unfurling rug after rug, each more exquisite than the last.

The only travel I'd ever done was to see the Big Banana in Coffs Harbour.

Baashir very kindly listened to my detailed description of the Big Banana. Everything interested Baashir. Curiosity is such an attractive quality. He said he would have to check it out. I said I wasn't sure how it would stack up against the Taj Mahal.

I never overhear a Scottish accent without quickly turning in the irrational hope that it may be Baashir. He gave me my first job, an interest in travel, a taste for red wine, and he invited me to a Swiss fondue party, which supposedly "changed my destiny."

I consider that phrase to be a logical fallacy.

Don't try to be funny, Cherry.

Chapter 84

It is Sue's sixty-fourth birthday and her family seems to be treating it as her wake, even though she is not only alive but apparently in perfect health: Caterina has sent her for still more tests, and nobody can find anything wrong with her. Nothing more can be done. She can't be treated for an illness she doesn't have.

"Your psychic has got it wrong," said Caterina. "I would bet on my life you're not a candidate for pancreatic cancer. You're just not. She's wrong."

"I agree," says Sue, and she truly does agree. She feels in excellent health, possibly the best health of her life. When she was bringing up the boys and working full-time she hovered permanently on the edge of exhaustion or possibly a nervous breakdown, and then along came menopause, which put her through the wringer, it really did, but for the last few years she's felt great. Not a single niggling symptom to worry her, and if she'd been asked that question in her fifties she could have listed a dozen. Honestly, she feels like she might be in better health than a lot of people at this party. Her youngest son, for example, has that run-down, glassy-eyed look he used to get after a sleepover. He's thirty-five, so she can't put him to bed, but gosh, she'd love to clap her hands and say, "Early night for you, buddy!"

They are at the family home in Summer Hill, the one that Sue and

Max bought forty years ago for a price that everyone now considers inconceivably cheap, but did not feel that way at the time. It was a damp, dark Federation cottage and Sue secretly hated it; it was years before they had the money and the time to turn it into the light-filled "character home" it is today.

Sue looks around her living room, where she and Max sit side by side in the middle of their faux-leather IKEA couch while their family swirls about them. "No! It's your birthday!" people keep saying when she goes to do something. Her glass is refilled. Platters of food she did not prepare are offered to her.

"You look great, Mum," said her eldest when he kissed her hello today, with a note of surprise.

"Darling, you know I don't actually *have* a terminal illness," she reminded him.

"And she's not getting one!" said her son's wife. "This psychic stuff is *ridiculous*. I don't believe a word of it!" Then her eyes filled with tears and she threw her arms around Sue and told her in a choked whisper that she was more of a mother to her than her own mother.

The rule in their family is no presents for adults except on milestone birthdays, but everyone has arrived with an elaborately wrapped gift accompanied by a heartfelt card. Sue is touched but annoyed by the expenditure of hard-earned money.

This is a preview of how her family would respond if she truly was struck by a serious illness, and of course everyone is behaving as themselves, just more so. The positive thinkers think positively, the worriers worry. Her husband, bless him, is the most worried but pretending the hardest not to be. Max is always frenetic with delight when the whole family is over and the house is filled with children running this way and that, while he plays music, tells dad jokes, and presides over the barbecue, but today he vibrates with so much energy it's like he's on speed.

The problem is that the boys and their partners have insisted that neither Sue nor Max do anything today, no barbecue, they haven't even been allowed to bake a cake. Sue knows they are doing this out of love and worry, but it means there is nowhere for Max to put all his pent-up energy.

"You know I'm fine," Sue keeps telling him.

"Of course you're fine," he says. "Why wouldn't you be?"

Well, he knows why. Like the rest of her family, except for the littler grandchildren, he saw the video of the girl in the car and he read about the elderly doctors.

Her youngest grandchild, a curly-haired toddler, reaches a sticky hand toward Sue's knee, and she doesn't try to save her good pants, just lets him grab her and hoists him up onto her lap. He presses the same sticky hand against her cheek and looks romantically into her eyes. A droplet of dribble hovers on his rosebud lips. His teeth are tiny, perfectly spaced pearls.

"Hello, beautiful boy," she says. She turns to Max so he can join her in shared wonder, but Max is looking at their two oldest sons on the other side of the room, their heads both bent over their phones, their expressions serious.

"What are you two looking at?" he says, a little roughly. "What's going on?"

Both men look up from their phones, both of them shove their phones guiltily into their jeans pockets, the dents of their dimples still visible in their unsmiling cheeks.

"It's nothing, Dad," says Callum.

"It's something," says Max. "Is it to do with your mother? Is it another—?"

Death. He means, *Is it another death?*

"No," says Callum. "Definitely not. Nobody else has died."

"Someone has set up a page on social media," says his brother. "That's all. For passengers who were on that flight."

"That's a good idea," says Sue. She holds out her hand. "Let me see it."

"It's not that interesting."

"So there *has* been another death?" says Sue.

"No," says Callum. He grimaces. "It's just that she's correctly predicted someone's diagnosis."

"Another lucky guess, that's all that is!" says Max.

"*Unlucky* guess," murmurs Sue as her grandson, sensing tension,
slithers off her lap and toddles off to find a parent.

Sue licks her finger and wipes away the sticky patch he left on her
cheek. "Let me see."

Callum hands her his phone. Max and Sue both put on their
glasses and read:

> *This page is for passengers, and their concerned loved ones, who
> traveled on the delayed flight from Hobart to Sydney on Friday,
> April 21, this year and may have been approached by a psychic of-
> fering to predict their "cause and age of death."*

"Well, she didn't *offer* to predict," says Sue. "She just did it."
Max grunts in agreement.

> *Since the tragic deaths of Kayla Halfpenny, Dr. Barbara Bailey, and
> Dr. Brian Bailey were correctly predicted by the psychic, we are in-
> terested in gathering information about the experiences of other
> passengers. We are also interested in tracing the psychic herself. If
> you have any information in this regard, or if you took photos or re-
> corded footage, please post below, or if you prefer, contact us pri-
> vately.*

"Let me see who set up the page," says Sue, going to the "About
Us" section. "Such a good idea."

"Doesn't matter," mutters Max.

"Just curious," says Sue. "Oh, would you look at that, it's the bride
and the young mother! They must have teamed up. That's nice. Young
women are such go-getters."

"Thanks, Mum," says her youngest son.

"Well, you're a go-getter too, darling," says Sue. (He's really not. He skates by on his looks.)

"Sue, let me see the posts," says Max.

They read the first one together.

> *My six-year-old son was an unaccompanied minor on this flight and the airline did nothing to protect him from this deranged woman. The Death Lady told him he would live until he was ninety-four. He now truly believes himself to be invincible, and is taking unacceptable risks on a daily basis. He recently BROKE HIS ARM (see photo) while doing dangerous parkour moves in the school playground. He informed me this morning he is taking up BASE JUMPING as soon as he is old enough. This is a DIRECT RESULT of the airline's negligence.*

Sue chuckles when she sees the accompanying photo of a little boy sitting on a hospital bed with a broken arm. He looks both ecstatic and wicked. She can well believe he's a future base jumper.

"Oh, well, that's kind of funny," she says.

"Not really," says Max. "Poor kid broke his arm."

"But it's rubbish. *All* children think they're immortal! It's got nothing to do with the lady!"

Sue looks up and sees that everyone is now looking at the page, either on their own phone or on someone else's device.

She reads the next post and can't help but snort.

> *TRYING TO FIND INFORMATION! I was told by the Death Lady I would die of alcohol poisoning, but I don't recall her mentioning an age. I don't know if she forgot because she was rushing or if she spoke too softly and I didn't hear it. I understand other passengers received both an "age of death" and "cause of death." I'd like to know my full prediction! It's only fair! If anyone was sitting near me and remembers hearing my age of death please contact me ur-*

gently. I am an attractive brunette of slim but curvaceous build in my early forties. I was wearing a Dolce & Gabbana leopard-print jumpsuit. I don't recall my seat number but it was an aisle seat near the front. P.S. I have recently begun exploring a "Sober Curious" lifestyle. If anyone wants to get together for a (nonalcoholic!) drink to discuss, let me know!

"She was the one who tried to get off the plane," comments Sue. "Poor Allegra had to deal with her."

"Who is Allegra?" asks Max.

"The beautiful flight attendant, I know you remember her."

Max grunts. He does.

"The next post is kind of sweet," says her daughter-in-law.

Sue scrolls to a picture of a woman holding a gardening fork, kneeling next to a rosebush, a watering can at her side, grinning at the camera, with a caption that says: *I GAVE UP MY MARRIAGE AND MY CAREER THANKS TO THE DEATH LADY!*

Sue recognizes her. She was the red-faced, frizzy-haired woman who suddenly called out, "Oh, can't someone do something!" during the delay when the baby wouldn't stop crying.

I don't know if the Death Lady will ever see this page, but if she does, I want to thank her. I have never believed in psychics, but when she told me I only had nine years of my life left to live, it gave me the most amazing clarity about how I wanted to spend the time I had left. I have changed my whole life for the better. I asked myself, When are you going to start living, Philippa, WHEN? And that's when I decided there was only one answer: TODAY, PHILIPPA, TODAY!! So I packed my bags, left my unhappy marriage, and left the city! Well, first I resigned from my high-stress corporate tele-communications job! Hooray! Why did I think I had to stay there forever? I don't know! I am now working at a garden center in regional Victoria and I have a new passion for PICKLEBALL. I also

*have begun a new relationship with someone VERY SPECIAL.
I have never felt happier or healthier. Thank you, Death Lady! You
were the kick up the bum I needed! Whether I get more or less
years than you predicted, I will never regret the life changes I have
made.*

"Go, Philippa!" says one of the daughters-in-law, punching the air,
but then she winces, "Oh, gosh, this one isn't so . . . cheerful."
Sue looks back down at her phone and reads:

*Hi, everyone, my name is Geoff. My wife, Sarah, was on this flight
and was told by the psychic that she would die of breast cancer at the
age of thirty-seven.*

 She was pregnant at the time with our baby boy

"Knew it was a boy," says Sue.

*and I thought it was a disgusting thing to say to a pregnant woman,
but Sarah wasn't worried. She brushed it off. She's very tough. That
was until the news came out about the young girl who died in a car
crash. My wife is only thirty-three and has no history of breast cancer in the family. She had no symptoms, so it took some convincing
for a GP to send her for a mammogram. I think in the end she probably agreed just to shut Sarah up.*

 *To everyone's shock the mammogram did show something of a
concern. Sarah had a biopsy last week and the results came in:
"triple-negative breast cancer."*

 *It's my understanding her cancer is treatable, but we will know
more about what lies ahead when we see an oncologist tomorrow.*

 *Okay, so here is my problem: My wife is adamant she will refuse
any "invasive treatment" as she is convinced any chemo/radiation
regimen will be unsuccessful and she is going to die anyway. She
wants to spend the time she has left "celebrating life," "making
memories," and ticking off stuff on some stupid "bucket list." Sorry,*

but I have ZERO interest in "dancing under the stars" like I'm in a bloody Ed Sheeran song right now. She is writing letters to our son to be opened every year on his birthday. I want her to focus on being ALIVE for our son's birthdays!!!

My wife had a friend who endured a brutal treatment regimen for many years and ultimately died anyway. She can't stand to think of this happening to her. I understand this, but I've tried to tell her every case is different. I am hoping the oncologist will be able to convince her, but I am terrified she won't budge.

I'm grateful to this psychic because if it wasn't for her there is every chance my wife's cancer might not have been discovered until it was too late, but at the same time I'm so pissed off. I can't drag my wife to treatment. I've never been able to make her do anything she doesn't want to do. She is as stubborn as a mule.

I am desperate for any help anyone can offer tracking down this "Death Lady." I have tried the airline, but they can't do anything because of privacy issues. I am hoping she would be happy to tell my wife that even if she does have psychic abilities she is NOT one hundred percent accurate.

I am also keen to hear from anyone who may have already outlived the Death Lady's prediction, thereby proving her wrong.

Fingers crossed: Nobody is one hundred percent accurate, right?
PLEASE HELP ME SAVE MY WIFE'S LIFE.
(I loved her from the moment I saw her.)

You poor man, thinks Sue.

She thinks of her conversation with the pregnant woman in the security line, how she spoke so cheerfully about her heartburn and swollen ankles, and now she's dealing with cancer, when she should be enjoying the wonder of her first baby. Of course there's never a good time for a serious illness. Nobody has time for it. Everyone has other plans.

Sue wonders idly if she should try to get in touch with the young woman, try to help convince her to get treatment, but of course that's

ridiculous, you can't meddle in a stranger's life and she has her own
family to worry about.

Right now they all look a little shell-shocked. There is no sound
except for the giggles of her two granddaughters who are lying on
their stomachs on the floor behind a couch playing Snap with an old
pack of cards.

She says, "Well, you know, she hasn't actually died—"

"Yet," says her daughter-in-law. "She's going to make the proph-
ecy self-fulfilling."

"Which is why it doesn't prove anything," says Sue. "Because—
well. Just because." This is like one of those awful "farmer crossing a
river" puzzles, where you have to work out whether to take the wolf,
the goat, or the cabbage first. Her head is starting to hurt.

"It means nothing," says Max. "No need for anyone to stress." His
leg is jiggling up and down next to hers. "Why don't we have some
music?" Then he says unexpectedly, "Sometimes I wish we'd never
gone on that damned trip."

"But we had such a great time." Sue fiddles with the apple charm
on her bracelet that she bought as a souvenir of their trip to the "Apple
Isle." She's sad at the thought of their camper van holiday memories
being sullied.

"I know we did, darling, I'm sorry," says Max. "We had—"

He stops. Sue looks at him, to check he's not having a stroke. His
dad's last half-finished sentence was "I feel like something is not—"
before he had the massive stroke that felled him.

"Jeez." Max rubs his hand across his face as if he's rubbing in sunscreen. "This whole situation is outrageous. Nobody should be taking
it seriously. The old couple were so old!"

"Just so you all know, I would never refuse treatment," says Sue.

Nobody speaks. Her youngest son spins his phone against the side
of his chair in exactly the same way Max did on the flight. She
shouldn't have said that. Maybe that makes it seem like she now
thinks a future diagnosis is inevitable.

Max stands, pulling on the legs of his jeans. "I'll just check the . . ."

He doesn't bother finishing the sentence. They all know there is nothing for him to check.

"You can't die first, Mum," says her youngest son with forced lightness after Max has left the room. "Dad wouldn't survive without you."

"Well, he *would*," says Sue. "He'd be very sad, but he'd survive. That's life!" She grabs her grandson just before he sinks his teeth into a giant wheel of Brie. She buries her nose in his sweet-smelling hair. Her big strong grown-up sons fear death, but they also think they are somehow protected—it's so far in their futures it doesn't really exist, it's only for people unlucky enough to make the news, for people in war-torn countries and natural disasters, for sick elderly grandparents, but not for *their* young parents, not for years and years. Her boys haven't yet discovered the awful fragility of life. They don't yet know that the possibility of death is always there, sitting right alongside you.

She says, "Your dad would have no choice but to carry on."

"*Snap!*" shriek her granddaughters.

Chapter 85

I'd been working for the National Parks and Wildlife for three years when Baashir hosted a Swiss fondue party for his fortieth birthday.

Obviously I was aghast to be invited.

Baashir was my boss and my friend, and I was so fond of him it virtually qualified as a crush, but I would know no one at his party except him. I would not have Jack to count me in and I had no doubt every guest would be older, more glamorous, and more interesting than me. Chances were high I would embarrass myself by speaking too much or not at all.

I feel tenderly now toward my twenty-two-year-old self. So upset to be invited to a party! Poor darling.

Look: I don't know why I'm pretending anything has changed. Just last month I was horrified to be invited to a "coffee morning" and it must have showed on my face, because the person extending the invitation felt obliged to apologize and say, "It's not compulsory!"

Embarrassing.

(I went to the coffee morning.)

Also embarrassing: I had never heard of Swiss fondue. I thought it was a type of dance. I asked my mother if she could teach me the steps to the Swiss fondue and she and Auntie Pat laughed longer and harder than necessary. My error really made their day. Each time they stopped, one of them started up again. I don't know how they knew about fondue, it's not like they'd ever been to Switzerland.

By the way, I've been to Switzerland multiple times since then and eaten fondue in some very fancy Swiss restaurants. Just so you know.

Gosh, humiliation takes a long time to fade, doesn't it?

I got sulky and said I wasn't going to the party anyway.

"You will hurt your friend's feelings," said Auntie Pat firmly. "Be brave, Cherry."

She'd been to war, so I could hardly complain about going to a party.

"Cherry, I see this party changing your destiny," said my mother, and both Auntie Pat and I put our fingers to our lips and said, "Shhh." We didn't want to hear from Madame Mae outside of work hours. Or ever really. We both tolerated Mum's profession.

The truth is, part of me badly wanted to go to that party. I was "in a good place" as people say now. I'd emerged from the other side of my grief. I loved my work, but my days, although very pleasant, were mostly the same and even those of us who love and need routine sometimes long to break it.

I wore a blue minidress and a matching blue headband that I had been told made my eyes look blue, with white knee-high boots. My eyeshadow was also blue, and probably too liberally applied, but I was twenty-two, so I expect I looked divine.

I found a photo of myself in my mid-fifties recently and remembered the sunny spring day it was taken, and how I felt grumpy because I wasn't happy with my appearance: something to do with my dress or my hair, I can't recall what exactly. When I looked at that photo, I thought, Cherry, you looked pretty good that day, not divine, of course, but good!

Perhaps ninety-year-old Cherry will say the same things about photos of me now, but it seems unlikely.

Never mind.

Baashir lived in an apartment in Newtown with purple shag carpet, red-glowing mushroom lamps, and violently patterned wallpaper.

The air was thick with cigarette smoke, sweet with cannabis, and pungent with the aroma of melted Gruyère cheese. Three earthenware fondue pots were set up at intervals along a wooden table with long bench seats like church pews.

"I want you next to Eliza," said Baashir as he handed me a Brandy Alexander and indicated a woman already seated. She had a high ponytail, eyes made up to look like cat's eyes, and a leopard print-patterned dress with a plunging neckline. Leopard print slinks in and out of fashion, but whenever I see it I think of Eliza and her creamy cocktail dusted with nutmeg.

She held out her hand and said, "Cherry, I've heard all about you! Baashir tells me your mother is a fortune teller and you are a genius."

(I'm not a genius. Baashir didn't really think I was one. I was just good at my job.)

It was difficult to step over the long bench seat in my dress. A man with Elvis Presley sideburns in a lime-green safari suit had to help me by holding my elbow.

Well. It was a wonderful night. I don't know if it was Eliza or the Brandy Alexander or if I was inhaling too much secondhand pot smoke, but my nerves melted instantly. I talked a lot, but not too much. I remembered to listen. "Remember to listen, Cherry," Mum had said to me as I walked out the door. "Don't get overexcited." It's terrible how people can know your flaws so well.

I laughed that night like I hadn't laughed in years.

You are probably thinking I would have had nothing in common with Eliza—with her abundant cleavage, eye makeup, and charm— but you would be wrong. We soon discovered we had multiple shared interests, like the Bermuda Triangle and *Dallas*. People were excited about the Bermuda Triangle at the time because of a popular book, but Eliza and I tried to share the theory put forward by Lloyds of London: the percentage of mysterious disappearances wasn't any greater there than in any other large area of the ocean with a high volume of air traffic and multiple shipping routes. "It's simple probability!" we both said. Nobody wanted to hear us. Nobody ever does. They preferred to talk about mysterious shipwrecks and planes disappearing off the face of the earth.

We were also both addicted to the television series *Dallas* and agreed the storylines were *Shakespearean*. Bringing up Shakespeare is an excellent way to justify your enjoyment of lowbrow entertainment. Even if, like me, you only ever studied one play at school (*King Lear*) and didn't especially like or understand it. People do it all the time now. Eliza and I were way ahead of the curve.

Eliza was the same age as Baashir, forty, and she was what my mother would have called, with both mild scorn and mild envy, a "career woman."

She was working her way up the ladder in an insurance company, and corporate ladders were tricky to climb back then. She told stories about having to train baby-faced boys who completed their training and the very next day were paid more than her. There was the casual expectation that she would be the one to organize tea, coffee, and snacks, no matter how senior she became. She had to endure being regularly patted on the bottom at the photocopier and, worse, she once had a boss who literally *patted her on the head* in a meeting. "I was thirty years old, Cherry!"

Can you imagine being patted on the head in a work setting?

Well, it will depend on your age and gender.

"But the *work*, Cherry, I *love* the work," she sighed, as if she were talking about a delicious food or a lover.

I had never met an unashamedly ambitious woman like Eliza, or at least not one who had ambitions to be as successful as a man in a man's world. My mother was ambitious, although she would never have described herself that way, and she was a businesswoman too, but she was working within the framework of the world of women. It was also important to her identity to give the impression Madame Mae wasn't a "business" like Mrs. Shaw's cake shop, even though Mum kept a careful eye on cash flow, raised and dropped prices as appropriate, and even offered loyalty programs where, for example, your fifth reading was free.

Eliza reassured me that things were getting better for women in the workforce. She said, "Women in the 1980s won't be enduring that kind of sexist behavior."

If you worked in an office in the eighties, please take this moment for a hollow laugh.

I asked if Eliza was married or had children, and she said she was divorced and had never wanted children.

I was on to my third Brandy Alexander by then and I found myself leaning in close to whisper in her ear, "Eliza, I don't think I want children either."

Eliza wiped a smudge of cream from my lip and whispered, "You don't have to have children, Cherry."

I have only been attracted to a woman once in my life and this was the time.

She asked me if I'd heard Loretta Lynn's song "The Pill."

I had not, and because there was no Spotify and she was joyously drunk, she proceeded to sing it, loud enough for the whole table to hear. She got to her feet and used a fondue fork as a microphone. She changed the lyrics to "Cherry's got the pill." (Cherry did not have the pill.) Loretta's song about how the contraceptive pill had liberated women and allowed them to enjoy sex without the fear of getting pregnant was considered outrageous for the time—some radio stations refused to play it. Baashir's guests only found the song outrageous because they disliked country music. People began pelting Eliza with bread cubes to get her to stop.

When the party finally ended, in the early hours of the morning, Eliza gave me her business card. She said I should call her about a job in her division. She said, "You can't count kangaroos forever, Cherry, you should have a *career*! You and I should be together in the boardroom, patting *their* stupid heads!" She patted a still-seated man's bald head to demonstrate, and he looked up, delighted, and tried and failed to grab her wrist.

I've wondered over the years what would have happened if I had called Eliza the next day; if I might have bravely climbed that rickety ladder and got myself into a senior management position. She died only last year. She never remarried, never had children. There were obituaries in all the financial papers. Eliza was a pioneer for women in insurance, she broke that glass ceiling: she was the first female CEO of her company, and she mentored countless other women. The photos showed a woman with short gray hair and glasses in a smart suit. If you didn't know her you would never have guessed she was once a gorgeous woman in a leopard-print dress singing into a fondue fork.

Although if you looked closely enough at the photo you could still see her sparkle, right there in her eyes.

Look a little closer at the next older lady you meet. You might see that sparkle.

Or you might not. Some of us are grumpy and sad. Some of us are in serious pain: our feet, our hips, our shoulders. Some of us are crazed with grief and regret for wrong decisions.

Never mind.

I didn't call Eliza the next day. It was years before I called her.

I never climbed that corporate ladder.

This is what I did instead:

I married the man in the lime-green safari suit.

Chapter 86

Ethan wakes on the morning of his thirtieth birthday to the sound of his phone beeping and Harvey's voice in his ear saying: *Didn't you think we would have achieved more by the time we turned thirty?*

"I'm blocking you from my brain, Harvey," he says out loud.

The text message is from an unknown number. It's Harvey's sister, Lila.

Thought about sending this from Harvey's phone but didn't want to freak you out. Happy 30th! (Saw it in Harvey's calendar.) I think you were his best mate. He might not have been yours. I know he could be kind of . . . Harvey. Anyway, here's a Harvey kind of pic I took for your pleasure.

It's a meaningless blurry close-up picture of a fence post. It's so Harvey that Ethan laughs out loud and then bursts into tears, and he keeps crying while he's showering and shaving and he thinks: *For fuck's sake, when will this be DONE?*

By the time he's ready for work, he is fine again. That's it, Harvey. No more, mate. I've got stuff to do. A life to live.

It's a good birthday. For a Monday. He suspects he gets more gifts and attention because people know his friend died, and also because some people genuinely think he hasn't got long to live. All the women on his team give him gifts with which to protect himself in a fight: a self-defense keychain with a "super-loud" personal alarm, a pepper spray in its own leather pouch, and something called a "multifunction stealth knife." They are clearly all designed for women as they are in pastel colors. The women present them as joke gifts, but then explain how they work. It is sweet and also terrifying.

When he gets home, the place smells of the chili Jasmine has been cooking for the nachos, and they eat crackers and black bean dip and drink strong margaritas in big glasses with salted rims. Jasmine has, of course, holidayed in Mexico.

Her birthday gift is a cushion featuring a pencil drawing of Jason Bourne. It's a private joke present! He therefore loves it, although he has no idea what to do with it.

Ethan allows himself to pretend, just for a moment, that they are a couple, and they talk about music and movies and wonder if their expectations for *The Sopranos* are impossibly high, and then she says—and it takes him a moment to be sure he didn't just daydream her words, because they couldn't be more perfect—"Oh! I forgot to tell you! I've broken up with Carter."

It's the best birthday gift he's received since he got the Masters of Magic kit with four hundred and fifty magic tricks when he turned nine.

"Your face!" Jasmine laughs. "You look so happy!"

"I'm sorry," says Ethan. "I was actually starting to kind of like him."

"No you weren't, Jason Bourne," says Jasmine. "Anyway, *I'm* sorry. I know he was staying over here too often and leaving his stuff everywhere. I just . . . I don't know what I was thinking, everyone tells me I have the worst taste in men."

"How did he take it?" Ethan feels like he might levitate he's so happy.

"Not great," says Jasmine. "He's doing that 'you owe me closure' thing. He wants to come over and 'talk it through.' I mean, I don't have anything more to say. I'm just . . . not feeling it. How many more ways can I say it?"

"He doesn't want closure, he wants to change your mind," says Ethan. He'd want to change her mind too.

"I've spoken to him five times today," says Jasmine. "I've tried to explain—"

"You don't owe him an explanation," says Ethan. "You weren't married."

"Right, and also I don't really have an explanation," says Jasmine again. "I'm finding it a bit stressful. It feels like he's got the potential to become a bit stalkerish. God, I hate the stalkers." She sips her margarita and says, "So, what are your views on fish?"

Ethan tries to keep up. "Like your dad's fish? Frozen fish? For . . . dinner?"

"No! Yuck! Disgusting. I'd never eat my dad's fish, sorry not sorry, Dad. No, I'm talking about aquarium therapy."

"Going to an aquarium?" He could take her to an aquarium. He likes aquariums. Not as a date, of course.

She runs her finger around the rim of her margarita glass and sucks off the salt. "No, I'm talking about getting a fish tank in the apartment. Apparently looking at tropical fish for just a few seconds lowers your heart rate." She shows him her phone. "Look at this guy! Isn't he adorable? It's a guppy. Apparently they live-birth their young! We could wake up one day and find all these tiny guppy babies have been born in the night!"

Ethan is looking at the guppy fish, imagining him and Jasmine as new parents of tiny guppy fish (Well, it's something. Harvey laughs so hard), when her phone begins to peal the chimes of Big Ben (her choice of ring tone this week) and Carter's face appears on the screen.

Ethan recoils. "Oh," he says. "It's—"

She sighs. "See? Sixth call of the day."

"Don't answer," says Ethan.

"He loses his mind if I don't." She answers, avoiding Ethan's eyes. "Hey, Carter."

She listens and says, "It's okay. I know. Don't be sorry."

She twists her knuckle near her eye and sticks out her bottom lip to indicate Carter is crying. Ethan can feel Carter's pain: the shock and disbelief when you're in love and you think the other person feels exactly the same way.

Terrible. Couldn't happen to a nicer bloke. He sips his margarita to prevent the Schadenfreude from spreading across his face.

"Why aren't you at poker with your friends?" Jasmine asks. She murmurs and clucks, like a mother talking to a toddler, and then she becomes careful and conciliatory like a hostage negotiator talking to the man with the gun. Ethan searches his memory. Has any woman had to do this for him following a breakup? Surely not.

Then she says, "I'm at home. I told you. I have not met someone else. I'm just at home."

Pause.

"Yes, he's here, he lives here, you know that." She looks at Ethan. "Well, yes, we are having dinner together because it's his birthday, but as I told you a million times there is nothing going on between us, and, Carter, it is perfectly normal for a man and a woman to live together and just be friends and nothing else."

Nothing else.

Pause.

"Yeah, okay, well, you can think that if you want to think that, but it's not true. I've got to go. No. That's not why! I'm hanging up, Carter."

She puts the phone face down on the table and dips a cracker into the black bean dip. "Carter says happy fucking birthday."

Ethan nods his thanks. "Sounds like he's really applying the ancient philosophy of Stoicism."

Jasmine splutters on her cracker, and then they are both laughing and it's maybe the best moment of Ethan's whole life, but that's when the apartment buzzer starts going off, over and over, over and over, like an alarm warning of something cataclysmic.

He doesn't need to say, *Is that Carter?* The fear on her face is his answer.

Here we go, thinks Ethan, and it feels just like after he kicked that soccer ball and watched it arc across the sky, heading inevitably, unavoidably, toward that Year 11 kid's big boofhead, and there was literally nothing he could do to change his terrible future.

Ethan has never enjoyed movie prequels because the ending is predetermined. All the way through the movie you know the villain is going to end up the villain. Sure, you might know his backstory now, you might feel a bit sorry for him now, but no plot twist can change his ending.

If Jasmine is in actual danger from her ex-boyfriend, tonight or at some other time, Ethan will have to put her life first. That's what Jason Bourne would do. That's what Ethan Chang will do.

Of course he will.

He hopes he will, because right now that buzzer sounds like a chainsaw, and he's honestly not feeling especially brave.

Guys like us aren't action heroes.

Chapter 87

David Smith. That was his name. It was one of the most common names in Australia at the time, and remains so. Perhaps your accountant or pharmacist or optometrist is a David Smith.

Anyhow, I shall tell you about my David Smith.

His name was dull, but his face was not. It was a striking face. A beautiful face. His father was British and his mother was Korean, and David had inherited his mother's eyes and black hair and his father's patrician nose and strong shoulders. His Elvis Presley sideburns were something to behold.

He was not as tall as Jack. Not so tall that people said "Goodness, you're tall." David was appropriately, authoritatively tall. We had exchanged a few polite comments at the Swiss fondue party, but I was too enthralled by Eliza to take much notice of him, and he knew the couple sitting opposite, so he mostly talked to them.

Anyhow, when it was time to leave somebody asked how I was getting home, and I said I would be catching a bus and train. No Ubers back then, of course, and taxis were only for wealthy people and special occasions. However, Baashir came over all paternal and frantic, "Young Cherry must not walk the city streets alone! Just *look* at her!"

That's when David spoke up. He said he lived close to Hornsby, and it would be no trouble and his pleasure to drive me home. Everyone except me was thrilled to have the problem solved. I had become suddenly exhausted. I did not think I could manage to make conversation with a strange albeit handsome man on what would be an hour's drive, all the way home from Newtown to Hornsby. If you are a fellow introvert you will understand. We're all the rage these days. Movie stars regularly describe themselves as introverted while being charismatic on talk shows.

The night had become chilly. David had a Ford Falcon, which smelled very masculine, like leather and cologne. His cologne was Ralph Lauren Polo Green. He put the heater on full blast, switched on an easy listening radio station, and didn't try to make conversation at all. He turned out to be a man who never made conversation for the sake of it and I always appreciated that about him.

You can probably guess what happened when I got into that quiet warm car.

Yes, that's right, I fell asleep.

I'd only told David the name of my street, so rather than waking me to ask for directions, he pulled over, got his street directory out of the glove box and looked up Bridge Street. I had not given him the street number, but he looked for, and found, the MADAME MAE sign on the letterbox. (Madame Mae had been a hot topic of conversation at the party. People were always interested in Mum's profession.)

"Cherry," he said quietly, and he touched my arm. "We're here."

I woke, and was confused and grateful to be home. I thanked him and he asked for my telephone number, which of course I gave him. He took me out to dinner the following weekend to an Italian restaurant in Glebe. That's the night when I wore my green crocheted dress. That's the night he called me a "bombshell" while he refilled my wineglass and said, "Tell me your life story, Cherry."

It's also the night I lost my virginity on a giant waterbed in Wahroonga.

Please don't worry about the refilling of the wineglass. I consented.

Goodness me, I consented.

My apologies if that was too graphic.

It's just that my relationship with David Smith was based very much on desire. It was truly all that mattered. Desire can be powerful enough to sweep away everything in its path: your good sense, your Catholic upbringing, your plans for the next day. It was all I thought about. You may be at a stage in your life where you have forgotten this, and even the word "desire" might aggravate you.

I understand that too. (But deep down you remember, don't you? I bet you do.)

Depending on your age and religious beliefs, you may also be confused. You may be thinking, What the heck? Why didn't you sleep with Jack Murphy, Cherry? Wasn't he your soulmate and wasn't it the era of free love?

Yes, I'm always confused when I watch those documentaries with the stoned happy hippies swaying in the fields. That wasn't my seventies. My friend Ivy occasionally wore a flower in her hair, but that was about it. Jack and I were well-behaved, conventional, conservative Catholics in suburban Sydney and we had made a mutual decision to wait until we married.

I think it was mutual.

Once I told Auntie Pat I felt guilty Jack died without ever experiencing sex. This was after I realized exactly what I had deprived him of. What kind of God would have approved of that? I thought she might tell me she felt the same way about the man she lost in the war, but I caught a look on her face and I understood she had not made him wait. I felt like a fool, once again taking the rules too seriously. She also pointed out, which I did not appreciate, that it was entirely possible Jack *did* have sex at some point in his life, just not with me.

He didn't.

Anyhow.

David was a junior cardiologist. That night at the Italian restaurant he told me about the widow-maker heart attack, how when the left anterior descending artery becomes blocked, it kills without mercy, and how the heart surgeon races against time to unblock the artery, restore blood flow, and save a life. He said all this while he held my hand and took my pulse. He was always taking my pulse, to prove what he could do to my heart: make it race, make it skip a beat. He said the heart skipped a beat when the upper or lower chambers contracted slightly earlier than normal and it wasn't anything to worry about, it just meant we should go home to his waterbed in Wahroonga.

We were married a little over a year after the Swiss fondue party.

It was a beautiful wedding and I was very happy with my hair, flowers, and dress. The only stain on the day was that little pollen stain on my hem, and that didn't matter.

Our honeymoon was at a resort in Thailand: blue water, blue swimming pools, blue skies. Dinner the first night was an amazing seafood buffet, like nothing I had seen before. There were platters of glistening oysters, mounds of prawns—

I'm sorry.

Please give me a moment.

I'm afraid I can't offer any more details as I feel queasy. I have avoided seafood ever since. I'm sure you have already guessed what happened.

You are correct. I suffered the most shocking case of food poisoning. I have never experienced anything like it before or since. David was fine. It must have been something only I had the misfortune to eat or the foolishness to choose from the buffet.

I thought I was going to die. I actually had no idea it was possible to be that violently ill.

David looked after me, of course he did, and made sure I did not become dehydrated or die, but he was a cardiologist, not a nurse.

He wasn't unkind. Just brisk. Certainly not cruel.

I'm trying very hard to be accurate here.

David was driven by self-interest. It was at the heart of everything he did.

Every one of us is driven by self-interest, of course.

Never mind. I'm not sure what point I am trying to make. It's something to do with *convenience*. I discovered on my honeymoon that David preferred not to be inconvenienced. Ever.

When he drove me home after the Swiss fondue party and so kindly let me sleep rather than waking me to ask for directions, I got an impression of him that turned out to be somewhat inaccurate. That can happen. I guess that was before he'd got me into his waterbed.

He did not exactly blame me for the food poisoning, but he did say under his breath: "Never eat the oysters at a buffet." He said this as if it were a truism, a rule of life that everyone knew except me. But he *saw* me eat them and never said a word! They were the first oysters I'd ever eaten! He made jokes about them being an aphrodisiac!

Anyhow, we agreed there was no point both of us having a terrible time so he signed up for lots of resort activities, which was sensible. One such activity was scuba diving. He fell in love with it. He canceled the other activities and decided our honeymoon was the perfect opportunity to complete a five-day Learn to Dive course.

Never mind, I thought, as I lay with my cheek pressed to the cold bathroom tiles. At least one of us is having a good honeymoon.

But on the fourth day, when I had recovered enough to lie on a deck chair out in front of our "villa" while David was out doing his first open-water dive, I found myself looking at the horizon and thinking of Jack Murphy and wondering if he would have been good in bed. I decided he would most likely have been marvelous.

Try not to think about former boyfriends while on your honeymoon. It's never a good sign.

Chapter 88

It's five a.m. on a Tuesday morning and Sue lies in bed, curled on her side, her pillow clutched to her stomach, while she watches the light in the room change. Max sleeps beside her, his back against hers, snoring the way he has snored throughout their marriage: soft and regular, in perfect time, like the ticking of a grandfather clock.

Something is not right.

It started the day after her wake-like birthday party. A kind of dull ache in her stomach. She put it down to eating too much spicy food at the party and drinking more than usual due to stress. It was just her middle-aged digestive system not being able to cope with a party. It was not a sign of something terrible. She told no one, went to work, and the feeling came and went, and she convinced herself it was all in her head. That night she had a long bubble bath, unusual for her, tried to make herself relax, went to bed early, told herself it was psychosomatic.

But the next day she felt even worse, and the pain seemed to be moving, possibly radiating into her back, and then: itchiness.

Itchy skin is on the list, along with abdominal pain, loss of appetite, fatigue, nausea, and vomiting. The awful list: *Early signs of pancreatic cancer.* The list that means it's happening. The Death Lady's prediction is coming true, just like all the others. *No getting off that roller coaster.* People used to say that to her when she was pregnant.

Sue has not mentioned her symptoms to anyone. Of course, she will take action very soon, but once she says the words out loud it will set everything in motion. There will be no going back. Appointments, forms, tests, and procedures. Poking and prodding. Pain and pain relief. Prescriptions, medication, side effects, medication for the side effects, more side effects. There will be waiting: for results, for phone calls, for treatment plans, for busy people to get back to her. There will be nothing else but the disease. She just wants a few more moments in her beautiful normal life. She now understands the pregnant woman from the plane and her desire to simply ignore her diagnosis, especially if she believes that she is ultimately going to die anyway. Sue sees it in the face of every patient at her work: Let me get back to my life, I don't belong here, I don't want to be here, I have things to do. They tell her what they were busy doing just before their life was interrupted by this trip to the ER. They want her to know: Out there I am somebody.

The nausea swells and recedes.

She was so lucky with all her pregnancies. No nausea at all. She got pregnant easily and she coped well. She's been lucky with her health. She's never had an operation. She's only been in the hospital to give birth.

Your luck has to run out sometime.

What's that awful statistic? One in two people will develop some form of cancer at some point in their life. It's her turn.

She finds herself thinking about their honeymoon. Not exactly glamorous. They drove to the Seal Rocks Caravan Park in Max's ute. It was all they could afford at the time. Her sons would never consider anything less than a tropical resort for a honeymoon. That's how it goes. Each new generation has higher expectations. Goodness knows what the grandchildren will expect for their honeymoons. A trip to the moon! Funny. She won't be there. She won't see them grow up. She got to see the kids grow up. Some people don't get that.

Gosh, though, how could their honeymoon have been any better? Salty skin and the smell of frying bacon and the sound of the waves and the stars twinkling down at them through the caravan skylight. Laughing in bed. They've always done a lot of laughing in bed.

She realizes she is thinking about their honeymoon because she and Max woke up each morning on their honeymoon at this time, when the light had this exact dreamlike quality, and they'd have dreamlike sex, and then fall back to sleep again.

Not that she feels like sex now, of course. God. She couldn't think of anything worse.

She reaches for her phone on the nightstand and checks the Death Lady Facebook page again. Maybe there will finally be good news.

A passenger has posted a photo of the lady. She has one arm out-stretched, ballerina straight, her mouth open, as if she is making an accusation. She looks noble. Like Joan of Arc. Sue doesn't remember her seeming noble. She remembers how she thought the lady seemed nice and ordinary, like someone she would know from her aqua aerobics class. Clearly, she's *not* an ordinary person. Clearly, she has extraordinary, terrifying, supernatural powers.

The caption says: PLEASE SHARE. DO YOU KNOW THE DEATH LADY??

There are multiple comments underneath.

> She looks like my first boss at the Commonwealth Bank. Mrs. Burnett. Back when we didn't use first names in the workplace! I actually thought she'd died years ago but it's possible I'm wrong.

> I know her. That's SALLY VANDENBURG. She was my local pharmacist when I lived in Hurstville. A very nice lady. Surprised she got into this line of work.

> That's my former Math Teacher's wife! Or her identical twin! Can't remember her name, sorry. Scary experience for those of you on the flight but she is obviously a fraud, don't let it upset you, get on with your lives, nobody knows what tomorrow may bring.

Pretty sure I know her. She threw a spring roll at me when I lived in Perth many years ago. For no apparent reason! Can't remember her name. Very rude hysterical person.

Can't help with identity of the Death Lady but my business partner and I met on that flight and came up with the idea for a new protein shake business. Follow the link for more details about Phil & Pete's Protein Shakes!

She reminds me of a woman who read my palm many years ago and told me I'd leave my marriage and find happiness. She turned out to be right. I'm sorry I don't remember her name and it may not even be her.

I am a psychic medium and spirit guide with over thirty years' experience. This is not the behavior of a genuine medium. Here is my link if you are interested in dealing with a professional.

Sue puts the phone back down. The nausea rises. She's reminded of labor pains.

"Sue?" Max wakes. "What's the matter?"

"I'm sick," she says. "I'm feeling really sick."

Max is out of bed in one swift movement. He puts his hand to her forehead.

"Need the—"

"Got it." He's back, lightning fast, with the infamous yellow bucket that has been used for decades of tummy bugs and too much party food and teenage boys making their first disastrous experiments with alcohol.

He is calm. He can't handle the *anticipation* of a crisis, but once the crisis is happening, he deals with it. Both his grandfathers were war heroes. Her darling husband has heroism in his blood.

He adjusts the quilt over her shoulders, brushes her hair out of her eyes. Her husband the plumber is actually an excellent nurse. She always forgets this because she is so rarely ill.

"I'm very sick," she says pitifully.

She also always forgets that she, the nurse, is a terrible patient: needy, whiny, not at all brave. She groans, puts her head into the bucket, and feels the comforting pressure of his hand on her back.

"I know, darling," he says. "We'll get you better."

He sounds so assured and confident, Sue almost believes him.

Chapter 89

The first year of my marriage to David Smith was blissfully happy!

You know, I really didn't see all that much of him.

He worked long hours and there was also his new passion for scuba diving: a time-consuming hobby. All that left time for was sex, and we always excelled in that department.

We lived in David's house, now also my house, in Wahroonga: a lush, leafy, cool, and shady parkland-like village, with trees that soared like skyscrapers and better-dressed, better-paid people than in Hornsby. Hornsby seemed a little *scrubby* to me now when I went back home. Wahroonga is actually only two train stops away from Hornsby, but you would think I had moved from a country town to a thriving metropolis.

The house was the color of clotted cream, a small, charming Edwardian-style bungalow with polished floorboards, ceiling roses, and bay windows. Mum and Auntie Pat were always in raptures over the abundant blue hydrangeas that lined the curved path to my front door. I considered them old-lady flowers, but I loved feeling grown-up and gracious as I gave them each a bunch with the stems wrapped in aluminum foil to take home with them.

It breaks my heart to remember the pleasure and seriousness with which I arranged and rearranged our wedding gifts in my clotted-cream house, like a child playing with her toys. *Oh, Cherry*, I think, *you dear little idiot.* I can still remember the weight and heft of a crystal bowl with no discernible purpose, the new cutlery so shiny I could see my face in the dessert spoons, the twelve-place dinner set: giant plates, smaller plates, side plates, so many, many plates upon which to serve so many different types of food! Each item seemed to anchor and validate me. I was a handsome surgeon's wife with a double degree and an interesting job that no one had suggested I needed to give up just now I was married (I was a career woman!), a twelve-piece dinner set, and a fantastic sex life. I owned place mats and saucepans. I wore a diamond ring. I had it all worked out. One day I would host a dinner party for twelve. Not yet, of course. First I would improve my cooking skills.

David's parents, who had, by the way, helped him buy the house, lived directly across the road from us. Neither of these two facts was mentioned by David in the early days of our relationship.

"I predict trouble," said my mother when she discovered the extremely close proximity of my in-laws.

"I don't remember making an appointment, Madame Mae," I said.

"Make sure you start as you mean to go on," she said. "Make your boundaries clear."

The day after we got back from our honeymoon, David went off to investigate a scuba-diving club in Manly, and while he was out my in-laws turned up on the doorstep. My father-in-law carried a toolbox so he could do any jobs that needed doing. My mother-in-law carried two fragrant covered baking dishes. I had just got my appetite back after the incident with the you-know-what.

(The oysters.)

(In case you'd forgotten.)

I threw the door wide open. I said, "Please come in!"

My father-in-law, Stephen, was handsome, distinguished, and kind, a retired bank manager with a calm, unruffled way of looking at the world. My mother-in-law, Michelle, was tiny, intense, and often hit me on the arm to make an important point. She had been a South Korean war bride and had chosen the Western name of Michelle to replace her Korean name, which was Hyo-Ri.

You will recall how much Mrs. Murphy disliked me, and I had been prepared for David's mother to feel the same way, but Michelle seemed to love me from the moment we met. She liked that I was good at math. "Math is very important." She liked that I was an incompetent cook. "No problem, I will teach you." She observed my lack of skill in the kitchen like it was a hilarious comedy act.

She preferred me to David's previous girlfriend.

"That girl was always trying to *hug* me," she said with a shudder. "She keep telling me, 'Oh, you're so cute, Michelle!' Like I'm a doll! Very strange girl!"

Needless to say, I never tried to hug her.

David had just one sibling, an older brother, an ear, nose, and throat specialist who had moved to London to look after British ears, noses, and throats, and then he'd gone and fallen in love with a British woman, so that was the end of him.

Not really. But effectively, because he was so far away and you couldn't Zoom or FaceTime, text or email, and flights were much more expensive then. Michelle was in need of someone to mother, and along came me. Another daughter-in-law might have felt suffocated. Not me. As an only child I felt more comfortable in the company of older people than I did with people of my own age. Michelle and Stephen became my dear friends. I adored them.

I rarely came home from work without finding a box of food left by Michelle on our doorstep: red rice cakes, fried chicken, soups and stews and kimchi. She made all David's favorites and then eventually she made all my favorites.

Once Michelle dropped off some ginseng chicken soup (I'd been sniffly) when my mother was visiting. Mum was horrified when Michelle went to the cupboard under the sink, put on my rubber gloves, took out the cleaning products, and began to clean my kitchen, without saying a word. That's how Michelle showed her love. She cleaned my house. I promise you I tried to stop her in the beginning. Normally I ended up cleaning alongside her. I had a very clean house.

"*Cherry!*" hissed my mother through clenched teeth. Mum was in a bad mood that day because she was doing the Sexy Pineapple Diet: a popular diet where you ate nothing but pineapple for two days a week. That day was one of the pineapple days.

(Dieting was a new development. Mum had always had a good figure and never gave a thought to what she ate, until the day she found she couldn't zip up a favorite skirt. She was aghast. It was as if the skirt had personally offended her.)

I managed to get Michelle to stop cleaning and Mum to stop panicking by initiating a conversation about Korean fortune-telling, obviously a topic of professional interest to my mother.

Michelle settled down to tell Mum all about "sajupalja," which can be translated as "four pillars of destiny." She peeled an apple with a knife as she spoke and handed us pieces on the end of her knife. She could never not be feeding someone. Mum took the apple, even though it wasn't pineapple.

Michelle explained that saju readers analyze the "cosmic energy" at the exact moment of your birth: the hour, day, and year.

"If you believe in saju, you believe your destiny is decided by the conditions of your birth," explained Michelle. "And therefore cannot be changed."

"Cherry was born at exactly three a.m.," said my mother. "The midwife said, 'Look at that! On the dot.'"

"Well, I am not a saju reader." Michelle looked alarmed.

"No, I wasn't—I was just mentioning—please go on," said Mum.

Sometimes Mum and Michelle couldn't quite get their footwork right in the dance of conversation.

Michelle told us saju readers can determine if couples are compatible by checking their "gunghap": marital harmony. If they are not compatible they're advised to change their first name, something that millions of Koreans have done and continue to do. She said some couples, if told they had bad gunghap, and if they were serious believers, would regretfully separate.

"I wonder if David and I are cosmically compatible," I mused.

"Of course!" cried my mother and mother-in-law at the same time, and I saw them exchange secret sparkly looks. Now they were in perfect sync. They both very badly wanted grandchildren.

A week after our first wedding anniversary David came home in an excellent mood, his cheeks flushed.

He'd done a night dive off Shelley Beach and seen a wobbegong shark, apparently a good thing. Then he'd been out for dinner at a new restaurant with his diving friends.

Meanwhile, I'd eaten dinner with his parents, played chess with his dad, looked at old photo albums with his mum, and then the three of us had watched a documentary together while we drank tea and ate Korean honey cookies that I had made myself in Michelle's kitchen, with minimal supervision. They were good. I was improving. David ate three of my honey cookies and kindly but erroneously said they were better than his mother's while I told him more than he probably needed to know about the documentary I'd watched with his parents. It was about Spitfire pilots.

Then we stopped talking and sat in our favorite corner of our sectional sofa, draped all over each other, limbs overlapping, hands entwined, my nose in his neck, his nose in my hair.

David brushed my hair out of my eyes and cleared his throat.

I thought he was going to say something of a sexual nature. My body was already responding on cue.

Instead he told me we were moving to Perth next month.

The phrase "the rug was pulled out from under me" aptly describes the disorientation I felt.

"Blindsided" also works.

David explained that he would be undertaking three years of

advanced cardiology training at the Royal Perth Hospital. We would rent out this house, and the hospital had already found us somewhere to live, *by the beach*. It was going to be a wonderful adventure. New friends! New restaurants! New diving sites!

I asked why this move to the other side of the country was being presented to me as a fait accompli.

"Because it *is* one, Cherry," he said. "I just want to be honest with you."

He said it would be wrong to pretend there was any possibility of a compromise. Moving to Perth was a necessary stepping stone in his career. It had to happen.

I said, "What about *my* career?" I was still working for the National Parks and Wildlife. I will admit I had thought it was probably time to do something different, especially as Baashir was leaving soon to go back on his travels, but I'd been distracted by getting married. It's a distracting thing to do.

He said, "Come on now, Cherry. You're not interested in a career. You could stay at that desk forever, happily adding and subtracting."

"Adding and subtracting?"

"All right, and multiplying and dividing." He grinned hopefully, as if I would find this witty, which I did not.

He said, "Anyway, we're going to start trying for a baby soon."

"Are we?" I said. I didn't remember discussing this either. Was it also a fait accompli? I guessed it was; certainly our mothers considered it one, and I longed to make them both happy.

"I don't want to move to Perth," I said. "I really don't."

I'm sure you know what happened. When a man's decision has momentum, it can rarely be stopped.

We moved to Perth.

Chapter 90

It is midmorning on a Wednesday and Allegra and Jonny are walking the coastal trail between Dover Heights and Watsons Bay. It's cool and beautiful. There aren't many people about, so it feels like this sun-shimmered expanse of ocean and these majestic sandstone cliffs are laid out just for them.

Allegra breathes deeply and notices a tiny muscle in her forehead has released, although she hadn't, up until now, been aware of its existence. Her face feels as smooth and carefree as a child's. Her back still feels good. No pain. She had always taken "absence of pain" as a right, not a privilege. It feels like a privilege now.

She posts a photo of the horizon and tries to think of a caption that isn't cheesy or pretentious or too obviously posted to make friends in the corporate world feel miserable about their career choices. Although isn't that the actual point of social media? To make everyone feel bad?

She posts it without a caption. Lets the photo speak for itself.

"Australia's first lighthouse," gestures Jonny as they walk past Macquarie Lighthouse.

He only moved to Sydney from Perth a couple of years ago, so he tends to carefully plan and research each "date," if that's what these outings are; Allegra is trying not to think about it too much.

She asks, "Will there be a worksheet for me to fill out later on?"

He bumps his shoulder against hers and she feels a moment of happiness so pure it's painful.

They walk on in silence and eventually stop at a lookout, where they lean their elbows on the wooden barrier and follow the progress of a jet on the horizon.

"Do you want to fly international one day?" asks Allegra.

They rarely discuss work because of her paranoia about the idea of their "relationship" going public.

"I do," says Jonny. "You?"

"That's always been the plan," says Allegra.

"So how did you get into the biz?" asks Jonny.

She lowers her sunglasses and looks at him over the top with raised eyebrows. "Did you just say 'the biz'? How did I get into *the biz*? The flying *biz*?"

He winces. "I know, I know. Give me a break, Allegra. Sometimes I feel like I've been body-snatched when I'm talking to you. I get nervous."

"You get nervous?" She can't believe he said that. "No, you do not."

"Sure I do. Sometimes. Because I like you so much."

There's that vulnerability again. Which every woman is meant to want in a man. The obvious thing to say would be "Well, I like you too, Jonny, you don't need to be nervous," but it feels pathetic.

She could tell him she feels nervous too. It's so awkward to be with him like this, outdoors in the sunlight, sober and dressed and talking about normal things. It's embarrassing! Nerdy. Also, very scary. Like peeling off a layer of skin. The only way she feels comfortable telling him she likes him is with her body, in bed, and surely she is making that very clear.

There is a flicker of a feeling she needs to investigate later. It's something to do with how he said, *Give me a break, Allegra.* Almost pleadingly. Is she protecting herself so effectively she's occasionally cruel? When this inevitably ends will he describe her to his next girlfriend as "a little toxic"? Imagine if *she's* the toxic ex? If *she* gets the villain edit?

She looks back out to sea and says, "Well, I've always had a kind of freakish love of flying. Mum thinks I was a bird in a previous life."

She hopes he doesn't now ask a respectful, earnest question about her cultural beliefs regarding reincarnation as if her mother is serious, although of course her mother is serious.

But he just smiles and says, "I think I was too."

Which is exactly the right thing to say, so she continues, "Mum took me on a domestic flight when I was two and she says when we took off I went crazy, clapping and shrieking, and everyone was laughing at me."

"That is very cute," says Jonny. He caresses the back of her neck beneath her ponytail with his fingers and she just about manages to keep the tremor of desire out of her voice as she continues.

"And then one day, I think I was about nine, we were on a flight to India and there was this flight attendant, who was so . . . elegant, she just seemed to glide down the aisle of the plane, and I had this sudden revelation: Wait, this is her *job*! She's literally getting *paid to fly*! I thought it was like a kind of glitch in the system—why wouldn't everyone in the world want that job?"

"So I was *this* close to being an accountant." Jonny holds up his thumb and index finger. "Same as my dad. I was okay at math and commerce, those kinds of subjects, so it just seemed, like, of course I'll be an accountant like Dad. I was fine with it. Even kind of looking forward to it."

"What happened?"

"One day at the dinner table my brother said to me, 'What job would you do if you could do anything in the world, Jonny?' I wasn't concentrating. I said, 'Pilot.' I said it so fast, without thinking, and then everyone went quiet, and my dad put down his knife and fork and said, 'Uh, Jonny?' I don't know why my brother asked that question but he just randomly changed my life."

"That's funny," says Allegra. "I'd say the same if someone asked me that question: Pilot."

She closes her eyes to enjoy the sun on her face. Mindfulness! Gratitude! Ward off that depression before it takes her down.

She opens her eyes and realizes Jonny is looking at her.

"Allegra," he says. "Did you hear what you just said?" The sunlight bounces off his dark glasses. He's too good-looking in sunglasses. It's a bit much.

For a moment she's confused, but then she gets it. "Oh, no, don't worry, I don't secretly dream of being a pilot. Absolutely not."

"Why would I worry?"

"Come on, let's keep going." She indicates the path, mildly irritable. She doesn't *really* want to be a pilot. Does she? Why did those words come out of her mouth? In front of an actual pilot? It's not like it's a secret dream of hers. It's certainly not a conscious dream.

He says, "Have you ever done a trial flight?"

"No, no," she says. "I don't know why I said that. It's not like you with your brother. It was like saying if I could choose anything in the world I'd be a rock star."

"You could be a rock star," he says. "You would be a very sexy rock star."

"Funny. I can't sing."

"A lot of rock stars can't sing, but, Allegra, you *could* be a pilot. Why is that not an option for you? Is it the money? Because there are programs—"

"I misspoke," she interrupts. "I'm happy with my career. Very happy."

He opens his palms in a gesture of surrender and she is relieved he is letting it go. *Think before you speak, Allegra.*

As they follow the coastline, Allegra sees the first security camera, the inward-leaning fence, the purpose-built phone booths that connect the caller directly to a counselor, another security camera, the billboards all trying to convey one message: *Please don't do it!*

"And here we have one of our most popular suicide destinations," she says with an outstretched arm, imitating his earlier tour-guide tone.

Jonny's face falls. "Wait. You're kidding. Is this The Gap? I didn't realize that was here." He scratches his jaw. "Maybe this wasn't the best place to suggest for a walk."

"You mean because of the prediction?" asks Allegra. "Do you think you'll put ideas in my head? Make it too convenient for me to 'self-harm'?"

He pushes his glasses up on his forehead so now his hair sticks up and he no longer looks like a movie star, just a mildly sweaty worried guy. She can imagine him in high school, one of those good-looking, well-behaved, a-little-bit-pleased-with-themselves boys, the kind who were always so surprised and abashed to find themselves in trouble. The kind the teachers always let off.

She says, "Don't panic, Jonny, I'm not going to make a run for it."

"I'd catch you," says Jonny gravely, and he grips the base of her ponytail, close to her scalp. Tight enough so it's firm but doesn't hurt. It's one of his moves in bed. He uses it to quite devastating effect.

"I'm a runner now," Allegra reminds him, with a quiver in her voice, and he knows what the quiver means. "Jay says I'm crushing it."

"What does Jay know?" Jonny's jealousy of Allegra's virtual treadmill trainer is an ongoing joke.

He drops his hand. "There haven't been any *more* deaths, have there?"

"No," says Allegra.

"And management was okay?"

"All fine in the end," Allegra says. "The captain said he knew all about it because we'd discussed it after the flight and *he* hadn't considered it significant. Nobody's safety compromised. Just one of those odd things that can happen."

"Vic is a good guy," says Jonny.

Trina had admitted she wouldn't have been so concerned by the incident if not for the fact that the lady's predictions were now coming true. Then she asked, "Did *you* get a prediction, Allegra?"

When Allegra told her, Trina said, "Good grief! So wait . . . you're twenty-eight now, right? That's a terrible thing for someone to say to you. That must have been so distressing! If you need anything from us, in terms of support, or, uh, you know, counseling—I mean, it's not real, obviously, but we take mental health seriously, so . . ."

It's possible Allegra would have received a sterner rebuke for not reporting the incident if it hadn't been for her dreadful prediction. Trina is just one of the many people treating her with kid gloves. She might miss all this tender loving care after she turns twenty-nine.

Although she won't miss seeing her poor parents so distressed. They are now aware of the three correctly predicted deaths. It's not like "the Death Lady" is the lead story on the evening news, but articles have been popping up online, and of course their eyes were caught by the clickbait headlines.

"So now I will admit I am a little worried," said her mother. "I am worried this awful woman *may* have some kind of special ability. Possibly. It is very unlikely."

"I am not at all worried," said her dad, looking extremely worried.

Her mother has been busy getting the deities onside, just like she did when Allegra and Taj studied for their final school exams. Allegra has received multiple special blessings: some at home, some at temple. Her mother has also been FaceTiming various relatives in Mumbai, and a cousin's wife's auntie has put them in touch with one of the best astrologers in India, so famous and well respected he regularly appears on television. This impressive person is studying Allegra's birth chart right now. Presumably in between television appearances. He will come back to them with his professional opinion.

Her father, meanwhile, thinks the treadmill is the answer. Endorphins! If Allegra goes more than three days without a run, he's on the phone to her.

Her brother is insultingly, actively unconcerned about her mental health and pretended to hide the knives when they were there one night for dinner. He suggested Allegra's bag should be checked for pills as if she were a psych-ward patient.

"This is not a joke, Taj!" cried her mother, but later that night Allegra caught her rifling through her bag.

They stop at another lookout and Jonny says, "Not thinking about jumping, are you?"

"Well, I am," admits Allegra. "But not because I'm suicidal. Doesn't everyone think about jumping when they're up high? A friend told me it's got a name: the 'call of the void.'" It wasn't a friend, it was the ex-boyfriend who dumped her after the seafood special. "He said something about a French philosopher calling it 'the vertigo of possibility,' like it blows your mind that you've got the freedom to choose whether to live or die."

"Sounds like a smart friend."

"Not really," says Allegra, and then she comes clean. "Idiot ex-boyfriend."

"Ah," says Jonny. "Sounds like a tosser."

As they head down toward Watsons Bay, Jonny clears his throat. "Oh! I've been meaning to ask you!"

Allegra's stomach drops. The man is a terrible actor. Whatever he is about to say is not something that he has just remembered, it is something important to him.

"My parents are having a fortieth wedding anniversary party. It's in a couple of weeks and I wondered if you'd, uh, like to be my . . . plus-one? Sorry, that sounds too formal. Do you want to come and meet . . . uh . . . do you want to come?"

Home visit! He's suggesting a *home visit*! The episodes of *The Bachelor* where the contestants do the home visits with the Bachelor's family are so painful to watch and obviously impossible to miss. Once they meet the Bachelor's family, the contestants are overly invested. They see themselves joining the family. They see their futures! But only one girl can win that future. At least two will have their hearts broken on national television. That's how they get the ratings.

Allegra feels genuine panic. The lattice-topped pie was only the beginning. Meeting the family takes it to a whole new level of official. If she meets his family she will be expected to introduce him to her family. She will have to tell Anders. She will have to *be* in this. No more holding back. No more pretending this doesn't mean anything, and once it means something, then she will have no cover, no defenses, and he can then choose, at any moment, straight after they've ordered the seafood special for two, to say, "This isn't working for me."

And if it hurt that much with that boyfriend, who was such a loser, how much will it hurt when Jonny does it?

"Oh!" she says. "Oh, right, when is it? I've just got a few things coming up so it's possible the date might not work." Now she's the one speaking in an awful, false high voice.

"It's fine," he says coolly. "Don't worry about it. Too soon to meet the family. Much too soon."

"No, I wasn't—"

"It's fine, Allegra." She has hurt and embarrassed him, and the sick feeling in her stomach tells her it's too late to protect her heart anyway. She's already overly invested. She's all the way in. She wants the rose. She badly wants the rose, and the viewers at home are covering their faces with their hands, mortified for her.

"Jonny," she says. She's an idiot.

There are no other contestants, Allegra.

She has to salvage this.

Allegra hears pounding footsteps. A runner gaining ground.

"*Allegra!*"

She turns.

It's Anders. He's at the crest of the hill, running like a maniac down toward her, and he's not a runner. His form is terrible. Jay would not approve. Arms flailing.

"*Al-leg-ra!*"

In an instant she understands. He's seen her post. A horizon without a caption. The location: Australia's most popular suicide location. So stupid of her. He thinks it's a goodbye post. He's probably been trying to call, but her phone has been on silent at the bottom of her bag because of trying to be present in the moment so as not to get depression, so as not to self-harm. He lives in the Eastern Suburbs so was able to get here fast.

A woman walking a giant dog is coming up the path behind Jonny in the opposite direction from Anders. The dog zigzags back and forth, frenziedly sniffing the ground: this way, now that way. The woman wears AirPods and is in the middle of a phone call.

"Is everything all right?" cries Anders as he gets closer.

He is about to clock the presence of First Officer Jonny Summers.

The woman with the dog decides to go to their left on the path they are blocking. Her dog decides to go right. Allegra tries to get out of the way of both of them while looking back and forth between Anders and Jonny. Her legs get tangled. Not with any object or person. Just her own indecision. She trips. Time goes into slow motion and there is long enough to think: *Why are you falling? There is no need to fall. Stop this. Choose not to do this.*

But it's impossible. Her arms windmill madly, her feet do a foolish, slapstick pitter-patter, and the next thing, she is on the grass next to the side of the path. She can feel the outline of her squashed backpack and all the items it contains digging into her flesh.

"You okay?" Jonny leans over her, blocking the sun.

She senses it, like the shadow of a shark beneath the water. *Oh, please, no. No, no, no.*

"Allegra!" Anders is there now, breathing fast, bent over, hands on his knees. "I was so worried! I thought—"

"I'm fine." She moves the tiniest fraction and there it is: huge, terrifying pain. "But I think I've done my back again."

"Oh, *no*," say Anders and Jonny at the same time.

She sees the next two weeks of her life unrolling and unraveling like a ball of her grandmother's knitting wool bumping down a flight of stairs. There is nothing she can do to stop it and this time she knows what's coming. The pain, the lack of sleep, the "pain management," the constipation from the pain relief, the ice packs, the heat packs, the laxatives, the long dull days, the slow incremental improvements, the physical therapy appointments. No more running with Jay on the treadmill. She will miss Jay so much.

When she hurt her back the first time there was novelty in the process. She'd never experienced any kind of significant health issue before. It was interesting! But the thought of going through it all *again* is not interesting, it's devastating.

Just like that, her beautiful day has flipped.

Anders is saying, "Fancy meeting you here, Jonny Summers!" in a suggestive, wink, wink, nudge, nudge way, but Jonny doesn't smile. His shoulders are stiff. Jaw set. Anders will only see the arrogant First Officer Jonathan Summers he thinks he knows. She's lost Jonny. It's too late to salvage things now. There are pivotal moments in life where you don't get a second chance if you mess up.

She closes her eyes and sees mustard-colored walls closing in on her.

Chapter 91

I told my mother I knew I would be unhappy in Perth.

She said, "Cherry! If you tell yourself you're going to be unhappy, you will be! You can *choose* how to see your future!"

She sounded like a self-help guru rather than a fortune teller.

"It's not like you're moving to Antarctica," said Auntie Pat.

"It's certainly not," said my mother. "It will be unbearably hot this time of year."

"That's helpful Mae," sighed Auntie Pat. "I thought you wanted her to think positively."

Her tone was mild, but my mother acted as if it was a terrible insult.

"Mind your own business!" This was a hurtful thing to say because I was just as much Auntie Pat's business as I was hers.

Auntie Pat didn't react. She lit a cigarette, exhaled smoke. We were at the kitchen table and Mum suddenly stood, walked to the refrigerator, opened the freezer, removed a bag of frozen peas, and squashed it over her face like she was suffocating herself with a pillow. She held it for longer than I would have thought possible, then threw the peas back in the freezer and left the room. We heard the slam of her bedroom door.

I thought I'd just witnessed an actual nervous breakdown, but Auntie Pat explained it was the Change of Life. She didn't lower her voice when she said "Change of Life," because she was Auntie Pat, but most people did at the time.

Mum was probably hungry the day of the frozen peas. She was still constantly on diets at this time. The Sexy Pineapple Diet I've already mentioned. The Grapefruit Diet. The Lemon Juice Diet. The Cottage Cheese Diet. The Cabbage Soup Diet.

She began to suffer terrible digestive issues.

"Well, of course you will feel sick if you eat nothing but cottage cheese!" Auntie Pat would cry when Mum was doubled over in pain: bloating, cramps. Awful.

It sometimes feels like she spent the last years of her life battling one dress size.

She won in the end, but the cost was unacceptable.

My mother-in-law was as upset about the move as me. Michelle wanted to move to Western Australia with us and continue to live across the road. She was ready to pack her bags right then and there, but my father-in-law said that was not the way life worked. They couldn't just follow the children around the world.

"We have our own lives to live!" he said.

Michelle said, "No, we do not."

But Stephen was just as adamant they should stay as his son was that we should go.

When we said goodbye to our families at the airport, a teary Michelle kept trying to stuff more foil-wrapped packets of food into my bag, while Mum nibbled on carrot sticks from a Tupperware container like a crazed Bugs Bunny.

"What do you see for us, Mum?" I asked, desperate for hope.

"I see your plane boarding." Mum pointed a carrot stick at the screen.

Which was fair enough. I couldn't dismiss Madame Mae's professional abilities for all those years and then suddenly request a prediction.

We arrived in Perth in the middle of a heatwave.

"It's a different heat, isn't it?" said David. "Much better than Sydney's humidity."

It's not that I'm a fan of Sydney's humidity. I dislike Sydney in February. But when I walked off the plane in Perth I felt like I'd walked into a preheated oven. I could not seem to catch my breath. "I feel like I'm suffocating," I said, and David rolled his eyes.

When one person in a couple wants to move somewhere and the other person has been dragged along unwillingly, you sometimes end up like fans rooting for rival sports teams.

David told me I wasn't giving our life in Perth a chance.

We had rented a two-bedroom apartment that looked out on Scarborough Beach. It was in a block of six apartments called Beachside Blue. On the day we arrived we were met by a woman in a wetsuit rolled down to her waist with a surfboard under her arm. Her name was Stella, her skin was tanned, and her bikini top was white. She welcomed us warmly, and I tried to be equally warm although I found her breasts unnecessarily buoyant.

Stella told us that every Friday night Beachside Blue "went off" with an epic rooftop party. Every apartment took turns "hosting," which meant you provided the alcohol and music. Most of the residents worked at the Royal Perth Hospital. She herself was training to be an obstetrician. Not only that, she was a scuba diver too! Wasn't that good news? Such good news. She said David should join the Underwater Explorers Club of Western Australia. She said the diving in WA was epic. They did a lot of shipwreck exploration.

Just in case you have missed the most salient point of this anecdote: *We had moved to an apartment block with a compulsory Friday-night party.*

Instead of watching documentaries with my beautiful in-laws at the end of my working week, I would be attending an epic rooftop party.

"We'll be there!" said David.

A solid wall of stifling heat greeted us in our new apartment. The walls were freshly painted a white so dazzling I felt I needed sunglasses. The apartment was fully furnished (so convenient!) with soft, sagging, faded couches, dingy cushions, and artificial bamboo plants in pots. Everything smelled faintly of ancient cigarette smoke. Normally I liked the smell of cigarette smoke because it made me think of Auntie Pat, but this furniture seemed to have come straight from a deceased estate, and I did not feel like it had been a happy home. I sensed bitterness.

"This is *amazing!*" David ignored the dazzling white walls and the unhappy furniture and went straight to the glass doors leading out onto the balcony.

"It is amazing," I said. I was still processing the idea of a weekly party and taking shallow sips of hot air. When would it be our turn to host? How would we know what alcohol to provide? What would I wear?

David said, "Cherry, what is wrong with you? This is paradise. We are actually in paradise right now."

It was an amazing view. Anyone would have thought so. Anyone who was not homesick already for the cool green canopies of Wahroonga. We looked out onto the Indian Ocean rimmed by white sand. The water was a tropical turquoise blue near the shore and became progressively darker as it reached the horizon.

"Feel that sea breeze," said David.

I could not. It seemed like that sea breeze was only for him.

David asked if I wanted to have a lie-down. The bed, at least, seemed to be brand new. He said while I rested, he might "bite the bullet" and go out right now to join the scuba-diving club suggested by Stella.

Something about the way he said Stella's name made me sense the hidden rustle of danger, like Grandma with the baby and the snake.

I said, "Maybe it's time I learned to scuba dive."

I did not have a desire to scuba dive. I have always been a strong swimmer, and I love the ocean, but I had never felt compelled to explore *underneath* the sea.

But I was prepared to do it. Just like Jack had been prepared to jump in the blowhole for me.

David said, "I don't think it would be your thing, Cherry. You'd be an air pig."

I didn't understand. He explained that an air pig was a diver with a much higher than average air consumption. You never want your dive buddy to be an air pig because your dive time is cut short.

"But how do you know I'd use more air than average?" I asked.

"Oh, sweetheart, you would! When you get nervous you breathe like this!" He impersonated me breathing, my chest rising and falling quickly. It was like seeing secretly filmed footage of myself.

David said, "I remember the first time I saw you walking into that god-awful fondue party. I thought I'd need to get you a paper bag."

The mortification must have been clear on my face because he said, "Aww, don't worry about it, Cherry, it's sweet, it's sexy, you've got that heaving bosom thing down pat. You're doing it right now."

"It was not a god-awful party," I said coldly. "It was a wonderful party."

I didn't become a scuba diver in Perth.

I became a drinker.

Chapter 92

"I hear you're moving to Tasmania and giving up work for a year!"

Leo's mother is on the phone, radiating misplaced joy.

"Mum, I really don't think we are, it's just an idea Neve has got in her head," says Leo. "She should never have told you that. Also, even if we *did* move to Tasmania, I'd still have to find a job."

He puffs up with pleasurable self-righteousness: this is an unequivocal marital misdemeanor. Every court in the land would agree. His wife should never have mentioned this *possible* plan to *his* mother.

It's late on a Sunday afternoon. Right now, Neve and the children are down at the beach. Leo had said he'd love to join them but should probably catch up on some work. Nobody said, "Oh, come on, Dad." Nobody whined, "You never come!" They threw towels over their shoulders and off they went into the warm spring-scented air. He could have gone, but then he would have been up so late tonight, and if he wants any kind of sex life, which yes, he does, it helps to go to bed at the same time as his wife. Every single decision in his life is a compromise.

"My friend Priscilla's son-in-law did exactly what you're planning, took a year off work," says his mother. "Priscilla said it saved his marriage."

Who *are* these people who can afford to just stop working for a year? He won't ask his mother because she will tell him. There will be a long story about how Priscilla came to be connected to their family. It's also possible he briefly dated Priscilla's daughter.

"I wish Neve hadn't mentioned it." He thinks of all the reasons why it's not going to happen. "The kids are settled here. They would miss their friends."

"They'll make new friends," says his mother placidly. "And their friends would be waiting for them when they came back home."

"Mum, it's not—"

"Yes, it's only an idea. I understand. I am capable of understanding this in spite of my advanced age. My hopes are not up. Although Neve says there's a chance you'll be here for your birthday so I've booked that new Japanese restaurant."

"Neve has been talking to you about *dates*? What, has she booked our flight?"

This is ridiculous. He has agreed only to consider the idea. You don't just move a thousand kilometers on a whim. A whim based on Leo's answer to a hypothetical question, where one of the fantastical presuppositions is that "money is no object."

"Of course she hasn't booked the flight," says his mother. "I hope my garden might be under way by then. My landscape gardener got started and then disappeared. I wish I hadn't paid him upfront."

Leo feels like his head might explode. "What? Please give me his details, Mum. I'll call him right now."

To take advantage of an elderly woman like that is egregious. At least Neve hasn't mentioned the prediction to her, and even if his mother has by chance read anything about "the Death Lady," she must be unaware that Leo was on that flight, because she has said nothing.

"No, no, I'll give him a few more weeks. I think he had an illness in the family. I guess if he really has disappeared we could sell his equipment on eBay," says his mother. "I might make a profit. Well, I must go, darling, talk soon, tell the children if they agree to move to Tasmania I'll give them one hundred dollars. Each! But they mustn't tell their cousins."

"We're not bribing them."

"Your hands are clean! I'm the one doing the bribing. Bye, darling!"

She's gone. Leo returns to his computer screen.

Neve is "preparing a proposal" for this hypothetical move. She is "crunching the numbers." She plans to have him unemployed by his birthday so he will not die in a workplace accident when he's forty-three. Leo suspects Neve might have his letter of resignation already drafted and dated, awaiting his signature.

Should he just let all this happen?

Ridiculous.

He looks at the Post-it note stuck to his computer.

Rod Van Blair and a phone number, in Neve's handwriting.

I know who you'd call, Leo.

She didn't have to think about it. She didn't check to make sure she had it right. They haven't talked about Rod in years, but it's like he's always been front of mind for both of them.

He remembers how confused his parents were when Rod wasn't at Leo's thirtieth birthday party.

"Where's Rod?" asked his dad, the only man at the party in a suit and tie, as he peered over Leo's shoulder.

"He's not here, Dad. We kind of lost touch."

That's what you say. You don't say "we broke up" when a friendship ends. You don't say "we're estranged" if it's not a family member. You say you "lost touch," as if you carelessly misplaced your friend, as if it's not one of your life's greatest failures and regrets.

Leo hadn't seen Rod in two years by then. He couldn't believe he was having a thirtieth birthday party without him. He hadn't enjoyed the party, and has refused to have one ever since. Parties are too stressful anyway.

"You *what?*" said his mother. "You did not lose touch. What happened?"

He never did tell his parents what happened.

The kids have sometimes asked about Rod when they look at the wedding photos. Rod was his best man and there are photos of them together at the reception, arms slung carelessly around each other's shoulders, ties askew, rumpled shirts and hair, young unlined faces.

"Just an old friend," said Leo. "We lost touch."

"Why did you do that?" asked Bridie.

Yes, why did he do that?

Leo and Rod had met on their first day at Sydney University. They were both studying for a Bachelor of Engineering (Honors) in the Civil Engineering stream. Neither of them had gone to school in Sydney, so they both felt like outsiders when other students hollered the names of friends across the quadrangle. Rod was from regional Victoria and Leo was from Tasmania so they probably both felt like country bumpkins, although both would have denied that at the time.

They ended up sharing a terrace house near the university. Rod taught Leo how to make a curry. Leo taught Rod how to do laundry.

Rod played squash and one of his squash friends became sort of friends with Leo too. And it was at that sort-of-friend's twenty-first that Leo caught sight of a tangle-haired girl wearing a Cartier watch. So basically Leo owes Rod his whole life.

When they were twenty-eight and had been each other's best mates for over a decade, Rod fell for a beautiful woman who constantly spoke to Rod in such a dismissive way it was painful to hear. She was a wicked witch, it was clear to all, but Rod was besotted, which meant, as Neve said at the time: the situation needed to be handled sensitively. Leo tried to tiptoe. He dropped hints over many months. He said mildly, "She sometimes seems kind of critical of you, mate." But nothing worked, and the relationship continued for over a year, and Leo had to watch as she sucked the lifeblood out of Rod; he was becoming less and less like the real Rod and more like a pale, anxious, second-guessing version of himself, which is why, one night at the pub, Leo lost patience. He did it out of love! But he'd had too much to drink and all his most unfortunate eldest-brother tendencies were on display and Rod responded like the defensive youngest brother he was, accusing Leo of being jealous, which, what the fuck, was an insult to Leo's *wife*. Leo had no reason to be jealous! Rod should be jealous of *him*! They ended up in a yelling match outside the Lord Nelson Hotel. There was chest shoving and swearing, red contorted faces and a security guard saying, "Oi! You two! Stop it!" The memory still makes Leo feel ill.

Some people who were at the pub that night said Leo was in the right, some people said he was not. Alliances were formed. The alliances didn't help, they only fed the fire.

Why didn't he get on the phone the next day, apologize, and end the thing? Rod was the only one who mattered in that group of friends, the rest have all fallen by the wayside. Rod loved Neve; he wasn't insulting her by calling Leo jealous. He was lashing out. He was in a really bad relationship and what he needed was Leo's support and understanding.

But the longer it went on, the more impossible it seemed. Leo told himself that uncomfortable emotional conversations are bad enough with your romantic partner, there's no need to suffer through them with your *friends*, life is too short, it shouldn't be necessary, et cetera, et cetera. Leo told himself it was for the best. If Rod wanted to waste his life with that woman, then so be it, but he couldn't be around her.

They haven't spoken since. Leo heard through the grapevine that Rod eventually broke up with his cruel, toxic girlfriend (Leo should have just waited it out), found his personality again, moved back to Victoria, and married someone else, apparently not a wicked witch. He had three children. He got out of engineering and ended up working for a global travel company. Leo hasn't heard anything else for years now. The grapevine no longer exists.

He has sometimes wondered if the reason he doesn't have many friends ("*any* friends," says Neve, which is rude and not true—he has friends, it's just that everyone is very busy) is because of his shame over what happened with Rod. Sometimes it still shocks him. He can't believe he wasn't best man at Rod's wedding. He can't believe they don't know each other's children.

If Rod was told he was going to die, would he call Leo? Leo is pretty sure he would. And Leo would be devastated. For Rod, and for himself, and for the time they'd wasted.

Or maybe Rod barely remembers him. He might say, "Who did you say you were?" People change. You can't go backward, only forward. They might have nothing to say to each other like those stilted, awkward conversations at school reunions where everyone is thinking, *No, but I'm different now.*

He unpeels the Post-it note from the computer, crumples it into a tiny ball in his hand. Neve should not be interfering in his life, calling his mother like that. But then he is flattening it out on his desk, and he's punching in the numbers on his phone, and he doesn't remember agreeing to do this, but apparently he is, he's running off a cliff without checking the depth of the water.

The phone is answered before he has time to change his mind.

"Hello, this is Rod."

A bit brusque, a bit deeper than Leo remembers, but essentially still Rod: just the tiniest suggestion of his dad's Dutch accent. It's unbelievable. Rod still exists. All this time Rod has always been available on the other end of a phone. As easy as this, and yet it's like Leo has done something metaphysically impossible.

Leo says, "Hi, Rod. This is . . . I just thought . . . well. It's Leo."

There is a long pause. A very long pause.

"Leo Vodnik."

This time Rod laughs. "I know who you are, Leopold."

His laugh catapults Leo back through time. He can smell Rod's chicken curry, he can taste the Carlton Draft beer they used to drink, and even the way he is sitting, loose and slouchy, tipped back in his chair, reminds him of the Leo he used to be, when Rod was his friend. He rests his feet up on his desk.

"Long time no see," says Rod. "All good?"

"Yeah," says Leo. "All good. What about you? Been up to much?" Because he sees how they're playing this, the comedic bit they're about to perform. They're going to pretend nothing has happened, no time has passed.

But then Rod says, in a different, urgent tone, the tone of an older man who has learned that bad things can and do happen, "Please tell me you're not dying, Leopold."

"No," says Leo. He puts his feet back on the floor before he falls and hurts his back—he's always telling Oli not to sit like this. "I'm not dying. Well." He sighs. He sees the lady on the plane, those pale blue eyes, the strangely familiar brooch. "According to a psychic I'm—"

He stops, because he suddenly remembers what the symbol on the lady's brooch signifies. Only Rod Van Blair saying "Leopold," a name no one else uses, could have excavated this obscure, specific memory from the crystallized layers of his consciousness.

He says, "It's a long story."

"Let's hear it," says Rod easily, as if they're sitting on the living room floor in their shabby terrace, a small bag of weed and a family-sized pizza box on the floor next to them.

Everything has changed and nothing has changed at all. Leo is filled with equal parts terrible regret for the time they have lost and sweet relief for the time they will hopefully have again.

He presses his phone hard against his ear. "It's so good to hear your voice, mate."

There is another pause, long enough for Leo to wonder if they've been cut off, and then Rod says, and he sounds a little congested, "Likewise."

Chapter 93

It's a strange experience to be married to someone who dislikes you but loves your body.

I do not recommend it.

It took me a long time to understand this. I don't know if David ever understood it about himself. It probably wasn't good for him either. Perhaps he tried to resist his feelings. Perhaps he woke each morning and told himself, *I will not find her annoying*, just as I woke each morning and thought, *I will not be annoying*.

I think this kind of relationship is only possible when you are young enough to fully inhabit your body. When you are older there is more separation between yourself and your physicality. Your body lets you down, it creaks and cracks and aches, it often feels unfamiliar, but back then my body was me, and his body was him, and if our bodies loved each other, that was enough.

Although, of course, it wasn't.

He was never cruel. Perhaps if his feelings had been articulated more specifically, I would have understood sooner the fundamental truth: *This man simply does not like me.*

When you live with someone who dislikes you in a mostly unspecified way, you begin to dislike yourself too, especially if you are someone, like me, whose self-esteem, at least regarding my personality, has never been high. A different person, a stronger person, would not have allowed her sense of self to be blown away like grains of sand in the brisk winds of Perth.

Perth is one of the windiest cities in the world.

Sometimes, even now, if I feel a hot dry wind, that strange time in my life comes back to me in choppy fragments, the same way a scent creates an instant memory.

Living at Beachside Blue was a little like time spent in a cult. As residents, we had our own culture, our own customs and practices. Nobody had children, and everyone was in their twenties and had come from somewhere else. Our families and childhoods were far away.

The Friday-night rooftop parties were like ceremonies: intense and dreamlike.

They began just before sunset. There were no skyscrapers around us. The sky and the sea were ours, and the alcohol hit our bloodstreams at the same time as the sun set.

Growing up on the east coast, I had seen pale pink-blue sunrises over the Pacific Ocean, but I had never witnessed the symphonic magnificence of the sun sinking over the Indian Ocean, turning it indigo and the light a molten gold. Being up on that roof as the colors spread like spilled paint across the sky was both sensual and spiritual, like being ravaged by God.

I'm sorry, Grandma, for that blasphemous remark, but that's how it felt.

Or perhaps it was just drunkenness, because, like many an unwilling party attendee before me, I discovered the solution to feeling awkward was to drink as much as possible, as quickly as possible. Not only did the awkwardness vanish but David much preferred me that way. Drinking improved my personality. I was not so uptight.

Before I'd moved to Perth, I'd been tipsy, but never drunk. I did not know a room could spin. I did not know you could wake up with unexplained bruises all over your legs and black nightmarish spots in your memory.

I drank Bacardi and Coke, vodka and orange, Tequila Sunrises and Harvey Wallbangers. Galliano was big at the time. The only food was bags of potato chips and pretzels. There was always plenty of beer, cheap wine, no soft drinks, no water. We didn't really drink water back then the way people do now. Most people smoked. There were drugs. The host was not required to provide them, but somebody always had something, of good quality, because most of the residents were medical professionals. I didn't bother with the drugs; alcohol did the trick.

We sank rows of empty bottles and cans into the gray dirt of a long-since-abandoned garden bed as if we were planting them. Three empty Eskies were lined up against a wall, and when it was your turn to host you had to fill them with ice and alcohol. (It sounds so silly now, but it felt so important at the time: this vital curating of the alcohol.)

A previous resident had hung colored Christmas lights around the edge of the terrace so that once the night turned dark people's faces were flecked with color. Someone's old portable cassette player remained permanently on the deck, and if you were hosting you were DJ for the night and brought along a selection of cassettes.

There was dancing. As you know, I can't dance, but when I was drunk enough I could sway on the spot in a way that one of the doctors told me was "mesmerizing."

There was a lot of flirting. David liked it when other men paid attention to me. He told me to read people's palms and I did. I pretended to read them, anyway. I could never really see their palms in the shadowy light. One night Stella and I kissed, cheered on by our partners and everyone else. I didn't enjoy it. She tasted of pretzels. I've never liked pretzels.

On very hot nights there was a plastic children's wading pool to cool your feet, or your whole self if you chose or slipped or were pushed. On very cold nights we lit a fire in a gallon drum.

People sat on the low brick edge of the balcony, their backs to the sea. There was no railing. It would never be allowed now. It was inviting trouble. I had a recurring vision of two people falling. One grabbing at the other's T-shirt sleeve. Both disappearing into the night. The drunker I got, the more I talked about this vision. Everyone knew my mother was a "famous" fortune teller, so it was a running joke that Cherry was predicting deaths, which made the men pretend to lose their balance, tipping their bodies back as far as they dared, which made the women scream, which made them do it even more.

Did I love those parties or did I hate them?

It's not clear. Each one felt like a fever dream. I guess the simple answer is I both loved and hated them.

At the end of each party David and I would lurch down the flight of stairs to our apartment, fall into bed, and have sex. It never got stale. It was often very angry sex. To be frank, and once again I apologize for being vulgar, the angrier we got, the better it got. It was like we were punishing each other for I don't know what. For our behavior at the party? For not being different people? For our aggravating habits?

I know I was aggravating.

For example, when I looked for something in my handbag, I bent my head into the bag to find the missing item, and in doing so I appeared like a "dithery old lady." When I sneezed, I made a squeaky sound, like this: *eee! eee! eee!* Nobody should sneeze like that. When I cleaned my teeth I tapped my toothbrush on the side of the basin multiple times. Once was enough. When I ran into the ocean I held my arms up like chicken wings. This made me look deranged. When I woke each morning I cleared my throat far more often than the average person. When I locked the apartment door I always forgot which way to turn it, and hence turned it the wrong way before I remembered the right way, and this was aggravating to witness. My taste in music and in fact all forms of popular culture was boringly mainstream, my underwear insufficiently sexy, my repartee insufficiently witty. I sometimes tried to be funny and I was not. David was witty. I was not. I should never try to be witty or funny. It was embarrassing to myself and to all.

I could go on, but I won't.

Gosh.

I see now that David's dislike was articulated quite specifically on numerous occasions! Or perhaps these were just quibbles, normal in any relationship, and the fact that I remember them all these years later is evidence of my overly sensitive nature, which was also annoying.

I do know my mother, who loved me very much, was also aggravated by my throat-clearing in the morning, but her annoyance was never laced with acid-like contempt.

You may wonder why none of this came out that first year in Wahroonga, where I assume I sneezed, tapped my toothbrush, cleared my throat, tried to be funny, et cetera. I think it was to do with his parents. David loved his parents, and his parents loved me. Hence, I was more lovable. Once we were out of the dappled green light of Wahroonga, and in the exposed fierce light of that white-walled apartment in Perth, David could see me more clearly.

Never mind. It wasn't all bad. I was very happy with my new job! I got a position at the Perth branch of the Australian Taxation Office. I worked in data matching in a team of mostly men. It was interesting because—

Well.

It's probably only interesting to *me*. I won't go on. I explained data matching to someone at one of the rooftop parties, in what I thought was very concise detail, but David could tell the poor man was desperate to get away from me and bored to death.

The Friday-night drinking seeped into Saturday night and Sunday night and eventually every night. I never missed a day of work, but I often slept away entire weekends while David was out diving, exploring fascinating shipwrecks. Stella became his dive buddy. She was not an air pig and breathed like a normal person. I'm sure those breasts helped with buoyancy.

I kept forgetting my contraceptive pill because I was so often tipsy or drunk and then, one day, I told David I might as well stop taking it altogether and we would try to have a baby.

David was thrilled. I can still remember how he looked at me when I told him. It showed me I was making the right decision. This would save our marriage. I could see he loved me again in that moment. It was him again. It was us again.

As you know, I was not especially keen on children, but David adored them. He smiled at babies on buses. He talked to toddlers in cafés.

I assumed I would like the baby when it came. I saw the baby as the missing variable in a tricky equation. A baby would make David love me. A baby would bring me my mother and my auntie. A baby would bring me my mother-in-law and father-in-law.

The months went by and I didn't become pregnant.

I continued to drink. There were no public service announcements on the radio about not drinking when you are trying to conceive. People knew about fetal alcohol syndrome so my plan was to stop drinking after I missed my first period. To be honest, I was relieved at the prospect of having an excuse to stop drinking. I was starting to suspect my drinking might be the cause of my constant fatigue and low-level depression, but it didn't seem to occur to me to just stop.

I was as surprised as every woman is when she stops avoiding pregnancy and doesn't immediately become pregnant. I don't know if I was disappointed each month, because there was always that tiny sense of relief, but I was bemused.

After a year, David said I should get some tests done to find out what was wrong with me. It was Stella, who was studying obstetrics, who said at one of the Friday-night parties that actually the man should be checked out first because it was an easier, less invasive test.

That's when we learned David had a zero sperm count.

There was zero chance of me becoming pregnant.

David had never failed a test in his life. He'd never failed anything. He'd never had his heart broken, never lost anyone he loved, not even a pet. His mother insisted that when David learned to walk, he never fell. Michelle said it was so funny, he just stood up and began strolling about the place.

I went to touch him, to offer comfort. He tossed my hand away.

He was furious. He had no coping mechanisms. I could see he badly wanted to blame me for this, but there was no rational reason to do so.

He said, "Don't you *pity* me."

And then I saw it come to him: a reason to be angry. He said, "I bet you're relieved. You never wanted children anyway. I overheard you tell that woman at Baashir's party."

I was shocked. I couldn't believe he'd never brought this up before.

I said, "Why would you have married me if you wanted children and you thought I didn't?"

He didn't answer. He said he was going for a swim and he didn't invite me to join him.

I watched him from the balcony as he walked across the scrubby dunes toward the sea, a red towel over his shoulder, his head bowed in an unfamiliar defeated way, and my heart broke for him, but it also occurred to me that the reason he'd never asked me about my feelings toward having children was because my feelings were never especially relevant.

I went back inside because our phone was ringing.

It was Auntie Pat telling me Mum was unwell and had been refusing to go to the doctor for months now. Auntie Pat said I should come back to Sydney right away, because Mum had read her own cards and determined she was dying, and Auntie Pat was so angry she could wring her bloody neck.

Chapter 94

Ethan is thirty and he's still alive. Each night he goes to bed and thinks: Still here, lady!

One month down. Eleven to go.

Most of his friends have stopped talking about it. The women at work who gave him self-defense presents no longer seem especially concerned.

All the online chatter seems to have died down again too. He's noticed before how fast the world moves on from a story without any further "bombshell" developments. His feed will be filled with articles about a missing person, a murder or a scandal, and then nothing, and you don't even notice until one day you think: Wait, did they ever find that missing person?

Presumably not.

His anxious plane friend hasn't forgotten. Leo checks in every four or five days since Ethan's birthday, which is nice, although obviously there is some self-interest involved because his forty-third birthday is approaching, at which point he needs to avoid a workplace accident.

Only eleven months before I prove her wrong, Ethan texts back to Leo's most recent message. Normally Leo responds with a thumbs-up emoji, but this time, to Ethan's surprise, he says, *Fancy a drink?*

They meet in the early evening at the Robin Hood Hotel: casual, laid-back; seems very unlikely anyone will try to assault Ethan at this time or location.

Ethan gets there first, and Leo arrives a minute later, stressed about something to do with parking and immediately launches into a story about how he recently got in touch with an old friend with whom he was "effectively estranged for many years."

"Good for you," says Ethan. He has no idea why Leo is telling him this story, but it seems appropriate to clink his glass against Leo's in a celebratory manner.

"Thanks!" Leo beams. "So, the reason I mention it is the lady's brooch."

It's really hard to keep up with this guy.

"Brooch?" Ethan has to think for a moment. "Is that . . . jewelry?"

"Yes, she was wearing a brooch, and it had some kind of symbol on it that I vaguely recognized, so I thought it had something to do with *me*, very narcissistic, I know."

"Okay," says Ethan.

"Well, I think I've worked it out. I'm pretty sure it's a mathematic symbol." He removes a beautiful fountain pen from his pocket, turns over his coaster, and writes. He holds up the coaster.

Ethan looks at it and says, "The Kronecker delta symbol?"

Leo points at him, delighted. "Exactly! I guess you studied it as part of computer science, right?"

"Sure, but why would she be wearing it? And, ah, what's it got to do with you?"

"Oh, well, it's just that it was developed by Leopold Kronecker, who was a mathematical genius. My name is Leopold, although everyone calls me Leo, but this friend I got back in touch with, we were at university together, and it just brought back this memory of us in a tutorial learning about Kronecker's theory and him saying, 'Leopold the Mathematical Genius!'" He puts on a deep booming voice as if he's saying *Leopold the Lion Tamer!* He chuckles fondly. "So *that's* how I remembered."

Ethan thinks. "But what could it signify?"

"No idea," says Leo. "I mean, it's just a useful way of simplifying a long, complicated expression. It's widely used: engineering, math, physics, computer science. Maybe she works in one of those fields?"

"You think she uses a mathematical formula to tell the future?"

"I don't know," says Leo. "All I know is that if she's wearing it on a brooch it must mean something to her." His phone buzzes, and he looks at it, frowning.

"Sorry, mate, I should go."

"Your wife?" guesses Ethan.

"My boss," says Leo, and he hurries off, no longer looking like he's celebrating anything.

When Ethan gets back to the apartment, the place is dark and feels deserted. It doesn't feel like Jasmine is out; it feels like she's gone.

He sits on the couch and stares at the brand-new fish tank Jasmine recently had installed. It takes up a full wall. The unique "aquascape" is loosely inspired by an amazing scuba-diving trip Jasmine once did in Mozambique. Ethan felt faint when he saw the casually discarded invoice. It cost more than a house deposit.

Gorgeously bejeweled tropical fish slide purposefully back and forth, without actually getting anywhere. With their fancy tails and unusual fins they remind him of ladies in an over-the-top period drama. Tiny luminescent fish dart between the rocks on the sandy bottom. It's quite remarkable, but is it reducing his blood pressure?

He thinks not.

His phone dings. It's Jasmine.

Hopefully she's home for dinner. He'll make something she likes.

But then he reads the message. She's texting from the airport lounge to let him know Carter is getting way too stalkerish and freaking her out, so she's giving him some space and going to stay with her brother in Paris for a few months. She was planning on spending Christmas in Europe anyway, so it makes sense to go early. Hopefully he'll enjoy having the place all to himself, oh, and could he please feed the fish?

For the first time since he's lived with her, he feels ordinary flat-mate annoyance.

I don't want to feed your fish, Jasmine. I don't like fish.

He texts back, *Sure, no problem. Have fun!*

Her text appears: *Thanks! PS: Flying commercial. OMG, I know it's better for the environment but SO much waiting!*

Is she for real? She must surely know he's never flown anything but commercial. He can't even answer that text.

Harvey chortles: *So, you're stuck feeding the fish heiress's fish while she's in Paris. This is really working out well for you, mate.*

There is a pounding on the door.

Someone's fist. He knows whose fist even before he hears Carter's voice: "Jasmine! It's me!"

He must have gotten someone to buzz him in downstairs, or someone held the door for him. It's not like he's an unfamiliar face around the place.

"I just want to talk!"

Ethan feels a surge of fury. It's Carter's fault Ethan now has the responsibility for these expensive fish.

"Jasmine!" Carter shouts, and bangs his fist over and over like he's trying to knock the door down. Does he truly believe this is an effective way to win back a woman's heart? It's bloody terrifying. "You owe me this!"

Should he call the police?

Ethan puts in his AirPods, turns up his music loud enough to give him permanent hearing damage, and waits for the snooty neighbor in the opposite apartment to do it first.

Chapter 95

You know what?

The fourth death really gets my goat, as Auntie Pat liked to say.

That's when everyone lost their damned minds. That's when articles about me began appearing in "respectable" publications.

That's when people began hunting me down. As if I were prey, as if I were a criminal, as if I were hiding, which I assure you I was not.

Chapter 96

Paula plays with her children on the living-room floor like a regular loving engaged mother. Dinner is in the slow cooker, the washing machine whirs in an industrious duet with the dishwasher. These are the precious moments that make up a life! All her thoughts are acceptable and pleasant. All her actions are normal and nonrepetitive. She is not obsessing. She is living in the present and she is not thinking about the fourth death, not at all.

"What a dee-yight-ful cup of tea." Willow doesn't sit, she crouches down on her haunches and purses her lips as she sips from a tiny plastic teacup: a regency matriarch in pigtails.

"Do you need more sugar, madam?" Paula's role in these games is often unclear. Sometimes she is a fellow guest but often she's the maid. She needs to be ready to pivot.

"Oh, yes, please, madam." Willow holds out her cup.

Timmy commando-crawls beside them, grunting with effort like a wounded soldier. He is much more graceful in the water than on land, but he's missing today's lesson because he has a head cold. Paula can see snail trails of snot on the carpet. He climbs into her lap, pulls himself up by her shirt, and flattens his snotty nose in her eye.

"Thanks, Timmy." She wipes her face.

"Mim, Mim, Mim!" Timmy babbles.

Swim. She is pretty sure he's saying "swim." She has not translated for Matt.

"No swimming lessons today," says Paula.

This is proof that Timmy's multiple secret swimming lessons do not fall under the definition of a compulsion. She does not need Dr. Donnelly. She knows what he'd say: *Life is unpredictable. Timmy might drown. Timmy might not drown. You are not your thoughts. Bad things can happen.* Blah blah blah. She knocks her knuckle against her front teeth.

His cold is not that bad. Just a sniffly nose. She could bundle both kids into the car right now and still make it. It might even make him feel better.

"Do you have a tummyache, darling?" Willow stands next to Paula, her little dimpled hand on Paula's shoulder, staring into Paula's face with motherly concern.

"We might take Timmy swimming," says Paula. She can already feel the relief it will bring, just being in the pool.

"Not swimming *again*!" Willow throws both hands up in disgust.

"Mim! Mim!" Timmy claps.

Paula's phone beeps with a message from her sister. *Dr. D still practicing. Hasn't retired! They offer telehealth. I remember you liked him. Just sayin'! Not interfering! Your life, etc. etc.*

There is a link to a psychotherapist's office: Dr. Donnelly.

It's like her sister can read her mind.

Dr. Donnelly came into Paula's life when she was seventeen.

She had just gotten her driver's license, was living her best life, studying for her final exams, dating her first boyfriend, when one day she braked at a pedestrian crossing and watched as people strode in front of her car, some of them close enough to touch the hood, but they didn't even glance her way. That's how trusting they were. How did they know they could trust her? How did they know she would continue to keep her foot on the brake, when the accelerator was right there?

What was to stop her slamming her foot on the accelerator?

Nothing.

She could mow them all over. The little girl in a tutu holding her mother's hand. The old man with a limp. Paula sweated and shook. Panic flooded her body.

She put the handbrake on. *Not enough.*

She turned the car ignition off. *Not enough.*

She got out of the car with her car keys. *Not enough.*

She *locked* the car.

The little girl in the tutu and the old man with the limp reached the other side of the road. She had not killed them.

She saw the person in the car behind her looking at her curiously. She raised a hand in apology, jumped back in the car. That became the ritual every time she stopped at a crossing. Sometimes people honked but that didn't matter.

It might have gone on forever. She might still be doing it now.

But one day it happened in front of her sister when she was giving her a lift. She tried so hard. She squeezed the steering wheel so tight. She told herself she wouldn't run anyone over with Lisa in the car. *But what if she did?*

After she got back in the car, Lisa looked straight ahead as if her bizarre ritual had been perfectly normal. They drove for a while in silence and finally Lisa spoke up, her tone mild and nonjudgmental. "Is it because you're scared you'll run them over?"

Paula nodded. Just the once.

"You would never do that," said Lisa. "I promise. I know you. You would *never* do that."

But Paula didn't believe her.

Lisa snitched to their parents. "I conveyed information," she said. "I did not snitch."

Up until then she'd always done her best to cover for her sister's weirdness. "Paula is just cleaning her teeth," she'd say when they were kids, when in fact, as their parents well knew, Paula was taking off all her clothes and putting them on again in the correct order because she'd messed up the first time around and her elaborate routine had to be followed exactly or else she couldn't leave the room.

When her parents heard about her street-crossing ritual they insisted she go to the GP and ask for yet another referral to someone who might help. Exiting the car every time she stopped at a crossing was a dangerous, unsustainable, frightening habit.

Prior to then, there had been various therapists over the years, none of whom helped much, probably because they never got the full story. Paula excelled at secrecy.

Nobody knew that the reason for the dark shadows under her eyes when she was ten was that she had to stay up late each night reciting her twelve times tables twelve times in a row. This, for some reason, would prevent Mittens, the family cat, from being run over. She didn't even like Mittens all that much.

Nobody knew that her refusal to touch a kitchen knife wasn't because of that one time she cut her thumb chopping tomatoes but because she was terrified she would suddenly plunge the knife into the nearest family member's throat.

Nobody knew that the reason she dropped Ancient History as a subject was because the teacher had a seating plan, and she had to sit next to a window on the second floor, and she could think of nothing else but throwing herself out that window, and the thought was so *incessant,* the only solution seemed to be *to just do it.* She remembers rationalizing it: *It won't necessarily kill me, just break my legs.*

It was in Dr. Donnelly's office that she first heard the term "obsessive-compulsive disorder" used as a diagnosis applicable to her, not as a lighthearted description for a tidy, uptight, germophobic person.

Dr. Donnelly was not a fan of reassurance. Unlike her sister, he promised her nothing.

He said, "Yes, it's true, Paula, you *could* run those people over."

He explained that many if not *most* people have thoughts like hers, but the OCD brain takes intrusive thoughts seriously. He said OCD sufferers often believe they are responsible for things they can't control, which is probably why she thought she alone controlled her cat's destiny. Even if she rationally knew this couldn't be true (because if it were, why not tell people what a good job she was doing, keeping the stupid ungrateful cat alive by laboriously reciting those tables), it *felt* true.

He got her to do exposure therapy. All different kinds.

She had to hold the sharpest kitchen knife to her family members' throats, for thirty seconds at a time. She had to slowly accelerate her car as close as she dared to her dad, while he gestured with his hands, *closer, closer, closer,* as casually as if he were just helping her park.

She had to stand in various high locations—the top level of the local shopping center, a cliff face on their favorite bushwalk—and instead of reassuring herself, *You're okay, you're not going to jump,* she had to tell herself, *You might jump, you might not.*

She and her family had to play a memory game with cards on which she'd written her intrusive thoughts and then match them up, to demonstrate that her thoughts were nothing special or mystical. She can still remember her sister triumphantly holding up two cards saying *I might push Lisa down the stairs,* thrilled to have matched up the two cards, not at all concerned that her sister thought about pushing her down the stairs.

These are not unhappy memories. There was relief because there was no more secrecy, and there were rules to follow and she likes rules. She was not ashamed or embarrassed. Nobody made her feel that way. Her family could not have been more supportive. And it *worked.* She saw Dr. Donnelly for two years, and she learned to live with her OCD.

But the more time that has passed, the more she has assumed that OCD is like a childhood allergy she has outgrown. She looks at Dr. Donnelly's name on her screen. Sees his kind face. She is too busy to make an appointment. She is a grown-up now, with two children. It's been years. She's fine. She knows the techniques. She could predict every word that would come out of Dr. Donnelly's mouth. She can keep a grip on this. Why pay for information she already knows?

Her phone rings in her hand as she's looking at her sister's text.

"Grandma?" asks Willow hopefully.

"Not Grandma." It's an unknown caller. Paula removes Timmy from her lap. He whimpers and wipes irritably at his nose.

Normally she ignores unknown numbers, but it could be a lead.

After the funeral at St. David's, where the psychic did *not* show up, or if she did, she managed to blend into the crowd, Paula and her new friend, the newly married Eve, had gone for coffee. They are kindred spirits: both of them are systematic and organized, compulsive (ha ha) list-makers, except Eve did hers on the Notes app on her phone while Paula did hers on a notepad. It has been enjoyable "working" with Eve on this investigative project. They had a Facebook page set up by the end of the day and have been in regular communication since then. Paula has been direct-messaging anyone who posts if it sounds like they might have genuine information. Eve is keeping an eye on the younger platforms like TikTok.

"Hello?"

The voice on the phone is cultured and confident. "Paula Binici?"

"Yes, that's right." Paula automatically sits up straighter, as if it's a work call.

"My name is Suzanne. I posted something on your page about possibly knowing the identity of the psychic on your flight. You messaged me."

"Of course." Paula scoots over to the coffee table, grabs her notepad and pen, and sits up cross-legged behind it. "I remember. You thought she might have read your palm once, many years ago?"

"Well, possibly, I could easily be wrong, it was literally fifty years ago, so . . . but as soon as I saw the picture I thought of her, and I can't even tell you why. I remember she was a sweet, very pretty little thing, with long straight brown hair and compelling eyes. Ice-blue. A kind of arctic blue."

Paula feels a shiver as she remembers the lady's pale blue eyes. "Kind of scary?"

"Scary? Oh, no, not at all. She was quite shy. Awkward. At first, anyway."

"So how did she come to read your palm?"

"I was married to a farmer at the time. He, well, *we*, lived on a cattle station in Queensland. Enormous. Over a hundred thousand acres. She was staying in the staff quarters, I think maybe doing some kind of . . . research? I just remember her in my kitchen, reading my palm. I don't even know how that came about, if I paid her or what, but I will never forget what she said. She said, 'I see you leaving.'"

"Leaving the cattle station?"

"I took it to mean leaving my marriage. I was very unhappy at the time."

"And you left?"

"I did. It was the right decision for both of us. He's happy with someone else. I own an art gallery. I think she might have said something about the art gallery too."

"So she got it right," says Paula. Timmy crawls over to her and lays his snot-slimy cheek on her leg. Paula holds one hand protectively over his head so he doesn't bang it on the side of the coffee table. He closes his eyes. His cheeks are flushed. Swimming is the last thing he needs today. "Her prediction came true."

"Sure, I guess. Technically," says the woman, "although, to be honest, I don't know if I would have left if she hadn't read my palm. I was so young and stupid and I had gotten myself in this strange passive state, but she was so adamant she could *see* this other life for me! It was . . . inspiring."

"I assume she didn't tell you how and when you were going to die?"

"Oh, no, I wouldn't want to know that!" The woman catches herself, and makes a "tch" sound.

"It's fine," Paula says. "And I think you said you couldn't remember her name?"

"Well, that's why I'm calling," says Suzanne. "Just this morning I was reading an article about that charity where they auction off a box of the first cherries of the season. It said Tanya Somebody-or-other had been crowned Cherry Queen. That's when it came to me. So funny the way the mind works."

"Her name was Tanya?" Paula is already writing it down.

"No," says the woman. "*Cherry.* Her name was Cherry."

Chapter 97

I've since learned some acquaintances came across my photo online and chose to do or say nothing, assuming if I wanted to be found, I would be. Presumably these are the people who wouldn't turn me in if they saw my face on a wanted poster, so that's nice to know.

Although I guess it would depend on the severity of my crime.

Chapter 98

Eve has just walked in the door from her waitressing job when her mother calls to ask if she's heard about the fourth death.

"He was some kind of up-and-coming YouTube star," she tells Eve. "He called himself Simon Says Be Kind. He did 'random acts of sunshine' like running up to people in the street and giving them a potted plant. Sounds infuriating. Imagine having to pretend to be grateful when some stranger thrusts a potted plant at you. Do you remember seeing him on the plane?"

"I don't think so," says Eve. She is looking him up on Dom's laptop as she speaks. She doesn't recognize him. He was a good-looking man, although he was one of those people who tilted his head and pouted each time he had his photo taken.

Simon Gallea was twenty-seven years old. The Death Lady correctly predicted he would die of an acute respiratory infection. He didn't want to worry people so he'd only told one close friend and never mentioned it to his followers. His followers say this selfless behavior is so typical of Simon!

There is talk of a Simon Says Be Kind march to commemorate Simon. *Let's make Simon's legacy a global kindness movement! Rest in peace, Simon, we won't forget your message!*

Interest in the Death Lady is now reaching fever pitch. Comments pour in as Eve watches:

Does anyone know how to book an appointment with the Death Lady?

I am DESPERATE to find the Death Lady.

I think it would really change my life if I knew how long I had left, I need to see the Death Lady!

I would like to give my mother a session with the Death Lady for her birthday. Does anyone know how I can arrange it?

Could someone please urgently post contact details for the Death Lady?

Surely someone is going to find her soon.

"Remind me when this Death Lady predicted I'd lose my only daughter?" says her mother, and there is fear in her voice, and Eve isn't having it.

"No," says Eve. "I will not."

Chapter 99

The first thing I noticed when I arrived back in Sydney at my mother's house was that the MADAME MAE sign had gone from the letterbox. I had been so embarrassed about that sign, before I came to accept it, and then, it seems, I'd apparently become proud, because I felt such a sense of loss when it was gone. Now our house was just ordinary, no different from anyone else's in our street. We were no longer special.

Auntie Pat opened the door. She had moved into my old bedroom. I wasn't aware of this.

Mum was up and dressed, but she carried herself carefully like someone in pain, although she insisted she wasn't feeling any. Her face was gaunt, but she was smiling, her eyes shiny with happiness to see me.

The last time I'd been home had been for Ivy's wedding (to my wedding photographer, I was her bridesmaid and was very careful with my bouquet and did *not* leave a pollen stain on *her* wedding dress). Mum had been slender then, but I'd been pleased for her, I'd thought it was all the dieting paying off. Now she was fragile and birdlike, her clothes hung off her, her cheeks were sunken and her eyes enormous. Still beautiful but terrifyingly frail. We'd been the same height and build for many years, but our hugs had always been of a parent and child. I had always leaned toward her. Now for the first time it was as though I was taking her in my arms.

Before I could express my concerns, she stood back and surveyed me and said, "You look terrible."

Auntie Pat said, "Yes, you do."

"It's a long flight," I said defensively. I was not the one who looked terrible!

"What's wrong with you?" demanded my mother, sounding not at all frail.

I didn't tell them about the Friday-night parties, or the way my thumping heart woke me in the middle of the night with a gasp of terror, or about my permanently dry, sour mouth and the dull feeling in my head that only went away with my first drink each evening.

I told them I was distressed because we had learned that David and I couldn't have a baby. I didn't tell them of my secret relief, and I didn't tell them I needed a baby to save me and my marriage from the dreadful abyss into which we seemed to be falling.

It turned out this was old news. David had called his mother and Michelle had called Mum.

David would have been just thrilled to know his mother and his in-laws had been discussing his sperm.

(He would not have been thrilled.)

They said it was going to be fine. Michelle had a plan, which she wanted to discuss with me, and Mum and Auntie Pat were already on board. David and I were to be brought on board too. The plan was that we would adopt a Korean baby, and our baby would be so very lucky, because unlike most adoptees going to white families, he or she would have a Korean grandmother and a half-Korean father. Michelle had already been calling adoption agencies. Auntie Pat was waiting to hear back from a friend whose daughter had adopted a baby from Korea, in case she had useful information. Mum had various distinguished people writing character references for us: the mayor, my high school principal, the head of the local chamber of commerce. (They had all sat for her at various points.) Of course, these references were probably not even necessary; David was not only half Korean but had a career in *cardiology,* saving lives, while I worked for the Australian Taxation Office, helping catch tax avoiders. We were clearly of excellent character and would go straight to the top of any list of desperate parents-to-be.

The mention of excellent character recalled a vision of our behavior at the rooftop parties, hands all over each other, in full view of everyone, staggering down the stairs to bed. It felt sensual at the time but so sleazy and vulgar in the morning, and reprehensible in my childhood home. What would my dad think? What would Jack think? I could not imagine either of them on that rooftop. Sometimes I wondered if my recurring image of two people toppling backward into the inky black night was symbolic. It represented David and me, but I only thought that when I was drunk; when I was hungover I had no interest in symbols or visions and I knew it meant nothing.

"Obviously this is only if you and David are happy with the idea," said Auntie Pat.

"Really?" I said. "We have a choice in the matter? We won't come home one day and find a little Korean baby on the doorstep delivered by the postman?"

"Very funny," said Auntie Pat.

"Didn't that happen to Betty Carroll?" said Mum.

"Betty's baby didn't come from Korea, Mae," said Auntie Pat.

(It was an open secret nobody was really bothering to keep anymore. The oldest Carroll girl, Bridgette, had given birth at fifteen to the fattest baby you've ever seen.)

"Oh, yes," said Mum. "Fancy me forgetting that." She frowned. "I think I predicted it too."

Another woman might have found it outrageous that Michelle was already making calls to adoption agencies on our behalf, but I liked the idea of pleasing my mother-in-law, and—this sounds terrible—I think it reduced my level of responsibility. If I couldn't take care of this baby Michelle was organizing, she would do it for me. She would help me keep the baby alive, and the baby would get me back into my clotted-cream house, where all my fancy dinnerware and wedding boxes were packed away along with my former self, while another newlywed couple paid us rent to live there. Also, I would be doing something "good" by helping out a child in need.

"I think I would like to adopt," I said. "If David is happy to."

Of course, we didn't know what we didn't know. We didn't know many of the Korean children adopted at this time were not orphans at all. We didn't know about unwed mothers being coerced into giving up their babies, or document fraud, or profit-driven adoption agencies. It did not occur to us to think about distressing questions of identity that might face these children when they grew up.

I watched Mum tentatively nibble a tiny corner of lamington as if it were a strange exotic food rather than her favorite cake, then put it back on her plate with a deep sigh of resignation.

I slapped my palms on the table and said there would be no more baby talk. We needed to focus on Mum and her health. This, after all, was the purpose of my visit. I said it was ridiculous that she hadn't been to the doctor yet, and Mum said, no need to get bossy, Cherry, because she'd been yesterday! Pat had finally worn her down.

Mum looked so pleased with herself. She was experiencing the glorious relief of having faced a fear. She'd believed going to the doctor would make her sick, but now she'd finally been convinced to go, she was convinced it would cure her. Sillier things have been thought.

They were waiting for a whole lot of test results. The doctor was being extra cautious. She probably just needed an antibiotic!

Auntie Pat avoided my eyes. I said, "I thought you read your own cards and you're going to die?"

She said, "Oh, we're *all* going to die, Cherry. I probably misinterpreted it. I am human, after all."

I asked about the MADAME MAE sign and Mum said she'd taken early retirement. It had started to become too tiring. Sometimes she'd been so tired she saw nothing, nothing at all, and she had to make it up. She said this as if we'd be shocked. Once again Auntie Pat and I pointedly avoided eye contact. *Didn't she make it all up?*

"All these women, looking at me with such *need* in their eyes, year after year," said Mum. "I couldn't take it anymore. Some of them became too dependent on me. They got addicted. That woman from the Southern Highlands wanted a *weekly* appointment. I said, absolutely not, you can come twice a year at the most. She wore me down and I let her book in for quarterly visits, but it just wasn't . . . healthy."

"Why were your customers mostly women?" I wondered.

"Because women are more in touch with their intuition," suggested my mother.

"Because women have less control over their lives," said Auntie Pat grimly.

For the previous two months, Mum had been "closing up shop," telling her regular customers that this would be their last reading with her. She was referring them all to a psychic who had set up an office in the local shopping center next to the dry cleaner. "She's talented and terribly energetic," said Mum. "She sees twice as many customers a day as I ever did. Charges twice as much too."

Mum's regulars had all brought along gifts to their last appointments: flowers, potted plants, homemade jams. There were cards on display all along Jack's floating bookshelves with heartfelt handwritten messages: *I owe my life to you, Madame Mae . . . I could not have gotten through these past difficult years . . . you guided me in my darkest hour . . . if it wasn't for you, Madame Mae, I would never have had the courage to chase my dreams.*

Reading them, I felt guilty. I knew Mum was successful. I knew Madame Mae was often booked out for months in advance, but I don't think I had been truly aware of how much she meant to people. This was like the retirement of a beloved teacher, therapist, or priest.

Her last ever reading had been at three o'clock the previous day. Unfortunately it had been with grumpy former bank manager Bill Hanrob, who came once a year, and whenever she said, "How are you, Bill?" he'd say, "You're the fortune teller, you tell me." Then he'd chuckle disbelievingly at everything Mum predicted. Every job has its negatives. (Yet he came back. Year after year.)

Tomorrow her office would be dismantled.

"I'm not sure what we'll do with all the space," said Mum.

Auntie Pat said nothing, but I could somehow tell she already knew what it would be used for.

"What about one last reading?" I said to Mum. "For me?"

Her face lit up and I wondered if I'd hurt her by never asking for a reading before. I deeply respected her fashion and skincare advice, but had it been disheartening to have so many people consider her an oracle while her own daughter scoffed?

"Yes," she said. "That's good. That's better. My last ever reading will be for Cherry."

I thought she might just read my tea leaves then and there at the table like she used to do when I was a little girl, but she said she wanted to do it properly. She left the room and came back dressed as Madame Mae: the patterned silk scarf around her head, the heavy eyeliner under her eyes, the dark red lipstick, the cape-like dress.

"Oh, Mae," said Auntie Pat when she saw her. "You didn't need to—you will tire yourself."

Mum ignored her.

"Mrs. Cherry Smith?" she asked in her singsong professional voice, but with a roguish lilt. "Here for your two o'clock appointment? I'm ready for you now."

"I'm a little nervous," I said, getting in character. This was something I'd overheard customers say, but I did feel a little nervous.

"No need to be nervous," said Mum. "All you need to do is relax."

She pulled back the purple curtain. "Please take a seat," she said. "Make yourself comfortable. It's important you are comfortable." She put a soft gold cushion behind the small of my back.

She switched on the lamps and used a nifty lighter I had never seen before to light the candles as well as a thin bamboo incense stick. The scent of frankincense filled the room. It's a woody scent, a bit like rosemary, and it helps alleviate anxiety.

She said, "Do you have a preferred method of divination? Tea leaves? Palm? Tarot?"

I said I didn't mind, and she said in that case, could I please give her a piece of my jewelry, my engagement or wedding ring, for example.

I tugged off both rings and gave them to her, glancing at my naked left hand as I did.

She solemnly placed the rings on a small silver tray on the table next to her. Grandma had given her that tray years ago for Christmas. She'd gotten one for Auntie Pat, too, and said, "You girls can swap if you like," and I think perhaps they did. It was a strange experience seeing familiar household objects become mystical in this setting and seeing my frustrating, headstrong, beautiful mother through the eyes of a "sitter," who had maybe caught the train and then walked nervously up Bridge Street, hoping to find answers in this ordinary house made extraordinary because of a little sign hanging from the letterbox.

She asked, "Did you bring a blank cassette for today's session?"

Then she caught herself. "I have a spare one." She took one out of a drawer and winked at me as she put it in the cassette player and pressed record. "You may have it for free."

I didn't know she offered recordings. It had been so many years since I had eavesdropped. She had gotten so polished and professional.

She sat down, took a deep breath, and said, "Cherry. That's a beautiful name. It suits you."

"My mother chose it," I said. (Being funny.)

"She must be very proud of you."

We smiled and I thought for a moment I might cry. It's strange how rarely you sit quietly opposite the people you love, without a menu or a meal or a drink between you.

She said, "Is there anything in particular you're hoping to learn or explore today, Cherry? A question you want answered? A problem you need solved?"

I thought for a moment and then I said, "Lately, I just don't seem to feel . . . happy."

(All these years later, when I listen to that recording, I hear my voice break on the word "happy." I've had the audio cassette recording transferred to a file I can listen to at any time. I press an arrow and there is my mother's long-dead voice, as if she is sitting right next to me, as if she is still available on the other end of the phone, and then there is my own voice, which sounds absurdly young, high and shrill, but recognizably me; it's as though I'm a bad actress, putting on a childish voice, or as if I have sucked on helium gas.)

"I can't see a future for myself," I said, "I just see a . . . big blank space."

"Is there anything you wish you could see in your future?" asked Mum, but I'm going to call her Madame Mae now, because if I'd told my mother I couldn't see a future for myself, she would have responded with exasperation and loving mockery: "Oh, you can't see a future for yourself, Cherry, you poor thing, with your university education and your handsome husband and that diamond ring on your finger."

I said I just wanted to see happiness in my future. Isn't that all anyone wants?

"So you need to make some changes," said Madame Mae.

"What kind of changes?"

"You will know."

In the recording you hear me shifting about in my seat. "*How* will I know?"

I was annoyed, a little contemptuous. It was as I'd always suspected, Madame Mae was simply a mirror, reflecting back whatever her customers so obviously wanted to hear. An untrained therapist who spoke in generalizations.

She said, "Will you close your eyes, please, Cherry."

Funny how she said my name now, with detachment, as if I were a customer, not her daughter. No more laughing about my mother choosing my beautiful name.

There was silence. I grew impatient. I opened my eyes a fraction, and saw that she had her eyes closed too. She breathed slowly and deeply, my rings now in the palm of her hand. I watched her for a moment and she spoke without opening her eyes. "Please keep your eyes closed and just breathe. That's all you need to do for the next little while, Cherry. Breathe."

I obeyed. I breathed slower, still slower, and I began to feel as if I might doze off. I wondered if any of my mother's customers had nodded off over the years, and what Mum did in those cases; did she clear her throat or nudge them gently with her foot? This silent breathing had also not been part of her routine when I eavesdropped. It felt as though my mother and I, or Madame Mae and I, went into a kind of meditative state.

There is plenty of research showing the efficacy of meditation in lowering blood pressure and reducing stress, and some believe expert meditators access a universal consciousness and therefore develop what could be perceived as psychic abilities. Is that what was going on with my mother that day?

She said, "I see so many things in your future, Cherry, so many beautiful things. They're all fluttering about me like butterflies, I hardly know where to start."

Mmmm, I thought skeptically, in my dreamy state. Pick a butterfly, Mum.

"I see you climbing up a mountain trail. Patches of snow. Glinting diamonds in the sunlight, and you see the spires of a castle, and you're laughing with somebody who makes you happy, and you . . . oh, that's gone . . . let me see . . ."

"Is it David?" I interrupted. "Is that the person making me happy?" *Do you see me leaving? Do I see me leaving?*

"I don't know." A pause. "It's someone you love."

Another long pause, then she said, this time with confidence, "You've already met the love of your life."

"So you mean David?" I felt relief. It would be convenient for all if my husband was the love of my life.

She paused and when she spoke again, she said, once more, a little uncertainly, "You've already met him."

Could she mean Jack Murphy? But what would be the point of telling me my deceased boyfriend was the love of my life? Didn't she always say, "They come for hope, Cherry. They should leave feeling happier and lighter than when they walked in my door." "Lighter in the wallet," Auntie Pat would say.

"I see a notebook. I see many notebooks."

"Right," I said. "I'll keep an eye out for notebooks."

In the recording you can hear my impatience. I wish I hadn't spoken like that.

"It's important you remember this: a marriage can change in ways you can't imagine, Cherry." Was that Mum or Madame Mae? A little acerbic. Could have been either. "You can bring it right back from the brink, if that's what you both want. And it can get better and better. Honestly. Better than you imagine."

Back from the brink. I saw again that image of the couple sitting on the edge of our apartment rooftop, backs to inky-black sky, falling into nothing.

"I see you moving, all the time, so much moving."

"Moving where?"

"Everywhere. On big planes and little planes, a train crossing a ravine over an arched bridge, a gigantic hot air balloon, a tiny car, driving along the coast, singing; I wonder where you're going? Back and forth, back and forth, here and there, but you're so happy."

"I'm going to become a travel guide?" I was being smart.

She said, "I do see a career change, yes. More learning. Late nights. Very, very hard. You will think you can't do it, but you will do it. You're very clever. A successful career. A little bit like mine, different from mine, of course, but there is a kind of . . . similarity. You will say, *I'm like my mother, I'm a fortune teller.*"

"Really?"

"It will be a kind of joke. I don't understand the joke. But I know this career will make you very happy. Proud. Well done, Cherry."

Her voice became quieter. She was tiring. I opened my eyes again and she looked exhausted, her shoulders slumped, my rings still held loosely in the palm of her hand.

"Will I have a family?" I asked. "Children?"

Another long pause.

She said, "I see a little girl. She will come on a plane."

That would have been so impressive if she hadn't already known about the potential adoption.

"She will come. Just when you need her the most. Her first name begins with . . ."

A long pause.

"It doesn't really matter, Mum . . . Madame Mae," I said. I always found the predicting of initials to be so pointless. A chip on the roulette table. You never know! If they get the initial right, everyone is amazed; if not, no one is that worried.

"B," said Madame Mae. "Her name will begin with the letter B."

"Wonderful," I said.

There was another pause, and when she spoke again, her words became garbled. It frightened me. I was worried Auntie Pat would be cross with me for suggesting she give me a reading.

"*The little girl won't stop the pain, terribleterrible pain nothing like it, IknowIknowIknow hurts so much, it's unfair, it's unbearable, can'tstopithurtingdarling . . . but she will help, she will be a reason to get up, likeyourlittleface gave me a reason, you just need a reason to get up, look for the notebooks, if there is a way, promiseIwillbethere keepbreathing keepbreathing that's all you can do.*"

She stopped.

Her face looked terribly old. There were beads of sweat on her forehead.

She opened her eyes, shook herself slightly, flicked "Stop" and "Eject" on the cassette recorder, and handed me the tape. She said, "That will be fifty dollars, Mrs. Smith." Her eyes lost their spooky glaze and she grinned at me. Madame Mae was gone. It was Mum again. "Only joking, you know I always collected payment upfront. Did you find that helpful? Do you feel more hopeful?"

She looks tentative and vulnerable, as well as spent. "I know sometimes people wish I could be more specific, more prescriptive, but that's not . . . that's not the way it works, of course." There was something so defensive about her, as if I'd come backstage to meet her after a performance.

And was it a performance? That's what I still didn't know.

I thought of all the books she had continued to borrow from the library; she'd taken her ongoing professional development requirements as seriously as a chartered accountant. I thought of the times she'd mentioned a new technique she was trying, and how she had always taken half an hour at the end of each working day to write a little reflection, I guess you'd call it, about her day's work.

"Yes," I said. "Thank you, Mum. That was wonderful."

I didn't know what I felt.

Mum got her test results a few days later. It was not good news, but of course you already know this. We all knew it. She'd left it too late. The silly diets had not been the cause of her digestive problems. The silly diets had masked the true cause.

"Six months," they said. "A year at the most."

Chapter 100

"So I understand you have a rather significant birthday coming up, Leo?" says Lilith brightly, as if she were speaking to a kindergarten kid excited to be turning six.

Her pantsuit today is the pale green of a not-quite-ripe avocado.

"I'm turning forty-three in November," says Leo. He knows where this is going. It's gotten crazy. Since the YouTuber's death, *everyone* at work seems to be talking about the prediction. The jokes have gotten out of hand. People give him a wide berth, even if he's in the office. They're joking. Or maybe they're not.

"You didn't think to let me know about this psychic prediction of a workplace accident?" says his boss now. She sits at her desk opposite him. There is a silver framed photo of Lilith with her husband and two children on her desk, angled so the person on the other side can see it. Presumably they are real people, but the husband has never accompanied Lilith to a work function, and their smiles are so plastically bright Leo sometimes wonders if she photoshopped herself into one of those photos that comes with the frame.

"I didn't take it seriously." Leo pinches his nostrils shut. Lilith's perfume is especially overpowering today. It's Calvin Klein Secret Obsession. He knows this because once he was in a department store with Neve and she was spraying perfume onto cardboard strips, and when she waved one in front of his nose he reacted with visceral horror. "Euww, Lilith!"

"But you made an announcement about it at a meeting." Lilith taps a fingernail on her desk.

"I was joking," says Leo, "you know, along the lines of 'so let's make sure we take workplace safety seriously'!"

"Which we certainly do," says Lilith.

"We certainly do," agrees Leo.

Lilith says, "So I'm thinking we keep you off-site as soon as you turn forty-three."

Leo's mouth drops. "I need to be on-site to do my job effectively."

"You can work around it," says Lilith. "FaceTime and so on." She waves an airy hand. "It's the only way. The feeling is that you're kind of, you know, cursed."

"Right," says Leo. "Well, that's kind of you." It doesn't feel kind, it feels like people believe his mere presence will cause an accident. "I guess."

"Obviously, we'll have to look at your key performance indicators in light of this new flexibility, discuss your utilization rate and so on."

"Obviously," says Leo. She means he will be expected to work longer hours. She means she intends to squeeze him and squeeze him like a damp cloth until every drop of him is gone and he's bone dry.

Leo says, "My wife wants me to give up work for a year."

Lilith smirks. "I assume you've told Neve that's not financially viable."

What does she know about their financial situation? He also doesn't like the way she always uses Neve's name in that strangely patronizing way.

"What's your husband's name, Lilith?" he asks on impulse. He gestures at the photo. "I've never met him, have I?"

Lilith pushes the photo frame so it's facing her. "John."

John! Likely story! He wonders if Lilith is an alien, imagines her going home each night and peeling off her face.

(Just one phone call with Rod and he can feel another younger, more lighthearted version of himself coming creakily back to life.)

(It makes him so happy.)

Last night Neve did an impressive presentation to the family about moving to Tasmania and Leo becoming a stay-at-home dad while Neve works at a new job with the Tasmanian Department of Education, a job she hasn't yet applied for but is bizarrely confident she can get. Where does she get that crazy optimism? The public service regularly places ads for jobs that have already been filled. Everyone knows that! The presentation included music and special effects. There were pictures of possible rental homes and nearby schools. One slide was devoted to "fun activities" the whole family would enjoy in Tasmania, along with spectacular pictures of bushwalks and beaches. (His soft Sydney kids have no idea about the icy temperature of that water.) One slide was called "Nana" with a picture of Leo's mother looking sad and hopeful. Emotional blackmail. The children didn't say yes, but they didn't say no either. Leo suspects his mother's bribes may have been offered and accepted. Also, and this wasn't covered in the presentation, but the children are smart: they know Leo "staying home" would avoid the possibility of a workplace accident, which was much worse emotional blackmail they'd probably tell their therapists about one day.

Leo said he would think about it.

"Think about it fast," said Neve.

She's been playing an old country song on repeat, called "Take This Job and Shove It." It's not exactly a subliminal message. Could he really change his whole life because of a psychic's prediction? One he doesn't really believe?

He thinks of his conversation with Rod, who said the prediction was bullshit, but that sometimes you don't realize how worn down a job can make you until you get out. He said he'd never regretted his decision to move interstate back near his parents and that he'd jump at the chance to be a stay-at-home dad for a year. Rod suggested he and his son, who is a year younger than Oli, could join them on the

Bay of Fires walk in Tassie, the thought of which makes Leo drunk with happiness. Delirious.

"Maybe our boys will become friends!" he said to Neve.

More likely they'll hate each other on sight. Leo isn't an idiot.

But you never know.

"Right. I think that's all," says Lilith.

Leo holds up a finger. "One more thing."

Chapter 101

The same day we got Mum's diagnosis, David called from Perth. He was very upset. There had been a terrible accident at the previous Friday night's rooftop party.

Two people, a man and a woman, had been sitting on the edge of the balcony, laughing and smoking and waving their arms about, when, just like that—it happened so fast, it was the strangest, most terrifying thing to witness—they fell. Together. Backward. Into the night.

The man was already dead by the time they got downstairs. They stabilized the woman—all those medical professionals together in one place, she got the best possible care—but she died later that night.

We didn't know the couple. They were friends of the trainee anesthetist in the apartment below ours. Visiting from Melbourne. The anesthetist was a mess.

"It was just like you described," said David. He sounded like he'd been drinking. I had not drunk any alcohol since I'd been home with Mum and Auntie Pat. I was sleeping and eating better. I knew I would still drink to the point of oblivion at my next Friday-night party. I could not imagine attending one of those parties sober. It was like I was a situational alcoholic. (This is not a recognized term.)

David said, "The man wore a white T-shirt and she was trying to grab at his shirt. Everyone says that's exactly how you described it."

I didn't remember saying anything about a white T-shirt, but I guess I *could* have said that when I was drunk. White is a common color for a T-shirt.

"So I guess you've got the family gift, Cherry," he said slowly. He had always been respectful about my mother's fortune-telling, as if it were an unusual religion she practiced, but up until now he had certainly not been a believer.

"It was dangerous," I said. I felt as if it were somehow my fault, as if I'd made it happen. "Drunk people sitting on the edge of a rooftop balcony. I wasn't telling the future. I was trying to warn people to be careful."

And as I have already mentioned, I had also wondered if it was a symbolic image. If the couple represented me and him.

"But you kept saying you could *see* it happening," said David.

"I meant I could *imagine* it happening."

I told David about Mum and he said he was so sorry, and I know he meant it because he was fond of my mother, but he was too shaken by the accident to focus properly.

"When are you coming home?" he asked.

It took me a moment.

I very nearly said, "What do you mean? I *am* home."

It's a very particular time in your life, when someone you love is dying.

The world doesn't stop for you. We know this, but in our hearts we are shocked. We are like famous people who say: *But don't you know who I am?* Except we want to say, *But don't you know what I am going through? How can you speak to me like that when my mother is dying?*

There are still red lights and rude people, long lines and lost keys. You can still stub your toe, and it will still hurt like the devil. The difference is that your reaction may be gargantuan. You may react with a rage-filled stream of profanity, the likes of which your aunt hasn't heard since the war. You may scream in your car at a red light and scare small children.

The dying person will not, by the way, always behave like a lovely dying person in a movie. She will not necessarily want to sit on the beach with a blanket wrapped around her thin body, looking wan and beautiful, her eyes wise and sad, a gentle breeze in her hair, while she makes profound remarks and looks at the sea. (I believe I may be describing a scene from the excellent, extremely sentimental movie *Beaches*.) She may in fact say, "Of *course* I don't want to go to the *beach*, Cherry, I feel so sick, why would you suggest such an *idiotic* thing?"

Your feelings can still be hurt by a dying person.

A dying person can still be vain. Stupidly vain. A dying person can take pride in her thinness, point at her hipbones, and say, "Look how skinny I am!" as if it's a nice bonus, and you can't shout, "You're skinny because you're DYING, you silly woman!"

You can still feel infuriated by a dying person, especially if the doctors make it clear an earlier diagnosis would have saved them. You can want them to feel remorseful for the catastrophic consequences of their foolish actions, even though they are paying the ultimate price, because it feels like *you're* the one paying it. Not them. They're getting off scot-free—back to stardust, or resting in peace with their heavenly Father, or rerouted to another body, whatever it is you believe—they're the ones leaving, and you will be the one left behind.

Macabre but necessary calculations are required. If your loved one is dying in a matter of weeks you'll want to spend as much time as possible with them. But how many hours a day is appropriate? (Can you have a day off?) If your loved one is expected to live for another year the calculations become trickier, especially if your home and job are on the other side of the country.

I wasn't required to be a carer for my mother. Auntie Pat was adamant that this was to be her job, but what respite care did I owe my aunt? I say this as if I struggled with the question at the time, but I fear it never crossed my mind. Auntie Pat was so capable.

Anyhow, Mum and Auntie Pat answered all these questions for me. They told me to go back to Western Australia for now at least, and I did as they said.

Everything had changed when I got back to Perth. There were no more rooftop parties. The entrance to the terrace was blocked off. The residents were all still shocked and somehow ashamed.

The anesthetist whose friends had died moved out and a couple with a very lovely baby moved in, which changed the whole "vibe" of the place. Even I could see that the baby was objectively lovely, and naturally my husband adored the child. It hadn't occurred to me that it was possible for a family to live there.

David and I applied to adopt a baby from Korea. It was a strange time, waiting for something good to happen, waiting for something awful to happen. I was grieving in anticipation, but Mum was still alive, and we talked every couple of days. Some of those calls felt forced and we got off the phone fast, but sometimes we talked in a way we hadn't before.

One day I asked her, "Was Madame Mae real, Mum?"

She sighed and said, "I did my best, Cherry." Which wasn't an answer. Another day, she said she was sorry for not going to the doctor sooner, and she hoped she could get to hold her grandchild. "You'll be a good mother, Cherry, I know you think you won't be, but you will." I said, "Is that Madame Mae or Mum?" She said it was Mum. Madame Mae had retired.

She didn't get to hold her grandchild, but she did get to see a copy of the photo we received of an eighteen-month-old baby called Bo-Mi.

It was a black-and-white picture of a beautiful, big-eyed little girl sitting on a bed, looking sideways at something we couldn't see as she played with the long ears of a toy rabbit, pulling them wide. I don't know why I loved Bo-Mi, or why I thought she would somehow transform me from a reluctant mother into a mother, but I did. I think I liked that she was serious, as if this one moment captured by the camera conveyed her personality. I thought a serious baby would suit me. I thought I could make a serious baby laugh.

In my accompanying letter with the photo, I said, *Look, Mum, it's the little girl you said would arrive on a plane and you even got her first initial right too.*

Auntie Pat called and said Mum cried when she saw the photo and was so pleased her prediction had come true.

"How is she?" I asked, because I was thinking of the other part of Mum's prediction that the baby would arrive just when I needed her the most.

"Well," said Auntie Pat, and I heard the pause as she inhaled on her cigarette. "She has good days and not-so-good days. I think you should make plans to come here next month, darling."

Michelle called and said the baby reminded her of both David and me. Of course the baby looked nothing like me, but Michelle insisted. "She has that serious look of yours."

David and I spent a lot of time lying in bed, staring at the photo together, handing it back and forth, analyzing it and finding new things to say. "I feel like she's quite intelligent," said David. He was besotted. I loved the love he showed this little girl.

I have lovely memories of that time. We were gentle with each other. Kinder than we had been before. Perhaps we were even a little vulnerable with each other.

Sometimes when we had sex, there would be a moment when we would look into each other's eyes, and it seemed like we were both trying to communicate something urgent and important, but we never said it out loud, whatever it was we were trying to say. Perhaps neither of us had the words.

I thought about my mother saying you could bring a marriage back from the brink and I wondered if that's what we were doing: carefully tiptoeing our way back from the cliff edge.

Then two things happened.

We got a phone call from the adoption agency saying there had been a mix-up. That photo we received should have gone to Mr. and Mrs. David and Cheryl Smith, not Mr. and Mrs. David and Cherry Smith. We were not to worry, though. We weren't going to miss out! Our baby, a boy, was only six months old, and a younger baby was always preferable, obviously, and this was an absolutely gorgeous little fellow. A new photo was on its way to us. "I just can't believe how similar your names are," said the woman on the phone. "What are the chances?"

I hope you now understand why, when I attended a team-building lunch at the Wok n' Roll Chinese restaurant the very day after we'd got the news about our baby no longer being our baby and a colleague referred to me as "Cheryl," I felt compelled to throw a spring roll at him. I am not proud of that moment, but I don't regret it.

My boss suggested I leave work early as I was obviously "not myself."

I sometimes wonder what would have happened if I had not thrown that spring roll, if I'd felt the urge in my fingertips but resisted it, and if I therefore had not come home much earlier than expected and seen David and Stella deep in conversation on the stairs outside our apartment.

There was nothing unusual about this. They both worked irregular hours at the same hospital and belonged to the same dive club. They were friends. Men and women can be friends, colleagues, flatmates or dive buddies without feeling the need to have sex! Of course they can.

And yet.

They were only talking. Not touching. Not standing inappropriately close. They were doing nothing wrong.

But I stopped and watched for a while, and I knew.

I can't tell you exactly *how* I knew.

Sometimes you just do. Even if you have the intuition of a potato.

Chapter 102

The YouTuber death pushes Dom right over the edge, just like Eve knew it would.

"Eve, if the only way to keep you safe is to break up . . ."

He doesn't finish the sentence.

They sit side by side on their couch. (They had two choices at IKEA, and of course they had chosen the more expensive one, because they are idiots. It already looks shabby and old.)

"You know it wouldn't be a breakup like when we were at school," says Eve. "It would be a *divorce.*"

He flinches at the word.

"We'd have to get lawyers. *Expensive* lawyers."

She's not sure that's true. It's not like they have any assets.

They slump silently on the couch, looking blankly at their phones.

Suddenly Eve puts down her phone. "So what if we do divorce, I marry someone else and *he* ends up killing me when I'm twenty-five? Did you think about that?"

It's a very mean thing to say because he obviously has not thought about it. His face first goes white and then red.

Dom is a very strong boy, but she's stronger.

Chapter 103

A divorce is like a death but without the comfort of a funeral or sympathy cards. No one brings you flowers, but even if your divorce is right because your marriage was wrong, it can feel like you are being slowly, painstakingly ripped in half.

Most studies of stress put divorce right up at the top, along with the death of a spouse, moving house, and a jail term. I'd find a jail term more stressful than moving house, but everyone is different.

David didn't try to deny it when I asked him about Stella. He vaguely implied it was my fault because I wasn't there when the couple fell off the balcony, which was traumatic (and also kind of my fault because I predicted it, although he didn't say that out loud, of course). What else could they do but go to bed together?

He probably felt guilty and I definitely felt righteous. We were upset about the baby girl and embarrassed by our distress, so we never properly articulated our feelings of loss. It was only a photo, after all. We could still adopt a baby.

Of course you probably think the cheating was just a symptom of the rot at the heart of our marriage and perhaps you are right. Once, I said, "You don't even *like* me, David," and he looked horrified, as if I'd caught him out in something far worse than cheating. He said, "Well, do you like *me*, Cherry?" I'd never really thought about it. I know that conversation sounds so odd. Relationships can be very odd. How did we end up together? It's a mystery.

Not really a mystery. It was sex. No need to overcomplicate things.

My in-laws tried to help, sharing stories of difficult times during their marriage. Auntie Pat suggested we go on a "Marriage Encounter" weekend, which is a popular program for married couples begun in Spain in the sixties by a Catholic priest. It would involve us going away with other couples and talking about feelings. We could think of nothing more horrific.

I shall not rehash the dying throes of our marriage: paperwork, admin, the canceling of our adoption, a division of assets, shouting, a vicious argument about the "good" saucepan. We kept having sex right until the end. We kept saying, "Last time." It took quite a while for the last time to be the last time. In fact, he was living with Stella at the time. (I don't feel guilty. She did it to me first.) (I do feel a little bit guilty.)

He's still living with Stella. He's a very successful, happily married cardiologist with children they presumably adopted or conceived through sperm donation, I can't tell you for sure, and grandchildren. I'm just a little footnote in their life.

I called him when his mother died. She and I tried so hard to stay friends, but it was impossible because Michelle's loyalty had to be to her son. She loved me but she loved her son more. Of course she did.

I forgave Stella for sleeping with my husband, but I never forgave her for stealing my in-laws.

In the middle of all that, my mother died: far too young. As you know. An unnecessary death. But I've been over this. Grudges aren't healthy.

It was a late afternoon in May, and Mum floated on a sea of morphine administered by Auntie Pat, who was haggard with exhaustion, barely able to stand upright, because she'd refused to let anyone else nurse her sister. An older, less self-absorbed version of me would have insisted I give her more respite. It's on my list of lifetime regrets.

I sat in the high-backed chair that had once belonged to Dad and from which Madame Mae had done all her readings. The light was softening, and Auntie Pat had said to me earlier in the kitchen, "Not long now, Cherry." She sat on the other side of the bed in the chair where Mum's customers had sat, hugging the gold pillow to her stomach.

There were long periods where nobody spoke. We could hear magpies singing, the far-off sound of a lawn mower, the steady drip of the IV, and an occasional huge yawn and corresponding jaw click from poor Auntie Pat.

Auntie Pat had warned me about the death rattle. It's when saliva or mucus collects in the back of the throat and the person can't swallow or cough. It sounds very unpleasant, like a loud gurgling or choking sound, but it doesn't mean the dying person is distressed. (Or so they believe.)

Mum never made that awful sound. Not everyone does. She always said she simply *refused* to snore.

Her breathing got erratic and then labored. I kept thinking she was gone and I'd hold my breath, but then her chest would rise again and I'd breathe again. At one point she waved two fingers like a conductor, her eyes still shut, and said, "Dancing the Swiss fondue! Wasn't that funny, Pat?"

"It was so funny, Mae," said my aunt, and she smiled at me.

I think maybe Mum could already see Dad and she was telling him about it, because she said, "Oh, darling, isn't she the funniest little thing?"

Those were her last words. They were excellent last words, Mum. Well done.

An hour later, she took a breath.

We waited.

There were no more breaths.

I like to imagine Dad waiting for her on the dance floor at The Cab, one hand behind his straight back, the other hand outstretched, ready to take hers, to swing her away.

The other night I dreamed I saw my parents dancing and they turned and saw me, and held out their arms. I ran to them, fast as the wind, like a child.

Chapter 104

Allegra, wearing a blue hospital gown—"underpants on, bra off"—lies face down in a small tunnel. She does not suffer from claustrophobia, but she now understands why people do, because this is not fun. She is wearing giant headphones. Michael Bublé is crooning love songs to her through the headphones. Her mother is a Michael Bublé fan, Allegra not so much. She holds a buzzer she can press if she needs to talk. A clip on her finger is attached to a long tube monitoring her heart rate and breathing. She rarely goes to the doctor, has never been admitted to the hospital. Everyone is friendly and kind, but she doesn't like the way they are in charge of her, the way she is in charge of her passengers. She recognizes something of herself in the authoritative boredom of their tones. Everything they say they've said a thousand times before. Every question Allegra asks has been asked and answered before.

Her back pain is far worse this time around. Nothing seems to help. She may require surgery. They just have to work out what's going on. She has never had surgery.

Her mother remains in a state about the prediction, in spite of the blessings, mantras, and the famous astrologer in India who could see nothing untoward in Allegra's birth chart.

She overheard her brother saying, "Mum, no doctor is going to prescribe Allegra antidepressants as a preventative measure based on some nutjob's prediction."

"But back pain causes depression, Taj!" said her mother. "And depression causes back pain! It's a loop! She's stuck in a loop! Now she can't work, she can't drive, she's stuck at home all day, she is a sitting duck for depression!"

"So we fix her back pain," said Taj. "We don't muck around with her brain chemistry."

Allegra is not suicidal, absolutely not, but in the same way she now understands claustrophobia, she also has a new understanding of suicidal ideation. There have been times when she would do anything to escape the pain.

A disembodied voice says, "All right, Allegra, we're about to begin! It's going to get very noisy, but try to relax and press the buzzer if you need me."

In spite of the warnings, she is still surprised by the loudness of the machine when it starts up. The noises are so comical she wants to laugh. Is someone playing a joke on her? They are like pretend sounds for a children's spaceship toy.

Eow, eow, eow, eow.

BOOM! BOOM! BOOM!

Thump, thump, thump.

Beep, beep, beep.

The fact that these strange sounds are interspersed by snippets of Michael Bublé makes it all the weirder. How did she end up here? She thinks of the moment she took the full weight of that caftan woman's carry-on bag, and then that day, when she'd felt so happy, Anders running, the dog on the lead, her legs tangling so unnecessarily. Nobody to blame for all this except herself.

She tries to remember all the MRI sounds so she can replay them for Jonny, and then she remembers that she and Jonny are not together anymore, or were never really together in the first place, she isn't sure. Of course, he didn't abandon her on the grass that day. He and Anders got her to her feet—she was nearly sobbing with the pain—and Jonny drove her home, got her into bed, and gave her two painkillers left over from last time. Her parents came over because she called them like a child. She didn't know what else to do. Who do people call if they don't have parents?

Jonny met her parents on the same day she made it clear she didn't want to meet his. He was warm and friendly with them and she heard him describe himself as "Allegra's friend." And then he left. He has checked in twice to see how she is doing. His messages are not cold, but they are not warm either. They are *neutral*. Neutral is awful.

Fool, fool, fool, she taunts herself, in rhythm with the MRI noises.

"I'm sorry you've had to take time off work again for me," says Allegra to her mother as she drives her home from the MRI.

"It is fine," says her mother with a shrug. "I am indispensable. They know it. And my family comes first."

Her mother has worked at the same insurance company for many years.

"How is the pain right now?" she asks.

"Seven out of ten." Allegra shifts in her seat. "It's bearable."

"We will get it sorted out. Put your seat back farther. Are you having suicidal thoughts?"

Her mother has been doing research and she has learned that you should not be afraid to ask someone if they are having suicidal thoughts. Allegra is sure the research is correct, but she's not sure you're meant to ask the question quite as often as her mother does. It's a little jarring.

"I'm fine," says Allegra. She reclines her seat back. "I'm not bursting with joy, obviously."

"Because of that boy?"

"No, because of my back," says Allegra. She sighs. "Also because of the boy. I mucked it up."

"Well, then you fix it," says her mother as she weaves in and out of traffic.

Allegra says, "It might not be that easy."

Her phone buzzes. It's Jonny. Her heart automatically lifts at the sight of his name, but then she remembers to steel herself for another neutral, we-are-friendly-work-colleagues-who-hooked-up-for-a-while-but-that's-all-over-now message.

It's a link, along with a text that reads: *At least try it in this life too.*

"Try it in this life?" She clicks on the link and laughs a little. It's a flight school offering trial introductory flights. He's talking about her being a bird in a past life.

"What is it?"

"Jonny sent me a link," explains Allegra. "He got the impression I want to train to be a pilot."

"How did he get that impression?"

Allegra tells her the story of her conversation with Jonny on their walk. "I'm not interested in training to be a pilot," says Allegra comfortingly.

"And why is that?" asks her mother. They stop at a light and her mother looks at her, her hands on the wheel. "Do you think because you're a *woman* you can't be a pilot?"

"Of course I don't think that," says Allegra. "Absolutely not." If it was any other woman than herself she would be encouraging them. The industry needs more female pilots.

She says to her mother, "You don't want me to be a pilot! You still go on about dentistry!"

"I haven't mentioned that in *years,*" says her mother. "I'd be proud if you became a pilot! If that's what you want, of course."

"It's not what I want," says Allegra. "I've honestly never thought about it. Not consciously, anyway."

"But then why did you say that to Jonny?"

Allegra says the same thing she said to him. "It's just the first crazy thing that came into my head. It's like saying, if I could be anything, I'd be a rock star!"

"You could not be a rock star," says her mother. "Your singing is terrible."

"Thanks, Mum."

"Seriously. It's very bad. I see the contestants on those singing shows and I say to your father, 'Why do their parents not set them straight?' But you *could* be a pilot, Allegra, you could be a very good pilot. You are a good driver, best in the family, better than your father, and you are so good with his coffee machine."

Allegra laughs. "So I should be a pilot because I can drive and work Dad's coffee machine?"

"It has as many buttons and switches as a spaceship. And you *always* wanted to fly. Do you not remember at your grandmother's house how you would run and jump off her back veranda with your arms out? It was terrifying to watch. Taj wouldn't do it!"

"I wasn't pretending to be a pilot," says Allegra. "I was pretending to be a plane."

"Well, you can't be a plane, Allegra, but you could be a pilot."

"You've never said this before, Mum."

"I didn't know it was your dream. I thought it was your dream to be a flight attendant."

"It was! It is! I love it."

"But just because you achieved one dream doesn't mean you can't now try for another. I've recently wondered if you needed a new challenge."

"Because you're obsessed with me not getting depressed," says Allegra.

"No! Before that! I simply thought it might be time for something new. Sometimes I worry you have become too . . ." Her mother looks for the right word. "Careful," she finally says.

"*Careful?* That was your favorite phrase when I was growing up, Mum: Be careful, Allegra."

"But now you're *too* careful. You dress like a rebel, but you are not one! Ever since that stupid boy broke your heart you have been so . . . tentative . . . with your heart, and now, it seems, with your dreams. *YOLO,* Allegra!"

"Ah, do you know what that means, Mum?"

"Yes, I do know what it means. It means you only live once."

"Which is a very strange thing for my Hindu mother to say."

"The acronym might mean that, but I think the message is: Dare to dream."

"Now you sound like Oprah."

Her mother sighs. "Also, that gorgeous young man likes you. He is sending you interesting links! And you have so much in common! Such beautiful faces and both just a little . . . *stupid*." She jabs her finger at her head.

"Thanks, Mum."

"Not intelligence-wise. But I find it interesting you both seem to need other people's permission to dream."

"Moving on," interrupts Allegra.

They drive in silence for a while.

What if she stopped being careful? What would that actually entail? Could she be a pilot? Could she allow herself to want that? What if she failed? What if everyone laughed at her? What if she doesn't have what it takes?

She looks at the reflections of the clouds in the car window.

What if she succeeded?

"I am wondering what that fortune teller is doing right now," says her mother. "I think about her all the time, but does she ever think about us? And the stress she has caused the families of her victims?"

"She could be on another flight," says Allegra. "Doing her 'cause of death, age of death' thing."

Her mother frowns. "That is the phrase she used? That is how she spoke?"

"Yes," says Allegra. "Didn't I tell you that? She'd say I *expect* . . . and then she'd give the cause of death, followed by the age of death."

"*I expect*," repeats her mother. "That's interesting."

"Why?" asks Allegra.

"Her choice of language. I wonder if she works in the insurance industry. Expect. Expectations? Life expectancy. Age of death. Cause of death."

Allegra doesn't answer. She is not interested in the lady. The lady means nothing. She is taking out her phone and texting Jonny.

Can we please talk . . .

Delete.

Thank you for the link . . .

Delete.

I actually really like . . .

Delete.

The problem is I think I maybe love you.

She thinks of herself as a little girl running as fast as she could and jumping off her grandmother's back veranda, arms straight and horizontal like wings. It wasn't really that high, but you couldn't see the ground before you jumped, you just had to believe it was there, and every time there was a terrifyingly glorious moment of freefall.

She presses send.

Her regret is instant. Her back clamors for attention. Her pain soars to a nine. Such a weird message. You don't say "I love you" for the first time in a text. You don't say "I love you" when you've not yet confirmed you're in a relationship. He'll go running for the hills!

Her mother says, "She sounds just like an actuary."

Allegra doesn't respond because she is looking at the words that have appeared so quickly on her phone it feels like magic, it feels like a miracle.

The ground was there all the time.

She just flipped her whole day. Maybe she just flipped her whole life.

It says: *It's not a problem, Allegra, and it's not a maybe for me.*

Chapter 105

I'm retired now, but yes, that is correct, I was an actuary.

In other words I was a "fortune teller of the business world."

An actuary uses probability, statistics, and financial mathematics to project the future. I love my profession! Quite passionately. I have delivered many speeches on its fascinating history! To be clear, I delivered these speeches at industry events, not to cornered people at parties.

Well, all right, there was one cornered person at a party, but he seemed very interested. I will resist the temptation to share it with you. (But you should look it up!)

People prefer jokes to history, so here are some actuarial jokes:

Old actuaries never die; they just get broken down by age and sex.

I find that quite amusing. You may not.

How can you tell if an actuary is an extrovert? He looks at YOUR shoes when he talks to you!

That one is a little offensive, as it makes fun of our social skills. It's true we tend to be analytical, introverted people and some of us are "boffins" who disappear into a back room and emerge forty years later for our retirement party, but that is no reason to call us "strange" or "weird." Everyone is different!

What is the difference between an English actuary and an Italian actuary?

An English actuary can tell you how many people are going to die next year. An Italian actuary can give you their names and addresses.

That one is insulting to Italians who are *not* involved in organized crime, which is obviously the vast majority.

Anyhow, this is how I became an actuary.

After my divorce and my mother's death, I went through a difficult period. It's possible I was suffering from depression. You would have thought Auntie Pat and I would have leaned on each other after Mum died, but we did the opposite. We drew away. I think Auntie Pat might have suffered a kind of breakdown. She made oblique references to it in later years. We eventually both apologized for abandoning each other, but I think we had no choice. We were like two drowning people. We needed to work out how to swim on our own. Auntie Pat went back to her own home the day after Mum's funeral. Mum's house was now mine. I didn't want it, but it didn't occur to me to sell it. That felt like bad manners. (I still own it. I have very nice tenants living there. I'm sorry to mention real estate, like a typical baby boomer. I know I'm lucky, although I would have preferred not to have inherited when I did.)

My dad used to say to my mother and me, "This too shall pass." We didn't find it helpful. In fact, I recall my mother stamping her foot over some baking disaster one hot Christmas Day, wiping her sweaty forehead with a tea towel, and crying, "Oh, *do* shut up, Arthur, it will only bloody pass after I've done it all again!"

Every day that year I woke up, cleaned my teeth, looked at myself in the mirror, and said, "This too shall pass, Cherry."

One day I was thinking about Mum laughing about the Swiss fondue, which led me to think about Eliza in her leopard-print dress. I was worried she wouldn't remember me, but she did, right away. We met for lunch in the city and I told Eliza I was looking for career advice, and she dabbed her mouth with a cloth napkin and said, "Right." She mapped out my future as decisively as Madame Mae mapped out the future of a woman needing to escape a violent marriage.

She said the Australian insurance industry needed more actuaries.

She said that unlike management positions, my gender would not hold me back because an actuary is an actuary is an actuary. I didn't understand what she meant at the time, but I do now, and she was right. She said the exams were *brutal* and she was right about that too. It was like signing up for a triathlon. I have never done a triathlon, but when I gained my final actuarial accreditation, I felt some affinity to those athletes who stagger, seemingly half dead, across the finishing line.

I worked in the insurance industry for many years, eventually at quite a senior level. I analyzed statistical data related to mortality and then developed probability tables to forecast risk and liability for payment of future insurance benefits. I studied historical data for patterns specifically in relation to CODs (causes of death). I do apologize. You're not interviewing me for a job.

I'm trying to say I spent my career asking and answering this question: *How and when will people die?* To put it as simply as possible, it was my job to work out how much an insurance salesman like Jiminy Cricket should charge someone like my dad for life insurance. To be clear: my job was *not* to determine how and when any one *individual* would die, but a group of individuals, which is why my actions on the plane continue to mystify—never mind.

I believe I'd been working in my first actuarial position for about eighteen months and enjoying it immensely when one Saturday morning while catching up on errands, I happened to walk by a Hornsby hairdressing salon called Hazel's Hair. I normally went to a salon in Wahroonga, but that hairdresser always remembered everything I'd said at my previous appointment. I think she wrote it down. I found that invasive.

So, on impulse, I went into Hazel's Hair. You'll be surprised to know that I rarely do things on impulse.

(That was a joke.)

(As I assume you would not be surprised.)

As soon as I walked in the door, a girl sitting behind the counter reading a copy of the *Women's Weekly* looked up at me and said, "Madame Mae's daughter!" Then she said, "Don't tell me, don't tell me!"

"Don't tell you what?" I said, confused.

"It's Sharon—no it's not, it's Cheryl! No, not Cheryl, Cherry!"

I didn't know her from a bar of soap. She knew me because of Mum's fame. It was Hazel, of course, who attended the same high school as me and would go on to become a significant person in my life, not solely because of her excellent hairdressing skills.

She cut my hair that day, and I liked the way she cut it, and we chatted and, eventually, after a number of appointments, we became friends. One day she invited me to a dinner party at her place in Terrey Hills. She said her husband, who worked at a university, was inviting some very "clever" friends, and I was clever, so I would fit right in.

Of course I was dismayed, but there was no way to get out of it because she was so keen for me to attend that she gave me *options*. I was available on every night she suggested because I had become a real loner. My friend Ivy had moved to America, and although I occasionally saw Eliza, she was part of a huge social circle and I'm more of a one-on-one kind of friend.

Well, as you know, I went to the dinner party. It was a terribly hot night and I kept reminding myself not to fall back into my old ways. I did drink a *little* too much, and as I've mentioned, I told everyone about Mum, but I didn't do too badly. I even enjoyed some parts of it. For example, I enjoyed it when the handsome man told me I didn't look like a potato.

If you recall, the night was nearly over and I was seated cross-legged on the floor. Hazel had fallen asleep on the couch, the bearded man was droning on, and the doorbell rang.

"Excuse me," said Hazel's husband, Tony, who I think was hopeful we would all go home soon. "That will be my brother."

His brother was borrowing some kind of gardening implement and he came in briefly to meet us and try some of the German Black Forest cake. Tony introduced us all.

Ned seemed like a perfectly pleasant man. Blue jeans. Glasses. Average height. Not much hair. A kind of impatient energy to him. I felt nothing in particular toward him, but when he saw me, his face lit up like a Christmas tree. He handed his plate back to his brother and crouched right down, balancing on the balls of his feet on the carpet, to look intently at me, as if he were a naturalist and I were an interesting botanical specimen.

He said, "Kronecker delta girl."

I had not the slightest clue what he was talking about.

Chapter 106

"Got to go," says Eve.

"Wait, where have you got to go?" Dom sits on the end of their bed, taking off his shoes. He looks exhausted. He started his day at five this morning.

"The restaurant," Eve reminds him. "It's Thursday, remember? I'll bring home leftovers."

It's a pizza and pasta restaurant and the boss encourages staff to take home leftover pasta at the end of the shift, which is excellent. Free dinner for tonight and tomorrow.

"Is it Thursday?" says Dom. "I thought it was . . . oh, I don't really know what day I thought it was."

She kisses his forehead. "All of this, the money, everything, it's going to get better."

"Is it?" he says, yawning. He is asleep before she even leaves the apartment. She thinks he only lets himself fall asleep properly now when he's alone. It's so, so stupid.

On the bus she checks the online chatter about the Death Lady.

Someone has posted: *Could she be an insurance actuary? My daughter was on that flight and the language she used made me wonder that.*

Yesterday, Paula sent Eve a message saying: *The Death Lady's first name might be Cherry.*

So Eve googles, without much hope: *Cherry Actuary.*

And there she is. As easy as that. All this time she was only a Google search away.

She's younger in the picture but there is no doubt: it's the lady from the plane. She wears a silk blouse and pencil skirt, pearl earrings and red lipstick, and she stands at a podium gesticulating at a Power-Point slide behind her. The caption says: *Cherry Lockwood delivers another riveting keynote address at the Actuaries Institute December Luncheon!* It was taken five years ago. She looks so happy. Not like a Death Lady at all.

Chapter 107

Ned Lockwood. That was his name. My hairdresser's brother-in-law.

Ned was a high school math teacher. A beloved teacher. If you had Mr. Lockwood you remembered him forever, even if you hated math, or especially if you did, because his were the only math lessons you ever enjoyed.

"He leaps about the classroom like he's doing a kind of interpretive dance," a student once told me, laughing, and I laughed too, because I'd been married to Ned for five years by that time and this was such an accurate description. Ned leaped about supermarkets, cocktail parties, and museums in exactly the same way.

Ned had studied for his mathematics degree at Sydney University at the same time as me, and one day, according to him—I have no memory of it, I so wish I did—we sat next to each other during a lecture on the principles of Kronecker delta. Ned's pen, even though brand new, ran dry and he asked if I had a spare one. Apparently I handed one to him without even turning my head, which was a little rude, but I was concentrating so hard on the lecture.

He said he fell in love with me at that moment.

That is not true.

We didn't even speak and he was engaged to someone else at the time and he went right ahead and married her! It didn't work out, thank goodness. She couldn't cope with his energy.

Oh, and by the way, even if we had spoken it would have meant nothing because at the time I had eyes for nobody but Jack Murphy.

Ned and I went to see a movie for our first date. It was the "classic" romantic comedy, *When Harry Met Sally*. I loved it, but Ned didn't have the patience for romantic comedy. He could not sit still or stop talking. The movie begins when the couple drives from the University of Chicago to New York, and Ned wanted to tell me about a drive *he'd* taken between New York and Chicago, and finally I whispered, "Go for a walk! I'll meet you in the foyer after." He was so happy to be given permission to leave. I'm sure the people around us were happy too. He was a stickler for good manners but was really very bad-mannered about talking in the cinema.

He said, "Really? Would that be all right?" It was so strange, because it was our first date, and yet I felt like I already knew him, as if I knew how to handle this man, even though he was unlike anyone I'd met before. I always preferred seeing movies on my own. (Years later, he did manage to sit through all of *Titanic*, which was a record, and he managed not to talk even when I could tell he was becoming agitated about Rose not letting Jack share her door. Afterward we had burgers and I told him I would have let him share my door. We would have sunk together to the bottom of the ocean.)

When I came out into the foyer after *When Harry Met Sally* Ned was waiting for me, and he took me in his arms, bent me backward, and kissed me like it was the end of the war. Mind you, that was our first kiss, a little presumptuous! (I didn't mind.) "When Cherry met Ned," he said, and then he took my hand and said we had to run, because he'd found this great Nepalese restaurant that didn't take bookings, but he'd convinced them to hold us the perfect table in the window, and we made it, then sat down, started talking, and never stopped.

Ned Lockwood. The most exasperating, impatient, intelligent, funny, curious, intense man. On our first wedding anniversary he gave me a beautiful gold brooch inscribed with the Kronecker delta symbol. I've worn it every single day since.

Chapter 108

"I'm so embarrassed, that damned Death Lady has turned me into a hypochondriac," says Sue.

It's a Wednesday evening and Max is driving her somewhere. He's planned a surprise and he's gleeful about it. It's not even her birthday. She's fairly certain she knows which restaurant he has booked.

Sue's illness turned out to be an ordinary virus. Her itchy rash was a red herring. It was an allergic reaction to a bath bomb given to her by her favorite daughter-in-law. She's fully recovered now. Full of energy once again.

"You were quite ill," says Max.

"Yes, but I wasn't dying," says Sue. "If I overreact like that again, slap me across the face."

Max grimaces at the thought of slapping her across the face. "You didn't overreact, darling."

"Are we going to that new Japanese restaurant the kids were talking about?" asks Sue.

Max ignores her guesses.

"I'm not angry with the lady anymore," he says. "I'm happy we've had some . . . chats."

It's not like they didn't have their "affairs" in order. Of course they did. They have proper wills and powers of attorney and all that horrible stuff in case one of them should become incapacitated. They are pragmatic people who have both lost parents, but maybe they never really looked death square in its cruel implacable face before, because once they got started, they discovered a lot they had not discussed, from the macabre—"Any thoughts on an outfit for your corpse?"—to the mundane, such as the location of passwords, keys, and paperwork. They've written preferences for their funerals. Max wrote: *Don't care, won't be there, your mother is in charge.* But still, that's something to show the boys if there are arguments.

Max says, "When you were sick, I was thinking, okay, if this is it, if the old bird's prediction is right, what would I regret that we hadn't done together?"

"The trip," guesses Sue.

"Nah, not the trip. I'm looking forward to it, but I dunno, could it really be that much better than our trip around Tasmania?"

Sue thinks of the fjords of Norway and the lights of Paris.

"We-*ell*," she begins, but Max is on a roll.

He says, "I decided there's only one thing I'd feel bad we hadn't done."

He is pulling into the parking lot of what seems to be a local community hall in a nearby suburb. Sue's heart sinks the way it occasionally does when Max looks on with anticipatory delight as she opens a gift of clothing she knows won't fit or suit her. She can see other couples of a similar vintage to them emerging from their cars and heading toward the open door. Surely he hasn't got them joining some kind of community group.

"Salsa dancing!" he cries.

"Salsa dancing?"

"Don't worry," he says. "We're all beginners! It's an eight-week course. I remember how you were so keen to try it. You were always bringing it up and I was always shutting you down, and I thought if I lost you, I'd be kicking myself, thinking, *Why didn't I just say yes, why didn't I take her dancing?*"

Sue can't remember ever expressing an interest in salsa dancing, but over the years she has at various times tried to come up with creative ways to convince Max to exercise more. He likes dancing at weddings. He's always first on the dance floor and comes home with the back of his shirt soaked in sweat. She probably thought the best way to convince him would be to pretend salsa dancing was her dearest wish, when in fact she'd really just like him to join a gym! Imagine if she'd died and the poor man had spent the rest of his life saying regretfully, *If only I'd taken my darling wife salsa dancing.* She gets the giggles, but of course she can't tell him.

"I can't dance in these shoes," says Sue. "Not with my ankle."

Max reaches into the back seat and grabs a bag. "Sneakers."

"You think of everything," she says, ruefully recalling the lunch she'd skipped in anticipation of the apparently amazing Japanese food she thought they were trying out tonight.

Of course, within five minutes of the first lesson Sue knows they are going to *love* salsa dancing like they love most things. They are Sue and Max O'Sullivan. They love life. We're good at life, she thinks, as they grin at each other while they clap the rhythm of the salsa: clap-clap-clap-pause, clap-clap-clap-pause. Her charm bracelet jingles as she claps. Each charm is a symbol of something precious from her life: each son, each grandchild. There will be room for a tiny salsa dancer.

Their instructors are a gorgeous lithe swivel-hipped couple, and Sue can feel every sixty-plus person in that community hall, even the ones clearly dragged there by a more enthusiastic partner, falling in love with them. She already knows from the wry comments and jokes being shared that she and Max will have made friends for life by the time they've finished this course. More friends! "My parents make friends every time they leave the house," one of their sons had said at a speech for their thirtieth wedding anniversary, and the room erupted with laughter and love.

Max has got the rhythm already, and he's having a go at the hip movement, even though they're just meant to be clapping. It's hilarious, and hopefully he's burning a few calories, getting his heart rate up—this might even end up saving his life, you never know.

She repeats one word over and over in her head as she claps: Lucky-lucky-lucky-pause, lucky-lucky-lucky-pause.

Later that night, while they're eating toasted cheese and tomato sandwiches for dinner in front of the television, Sue sees on Facebook that another passenger has received a diagnosis of a serious disease he does not specify, but which was correctly predicted by the Death Lady. However, he intends to prove the lady wrong and beat the disease and then send her a thank-you card. That's the spirit.

She carefully puts down her phone, says nothing, and turns her attention to the television. She and Max laugh together at a rerun of *Frasier*. Niles is their favorite. He's so funny. Max laughs so hard he has to wipe tears from his eyes.

No more fussing. She will simply cherish every moment she's allocated until there are no more.

Chapter 109

You could say that Ned and I lived happily, for the most part, ever after.

Ned thrived on change, I thrived on routine, but we were committed to making it work because we had both come out of bad marriages and we wanted this one to stick.

We never had children. I told him early on that I did not want to be a mother, and he said that was fine with him, his students were like his kids and he couldn't imagine coming home to more "Sir! Sir!" I didn't think his own children would have called him "sir," but I didn't point that out.

We became avid travelers. I was in charge of packing and all logistics in regard to flights, bus, and ferry timetables. He was responsible for restaurant bookings and activities, both cultural and adventurous.

I will follow the lead of my old boss Baashir and share only a small selection of concise travel stories:

We did a hot air balloon safari over the Serengeti and our operator passed out! (He regained consciousness but it was touch and go. Ned said he could have gotten us landed, but I don't know about that.) (If he'd done that survey he would have said he could have landed a commercial plane in an emergency.)

We snorkeled with manta rays in the emerald-green waters of

Raja Ampat and a man on the boat was extremely rude to me and Ned yelled at him. We rode on camels at sunset in the Agafay Desert and Ned's camel bit him on the nose and I yelled at the camel.

We saw mountain gorillas in Uganda and orangutans in Borneo. Ned got pickpocketed at the Trevi Fountain and I got pickpocketed when a man accidentally spilled his drink on me in Buenos Aires. (It wasn't an accident.)

We raced through most museums and art galleries at breakneck speed except for the Mathematikum in Germany, where we did every single interactive exhibit and Ned took copious notes for teaching ideas.

You may recall my mother predicting I would see the spires of a beautiful castle with someone I loved, and it could have been at Schloss Vaduz in Liechtenstein—we laughed a lot that day and there was definitely snow on the ground—or perhaps it was the hike ending at King Ludwig's Neuschwanstein Castle in Bavaria, which Mum would have been more likely to have seen on a wall calendar. Although I was annoyed with Ned that day, so maybe not.

His impatience could annoy me. He could not bear to wait or line up, and it's inevitable when you travel. My so-called rigidity could annoy him. He wanted me to be more spontaneous, take more chances, and stop scanning every situation for possible risks. (That was literally my job.) He bounded up to strangers like a Labrador and asked them if they knew a better way, a shorter line, a faster option. Sometimes they did and he was triumphant, and sometimes they didn't and I rolled my eyes.

We lived for five years in an apartment in Sydney with a view of the Harbour Bridge, for three years in a stone-built cottage (circa 1630!) in Oxfordshire, England, with a view of a bubbling stream (there were swans! We couldn't get over it), and for one year in a one-bedroom Brooklyn brownstone with no view at all, for a rent you would now find unbelievable.

One year we got into role-play, one year we got into tantric sex (very time-consuming), and one year we got bored of sex and stopped for a while. One year we became obsessed with health food and exercise, and another year we got into fine dining and theater. One year, our twentieth year together, everything went wrong. Auntie Pat died, Ned's mother died, Ned and I both had health issues, our car was stolen, and we couldn't seem to catch a break. We bickered constantly, then we shouted, and then we stopped talking, and that was awful because talking was what we did best. We went to a counselor, who we both hated at first, but who we grew to love, and she helped us drag ourselves back from the brink. It's possible, just like Mum said it was, and then everything feels richer and deeper because of your awareness of what you so nearly lost.

Ned retired from teaching and I moved into a consultancy role, which meant I could work from anywhere doing the hours that suited me. We moved to Hobart and bought an ordinary shabby redbrick house with an overgrown garden and magnificent views of the Derwent River and the Tasman Bridge. I said, "No more moving. I'm done. They'll have to carry me out in a box."

Honestly I was just sick of the change-of-address forms.

Ned shook my hand. He said, "No more moving, Cherry."

On our first night our neighbors came over to introduce themselves. Their names were Jill and Bert. Jill carried a magnificent pavlova filled to the brim with cream and chopped strawberries and bananas. Her signature dish. It was a funny thing to take to a new neighbor because it had to be eaten right away and there was too much for two people, and what if we weren't hungry? What if we were lactose intolerant? Anyhow, that was my darling friend Jill: so foolhardy! We felt compelled to invite them in. Ned gave me a comforting look that communicated: Don't worry, I'll get rid of them fast.

But they stayed until midnight, and we drank the champagne our real estate agent had left for us while we polished off the pavlova. When I look back on that night it's like remembering the night we all fell in love.

To be clear: We didn't begin a polyamorous relationship, if that's what you're thinking! (Each to their own, but no thank you.) We just clicked in an entirely conventional but somehow very special way. The four of us seemed to balance one another out, like a beautiful equation. Euler's identity is considered the most beautiful equation in the world and is often compared to a Shakespearean sonnet, but a simpler mathematical analogy probably makes more sense. We were like a square. A square is mathematical perfection.

We were different. Jill and Bert, for example, did not like to travel outside of Australia. They only visited the mainland under sufferance to visit their three grown-up kids. Bert had a flying phobia. Jill had to dose him up on Valium to get him on the plane.

Jill had been a high school librarian and she was always trying to find Ned and me books we would like, as if we were reluctant young readers at her school. We preferred nonfiction, and when Jill told us fiction was "the lie through which we tell the truth" (she was quoting Albert Camus), we said truth is stranger than fiction (she told us we were quoting Mark Twain, and that wasn't the point). Bert, like me, was still working when we met, in construction, which was fortu-itous, as he helped Ned with some of his more overambitious renova-tion projects.

Because we lived next door we could get together at the drop of a hat. We played board games on cold winter nights in front of our fire-place, and we had barbecues in the summer on their back terrace. We discovered a shared love of hiking and camping, although as we got older our lower backs preferred we stayed in lodges. Tasmania has some of the best hikes in the world, and I'm confident the four of us did every one of them.

I think we moved next door at exactly the right time for Jill and Bert, because they had just become classic empty-nesters. Their chil-dren had all moved to the mainland for careers and opportunities. Jill and Bert were hoping lower house prices and free childcare would lure them back when the grandchildren arrived.

Ned and I still traveled, but Jill and Bert took care of our house when we were away, and when they were away visiting their children we looked after Bob, their adorable German shepherd.

Our friendship never got too much, which it could easily have done. We seemed to know when we needed to give one another space.

One day I came down with a very bad head cold, as I do every couple of years. The four of us had planned to go for lunch at a vineyard and I told Ned he should still go.

While they were gone, I lay on my bed and the thought came into my aching head: *They're not coming back. I'll never see them again.* It was the same cool precise voice I'd heard when Jack was going away to Vietnam.

Jill and Bert drove a white Toyota Camry. Jill was driving home so the men could try lots of wine at the vineyard. She had a bit of a lead foot.

I saw it happening. The men a bit raucous after the wine-tasting. Jill distracted. Just for a moment, as she took a sharp bend too fast. The car flipping. Three times before it settled. *Bang, bang, bang.* All three gone. Only me remaining.

When the knock on the door came, I was not surprised. I knew it was the police, and I knew they would ask if there was anyone I could call, and I would have to say no, there is no one. Everyone I loved most in the world was in that car. I went to the door slowly.

I wanted to stay in my life for just a few seconds more.

It was Ned. He couldn't let himself in because he'd forgotten his keys. He was so taken aback when I collapsed sobbing into his arms. He said Jill did take some of those corners too fast, but she was a good driver and he never felt unsafe. I said the pain when I thought I'd lost them all had been unbearable. I didn't think it would be possible to go on. I felt that I would have to kill myself. He said I mustn't think about it, I had not inherited my mother's gift—if she even had a gift—and everyone imagined terrible things, but that didn't mean they were going to happen. Jill was deeply offended when she heard about my vision and said she had an impeccable driving record, thank you very much.

Four years went by. More hikes with Jill and Bert. Our pace as brisk as ever, even after Jill hurt her ankle. She was good with her rehab, she got better. More board games. Ned and I did a road trip on the East Coast of America and visited my old friend Ivy and her husband, as well as some of our friends from when we'd lived in Brooklyn all those years ago.

Jill and Bert had their first grandchild, and two of their three children moved back to Tasmania as they had always hoped. Ned's nephew (Hazel and Tony's eldest) got married and Ned was MC at the wedding, and he was marvelous, hilarious, everyone said so. Where *did* Uncle Ned get all that energy?

I think it's possible I was as happy as I could possibly be during this time. That vision had really affected me. I felt there was another universe running alongside me, where Ned, Bert, and Jill really had died just as I foresaw, and I was grateful every day to have remained in this one. I remember once, on a Sunday morning, splashes of sunlight on our kitchen floor, a Coldplay song on the radio, I bit into a piece of multigrain sourdough toast with peanut butter and I looked at Ned's broad back as he stood shirtless in his boxers, chopping up celery for his awful morning smoothie; it was just another normal morning, nothing special, but I felt the most extraordinary feeling of bliss, euphoria, and contentment combined. I have never forgotten it. On the days I believe in heaven, I believe it's like that moment.

Then Ned pressed the button on the blender so I couldn't hear the chorus of the Coldplay song and I cried out in exasperation, "*Ned!*"

Now I will tell you what happened on another Sunday morning four months before the flight that made me famous.

Chapter 110

Ethan is at the Opera Bar. He's found a good table with an unobstructed view of the harbor, and he's ordered a big bowl of fries and a beer.

He has secretly avoided bars since the prediction, but the mood here is so congenial. There are office workers, backpackers, families, and theatergoers. There are *children*. Nobody looks like they want to pick a fight with him, or with anyone, in fact. All he can hear is laughter, conversation, the squawk of seagulls and coo of pigeons, the toots of ferry horns as they come in and out of the wharf at Circular Quay. It's the end of a soft-breezed spring day. He's definitely not going to be assaulted tonight.

He's waiting to meet Harvey's hot sister and a friend, or cousin, or something, he's unclear on the identity of the other woman, but they have both come up to Sydney from Tasmania for the weekend, and Lila texted and asked if he wanted to meet for a drink. To toast Harvey, she said.

The waiter drops off his bowl of fries and a seagull settles on the railing and looks Ethan straight in the eye.

"Not for you," says Ethan, and he looks for the guy in the yellow vest patrolling the concourse with a kelpie on a lead. The kelpie wears a Bird Patrol collar and appears to love his job shooing away the seagulls, which used to be a big problem at this bar. Ethan remembers being here with Harvey when he threw a handful of tomato sauce packets at a marauding seagull. The girl Harvey liked had accused him of animal cruelty. Poor Harvey. He was so downcast. He'd thought he was being chivalrous.

Ethan has finally told his parents about the prediction.

"That's not going to happen." His mother was adamant. "Absolutely not. You're not the type."

"I worry more about your sister," said his dad. "She's the one who should be arming herself. Give all that self-defense stuff to her."

Ethan, mildly offended by the lack of parental concern, was tempted to quote the statistics relating to the death of young adult males by assault versus females, but resisted. It's *good* his parents aren't worried.

Neither is he.

He sees a text from Jasmine. *Fish okay?*

He sends her a thumbs-up, then puts the phone face down again. He's become fond of her fish in the three weeks since she's been gone, but interestingly his crush has been fading day by day into an embarrassing memory. She'll be one of those friends who come in and out of his life, but she's not for him. He doesn't know what he was thinking, to be honest. He could never be himself with her. His personality isn't big enough to match hers. When he was in her presence he was more like a fanboy than a person. He's enjoying living on his own. He's so much more relaxed.

"Ethan?"

Ethan looks up and sees two women walking toward his table.

One of them is Harvey's hot sister, Lila. She's still hot. He didn't imagine it. But his attention is on the other woman. Dark hair in plaits, wearing shorts and a long-sleeved loose shirt, tanned legs and sneakers. She's laughing at the kelpie.

Ethan stands. Nearly knocks over his bowl of fries. Straightens his glasses.

Afterward he will marvel at the clarity of Harvey's voice in his head. *This one, mate. Not the other one. This one.*

Chapter 111

Ned and I booked a Jewels of Europe river cruise for my seventieth birthday. We thought it would be relaxing to have someone else making all the decisions for a change. "If we hate it, we'll ditch it," said Ned, although I knew we certainly would not ditch a cruise on which we'd spent so much money.

I should tell you that Ned had recently developed a new interest in "longevity." He wanted to live until he was a hundred and he didn't see why he shouldn't. He'd been reading up on the blue zones, the five regions in the world where people live longer than average. He was always quoting statistics: Sleeping less than seven hours a night can increase your risk of death by twenty-four percent. People with a clear sense of purpose live up to seven years longer than those who don't have one. Cold therapy prolongs the lifespan of mice by up to twenty-one percent. I found this all very interesting, as I have a professional interest in the issue of life expectancy, but I did not think we should invest in an ice bath, I felt there wasn't enough data.

He wanted us to give ourselves Apple Watches for Christmas so we could monitor our heart rates and so on, but I resisted. I love data, but I suspected that with Ned's obsessive personality we might talk of nothing else. We gave ourselves new luggage instead.

Ned ate superfoods, fasted, took cold showers, and went to the gym. He was always very fit and slim (people who never stop moving tend to be that way) and he'd been a loyal member of the Fast Fitness Gym for the past three years. He did weights and cardio. He had regular health checkups and his cholesterol was good. Better than mine.

One day he mentioned that he had been feeling a little more breathless than usual on the treadmill. He wondered if it was just that he was getting old. He wasn't experiencing chest pains. He would have taken chest pains seriously. Our GP wasn't overly concerned but gave him a referral to a cardiologist just to be sure. "You're no spring chicken, mate," he said. He could say this because he was the same age as us.

The earliest appointment we could get ended up being the day before we left for our trip. We were flying to Sydney and then transferring to the international airport where we would fly to Budapest via Doha. I do remember saying to Jill, "Let's hope there's nothing wrong with Ned!" Of course we never traveled without comprehensive travel insurance. It wouldn't be the end of the world if we had to cancel.

I would have gone with Ned to his appointment, but I had my own appointment with the optometrist. There are a lot of appointments when you get to our age.

The cardiologist kept Ned waiting for an hour.

Specialists often run late. I do not know why. It is just life.

I wasn't there to distract him. I can imagine him, impatiently tapping his good new shoes. They were *Armani*! He kept telling me this. He wasn't really a designer-label person, but he got these shoes "for a steal" in a closing-down sale. I teased him about how often he gave them admiring glances, but the shoes wouldn't have been enough to distract him during the wait. It would have been agony for him. He would have been shifting around in his seat, looking at his phone and sighing, perhaps striking up a conversation with another patient, but obviously there was no one interesting enough to keep his attention, because finally he went to the cardiologist's secretary and said, "How much longer, do you think?"

Perhaps she was having a bad day. It would make me feel better if there was a reason for her rudeness. A cause and effect.

She snapped, as if Ned were a child who had interrupted a busy adult with an irrelevant request. "No idea. It will take as long as it takes."

Manners matter.

They really matter.

If she'd just said, "I'm so sorry, Mr. Lockwood, it shouldn't be too much longer."

(Sometimes in my dreams I shout at that secretary, like I've never shouted at anyone in my life.)

My husband could not abide bad manners, all his students knew that. He left.

I was cross when he told me he'd walked out of his appointment (bad manners, Ned!), but I must not have been concerned, because otherwise I would have insisted we cancel the trip. We both thought the cardiologist was just a box-checking exercise. Ned knew he was fitter than some of the blokes at the gym who were twenty years younger. He hadn't noticed the breathlessness the last time he went on the treadmill. We agreed he would have the checkup after our trip.

Some physicists argue that every event with multiple outcomes splits the world into alternate realities. It's called the "Many-Worlds Interpretation" and, if correct, it means there is another reality where Ned sits back down, waits for his appointment, and the cardiologist rushes him in for a stent that very day.

I don't know what the bearded determinist crowd would have said about this theory, because according to them, Ned could only behave as he actually *did*, but you know what? Ned didn't *always* succumb to his impatience. Sometimes he endured an unacceptable line. Sometimes he chose not to take bad manners personally.

You could have behaved differently, Ned, my love.

There was another possible outcome.

But in my reality, the only one I know, this is what happens: Ned falls asleep on the flight from Hobart to Sydney and never wakes up.

And while I'm saying, "Ned, wake up, we've landed" (and I know, I *know*, but I keep saying it over and over, and shaking his arm), our friends Jill and Bert are driving to their grandson's first birthday party, and Jill has a pavlova on her lap. Bert is driving, not too fast.

The driver negotiating the hairpin bend in the opposite direction isn't drunk.

She's just careless.

I lost all three of them on the same day, just like I foresaw.

Does that make me psychic like Mum?

Or just human? We all imagine terrible things. It's a way of preparing ourselves, or a way of protecting ourselves: if I imagine it, it surely won't happen.

But that's the thing about life: both your wildest dreams and your worst nightmares can come true.

Chapter 112

She is Lila and Harvey's cousin. Her name is Faith. She designs computer games for a living and looks after people's pets when they go away. The pets stay in their backyards and Faith visits and feeds them, plays with them or takes them for walks. She took care of a snake last week. One of her computer games just won a major award so she might be able to cut back on the pet business soon, although she enjoys it. She is the sister of the cousin with whom Ethan shared the plate of mini vol-au-vents at Harvey's funeral, and she wasn't there because she was overseas at the time and her flight got delayed.

She is funny and interesting. She makes Ethan feel funny and interesting.

They talk about Harvey a lot. Raise a glass to him. Over and over.

When Faith goes to the bar for their third round of drinks, Lila leans forward. "I don't know if I should tell you this, but Harvey was going to introduce you to Faith at his thirtieth," she says. "He'd been going on about it for years. He reckoned you two would be a perfect match."

"He never mentioned her." Ethan glances back over his shoulder.

"He said he wasn't going to say a word because that would put you off. He was so excited, said he was a shoo-in for best man."

"Well," said Ethan. This is moving fast. "I mean—"

"Oh, sure, sure, let's see how it goes. Maybe ask her out on a date before we send out the wedding invites."

"And, um, Lila, doesn't she live in Tasmania?"

Lila lowers her voice and mutters in a fast, low voice, "Thinkingof-movinghereinthenewyear," just as Faith arrives back with their drinks.

"Do you think that's Harvey checking in on us?" Faith nods at the scowling seagull on the railing.

"I think I saw him earlier," says Ethan.

He is thinking about the day he had his cards read, and Luca was supposedly channeling Harvey and he said Harvey was telling him to have *faith*. Didn't he use the word "faith" multiple times?

Another coincidence? How many coincidences before you start to wonder? Or is the whole paranormal industry based entirely on coincidence? He thinks of that long-ago statistics class, when two girls seated together were *amazed* to find they shared a birthday, and even after the lecturer explained the math of it, they thought it must mean something and became best friends. Maybe they're still best friends.

"Oh, gosh." Lila studies the seagull. "That is *such* a Harvey expression."

It looks for a moment like she can't get her breath and Ethan wonders if she is about to cry, but then he realizes she is laughing. She has her brother's identical silent wheezy laugh. It strikes him as somehow beautiful that Harvey's wonderful weird laugh is still here in the world. It hasn't vanished after all, and it might live on for generations in Lila's children.

Ethan catches Faith's eye as she watches her cousin fondly.

"Lila, Harvey, and Uncle Tom all laugh the same way, and when the three of them laugh together, it's wild," she says. "I mean it was wild." Her voice cracks and Ethan feels his sinuses block.

"Um, can't you see your friend is choking? Right in front of you?"

A woman walking by in towering stilettos, dressed up in formal wear, perhaps for a black-tie wedding at the Opera House, stops to bang her palm against Lila's back.

The seagull jumps about excitedly.

"No, no, it's okay, she's just choking," says Ethan, meaning to say, she's just *laughing,* and then he can't get the correct word out. "No! I mean, I meant, I mean—"

"Well, I *know* she's choking!" says the woman.

Now Lila, Faith, and Ethan are all laugh-sobbing, their faces crumple-wrinkled like old peaches as they rock with laughter and grief. They're a hot mess.

"They're *drunk.*" The woman's friend drags her away.

"Ah, Ethan," says Faith as they are finally regaining their composure. She is looking over her shoulder. "Do you know that guy? Because he looks kind of . . . mad with you."

Chapter 113

Well. It has been difficult.

I thought I had experienced enough loss in my life to have developed some kind of skill or expertise in coping with it, but it seems I have not. Not at all. I have found it impossible over these last months to get a grip on my grief. It's big, slippery, and mean, not beautiful and profound. I do not look wistfully at sunsets. No. I often break things. I swear. I'm brittle and vicious at times. You should have heard me on the phone to that travel insurance company.

We had Ned's funeral in Sydney.

"I guess it's more convenient, he's already here," I said to Hazel, and then I laughed, and couldn't stop laughing, and poor sweet Hazel didn't know if she should call a doctor.

Nobody expected it. He was so fit and healthy, to pass away of a heart attack while he napped just did not seem like something Ned would do.

Do you know what I did the day Ned died? I called my ex-husband, David. Isn't that peculiar? I don't know exactly what I wanted from him, but I seemed to need to tell him all about Ned, as if, because heart attacks were David's field of expertise, he could offer a solution; he would find a way to give Ned a different ending. He seemed to understand. He told me half of all cardiac deaths occur in people with no history or symptoms. He said the cardiologist might have saved Ned, but not necessarily. Ned's EKG might have been normal and he might have told him to book in for a stress test and angiogram after his holiday, or, yes, he might have told Ned not to get on that plane. He said he didn't think an Apple Watch would have saved his life. He said, "I'm so very sorry, Cherry."

The morning of the funeral I looked at our river cruise itinerary. That day we had a choice of two full-day excursions: Salzburg or Český Krumlov, a medieval town with Gothic, Renaissance, and Baroque architecture. I think we would have chosen the latter as we had already been to Salzburg. It's funny how the mind works, how I kept thinking about which excursion we would have chosen, as if it mattered.

It was a big funeral. Many of Ned's former students attended, including people in their fifties who Ned had taught more than thirty years ago. One man, who'd been in one of Ned's classes when we lived in the UK, flew all the way to Australia for the funeral. I said, "Oh, goodness, that wasn't necessary." Rude of me. He said, so sincerely, "It was necessary because Mr. Lockwood changed my life." And then, well, I felt so *proud* of Ned, I couldn't stop crying. It was very embarrassing.

I kept looking about for Jill and Bert, and then remembering. I thought I could get through this if I had them by my side, and then I thought I could get through their loss if Ned and I were grieving them together.

But I could not get through all their losses on my own.

I thought: What did I do to deserve these tragedies? This is too much. This is *grossly* unfair.

I still think that, sometimes, even though I know full well I am exemplifying the just-world fallacy, which is the erroneous belief that the world is fair. We are socialized to think that. It makes the world feel more predictable if we believe good behavior is rewarded and bad behavior punished. The problem is that we then subconsciously believe people who suffer must deserve it. It's what allows us to look away, to turn the television off. People sometimes say that everything happens for a reason. No. No, it does not. There was no reason for these terrible things to happen together. No reason at all. They just did.

There was a big funeral in Hobart for Jill and Bert. I did not attend. It was the day after Ned's funeral and I was still in Sydney with Hazel and Ned's brother, Tony.

Jill and Bert's middle daughter, the one they called "our smart one" because she was a lawyer, wrote a lovely sympathy card saying Ned had meant the world to her parents. I wrote and said Jill and Bert talked about her and her siblings and their new grandchild all the time, which was certainly true; sometimes we had to quite forcibly change the subject.

I went home after a week. I sold the house. I did an enormous clean-out and gave away all of Ned's clothes to a local charity shop, as well as my first wedding dress, which I had pointlessly been keeping all these years. (For my second wedding, the one that mattered, the one to Ned, I just wore a nice blue sheath dress, which I wore to death and eventually threw away.)

I bought this house in Battery Point, sight unseen, from a buyer keen on a fast sale, and then I thought: Right. Let's get this grief thing done. You've done it before. Do it again.

But experience makes no difference; you cannot project-manage grief.

I remembered how Mum and Grandma and Auntie Pat took care of me when I lost Jack. I took myself for long walks. I ran myself baths. Sometimes I ran a bath, sighed, and then pulled out the plug without getting in. I couldn't rub my own back, so I booked myself in for a massage, but goodness, that was a mistake. I sobbed so hard I thought I'd be sick. So embarrassing. They didn't want me to pay, but I insisted.

I remembered how *Number 96* had been such a good distraction so

I tried to find a new series, but it made me miss Ned too much. We loved so many series. "I wonder how Jackie is doing?" said Ned once, and I thought, Who do we know called Jackie? He meant *Nurse Jackie.*

I woke up crying, I went to bed crying, I cleaned my teeth crying. There were some days when the pain was so physical, I felt like I was being squeezed to death in some kind of medieval torture device. Then there were some days, normally after a big crying day, when I felt nothing at all, like I was fading slowly away.

Ivy kept calling from America, but I didn't return her calls. She didn't give up. She kept leaving messages, which was nice of her.

I know I didn't drink enough water during this time and I take responsibility for that.

It is a strange experience leaving on holiday with your husband and returning with his ashes in a Styrofoam box. I didn't pay for the fancy gold urn. I didn't see the point. The plan was to scatter the ashes somewhere meaningful, but I couldn't think of the right place. We had led such nomadic lives. Then Tony emailed and suggested a scenic lookout on the New South Wales south coast near the caravan park where he and Ned used to stay as children on summer holidays. I know Ned had (relatively) fond memories of those holidays. (He said he was often bored out of his mind, but Ned was easily bored.) So I agreed to fly to Sydney with the ashes and we set a date after Easter.

Hazel wanted me to spend Easter with them, but I said no thank you. I had plenty to do. When someone dies there is a mountain of paperwork. I was ruthless with it. "My husband has died," I said coldly to various people in call centers, and I cut them right off when they offered condolences. "This is what I need you to do."

However, I had great difficulty canceling Ned's gym membership. They kept insisting *the member* needed to personally come into the gym. That was their "procedure." When I patiently explained why this was literally impossible, they would promise to "look into it" and "get back to me," but they never did, and they continued to charge membership fees to our credit card, and I got testier and testier each time I called and had to go through the whole rigmarole again.

The day before the flight I talked to yet another cheerful dimwit. "The member needs to come in personally to cancel their membership," he said. "It's right there in the terms and conditions."

I lost patience. I grabbed the Styrofoam box. I drove to the gym, muttering like a madwoman the whole way.

"Here he is!" I shouted, and I slammed the box on the counter.

"I beg your pardon?" said the young receptionist.

I'm ashamed to say I shook the Styrofoam box in her face. "He's here to cancel his membership! As per procedure!"

She peered at the box and then she saw the small gold plaque on the lid: *Edward Patrick Lockwood*.

"Wait, is that *Ned*?" she said, and she lost all color in her face. "You don't mean Ned Lockwood died?"

"Yes!" I shouted. "That's what I've been telling you people for weeks on end! He died! So he doesn't need his goddamned gym membership anymore!"

Isn't that dreadful? The swearing, I mean. My grandfather would be rolling in his grave.

She burst into tears. Then an overly muscled young man came over to see what was going on and when he found out about Ned, *he* cried! I thought, For goodness' sake.

It turned out nearly everyone at the gym that day knew and loved Ned. He'd been helping the muscly guy with his math subjects for his university degree. The people I had been speaking to on the phone had all been at a central call center and had nothing to do with this local branch where Ned was a beloved member.

Anyhow, they canceled his membership, so at least I could check that off my list.

I stopped at the grocery store on the way home. I left the ashes on the passenger seat.

"You stay there," I said.

I went into the grocery store and filled my basket, but then, when

I was at the checkout, I realized I had bought pistachios. I do not like pistachios. I only ever bought them for Ned.

"Oh," I said. "I don't need those. Sorry."

The young girl sighed and huffed and reversed the transaction, as if it were the biggest inconvenience of her short life to date. She tossed the pistachios into a basket at her feet in an unnecessarily aggressive manner.

The next item on the counter was Monte Carlo biscuits, and I thought of the day Bert bit through both layers and said, "I like to live dangerously, Cherry," and I recalled that was the same day Jill and I tried to do the sit-to-stand longevity test.

"Guess we're dying young," said Jill.

"Too late for that," said Bert, and Jill threw a cushion at him, which he caught one-handed.

"Forget it," I said to the checkout girl.

She held up the biscuits. "You changed your mind on these too?"

"Just—forget it."

I left the grocery store. I ate nothing that night and I think it's possible I didn't drink any water at all, except perhaps when I cleaned my teeth, which I definitely did. I continue to clean my teeth each time my world crashes to pieces.

The next day I took a taxi to the airport.

Chapter 114

"What is this?"

Paula doesn't look away from the bathroom mirror. She is putting on mascara, which she hardly ever does anymore. Her former colleague, Stephanie, asked if they could get together for a drink. The last time they saw each other was at Stephanie's parents' funeral at St. David's around this time last year. That devastating day when Paula feared she would burst into inappropriate sobs.

"Paula?"

This time the tone of Matt's voice makes her look away from the mirror. He is holding a pile of loose paper, and she knows immediately what it is. She should have hidden it better. She'd just shoved each page in the bottom drawer of her desk, exhausted each night, glad it was done.

He brings it over to her and she sees her own handwriting, cramped but perfect, filling the paper.

Timmy will not drown.

Timmy will not drown.

Timmy will not drown.

Write it down a thousand times a day and he will not drown.

"It's nothing," she says. "It's just, you know, something I do to calm myself down when I get too worked up about the prediction."

"But it must have taken hours, Paula," says Matt, leafing through the paper. "Hours and hours."

"Daddy!" bellows Willow.

"You'd better go to her before she wakes up Timmy." Paula applies lipstick. She looks at the dark shadows under her eyes. No concealer can fix that.

"But I'm just wondering," says Matt, and he is being so careful, tiptoeing through marital landmines, "I'm just wondering if this could be a . . ." He clears his throat. "A compulsion."

How does he even know that word? Has he been talking to her sister? Googling?

"Yeah, so I'm a bit OCD," Matt had said to her, on one of their early dates, when she first visited his apartment and saw his pantry with the spice bottles all lined up precisely, like soldiers standing at attention, in alphabetical order.

People say that sort of thing all the time. Anyone who is meticulous, or extra clean, is "OCD."

She told him soon after about her diagnosis. She wasn't on medication anymore, she explained, but she did have to keep an eye on it. Matt had assumed it was handwashing, but she explained that her compulsions varied. He was respectful, asked questions, and she never heard him say "I'm a bit OCD" again. But they haven't talked about it in years. Sometimes she has wondered if Matt has forgotten about her diagnosis or if he thinks she exaggerated it.

"It's under control," she says.

"But do you feel like you have to do it? Or Timmy will drown? And it seems like you do it every day?"

Of course she dates each page. She's a lawyer. She has been doing it every day since the flight in April. It's November now. There are a lot of pages.

"Can we talk about this when I get home?" asks Paula. "I'm running late."

"Sure," says Matt. "But I think we really *should* talk about it."

"I just said we would!" she snaps.

He holds up his hands in surrender. As he leaves the room he is straightening the sheets of paper into a neat pile, as if it's important documentation for a future meeting.

"How are you?" asks Paula distractedly, when she sits down at the table across from Stephanie, and as soon as she says it, she realizes her tone is wrong.

She has become so self-absorbed that for a moment she literally forgot about this woman's terrible loss. She should be reaching across the table for her hand and saying, "How *are* you?"

But Stephanie doesn't seem to notice Paula's tone is too casual.

"I'm doing okay," she says. Her voice wobbles and then rights it-self. "Taking it day by day. Some days are better than others. Recently I've been making an effort to be more . . . social."

Paula should have called her. A kinder person would have called to check in, even if they were just work colleagues. At least sent a text.

"I should have called," she says.

"No! You're busy with your kids. Tell me about you."

Paula finds herself telling her everything, perhaps in an attempt to justify why she has been distracted. Stephanie is a good listener.

Her phone beeps. It's Eve.

"Read the message!" says Stephanie. "This is all so fascinating." She turns around in her chair to get the attention of a waiter on the other side of the room. "Let's order more drinks."

Paula reads the message out loud. "Her name is Cherry Lock-wood. She used to be an actuary—"

Stephanie's head snaps back around to face her. "I know Cherry Lockwood."

"You *know* her?"

"She and her husband were best friends with my parents."

Chapter 115

I have thought a lot about what must have happened to me on the flight.

I think it's possible I suffered from "delirium" due to dehydration. I believe I was severely dehydrated that morning and I've been told I refused all offers of water during the delay. People my age are susceptible to dehydration and it can lead to the sudden onset of delirium, resulting in confusion and hallucinations.

I have also considered the possibility I suffered a psychotic break caused by grief. This is rarer than delirium, but it happens.

In my day we would have said I suffered a "nervous breakdown," but the new term is "mental health crisis."

Grandma would have said I had "a funny turn."

I have tried to remember everything I can about the moments while I was still lucid.

I know I got an awful shock when I saw the fair-haired flight attendant because he was there the day Ned died. I will never forget that boy's grim, frightened expression as he leaned over Ned, pressing two fingers to Ned's darling neck, which I loved to kiss, which smelled so good, right near the little dark spot we were keeping an eye on. I knew there was no pulse to find. I knew the CPR wouldn't work. I knew the paramedics who came on board wouldn't save him. I'm sure the young flight attendant would not have forgotten the day one of his passengers died, but perhaps all his attention had been on Ned's face, not mine, or perhaps ladies of my age all look the same to him, because he looked right through me when I boarded. It added to my feeling of unreality, as if I'd dreamed the whole thing, as if I'd never been married to Ned.

I had Ned's ashes in my carry-on bag, above me in the overhead bin, and yet there was an empty seat right next to me, the only empty seat on the plane, as if it were waiting for Ned, and then the man across the aisle from me, who I now know was Leo Vodnik, wore the very same stylish shoes as Ned, and tapped his feet in an identical impatient manner, while he sat next to the couple who reminded me of Jill and Bert, and I saw the Jewels of Europe—well, never mind, none of this matters.

I did what I did.

When I got to Hazel and Tony's house in Sydney after the flight, I didn't technically faint, or collapse as such, but Hazel says I sat on her couch and "toppled sideways like a tree."

Embarrassing.

She put me to bed in her guest room, and I stayed there for a week, like an invalid suffering from consumption. It was decided (without anyone asking me) that the scattering of Ned's ashes would be postponed until I was well enough.

I lay in bed and listened for Tony's voice because, although he and Ned are nothing alike in looks or personality, their voices have always been eerily similar. Hearing Tony's voice didn't upset me. I found it comforting.

Goodness, my in-laws were kind to me that week. Sometimes over the years I had wondered what Hazel and Tony truly thought of Ned and me, traipsing about the world while they stayed in one place and brought up a family. There were long periods when we had no contact and then we'd breeze in at Christmas, with our gifts and stories. Just as their children got close to us, off we went to live in another city or country. Tony and Hazel might have secretly rolled their eyes at each other while we talked about tandem skydiving and trekking in Nepal. Families do secretly roll their eyes at each other, but never mind, it doesn't matter if they did. There is no doubt they treated me like a loved family member that week. I am ready to do the same for them when and if they need me.

When I felt well enough, we scattered Ned's ashes at the scenic lookout Tony suggested. He told a lot of stories I'd never heard before about boyhood adventures involving bikes and surfboards and sand dunes. Tony said his little brother Ned made any activity ten times more fun.

I thought, Twenty times more fun. A hundred times. Maybe a thousand times.

Ned and I had thirty-four beautiful years together. That's longer than my dad's lifetime. Longer than Jack Murphy's lifetime. Longer than Kayla Halfpenny's lifetime.

I remind myself of this whenever I feel particularly cross with him for walking out of that damned appointment.

Chapter 116

Ethan turns and there is Carter. He's clearly drunk. His eyes are unfocused. His too-tight buttons-straining-over-pecs mulberry-colored shirt has come loose from his jeans. He must be returning from the bar because he holds a bottle of boutique beer in one hand and a slopping glass of white wine in the other. With the studied carefulness of a drunk he places both drinks down on Ethan's table and proffers his fist for one of his ridiculous fist bumps.

"Mate! Long time no see! How are ya?"

He seems amicable. Not angry. Perhaps it will be fine.

"I'm good, Carter," says Ethan. "Good. How are you?" Careful, careful, just tread carefully.

"So, you going to introduce me or what?" He gestures at the two women, who both offer the classic fixed fuck-off-please smiles Ethan's seen so many women give twats in bars.

Ethan introduces them, and Carter lurches forward and takes each woman's hand in a faux courtly manner and *kisses it*, the way drunk tossers sometimes do. Ethan tries to say sorry with his eyes. He knows both women know they can't refuse: that it's safer to let a guy this drunk slobber over their hands, because his mood can turn on a dime, but it's wrong, it's so wrong, and he feels the bubble of fury low within his stomach.

"Anyway, we were about to make a move," he says.

"Yeah, we've got that booking." Faith wipes the back of her hand on her shorts.

"So you heard from Jasmine?" asks Carter. "Since she's left the country? She's blocked me, but I bet she's still in touch with you, right?"

"She's my flatmate," says Ethan. "So . . . you know, I'm feeding her fish."

And here it comes. Anger floods Carter's face. "You're *feeding her fish*. I think you did a bit more than that, didn't ya?!"

The volume and vitriol are enough to still surrounding conversations.

Ethan thinks about the "stealth knife" in his pocket, but at what point is he meant to use it? This point? Or does he wait until he's attacked? When it's too late.

The two women stand. They push their chairs back in.

"We've really got to go," says Lila. "It was nice to meet you, Carter."

Carter stares at her for a moment, distracted, but then a thought crosses his mind.

"You fucking him?" He points at Ethan. "He fucked my girlfriend, you know. Right under my nose."

"Okay, that's enough," says Ethan. "You're deluded, mate. We're leaving."

"Or maybe you didn't, but you wanted to, didn't you, you badly wanted to, sitting there in your room—" He uses his fist to make a crude gesture.

Ethan has never felt rage like it. Carter is contaminating this night. This perfect night.

He feels Faith's hand on his arm, pulling him away. "Let's go, Ethan."

"Yeah, nice to see you, *Ethan*!" Carter calls after them. "Say hi to Jasmine, *Ethan*!"

"Don't look back," says Lila, and it seems like they are free, they are walking away from the bar toward Circular Quay, weaving in and out of the crowd, but then Ethan knows somehow he should turn and time slows right down, and this is it, it's happening. Carter is coming for him, like he's wanted to do for so long, fist clenched, elbow back, and Ethan has never been punched, *guys like us don't get into fights*, will it hurt? Will he fall and crack his head? It happens, Dad, nice guys sometimes die in fights they don't start, then white-feathers-flapping-squawking the seagull is flying straight at Carter's murderous face, as though Carter's head is a French fry it's determined to steal, and the guy with the bird patrol dog says, "Oh shit!" and the dog bounds forward as Carter staggers back, thwarted.

"Run!" says Lila.

"Thanks, Harvey!" calls out Faith.

They're running under the silver moonlight and the city lights reflect off the shimmering harbor and Ethan isn't dead, he's alive, he's so amazingly, gratefully alive, and he doesn't remember it happening but Faith seems to be holding his hand.

Chapter 117

After we scattered Ned's ashes, I flew back to my strange lonely new home with no idea that all those passengers were leading lives clouded and complicated by my predictions.

Grieving is hard for a task-focused person. You can never wrap things up.

One day I had a sudden memory of Auntie Pat saying to my mother, in the months after Dad died, "You need to try some kind of new activity, Mae, something you have never done before."

Mum took up fortune-telling, which is not what Auntie Pat meant at all. She meant a hobby.

So I looked up activities at my local community center. I tried line dancing, a philosophy club, a Knitting for Beginners course. I hated them all. Why did I think I would suddenly become a dancer, a philosophy student, or a knitter? It was like I thought grief had given me a new personality. It had not.

Then I tried aqua aerobics.

I loved it. I liked exercising in water, I liked the music, I liked the energetic young instructor bouncing on the side of the pool. I told her she reminded me of the vibrant rock star Pink and she seemed pleased.

I chatted to other members of my class as we dressed afterward in the change room, and one day a woman called Mira, who I had taken against ever so slightly because the buoyancy of her breasts reminded me of Stella, and she wore high heels to aqua aerobics, which I found ridiculous, mentioned that some people got together for coffee afterward.

I must have looked horrified because she said it wasn't compulsory, and then I felt embarrassed and explained I'd only recently lost my husband.

"Ah," she said, and do you know what she did?

She came over and wrapped her arms around me. I hadn't quite finished dressing. She was fully dressed and in her high heels. (I think she actually can't walk without heels.)

She smelled of a beautiful fragrance. She said, "I know what this time is like."

I did not know how badly I needed this.

She became my new friend.

Friends can save your life.

It was a few weeks before we realized how close we lived to each other, and of course we were amazed, although it was statistically likely seeing as we had met at a local aquatic center. I can see into her backyard from my house. She was the woman who waved at me from her back veranda the day of the flight. We can walk to each other's homes.

Her husband had died two years before and she said she still felt angry at times about all the plans they had made that would never come to be.

We both agreed we were not "merry widows"—we would never be merry about the loss of our beautiful husbands—we were "angry widows," and we joked about forming an Angry Widows Club. (I do not want to form a club of any sort.)

Mira said her husband had worked so hard, all his life, long hours in his own jewelry store, and she used to tell him he was a workaholic, and he would say he would rest when he retired.

She said her son was turning out to be just like his father, nothing but work work work, but her daughter-in-law, who she loved, although she wore the ugliest shoes you have ever seen, was trying to convince him to give up work for a year and move to Tasmania, and she thought he might have agreed, fingers crossed.

Chapter 118

One November morning, seven months after the flight, and about a week before the anniversary of Ned's death, as well as the deaths of Jill and Bert, someone knocked on my door.

I considered not answering it because I was not doing well that day.

You may know this and I'm sorry if you do, but there is a feeling you experience as the anniversary of the death of a loved one approaches. Your body seems to know it before you do. It is something to do, perhaps, with the weather, the flowers that bloom, a certain smell in the air, and you begin to feel a sense of anticipatory loss, almost fear, as if it's going to happen again.

I opened the door and found myself face-to-face with a man's torso.

I looked up. Farther up. He was a tall, muscled man with a gray buzz cut. The man who helped me with my bag on the plane. He resembled an older version of "Thor," the fictional superhero portrayed by the astonishingly attractive Australian actor Chris Hemsworth.

His name was not Thor. He introduced himself as "Ben," but I got the feeling it wasn't his real name, so let's call him Thor.

He gently told me what I'd done on the plane and seemed unsurprised when I said I had no memory of it. I pressed my hand to my mouth as he spoke. It was the same sick shame I used to feel when people told me about my drunken behavior at those rooftop parties. In spite of my shock, I never suspected Thor was lying. It all made sense. I remembered the expression on the beautiful flight attendant's face when we landed, how she'd treated me as if I'd had some kind of medical episode. I remembered how the little boy had been staring back at me, and children rarely show an interest in me. Also, there was something so eerily familiar about what Thor described—not that I suddenly remembered my actions, but as if I could remember once dreaming them, and who else but me would talk of "cause of death" and "age of death"?

He seemed to already know everything about me: my career, the loss of Ned, even the loss of Jill and Bert. I believe he is a retired intelligence officer of some sort, although he is vague about the details.

He said he'd been following the story and was becoming increasingly concerned. He said I'd correctly predicted three deaths and now there had been a fourth.

I gasped when I heard my predictions had come true.

I remembered the young girl and the elderly couple from the airport. It was frightening and distressing to hear they were now dead and that people thought it proved I had supernatural abilities. I felt that dreadful sense of responsibility I'd experienced when I learned about the two people falling off the rooftop terrace.

Thor seemed angry about the fourth death. I didn't understand. I didn't understand any of it. He showed me the news articles appearing online. He said he believed my identity was about to be exposed, probably any day now, and that people were looking for me, and he didn't want me to walk out my front door one morning to a crowd of journalists pushing microphones in my face. He said, if I liked, he could help me release a public statement explaining I was not a psychic. "Because you're not, are you?" I said I was not, and that it seemed like I needed to release an *apology*. He said it was up to me how I worded it.

He also said he had a safe house where I could stay until the story blew over.

(Look. He didn't really say "safe house." He said "investment property." It's just that he really did have the rather exciting manner of someone working in international espionage.)

He said he would leave me to think about it for a few hours, but he'd be back. He suggested that I not answer my phone in the meantime. He said he needed to look into the fourth death.

I watched him go. His cape didn't swirl, as he wasn't wearing one, and he's not really a superhero. He's just one of those heroically helpful people. He certainly rescued me.

Well, my head spun after Thor left. I literally spun in circles for a while. I was distraught, confused, and incredibly embarrassed, and I very badly needed Ned, but of course if Ned had been there none of it would have happened.

Finally I thought, I will walk down to Mira's place and tell her.

Mira answered the door incandescent with happiness. Her son and his family were in Tasmania, looking for rental homes in the area! Her son had resigned! His evil boss had gotten the shock of her life! I couldn't get a word in, she was so excited.

She introduced me to her granddaughter, Bridie, who was sitting on the couch engrossed in her phone. In spite of my agitation, I managed to ask Bridie if she was pleased to be moving to Tasmania and she took a moment to think, and said, "Maybe." She seemed like a serious little girl and I liked her. Her mother and brother were out visiting a local soccer club.

Mira went to the kitchen to make us some tea. She said her son was in the garden.

I walked out onto her deck. A middle-aged man was walking around Mira's backyard in an anxious, perturbed kind of way. I understood, as I was also a little anxious about Mira's backyard. I believed she'd been scammed. She'd paid upfront and this man had done nothing but left a very old, dilapidated-looking excavator parked on the edge of a half-finished, pointless-seeming deep trench.

Mira's son did not see me at first, but as I watched, I recognized him. His curly hair is so distinctive! It was the man who had sat across the aisle from me on the flight, the one with the same impatient-tapping fancy shoes as Ned.

At first I thought, Oh, isn't that interesting, what a coincidence, Mira's son, who she talks about so often, the one who works too hard like his father, was on the same flight to Sydney.

The sun was out, but there had been relentless rain the last few days, and Mira's backyard had turned to mud. I watched as he stopped to look down, probably concerned about the state of his shoes. (Like mother, like son.)

He scratched his jaw.

On the same flight.

That's when it hit me. If he was sitting across the aisle from me, then could I have given him one of those "predictions" Thor had just told me about?

If so, what in heaven's name had I said to him? To my delightful new friend's son? Color flooded my face. I was mortified, horrified. I wanted the ground to swallow me up. It was like coming face-to-face with another resident in the stairwell of the Perth apartment block, and thinking, *Oh my goodness, I hope I didn't kiss you last night.*

He looked up and saw me standing on his mother's back deck.

His mouth dropped. He clearly recognized me too. He looked like he'd seen a ghost. We stared at each other for an endless second and then I caught a movement out of the corner of my eye.

At first I thought I was imagining what I was seeing: the excavator falling sideways in slow motion, like a toppling tree, like me on the couch at Hazel's place, toward Mira's son, who was still staring up at me, transfixed, apparently frozen on the spot.

It was going to hit him.

I'm so glad I remembered that his name was Leo and I wasn't too shy to use it.

I shouted, "LEO, WATCH OUT!" and pointed.

He turned his head. He swore.

He jumped nimbly to the other side of the muddy trench just in the nick of time.

Chapter 119

Look. There is no need for everyone to get too excited about this. It might not have killed him, and even if it had, I don't believe it would have fallen under the classification of a workplace accident because it wasn't Leo's workplace.

Chapter 120

The up-and-coming YouTube star wasn't dead.

Thor suspected it and it turned out he was right:

Simon Gallea, aka Simon Says Be Kind, *faked his own death to get more followers and sell more merchandise.*

Furthermore, *he wasn't even on the flight.*

Can you believe it? He made it all up! So much for his "random acts of sunshine." Faking your own death doesn't seem especially kind to me. I never made any kind of prediction for him because I never met the little brat!

People were furious with him and their fury was actually quite a good distraction. It took the attention away from me. His trickery somehow made my fortune-telling abilities seem even less likely. People conflated us. When the Death Lady came up in conversation there were cynical, knowing comments: "Wasn't that plane incident some kind of fraud?"

In spite of the abusive messages and angry breakfast-show hosts, or perhaps because of them, Simon got the notoriety, the "merch sales," and the thousands of new followers he coveted, so he couldn't care less.

Chapter 121

Cherry Lockwood, "the Death Lady," opens the door of her tiny charming home in Battery Point—it's incredible, she's been just a ten-minute drive away from Paula all this time—and says unnecessarily, "You're here!"

Paula's friend Stephanie has insisted on bringing her over to meet Cherry. "She can reassure you."

Paula should not need reassurance. It's been a week since Cherry's "statement" went out in the press, assuring the world she is not a psychic and apologizing for the distress she caused. Paula felt exactly nothing when she heard this. There was no relief, not even when she learned one of the deaths was a hoax, and she has not changed her actions, although she has had to be more secretive, because Matt is monitoring her.

Stephanie and Cherry hug awkwardly. Stephanie is a hugger, but Cherry is clearly not.

Stephanie steps back. "Cherry. This is Paula."

"Hello, Paula."

Those same pale blue eyes, but without that scary blankness. There is more color in her cheeks and her face seems fuller, less sunken than when Paula saw her on the flight. She wears black jeans and a pretty collared blouse. A tiny brooch. No other jewelry. Lipstick that matches the pink in her blouse.

She is nervous. "I'm talking too much," she says, and keeps talking too much, about the house and its history, something about biscuits, and how she cooks as badly as she dances and she wishes she could make pavlovas like the ones Stephanie's mum used to make, those pavlovas were to die for, and then she stops and says, "Well, I can't believe I just said that," and Stephanie laughs and hugs her again. Apparently they don't know each other all that well, but Stephanie says her parents adored Cherry and Ned.

That's why Cherry's face was familiar to Paula on the flight, because she'd seen multiple smiling photos of her in the devastating slideshow Stephanie and her siblings played at their parents' funeral.

Cherry makes tea, puts out a plate of Monte Carlo biscuits, but remains standing, clasps her hands, and says, formally, "Paula, I am profoundly sorry for what I said to you on that plane. I have no ability to see the future. It was pure chance any of my predictions came true."

"Thank you," says Paula, and she smiles as if she's grateful, but she still feels nothing. She *believes* Cherry, but it's as if her abilities are of no consequence. She knows she will keep up the swimming lessons, she will continue to write out her lines.

"So, Timmy will definitely *not* drown!" Stephanie claps her hands together.

Cherry clears her throat. "Obviously I can't guarantee that."

Stephanie hisses, "*Cherry!*"

Cherry says, "Well, the child needs to learn how to swim, Stephanie! You still need to take steps to mitigate risk!"

Stephanie says, "Yes, but—"

"And make sure he avoids blowholes. I once saw a young boy drown in a blowhole. I've never forgotten it. A terrible, terrible thing. He was a good swimmer too. Just because you can swim doesn't mean you can't drown."

"Okay," says Stephanie. "Maybe don't mention—but listen, the point is, you have no psychic abilities."

"Absolutely not," says Cherry. "Even though my mother was a very successful fortune teller."

"Oh my God," sighs Stephanie.

Paula says nothing. Her attention is caught by a framed photo on the shelf next to her. It must be Ned, Cherry's husband, the man who died on a plane the same day that Stephanie's parents died, causing Cherry to break down as she did. He's a gray-haired, sun-tanned senior citizen with both arms slung back behind him over the railing of a ferry, azure water and misty mountains behind him—maybe Italy?—smiling with laid-back love at the person taking the photo, presumably Cherry. Something about him reminds Paula so strongly of her old therapist, Dr. Donnelly, although the two of them look nothing alike really. It's something about their kind intelligent faces and nicely cut gray hair.

"Paula?" says Stephanie.

What did Paula think meeting this poor grieving woman would achieve?

"Your OCD doesn't care about logic," Dr. Donnelly used to say. "You can't reason with your irrational thoughts."

That's exactly what she'd been trying to do.

She focused so much energy on finding Cherry, as if a different prediction from her would be the solution, but even if Cherry *was* a genuine fortune teller and even if she said, "Good news! All those swimming lessons have paid off, here's my new prediction!" it would make no difference. It would be just like when her sister told her she wouldn't run those people over at the pedestrian crossing. *Promised* her! But it made no difference.

Paula has been pretending this has nothing to do with her OCD, when it has everything to do with it. "This condition may always be a part of your life," Dr. Donnelly had said to her all those years ago. "Like asthma or eczema. But you can manage it."

He'd warned her that her OCD might flare up in times of stress.

It's stressful being a full-time mother of two young children. It's stressful hearing that your son might drown.

This is not about Cherry's prediction. This is about Paula and her anxious mind finding ways to live in a world filled with unpredictability and uncertainty. Yes, she's smart, yes, she knows all about the techniques, but sometimes, as Dr. Donnelly accurately predicted all those years ago, there will be times in her life when she might need a little help. "And there will be no shame in that, Paula," he'd said at their last appointment, as if he knew exactly what she was thinking, *No way, I've got this sorted now, sayonara, Dr. Donnelly!*

"I'm so sorry about your husband," she says to Cherry, gesturing at the photo. "He looks like a lovely man."

"He was a lovely man." Cherry picks up the photo. "Look at him grinning! He'd just made me run to catch that ferry." Her face is momentarily so grief-stricken Paula has to look away, but then she sees the same dreadful grief reflected on Stephanie's face, and she looks instead at the very nice rug on the floor.

"May I see a recent photo of Timmy?" asks Cherry. She's perfectly composed again. "And your little girl?"

"Of course." Paula takes out her phone.

On the way home she will call Matt and tell him he doesn't need to worry, she's making an urgent appointment with Dr. Donnelly, who will help her get back on track, and also she's going to ask Stephanie to keep an eye out for any part-time contract law positions because the blissful moments of motherhood aren't enough, and it's a first principle of law that a mutually agreeable contract offers both parties *certainty,* and she has to get that elusive feeling somewhere.

Chapter 122

Over the years, when people asked my profession and I said "actuary," they did one of three things.

Their eyes lit up with interest because they misheard me and believed I said "actor" and they wanted to know what they might have seen me in.

They frowned, perplexed, and said, "What's an actuary?"

Or, if they had a glimmer of understanding of the role of an actuary, they would make this jokey request: "So tell me, Cherry, when am I going to die?"

"Funny," I would say (although it wasn't), but you know what? I always answered the question in my head. I never said it out loud, but I would do a quick analysis of the data available. The person's age, gender, weight, whether they smoked, their wealth and social status, their hobbies (if I knew they engaged in extreme sports, for example), lifestyle, diet, and so on and so forth, and I would come up with a cause and age of death. For my own amusement.

Were my actions on that flight a strange version of that peculiar secret exercise? Was there any method to my madness?

To be very, very clear, this is not what an actuary does and I remain deeply embarrassed for bringing my beloved profession into disrepute that day. We do not point our fingers at individuals and tell them how and when they will die, rather we make educated predictions regarding the probability that any individual, belonging to a particular cohort, will die before their next birthday.

Were my predictions related to the fact that the focus of my work before I retired was mortality forecasting by cause of death? Was all that data swirling madly in my head like debris in the terrifying weather phenomenon known as a "twister"? (I am thinking now of the excellent movie *Twister* starring the talented actress Helen Hunt.)

Did I develop my own set of random assumptions by utilizing the very little information available to me?

For example, Leo Vodnik had held a magazine titled *Construction Engineering Australia*. Men are ten times more likely than women to die at work. Is that all it took for me to predict a "workplace accident" as his cause of death?

Ethan Chang had his arm in a cast. Was it his injury that made me choose "assault," together with the fact that injury and violence is a leading cause of death for young adult men?

I know I watched Kayla Halfpenny at the airport and saw her knock over her drink and then her phone. Was it my observation of the sweet girl's clumsiness together with the fact that road traffic injuries are one of the leading causes of death among young adults that led me to say "car accident"?

Did I simply make random choices? Is that what led me to pancreatic cancer, the most feared cancer, for the vibrant woman who reminded me of my friend Jill, and breast cancer for the pregnant woman?

Did I temporarily believe I was Madame Mae? I must have been thinking of my mother, because I kept saying "fate won't be fought."

Had I somehow become a strange alchemy of the two of us?

Both of us, after all, specialized in predictions.

There are certain events in my life that I believe may have had a profound effect on me. For example: the little boy who drowned at the blowhole when I was a child. I have never forgotten the sound of his mother screaming. That boy had brown eyes and dark hair. When

I saw that dear little brown-eyed, dark-haired baby, did I think of that poor boy and therefore predict the baby would drown at the same age?

Did I look at the young bride, Eve, and remember the charming woman who came to my mother for readings, who was so excited about her forthcoming wedding, the first wedding I ever attended? Did I think of the time I saw her at the shops, her inner light snuffed out, and remember how she died in a fire believed to have been lit by her husband?

Why did I choose self-harm for Allegra, the beautiful flight attendant? Was it simply that I saw repressed pain in her eyes from the back injury I now know she suffered on that flight? Was it because I knew the rate of suicide in young females has been steadily increasing over recent years?

Was I thinking of death as I boarded the plane and contemplating the fact that everyone on that plane would one day die, and wondering what their causes of death would ultimately be?

Well. That's the only one of my questions I can answer with certainty. Of course I was thinking of death. I had my husband's ashes in my carry-on bag. I was missing my two best friends. I was thinking of every person I had ever lost throughout my life.

I was crazed with grief.

At times I am still crazed with grief.

All I can do is sincerely apologize and make this clear: I am not a psychic. I am a bereaved retired actuary who suffered a mental health crisis on a flight.

Chapter 123

Eve is at work at the medical center. She forwards the latest news story—"Death Lady Continues to Deny Special Powers"—to Dom as a patient approaches the reception desk.

There was no need for bribery in the end. One hundred bucks saved. Just as she and Paula identified her, the Death Lady released a public apology, explaining she'd had a mental health crisis on the plane. She was not a psychic, she was an actuary and had no special abilities.

Dom is okay. He hasn't snapped back to his normal self. He's still worried about money and he's still worried about hurting her in his sleep, but there is no more talk about breaking up.

"I need to change my address," says the man.

"No problem," says Eve, and she smiles radiantly. The woman who trained her said it was important to always be kind and polite to patients, because some of them were nervous, and some were feeling sick, or in pain, and yes, some were just awful people, but you couldn't tell by looking at them. "So be nice to everyone, please, Eve."

Clickety-clack, clickety-clack on her keyboard.

"Yeah, I'm moving back in with my parents to save money," says the patient with a sigh.

Eve looks up at him. He is a businessman. He is literally wearing a tie. She looks at his date of birth on his file as she changes his address. Ten years older than her. If *he's* having financial problems, why does Eve feel such shame and self-loathing about their spiraling debt? Some people don't have family, but Eve and Dom do. They are lucky. Yes, they messed up, yes, it's embarrassing, but it's not actually the end of the world, is it?

"All done!" she says, and smiles again, and the guy looks at her for a moment too long, as if he's about to ask her out, so she angles her left hand to let him see her wedding ring—*on your way, buddy*—and he gets the message.

The solution is obvious. They will ask Dom's dad if they can please temporarily move into Dom's old bedroom and, two birds with one rock, or whatever it is, Dom can stop worrying about hurting her when he sleepwalks because *his dad will be there to save her*!

Their lease is nearly up. Luckily they only got a six-month lease, which Eve's mum said at the time was bad but turns out to be good, so maybe you're not as smart as you think, Mum.

A message arrives on her phone from her plane friend, Paula Binici. They have been trying to decide if they should close down their Death Lady social media accounts now that they have successfully tracked down Cherry Lockwood, like literal detectives, although some guy from the plane got to her first. Paula said it was typical for a man to swoop in at the last minute and take all the credit, but that's not really true, because he didn't take any credit at all.

People are still posting constantly. Some refuse to believe Cherry is not a psychic: *Get real, people, she predicted three deaths! Her mother was a famous fortune teller!* Paula says it might be good to keep the page so they can moderate comments and so people can post when Cherry's predictions (hopefully!) are proved to be wrong.

But this message from Paula is about something else: *I just remembered the person next to me on the flight was an expert in sleep disorders. Tracked him down (easy after Cherry). He is lovely. Said you or Dom can call him any time, he can definitely help. Warning: strong Scottish accent. xx*

Eve hasn't smiled this hard since her wedding day photos.

For better or for worse. That's what they said in their marriage vows. She hadn't expected it to get worse so soon, but it's going to get better.

She thinks of Kayla Halfpenny. Eve knows from her online sleuthing that Kayla's friend, the one who filmed the TikTok LIVE of the car accident, is out of the hospital and is doing school talks about road safety, together with Kayla's boyfriend, the overly tall skinny boy from the plane. It's a way of honoring Kayla, but it seems like they are also dating. They will probably have a baby one day and name it Kayla, or at least make Kayla the second name, which is nice, beautiful even, but it's also kind of shit, because it proves when you're gone you're really gone, and everyone else will keep on having lives, feeling sad about you but also having fun, and your best friend might miss you but she might also date your boyfriend, which you can't complain about because you're *not there,* and Eve feels like there is some life lesson there. Maybe it's just: Live your life, Eve. Live it hard.

She feels a surge of strength and optimism and power. She is Wonder Woman, she is Barbie, she is Ruth Bader Ginsburg, she is Taylor Swift—

"Hello? Anyone home?" A patient reaches over the reception desk and waves her hand in front of Eve's eyes.

"Sorry," says Eve. How embarrassing. "How can I help you?"

She is *Eve Archer-Fern* and the future is in her hands.

Chapter 124

You can't always choose your future. Not in a world of risk and uncertainty. No matter what the self-help gurus tell you. You can only attempt to guide it in the right direction, like a willful horse, but accept there will be times when it will gallop off in a direction not of your choosing. No one can tell you what lies ahead with one hundred percent accuracy. If your doctor tells you ninety-nine out of one hundred people die of your disease, you most likely will die, but you might also be the one who beats the odds, and if you do, you will believe yourself special and blessed, and your loved ones will believe the fervency of their prayers for you paid dividends, but it's just math. It's all just math.

It was a great relief when my predictions began to fail.

People outlasted the awful deadlines I'd given them. They posted photos of their birthday celebrations. Sometimes their captions said things like *Suck it Death Lady!* but I was still happy for them.

The woman who was pregnant on the plane, the one who had been refusing treatment because she believed it would make no difference, decided to accept her oncologist's advice. She is now cancer-free. Her husband wrote me a very nice letter telling me I'd saved his wife's life and enclosed a photo of their sweet, enormous baby.

Some people also sent messages telling me that serious illnesses had been picked up early thanks to my predictions.

One family had all their smoke alarms checked after I predicted a house fire and a short time later those smoke alarms saved their lives.

And then another woman, who I had predicted would live until ninety-four, died suddenly in her sleep, at the age of forty-five, so that was very sad, but also quite helpful.

I saw photos. She was the caftan-wearing woman who didn't apologize when she knocked my head with her elbow.

After a while, people began to call me a "fraud," which, you know, would have made me laugh if I didn't still feel so terrible.

Chapter 125

Allegra and her brother sit opposite each other across a red laminate table in a noisy shopping center food court, eating "Mighty Mega Burgers with the lot."

They've just successfully purchased gifts for their parents' birthdays, which fall only three days apart, so are always celebrated together. A bracelet for their mother, a new shirt for their father, possibly identical to the one they bought him last year, but he won't mind, he loves multiples of his favorite possessions.

Whenever Allegra and Taj are alone together like this, they have a defiant childish ritual where they indulge in the type of greasy junk food their mother consistently denied them as children. Taj has already texted a photo of the burgers to their mother, who has responded: *Yes, yes, I know, you had such deprived childhoods.*

"Your back still good?" Taj licks grease off his fingers.

"Yes," says Allegra. "Touch wood."

Taj cups his hands behind his ears. "*Nazar Na Lage.*" He's imitating their grandmother's way of expressing the same sentiment.

It feels like an achievement she could list on her CV: *I avoided back surgery.*

Her specialist had been prepared to operate but said, "I'm your last resort, Allegra." He said there were no guarantees. Taj told her unsuccessful back surgery is so common there's even a name for it, "failed back surgery syndrome."

So she threw herself into nonsurgical treatments: acupuncture, physical therapy, exercise. By her twenty-ninth birthday she was pain-free and back at work. Jonny and Anders both joined her for dinner at her parents' place. This time last year that would have seemed impossible: all those worlds colliding, all of Allegra's different "selves" needing to be simultaneously present, but it was fine, sure, it felt a little weird, but mostly comical to find herself in her parents' garage with Jonny and Anders while her father pointed out the supposedly unique features of his treadmill. Jonny, genuinely interested, crouched down with her dad to study the fan pulley belt, while Anders pulled elaborate secret faces at Allegra over their bent heads.

Anders has magnanimously forgiven her for dating a pilot, although not for keeping it a secret, and he's even made some lavish concessions, such as, "Maybe he's not as bad as I thought."

Her parents said they stopped worrying about the self-harm prediction when they saw the public statement issued by Cherry Lockwood. They were even more mollified when Allegra received a personal handwritten apology from Cherry, sent via the airline, but Allegra thinks her mother, at least, didn't truly stop worrying until Allegra had outlived the predicted age of her death. At this point she rewrote history and said *at no time* was she concerned, not at all, she always knew the lady had no special abilities, in the same way she correctly surmised that she worked in the insurance industry. Then she said, "In fact, if I had to guess which of my children might be susceptible to depression I would have thought it would be your brother, not you."

"But why?" asked Allegra. "Taj is always happy."

"That is why," said her mother. "Your grandmother was the same."

But then she refused to say anything more. She said she was sick of the subject. Allegra didn't push, but lately she's been thinking about something she read when she was researching depression: a phenomenon called "smiling depression." Apparently some sufferers show none of the typical characteristics of depression. They have an extraordinary ability to conceal and mask their true feelings. Even the people closest to them have no idea. They seem content. They are often very successful people.

Now Allegra studies Taj as he works his way through his burger.

"How are you?" she asks.

"Good," he says with his mouth full.

"You ... happy?"

"Ecstatic," he says blandly.

He seems fine. He probably is fine. She scans his familiar face. Her annoying, good-looking, cocksure big brother. The confident one. The clever one. When they were growing up, there were times she idolized him and times she truly hated him, but he was always on her side.

"Karma is a bitch," he'd said when they learned of the sudden un-expected death of the caftan-wearing passenger who had caused Al-legra's back injury. He would have gotten a lecture about the true nature of karma if he'd said that in their mother's earshot.

"You seeing anyone?"

"Not right now." Taj looks past her shoulder, as if he's fascinated by something going on at Sushi Hub.

Both pilots and flight attendants need "situational awareness." They need to always know what's happened, what's happening, what might happen. They need to know when to trust their intuition and when to ignore their natural instincts. She's a good flight attendant. She might one day be a good pilot. A few weeks ago she applied for a scholarship program offered by the airline to cabin crew. Jonny still talks about the expression on her face the day she did her introduc-tory flight. He says he'll never forget it. He talks about it as if it was something wonderful that happened to *him*. She has never been loved by someone who is happy just to see her happy.

Is her brother happy?

"Ready to make a move?" Taj drops his half-eaten burger on his plate. They never finish the bad junk food, and to be honest it always does leave them feeling a little ill, just like their mother promised it would when they were kids. It's her fault. She's cruelly spoiled their palates with all her quality food.

Allegra thinks of Cherry Lockwood's apology card: *I'm so sorry our paths crossed in the way they did. There was no reason for what I said to you.*

But what if there was a reason their paths had crossed?

Jonny told her one of his earliest flight instructors said that the difference between a pilot and an aviator is lightness of touch. An aviator doesn't yank or jerk the controls. An aviator doesn't move the controls. He—or *she*—applies pressure, and only ever as much pressure as needed.

Allegra crumples her napkin and drops it on her paper plate. She doesn't lean forward, toward her brother, she leans back. Not too serious, but no jokes.

Her tone is as light as a fingertip.

She says, "Taj."

Chapter 126

When you live with someone you love, you share all your most trivial concerns: *what time should we eat, what time should we leave, what should we watch, I thought they said that rug would be delivered by now, we've run out of black pepper, do I have time for a shower, can you buy dishwashing soap, are you tired, are you hungry, did you see the news about that politician, that atrocity, that accident, that disaster, you won't believe what I just read, I'm going to bed, listen to this, it's so funny, are you eating the rest of that, I'm calling about that rug, what time will you be home, I'll meet you there, I'll see you when I'm back, will you have eaten, I won't have eaten, we made the right decision about that rug* ... on and on it goes, an endless daily stream of tiny decisions and opinions and thoughts shared, and you don't even know it's keeping you alive.

Without Ned I had to find a new structure for my week and my life. I had to find people with whom I could share trivial concerns, because they must be shared—obviously not that I needed pepper, but you must have one person in your life to whom you can complain about the frustration of your local store continually changing the damned location of the damned condiments. (Why? Leave them be!)

Ivy and I set up a time for a weekly phone call. It's her Sunday evening in America, my Monday morning in Australia, and we talk for up to an hour, often about childhood memories, like the time Mr.

Madigan took care of his friend's cattle dog, who was thrilled when Miss Piper "walked" her dairy cows by the house and within minutes had efficiently rounded them all up into Mr. Madigan's backyard, where they crashed about demolishing his wife's garden, while Miss Piper shouted, "Buttercup! Buttercup!" What a hullabaloo.

Those calls bring back the barefoot freckle-nosed mulberry stain–fingered version of me that existed before men and grief and heartbreak. She's still here! Although I'm not sure I could climb a tree the way I once did so effortlessly.

Tuesday is aqua aerobics with Mira, followed by non-compulsory coffee.

Mira generously lets me share her beautiful family, who have moved back to Hobart, and often invites me to family events (I do not go to *every* event, don't worry, just now and then). One Sunday Bridie was struggling with her math homework, and I said, "I could maybe help you, Bridie."

She whispered, "I'm too dumb for math."

It broke my heart and I can't tell you how much it made me miss Ned. You know I am not good with children, but I decided I would go through his notebooks and look for ideas that might help me help Bridie. He never went anywhere without a small hardback notebook in his pocket, where he could jot down ideas and thoughts and lesson plans, even after he retired.

He kept the notebooks in a shoebox. There were more than forty of them.

I picked one at random and noticed the acronym "OGT" kept appearing, and I was initially puzzled until I remembered a long-ago conversation with Jill and Bert, when Jill had mentioned "gratitude journaling." It was meant to be so good for you, reduces inflammation, can help you live longer, and so on, and Ned said, "I've been doing that for years." He said he went through a period after his divorce when he got very down, some days he had to drag himself out of bed, and he decided he would try to find "one good thing" every day and write it down. He still did it most days, he said. I had forgotten

that. If I hadn't looked through the notebooks I might never have remembered.

He didn't date his notebooks (annoying man), so I never knew
what year I would find myself in when I picked up a notebook, but so
often the "one good thing" involved me.

Cherry's eyes
Cherry in the blue dress
Cherry yelling at the camel
Cherry's legs
Rainy day, talking to Cherry about memories of our dads
Singing with Cherry in the car
Cherry in the green straw hat
Sunflowers in Tuscany, talking about the Fibonacci sequence with Cherry
Cherry says she'd share the door with me
*Long talk with Cherry about mathematical Platonism and her mum
and God*

I can't remember a green straw hat (seems unlikely to me, it was probably blue) but so many of his One Good Things brought back memories.

Like that long talk about "mathematical Platonism."

We lay in bed on a Sunday morning because we had nowhere to
be and talked about the belief that mathematical truths are discovered, not invented, because they already exist, which, if correct,
means reality *must* extend beyond the physical world. We talked
about the idea that math is a sense like sight and touch, and if that is
true, well, then, was it also possible my mother possessed another
sense that gave her the ability to access another reality? I wondered if
my love of math and her love of the spiritual could therefore coalesce
in a way far more beautiful and mysterious than my cynical belief
that she used data and probability to make her predictions, no different from an actuarial table.

And then we wondered if we were just stumbling our way toward

God or enlightenment, or was that just a way of saying we didn't know, and it was all so interesting, but then Ned sat bolt upright and clapped his hand to his forehead, because he remembered we *did* have to be somewhere: Aldi was having a special on camp chairs.

I remember us running about madly, throwing on our clothes, and a testy argument in the car about air vents.

From the sublime to the mundane, all before breakfast.

By the way, I wasn't always the One Good Thing.

Sometimes it was *steak*.

Sometimes it was *Golf with Bert*.

Jill's pavlova appeared more than once.

I keep Ned's notebooks by my bed now and allow myself to pick "one good thing" every night before I go to sleep (always on my side of the bed, I give the pillow on his side a little pat good night), and so often it brings back another memory I'd forgotten, and I think about time, and how much we don't understand about how it works, and I do my very best to travel back through my memories, and sometimes if I try hard, but not too hard, if I just let it happen, I'm back there, in the moment, with Ned.

You may remember my mother mentioned "notebooks" when she did her last ever reading. *Look for the notebooks.* I didn't think of it at the time, but a few weeks after I found them, I dreamed of Mum. She was dancing about our old kitchen with the purple grape wallpaper, singing, "Told you so, I told you so!" (she so loved to be right) and I said, grouchily, as I seemed to be a teenager in this dream, "Told me so *what?*" I woke, and the first thing I saw was one of Ned's notebooks, where it remained, face down on my chest. I often fall asleep like that, hugging his words instead of him.

I put the notebook on my bedside table and thought, *Yes, you were right, Mum.*

Then I looked at Ned's empty side of the bed, the sheet so smooth and cold, and thought, *Sure the notebooks are lovely, Mum, but you didn't think to warn me to keep an eye on my husband's precious heart?*

She didn't respond.

Mum and I continue to have a somewhat fractious relationship.

The notebooks also gave me ideas for lesson plans for Bridie, and she began coming here every Wednesday afternoon for math tutoring.

I am no Ned. I'm not a natural teacher, but never mind, I'm improving along with Bridie and I think we're getting somewhere. My favorite part is just chatting with her. She wants to be an actress. Not an actuary. An actress. Her father and I agree she will win all the Academy Awards on offer.

One day Bridie finished eating her Monte Carlo biscuit and said, "I love Wednesdays."

I assumed she was talking about another activity in her day, perhaps at school, but she meant *me*. She meant she loved Wednesdays because she came to me.

I said, "I love Wednesdays too, Bridie." And then I told her about Mum, and how she told my fortune all those years ago and said that one day a little girl would arrive on a plane just when I needed her the most and her name would begin with the letter B.

She studied me with such a serious expression, the same expression as the only little girl I'd ever imagined mothering had, and then I saw it dawn on her, and slowly she said, "Wait, Cherry, do you think she meant *me*?"

I said, "Yes, Bridie, I think she meant you."

Epilogue

"Timothy Binici, this is your first Olympics, you must be so excited."

The boy is seventeen, tall and broad-chested, dark hair cut short, swimming cap and goggles in one hand. He lowers his head to speak carefully into the microphone. "Very."

"Now I hear, and correct me if I've got this wrong, but I've been told you could swim before you could even walk? Is this true?"

"It is true. When I was a baby a fortune teller told my mother I'd drown when I was seven," says Timmy. "So she got me into swimming pretty early."

"That's amazing!" cries the sports reporter. "And you obviously proved her wrong because you clearly did *not* drown when you were seven."

"No, but when I was seven, I went on a school excursion and got knocked off a rock platform into the sea by a freak wave, fully dressed. I *should* have drowned. Most kids my age *would* have drowned. But I was a super-strong swimmer, so here I am."

"Well, I'll tell you what, shout-out to that fortune teller, Australia thanks you!"

"You're welcome," says Cherry Lockwood from her armchair in front of the television. "Now bring home the gold, Timmy."

She is on her feet, both fists in the air, when he does.

It is only when we truly know and understand that we have a limited time on Earth and that we have no way of knowing when our time is up that we begin to live each day to the fullest, as if it were the only one we had.

—Elisabeth Kübler-Ross

Acknowledgments

A huge thank-you to my incredibly talented editors: Amy Einhorn, Claire Craig, Maxine Hitchcock, Danielle Walker, Brianne Collins, Lori Kusatzky, Madeleine Woodfield, and Bhavna Chauhan.

Special gratitude to Catherine Nance, Aimee Thompson, Nam Hyun (Natalie) Kim, and Jocelyn Milward (author of the thought-provoking book *Zero, Infinity and Me*), who gave their time so generously and patiently to answer questions about their respective professions. I am also indebted to George Gates, Jolie Futterman, and Rochelle Blacklock for sharing personal anecdotes that helped me create fictional lives for my characters. Thank you Lena Spark for answering medical questions for fictional purposes while our sons played football (causing you to miss seeing an excellent goal save. Sorry!).

Thank you to my fabulous publicists: Tracey Cheetham, Gaby Young, and Dyana Messina. Thank you to my wonderful literary and film agents: Fiona Inglis, Faye Bender, Jonathan Lloyd, Kate Cooper, Sam Loader, Jason Richman, and Addison Duffy. Thank you for the memories, Jerry Kalajian. Thank you to all the amazing sales and marketing teams, booksellers, and bloggers, who help readers find my books, with special thanks to Julie Cepler, Rufus Cuthbert, and Ellie Morley.

Thank you to Caroline Lee for fantastic narration of my audiobooks. Thank you to my amazing translators around the world.

Thank you to my sisters: Jaci, Kati, Fiona, and Nicola. Thank you, Jaci, for being my first, fastest reader and giver of extravagant compliments. Thank you, Kati, for your generous help with proofreading. (My sisters Jaclyn Moriarty and Nicola Moriarty are both incredible authors. Look for their books!) Thank you to my brother-in-law Steve Menasse for patiently handling all things online and technological for me.

Thank you so very much to my readers for your stupendous support. I promise I never take it for granted, and your kind comments truly mean the world to me. It's now been more than twenty years since my first novel was published, and I have some readers who have been with me since the beginning and some who weren't even born then. I love seeing mothers and daughters at my events along with book groups and friendship groups. Two readers once told me they first became friends after they got chatting in the signing line at one of my previous events from years before. That made me so happy.

Sue Fern contacted me after reading *Nine Perfect Strangers* and told me about the devastating loss of her gorgeous son, Dom. It was my pleasure to honor Dom's memory by giving his name, Dominic Archer-Fern, to one of my favorite characters in *Here One Moment*.

Thank you Dad for butterflies and parking spots and for popping into my head whenever I need you.

Thank you to all my fellow Australian authors, with special thanks to my friends Ber Carroll (now writing as B. M. Carroll) and Dianne Blacklock (now an editor extraordinaire).

Thank you to my beautiful mother, Diane Moriarty, and her friend, my beautiful godmother, Sandi Spackman, for sharing so many details and stories of their glorious tree-climbing, blackberry-picking childhoods on Sydney's upper north shore.

Speaking of lifelong friends, I have dedicated this book to two of mine: Marisa Colonna and Petronella McGovern. We met in our twenties as work colleagues and fingers crossed, we'll still be laughing together in our nineties. Thank you for your friendship and support.

Last but never least, all my love and gratitude to Adam, George, and Anna. I got so lucky. Thank you for all the beautiful, precious moments. Thank you also for the not-so-beautiful moments because they provide great material.

* * *

When Neve mentions an article she read about deathbed regrets, she is referring to Bronnie Ware's wonderful memoir, *The Top Five Regrets of the Dying*. The following books were also helpful to me in my research: *The Joy Thief* by Penny Moodie, *Fooled by Randomness* by Nassim Nicholas Taleb, *A Taste of Ginger* and *A Bit More Ginger* by Hedley Somerville, *Baby Boomers* by Helen Townsend, *Psychic Blues: Confessions of a Conflicted Medium* by Mark Edward, and *Palm Reading and Tarot for Beginners* by Rebecca Hood.

All errors are, of course, sadly mine.

About the Author

Liane Moriarty is the author of the #1 *New York Times* bestsellers *Big Little Lies*, *Apples Never Fall*, *The Husband's Secret*, and *Truly Madly Guilty*; the *New York Times* bestsellers *Nine Perfect Strangers*, *What Alice Forgot*, and *The Last Anniversary*; as well as *The Hypnotist's Love Story* and *Three Wishes*. She lives in Sydney, Australia, with her husband and their two children.